STORMBUCKLER AND THE LEVISCOPIC ENGINE

NEIL MACH

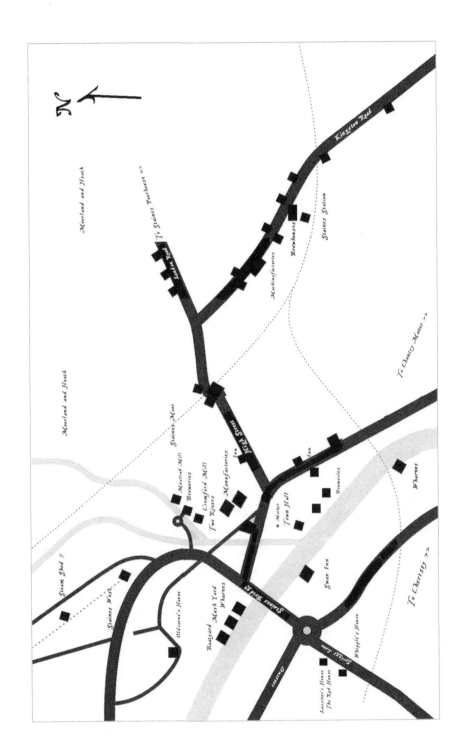

N

Moorland and Heath

Moorland and Heath

To Staines Poorhouse >>

Kingston Road

London Road

Staines Station

Staines Moor

Brewhouses

Machinefactories

To Chessey Manor >>

High Street

Inn Street

Manured Mill

Browerics

Crawford Mill

Manufactories

Two Rivers

Steam Shed ?

Staines West

Oldacre's House

Boatyard

Marsh Yard

Wharves

Staines Bridge

Mews

Town Hall

Browerics

Inn

Wharves

Swan Inn

To Chertsey >>

Spring Lane

Whipple's House

Lassiter's House

The Red House

Passim

I

2

The main residence had a large, pale mouth that jutted into the faint light and could only *just* be seen from the bockety doorway of the poorhouse's *only* dirt-closet. Stormbuckler had lived in Staines Town poorhouse all his life. He was surrendered into its custody as an infant.

The early light hit the arched entrance, almost petrified in the smoky air, so the ceiling of the structure resembled a huge fin rumpled onto the spine of a moribund fish. A lengthy backbone of work-rooms and other industrial structures connected the main buildings, which housed a dining area, midwifery, a dough room, a charcoal lodge, and the main workshop. All of these constructs had been ornamented with rows of pointed tiles, giving the poorhouse the appearance of jagged fangs running along its length. The day had not properly begun because the poorhouse bell had not yet rung. A shady crow hunkered over an oak tree's ribs, ready to scream her wake-up cry.

In the toilet, inmate Stormbuckler leaned back against the shattered seat and measured four fingers from the jerry-cabin walls. He retrieved a clump of moss that had been lodged in the hole on a previous visit. Then he plunged his broken fingernails into the soft earth and prodded around until he found a hole the size of a desiccated bumblebee. He shook his finger into this hole till he located the treasure.

He drew a smelly muslin bag corner from the soil.

This was the location of his buried purse. He shivered a smile as he removed the mouldy bag from entombment. Stormbuckler knew he could enjoy the delight of his bits and pieces by caressing their lumps inside the tatty ragbag. The contents of his meagre haul provided him with a rare sense of comfort. He knew it was just a simple pouch, but it held all of his worldly possessions: cartilages from a dead bird, milk teeth from his own gums, a jumble of polished stones, a splinter of horn, a sliver of antler, and his favourite treasure of them all: a gruff and scratchy cockle. Stormbuckler removed the shell from the bag and massaged the puckered ribs and irregular corrugations, hoping to contrast the crispy sharpness of the outer shell with the sugary sheen within. He moved the crusted casing closer to his nose for a proper sniff, then passed it across his cracked lips.

The crow hammered her wings in furious agitation, delivering a *car-carr* alarm call that would have wakened the spirits. At once, Stormbuckler tossed his shell on the dirt-closet floor, within the confines of the small closet, then reached for his other treasures, still in their muslin bag, but the rickety half-door swung open in a flurry of wood chips and fresh air, exposing his guilty face.

Outside the dirt-house door, there came a hoarse cry. 'Come fast.'

Stormbuckler stood to quickly place his stump over the bag he'd dropped.

A young guy emerged from the shadows to confront Stormbuckler. He exhaled through half a row of mud-brown teeth, and his lips were chapped.

Next came a woman's voice: 'Aha, so the buffle-head is *there* is he?' The meaty-boned woman approached the door. She was wrapped in ripped cassocks. Stormbuckler immediately recognised her as Mrs. Pinsetter, the matron of their home. He bent to recover his treasure bag, but it was too late.

'Leave it,' shouted the matron, pushing the privy door all the way open to examine the spectacle before her. She brought the lantern light to her flabby chin: 'By corks! What do we have here? With a swing 'o the shite-house door I see an aproneer and with his awards is he, ever? Did you see? Is this place where you hide your treasures, boy? In a stench house? What stink... what a merry stink this is. Grab it, Seedpod, grab the bag from under his *thingy*, will you? Confiscate the plunder.'

Mrs. Pinsetter's helper, a boy known to all as Seedpod, bent in the murk to remove Stormbuckler's stump from the fallen bag. 'Change position, oaf...' he grunted.

Mrs. Pinsetter hissed as Master Stormbuckler made a grumpy sound of resistance: 'You're in a lot of trouble already, boy. In a foul odour. I can't image how much pain and suffering you'll go through if you don't remove your pad from that sack of dirt *right now...* move it or be punished beyond a demon's most depraved imagination, you bedraggled scamp.'

So Stormbuckler removed his bad limb from the muslin bag, and Seedpod snatched it away, passing it to Mrs. Pinsetter, the matron to examine in her blotchy fingers.

'Well, what do we have we here?' she inquired, as if they had recovered the world's most marvellous find. 'Does this bag contain gold beads, or turd lumps, I wonder?'

She handed the lantern to Seedpod, who held it over their prize, so they might study the contents,

'Bones,' Stormbuckler explained.

'Bones? Are they golden bones from ancient Calabar? Or eagle bones from the Diamond River? Or are they merely the *crazy bones* from inside your head?'

'Bones, ordinary bones.'

'We'll see, Seedpod, won't we? Will you restrain him? We'll pull him inside while you go fetch Reverend Burney. He'll know what to do with a malefactor. But I doubt the Reverend will be moved to mercy at this awfully early hour.' Seedpod chuckled at the truth of this comment. 'So take him *firm*, will you?' the matron added. 'We don't want the stinking varlet to jump or flounder, do we?'

'He's not going anywhere, mistress, I'm tight on his arm.'

4

'Good, *good*. Bring him to the light. Bring him to the house. Bring him to the parlour.'

~

Shortly after eight o'clock, Reverend Burney, the guardian-warder of Staines Parish poorhouse, arrived. That meant that for more than an hour, Stormbuckler had waited on his one healthy foot. Meanwhile, Mrs. Pinsetter consumed two salted herrings and a bottle of warm malted beer.

When Reverend Burney finally arrived, he stumbled into her office-cum-parlour, his crimson neck and claret expression revealing a general state of worry and pother. 'What is the rumpus?' he inquired, wiping his greasy brow with a slippery red handkerchief.

'I'm sorry I called you *early*,' Mrs. Pinsetter said, from the easy comfort of her wicker chair, 'It's the boy we nicknamed Stormbuckler. Do you know him? He's a hoarder and a thief, I found out. I discovered his secret cache of trove.' She raised the muslin bag so the minister could see it. 'See, here? *Look*.' She grasped Stormbuckler's bag in her oily pink fingers while she squinched her nose as if she were holding a soiled filth-rag.

'What is it?' the clergyman asked, not daring to get closer.

'The boy's personal belongings.'

'Belongings? Did I hear you correctly? Did you say *belongings*? Is this correct boy? How do you have belongings? Don't you know you're a resident of a poorhouse?'

'Sir, I think I can explain, sir. They are merely *bones*,' offered young Stormbuckler.

'I need to light up and think,' the pastor said with a frown. He took a seafoam pipe from an inside pocket, then grabbed a candle from the hearth to ignite his bowl. 'Belongings, are they? Where do you get belongings? Tell me... what gives you the right to have *belongings*? Don't you know you are *not* entitled to belongings? That's why you are here, *fool*... You're a poorhouse orphan and *thusly*, you are entirely *without* any belongings...'

'Yes sir, I know, sir. I'm deeply sorry, sir. It's merely dust and bone, sir. Merely a bag of *not much*.'

'Is it now? A bag of not much? And where does this *not much* come from, boy? It comes from some-*one* doesn't it? Or it comes from some-*who*. It certainly comes from some-*where*. You know, boy, in a poorhouse, everything always belongs to *someone else*. I'd hazard a guess that an orphan living in a poorhouse rarely has his *own* belongings. Do you see?'

Stormbuckler shook his head, to deny anything had been stolen, but the matron chipped in: 'The boy said the bones came from a bird... In less ways, that's what he told me.'

'Indeed.' The minister took his first puff of his pipe.

'Will he be rewarded for this transgression, Reverend?' The matron raised a withered flower to her lips as blue smoke filled the room. 'Will he receive punishment for this egregious infraction of poorhouse rules? Will you now ask the sinner to pay for this sin? Only, I would like to watch the scoundrel squirming as you punish him. If I could, Reverend, I would really like to watch him suffer as he gets what is coming to him. Will you reward this sin with a lick from the birch? I would very much like to watch as you allow the birch to bite his raw skin.' The matron gave a lascivious leer. In her turgid cavity, Stormbuckler saw a row of ruby-red gums.

'Well now, *well now*, please wait a moment dear lady. I need to think. To think and to smoke. To smoke and to contemplate. To contemplate and to deliberate...'

'Would a glass of warm milk dashed with a drop of sour brandy help those reflections?' the matron asked.

'I daresay it would,' offered the Reverend, with a sigh. 'I dare say it would help *a lot*.'

'In that case, I shall fetch the milk myself,' Mrs. Pinsetter suggested. 'I can bring a beater with me, too. Because I'm sure you'll find good use of a strong beater on this wretched child.' Mrs. Pinsetter left the room and, once she had shuffled out of sight, down the passage, her wide steps slapping on flag-stones as she waddled, Reverend Burney indicated that the child might sit on the floor.

'Here?' asked Stormbuckler.

'Of course, *here*. Place cold bones on cold stone, boy. That's the spirit...'

Stormbuckler sat cross-legged while the guardian-warder collapsed into Mrs. Pinsetter's wicker chair and blew on his pipe. 'It gives me no pleasure,' the man said. He took a long puff, and the smoke curled into the stuffy air. 'No pleasure at all. Because I had high hopes for you, lad, even though you were a cripple. Even though you were a cripple, with a mother in heaven, and a father re-moved, and even though you have been fated by misfortunes, I *still had* high hopes. Do you know why? It's because you are the brightest star in this sad little constellation. And you are the most submissive lad in this poorhouse family. Yet — and it's fair to say this — your *eccentric* ways get you into much trouble and over-and-over, don't they, boy? I don't know why this is, Stormbuckler. I don't know why it is at all. Why are you so strange?' The clergyman took the muslin bag from the matron's tabletop and held it between his fingers. 'What am I to do with you? You know all these objects possess value, don't you? And you know that you *must* offer belongings into the safe custody of the matron, don't you? So why do you have such things? Why keep items in a bag?'

'Sir, the bag contains stones and bones. That's all.'

Reverend Burney raised his hand: 'I do not require an explanation. All I want from you is sorrow and repentance.'

'I am sorry, sir. Truly, very deeply sorry. So remorseful.'

'You say these things to save yourself, don't you? But there is no substance in your words. What will I do with you? What should I do with you?' Stormbuckler looked at the ground as he dared *not* speak. 'Well, the birch is required. That is obvious,' added the guardian-warder. 'And the woman will demand a proper thrashing, won't she?' The clergyman mulled-over his options. 'She wants to see blood and scars, boy...' Stormbuckler took a breath and felt his heart pounding. 'The woman will be back in a moment, with milk. After that, she will keenly watch while I administer the penalty for this sin. I warn you in advance, dear boy, my penalty will be *pitiless*. Because I need to send a message about *belongings*. What would happen if every inmate decided to reward himself with belongings? It would bring mayhem, wouldn't it? Can you imagine the pandemonium if the poorest in society were allowed to hold possessions? It would cause great upset to the social fabric, wouldn't it? There would be *no distinction* between the wealthy and the poor, would there? Can you imagine what would happen if the impoverished were allowed to possess their *own* things? That's *not* how God, or heaven, likes things to be, down here on earth. No! God and heaven want to see a fair separation between those who flourish and those who, like you, are predisposed to being impoverished. Otherwise, there'd be no point in going to heaven, don't you see? Heaven is for the lower classes... so that's why people like you should maintain their natural stance and refrain from exaggerating a lowly position. Those rules accord with God's intention for the poor. In other words, boy, what you describe as a *small bag of nothing* is actually a bag of blasphemous *effrontery*. This bag is a representation of obscene antichristian turpitude. And that is why you *must be* very severely punished..'

'Yes sir,' mumbled Stormbuckler. 'I didn't know it was *that* serious.'

Just then, the parlour door scraped open, and Mrs. Pinsetter pushed her wide hips through. She held a drinking vessel in one hand, with a yard-broom under a malodorous armpit.

'Don't get up...' she said, because Reverend Burney had made himself quite comfortable with his behind stuffed into the cushions, of *her* chair. 'I will bring the milk *to you...*' she insisted. ' Then I will get the miscreant ready for his punishment. We will want him lashed to the livery cupboard; I suppose? I will bring a rope for the tying, if you wish. Will you have his eyes blindfolded and his mouth gagged? Will you want him stripped? Do you want me to undress the boy? I can peel him *now* if you wish.'

Reverend Burney inhaled the last of his smoke and took his cup. He swigged the liquor, then brushed white droplets from a well-groomed moustache. 'One moment please Mrs. Pinsetter. I will ask the Lord God to give me strength before I deliver sentence.'

'Very well, Reverend, I did not intend to apply any pressure on your holy duty, or hurry the Almighty along... In spite of that, though, I ought to remind you that those who are ready to work are ready to work *now* and they wait on early sentence to be delivered so they might start their working day. We perhaps should not tarry any *longer* than need be. The poorhouse labouring day is already begun yet we are paused here... inexplicably —'

'Really?' This came as welcome news to the Reverend who smiled with enthusiasm. 'Have the inmates eaten, one and all?'

'Yes, they ate bread and porridge before prayers...'

'And this one? Stormbuckler. Did this sinner eat?'

'No, of course he did *not*,' Mrs. Pinsetter said with a frown. 'He awaited his correction. He awaited the penalty. And, by the way, I notice he *now* sits. Though I had him stand waiting, for penitential reasons...'

'Yes, you did, good lady. I thank you that you had him standing. I am grateful to you, as always. The poorhouse is indebted. We *all* are...'

'Well, yes, I suppose.'

'And now I have decided upon the nature of the scoundrel's correction. Let me tell you this, I am unbending in this decision. I shall inflict a punishment that will suit the awful narrative of his crime...'

'Good, *good*,' said Mrs. Pinsetter. She licked her blistered lips. 'Shall I unclad him, and have him exposed? Shall I strip the fruit now? Shall we divest him, bind him, and then gag him? Yes! We ought to blindfold him and rope him to furniture. Or would you prefer if we dragged him naked into the public workshop? So that everyone can witness his unclothed and full-hearted whipping? Yes? Would that be even better?'

'Take his shirt from his back and call your attendant... Call young Seedpod, because we will need his help.'

'Oh, perfect.' Mrs. Pinsetter had merry eyes when she went to the door to shout for her attendant. Of course, Seedpod came right away because he rarely strayed far from her side.

Reverend Burney rose from the wicker chair and banged his pipe against a table leg. They he watched as ashes heaped onto the matron's stone floor. 'Right boy, ' he said. 'Get yourself up. As Mrs. Pinsetter has suggested, you will be secured and taken to the workshop.'

9

'To the workshop sir?'

'I don't want chit-chat from you. I don't want insolence. Do you understand?'

Stormbuckler nodded.

~

Reverend Burney went to the foreman's stage that stood at one end of the oakum picking shop. Stormbuckler had been dragged into the workshop by Seedpod, while the matron trailed behind. The cleric climbed onto the central platform and coughed loudly to take control: 'Bring the rapscallion here...' he shouted. The clergyman examined the gathered faces to ensure that everyone was able to hear. Seedpod gave Stormbuckler a resentful pinch on the fleshy part of his arm as he pushed the lad up the wooden steps to take pride-of-place by the Reverend. 'Wait by, will you, Seedpod?' asked Reverend Burney. 'I shall require your services in a while. Will you, Mrs. Pinsetter, kindly bring an oakum sack?'

'Reverend? A sack did you say? Did you perhaps mean a rope and a stick? I can bring a rope and stick if you require... though I thought I misheard your request. I though you said a sack.'

'You did not mishear me, lady. It is true that I said *sack*. I require a large sack. The boy is to be bagged.'

'Bagged, sir?' asked the matron, her eyes widened.

'You'll see.'

While the Reverend Burney addressed the crowd, the matron went in search of a sack.

'The poorhouse rules are unambiguous,' declared Reverend Burney, in his address to the congregation. 'This institution offers parochial help to the *poor of the parish*. But I believe it is prudent to remind you all of the definition of *poor*. Do you understand what poverty means? Without a doubt, being poor means being empty-handed and propertyless. You must all keep in mind that entry to this Christian house is restricted to the *poor of the parish*. Admission is by Christian favour *only*. Do you understand everything I've said thus far?'

There was a general burble of assent. Men nodded, women sighed, and youths grunted in their vogueish style.

'I ask you this,' the Reverend continued. 'Is a person genuinely *indigent* if they control personal belongings?'

'No,' said Seedpod, loudly. The gathering seemed to agree. Inmates nodded, some murmured. All shuffled their feet.

'How can a person be a pauper if they keep belongings? It's a condition of entry, is it not? A condition that have-nots have not? Do y'see?' Reverend Burney smiled at his own clever wordplay, then he went on: 'For a person to be needy, he must be without bean and grain. That is quite literal. I know the Lord secures justice for the poor and upholds the cause of the needy. But I also know, in my heart, we should never test our Lord...'

'Hear ye, *hear ye*...' said a sycophant at the front. 'We are blessed *because* we are poor. We are blessed *because* we are meek. We are blessed *because* we are the *have-nots*.'

'Exactly,' agreed the clergyman. 'But this person, the one you know as Stormbuckler, dared to test the Lord. He has questioned everything that is pure and forgiving. He kept a little reward back for himself, a treasure bag. The matron found his luggage this early morning. She found his bag of *belongings*. A bag filled with personal items. Yes, this person did keep things! This miscreant owned mementos so he could indulge in secret pleasures.'

Several women gasped at this monstrous depravity. The clergyman paused, to allow everyone to take-in the information, 'That's accurate; this boy engaged in solitary revelry. Private hoggery is obviously against all the best customs of this parish poorhouse; I don't need to remind you of that.'

Mrs. Pinsetter arrived by the stage with a large hemp sack. 'Now, Reverend?'

'Yes, bring it here, matron.'

Seedpod cried-out in undisguised pleasure.

The sack was handed to Reverend Burney, who opened it with an elegant flourish. 'Get in, boy...' he instructed.

Stormbuckler looked into the sack then gazed at the cleric suspiciously.

'Quickly now, get in, we don't have all day. Get in the sack this instant. Get your body completely inside.'

Stormbuckler took the corners of the sack and swung his prosthetic foot into the bottom. After that, it was easier to move his healthier leg inward. He wriggled both knees inside too, then pulled the bag right up to his waist. 'Further. Deeper. *All in.* Get yourself all in,' shouted Reverend Burney. 'Right up to your neck, *up to your neck.*'

'We'll throw him in the river, won't we?' Mrs. Pinsetter exclaimed with growing excitement on her reddening cheeks.

And as he envisioned the suffering the fellow youngster would be going through in the dark of the sack; Seedpod grinned in cold pleasure and rubbed his hands together.

But Reverend Burney ignored the matron and directed his attention to Seedpod: 'Find a suitably strong needle and stout twine, will you? Find it *now*. We will sew the prisoner *into* the bag. I want him well stitched inside. Find the needle right away to complete the task.'

'Oh, splendid,' said Mrs. Pinsetter with a broader smile. She addressed the gathering: 'We will drag this sack to the river. And, there, we will throw this wrongdoer into the shivering waters of salvation. Let's see if this hoggish boy can be saved from sin, huh? Let's see if he can survive trial by dark waters...'

'No,' shouted Reverend Burney. The audience gasped. 'That would be contrary to Christian spirit...'

The matron nodded and responded, 'Well, of course. I hadn't really meant it.' Nevertheless, she tapped her foot in dissatisfaction.

Seedpod returned with needle and twine. 'Good, *good*. Get to work. Stitch him in. Stitch him inside his encasement,' shouted the Reverend.

Seedpod pushed Stormbuckler's head into the covering then bent-over the top seams. He made several long stitches with the brutal needle. From time-to-time, Seedpod 'accidentally' pinched Stormbuckler's body to get him to budge a little bit, inside the sack. He occasionally stabbed the boy with the blunt end of the needle. The clergyman witnessed these happenings and shook his head to make the little tortures *cease*. So Seedpod didn't stab anymore. But he pushed and shoved just as meanly as before. Finally, Seedpod stitched the bag fully shut and Stormbuckler's body could no longer be seen by the audience.

'The boy is now bagged,' announced Reverend Burney. 'And he will remain bagged for seventy-two hours. May this be a lesson to you all. Any person found in possession of belongings will be bagged. You have been warned.'

The cleric stepped from the stage and the congregation started to move-away to start their individual functions.

'I must admit I am baffled by your chosen course of action,' suggested Mrs. Pinsetter as Reverend Burney stepped from the stage. 'At the very least I imagined we'd flog him before you put that bag over his head. Wouldn't that have been appropriate? I think it *would*...'

'I suppose you would have preferred it better if we had thrown the sack into the river, from the stone bridge?'

'Yes, well...' the matron paused for thought, 'I admit the idea crossed my mind. Though, of course, such action would be unchristian... though, perhaps, if it were up to me —'

'Yes, fine, and good Mrs. Pinsetter,' said the cleric quickly. 'And it's wise to admit to such desires. And nobody would criticize your thoughts, least of all me. But, you see, it was not up to you. It was up to me. And I am a man of cloth and must practice good Christian procedure. Like you, I admit that flinging the scoundrel into black-water would seem an appropriate sentence... but nevertheless, also in my opinion, I think that having him stuffed into a rough bag and abandoned in a dusty corner, will have a discouraging effect on the *other* paupers, not to mention the boy himself, who will have time to meditate on the foulness. I think this novel form of punishment will be more effective, in the long run, than simply throwing a mortal body into the healing waters of redemption.'

'I hadn't thought of it *that way*...'

Reverend Burney nodded, then he yawned. 'Call me again in seventy-two hours. I'll cut the boy free from the sack *myself*. I will remove the thread and release him. Let it be known that no person should feed nor water him until I complete his liberation. Is that clear?'

'Yes, perfectly.'

'Excellent, get Seedpod and find another strong ruffian, so the bag-boy can be heaved into a dark corner of the workshop, in plain sight of others. Then take me to your parlour for bread and cheese.'

'Of course, Reverend Burney, it will be my distinct pleasure.'

It was hard to be certain, but it was surely *after midnight* when Storm-buckler picked up a gentle pacing that seemed to be coming closer to his position. He didn't know precisely where he'd been hauled, although he was inclined to think that the sack had been dropped into an unoccupied corner of the oakum picking shop — a place that was out-of-bounds to all but the matron and her staff. He prayed it wasn't Seedpod who'd showed up to pain him, because if it was, he'd be incapable of defending himself. If the coming character was Seed-pod, he predicted the outcome would most likely be torment.

Stormbuckler discovered, during working hours, that he retained a blurred sense of daylight because light penetrated the weave of the sackcloth. Nevertheless, once true blackness arrived, he saw *nothing*. He likewise discovered that his sense of hearing developed more acutely the longer he spent in the sack, and the dimmer it became. So, he seized his breath, listened closely, and focused on anything that might provide information about the character who imminently moved towards his confined body. The visitor tiptoed nearer the sack and Stormbuckler supposed it was a *somebody* who could be light on their feet — perhaps a child or a short woman. With relief, he figured-out that, whoever the threatening person was, the character was too subtle to be either Seedpod or Mrs. Pinsetter. The midnight prowler struck the side of his sack and Stormbuckler heard a modest breath before the person whispered: 'Stormbuckler? Can you hear me?'

'Yes,' he muttered. 'Who is it?'

'It's me. It's your friend. It's Tom Bisbee...'

Tom was Stormbuckler's sole ally in the poorhouse. They had known each other since before either of them could properly remember. They squatted jointly at mealtime; they knelt closely at prayer time. And they slept abreast on mats, nudged tightly, at bedtime. 'Why are you in this place? Return to your bed. If they discover you here, you'll get us both into a mess of trouble.'

'I stopped by to see what you needed. Food?'

'They will skin you alive if you feed me. Step aside. Go back to your sleep mat. They will throttle you if they discover you here.'

'Is there anything that you need?'

When Stormbuckler took a large breath, he felt a teardrop form in the corner of his eye. He had the impression that a heavenly thorn had pricked his heart: 'Bless you Tom, *bless you*,' he sobbed. 'Water is what I need.'

Tom Bisbee paused and thought for a moment before deciding what to do. He said, '*Wait*, I have an idea.'

'Wait? What a cockchafer you are, Tom Bisbee!'

Tom moved away but returned soon after. 'Can you place your mouth to the place where I push.' He lightly touched Stormbuckler's bony elbow. They both giggled. So Tom said, 'Not there! A little higher. Will you get your lips about *here*?' He prodded by Stormbuckler's neck.

'Go on then...' Stormbuckler whispered. Tom prodded some more at the hessian sack and Stormbuckler moved until he got his face close to where the prod was most keenly felt. He perceived a trickle of water that entered through the fabric. He moved his lips to the moisture and sucked. He managed to drink at least a mouthful of water before Tom spoke again, 'I wetted a cloth and squeezed it, do you want more?'

Stormbuckler used his most commanding voice. 'Take notice, mate. I appreciate everything you've done, but it's simply too much. You will pick up a horsewhipping, or worse, for this measure of loyalty. So, I beg you to withdraw immediately and go back to your mat. Please don't place yourself in any more jeopardy... just for me.'

On the other side of the burlap, Tom Bisbee answered: 'Fair enough. I'll take off now. But I'll come back tomorrow at the same hour.'

Stormbuckler whimpered as soon as he realised his friend had snuck off.

3

Mrs. Oldcorne of Priory Lodge called for her lady's maid.

Mrs. Oldcorne tinkled a bell, and the girl showed up at her door, to arch a knee. Mayotte was considered the only parlour maid at Priory Lodge to be resourceful enough to *act* as a lady's maid, when the occasion merited such a luxury.

When she was out in town, Mayotte invariably sported a refined appearance and was understood to be punctual, virtuous, and amenable. These were, of course, the capacities expected of a first-rate lady's maid. Yet Mrs. Oldcorne would advise any person who would listen, 'Howsoever she might appear, the girl is not a top-tier maid on account of her swarthy presence and roughly foreign variety. But Mayotte volunteers satisfactory service... and these days that is all anybody can hope for. '

'Ah, there you are, young woman,' said Mrs. Oldcorne. 'Quickly now, I wish to capture Mr. Lindwürm before he goes to church. Are we ready?'

Mayotte had earlier decorated her mistress's hair, put her in a Sunday gown, and had completed delicate finishings to her face. Now she produced a sweet little choker that matched the pair of gloves she'd found.

'Oh, what have you there?' asked Mrs. Oldcorne.

'Your pearl and velvet choker, Madam. I think it will match the shades of your gown and catch the twinkle of your eye.'

'Do you think?'

Mayotte smiled, 'Oh *yes*, Ma'am...'

The maid approached and fixed the narrow collar around the older woman's throat. The maid turned the choker around until the row of sparkling pendants matched the grooves in her mistress's gullet.

'Right, let's look at *you*,' said Mrs. Oldcorne, forcing the maid back to get a better view of her servant, examining her through Lorgnette spectacles. Her parlour maid wore a cast-off cotton day-dress, hand-stitched in blue gingham. It was neither extravagant nor simple. Which meant it was ideal for a social situation. 'Yes, girl, you look charming in my old frock. The chequered sequence throws you a slimmer outline. And your ghastly brown limbs are successfully tucked away from general view... I see that you've buried your ugly ankles too, very good.'

'Thank you, Ma'am.'

'Do you have my brush and spare comb? And my prayer book, should I need it?'

'Yes.'

'Well, let's go then, shall we?'

Mrs. Oldcorne insisted they got moving *right away* because she designed to interpose herself at the front porch of Mr. Lindwürm's ragstone manor, just as the millionaire left for church. She appreciated this would be an intrusion, so required the interaction to occur as if it were a *happy accident.* 'We'll take the two-person carriage. That way we can be sufficiently independent, yes?'

'Of course, Ma'am.'

~

On the approach to the tycoon's home, Mrs. Oldcorne explained everything there was to know about their newly installed neighbour, the American enterpriser, Mr. Asher-John Lindwürm: 'Of course, he'll become lord paramount of the area,' she explained. 'Although, being unfamiliar to our English ways, he won't recognise this *yet*. He's a stranger to our lands, you see, still a newcomer. Though his aide-de-camp has been in town for several months. His trusted assistant is an Englishman, by the way, a man who handled the mechanical businesses while Mr. Lindwürm organised his domestic interests across the Atlantic. Mr. Lindwürm is an industrialist and self-made *steamillionaire* and already retains the town mill and manufacturing plant. He arrived this month with his new spouse, who is an American by birth and ancestry. The less that is stated about the bride, maybe, the better, *methinks*. I steadfastly assume that Mr. Lindwürm will call for my help whilst he's here in our town because he will learn that I have uncommon and very privileged access to *genuinely* influential individuals. As you know, your master is the Pageant Master to the imperial household, so he and I have access to the Royal Court, down the river, at Windsor. Consequentially, I've decided to serve as our magnificently wealthy new neighbour's top lobbyist. Being a speculator and fortune trader by instinct, Mr. Lindwürm will see the benefit of taking advantage of the higher social echelons... and he will be happy to benefit from my professional guidance. I'll gain him access to the royal patronage he needs. This ought to be a greatly beneficial 'chance' meeting for both of us.'

When they reached Mr. Lindwürm's dwelling, Chantry Manor, it surprised Mayotte to discover there was no suggestion of a carriage being readied for Mr. Lindwürm's impending onward journey to church. Mrs. Oldcorne checked her own carriage by the front gate-columns of a faded Palladian-style villa and from there she regarded the wearied cobblestone entrance. 'That's odd...' she rubbed her chin. 'I don't see anyone about.' She slipped the reins and flicked her wrists. 'Be a good girl and identify someone to take our horse, will you?'

Mayotte tiptoed down the steps and hurried into the drive, carrying her petticoat above her ankles. Quickly thereafter, she returned with a footman, who arrived dressed in livery. The fellow took their animal and Mayotte helped her lady from the seat of the carriage. 'Where is your master?' enquired Mrs. Oldcorne. 'I wish to bump into him before he starts for church.'

'Ma'am, Mr. Lindwürm is a *Wesleyan*...' declared the footman.

'Really? And what is *that* supposed to mean? Don't non-conformists attend church?'

'Ma'am, the master attended chapel... *earlier*. He went to the open table... that's before seven.'

'Already? Before seven you say?' Mrs. Oldcorne tugged at Mayotte's sleeve. 'Come along. We'll call on him, *anyway*. What harm can it do?'

They left the footman standing by their carriage and hastened up the straight drive towards a crumbling portico. A butler attended them at the entrance and drew them into a lacklustre morning room. 'I shall call Mr. Lindwürm,' the retainer stated, though without any pinch of a smile. 'Please select a seat. I understand my master is in the *garage*...'

'Garage?' blurted Mrs. Oldcorne. She gave the butler a puzzled expression. 'Do you suggest the home's owner is in a garage?'

'Ma'am, he will be in his mechanic's shop. He refers to it as his *garage*. Mr. Lindwürm spends the most of his days there. I'll go get him right away.'

They waited in the undistinguished morning room. Mrs. Oldcorne sat by an unlit fireplace with her gloves folded, and Mayotte stood by the open window to observe sparrows playing in a holly shrub.

A mundane-looking man in his mid-thirties with short black hair and rolled-up sleeves then scuttered into the room and asked, 'What's this, what's this?' He possessed a mild American brogue, as he examined the two women. 'Who are you? When did you show up?'

Mrs. Oldcorne began to rise, but Mr. Lindwürm motioned for her to stay down while he wiped his hands on what looked like a claggy tray cloth. She explained their appearance in his home by saying, 'I thought I would grab you before you left to church.'

'It's fine...' he said, although Mrs. Oldcorne knew it was clearly *not fine*. 'Didn't my man tell you I already attended chapel? I joined the early service. Also, he ought to have warned you that I'm working *right now*. That's why you presently find me in a state of unreadiness to welcome house guests... I'm afraid I am not in the proper mood to tackle visitors at this hour on a Sunday morning. But since you have *incontinently* invited yourselves hither, might I offer you something? Coffee? I'm sorry there's no fire in the hearth, but, as I say, I don't expect *unannounced* visitors...'

'Um, no thank you... we're off to church. In fact, it's a sin to ingest before holy communion...'

'Is that so? How strange your customs are to me. It is a sin to ingest before communion yet not a sin to make unheralded domiciliary visits. Well, I'm sure I'll eventually adapt to your rituals. But what can I do for you, ladies? Why, indeed, are you here?'

Perhaps, because he kept referring to her maid, Mayotte, as a *lady* and had likely not realised she was just a plain servant, Mrs. Oldcorne looked at the foreigner with increasing expressions of frustration. It was completely unheard of, certainly in polite social circles, to bring a maid into casual conversation and to treat her equally. Mrs. Oldcorne exhaled heavily before saying: 'May I begin, sir, by apologising for my disruptive *stop by*. I'm off to church with my *maid*, as I have already stated...' She raised her voice slightly, emphasising the word *maid* so the nonconformer might take better notice of it. 'I wanted to stop over and see how you were doing since you are a new neighbour. I wanted to see if you were adjusting well to this parish...'

'How unusual. Well it's nice to have unexpected visitors.' Asher-John Lindwürm smiled at Mayotte, 'Even still, if you had let me know in advance, I would have preferred your visit. Then, we might have enjoyed lunch together or another amusing activity. However, I'm sorry, but I am quite unable to accommodate you this morning; too busy. Did you tell my wife you might come by?'

'Wife?' said Mrs. Oldcorne. She sounded surprised.

'Yes, sorry guys but it's the form where I come from. Back in America, we tend to tell the mistress of the house if we intend to make a social visit. I guess you guys don't have the same sense of etiquette 'round here? I don't know how it works in this neck...'

'Yes, well, I make another apology for my lack of formal appropriateness. I just wanted to *bump* into you, as it were. We won't stay awfully long.'

'It's fine,' Lindwürm said again. 'So, what's this all about? Why the bump?'

'Um?' Mrs. Oldcorne wasn't prepared for such blithe forth-right-ness. 'I only wanted to *say*...'

'Yes?'

'Um? Your enterprise. Um? Your company. Um, your works in town and the mill and so forth; I wanted to talk to you about *oppor-tunities*...'

'Opportunities? Like what?'

'Um, my husband is the Royal Pageant Master. You probably knew that. I am a lobbyist.'

'Are you? That's great.' Asher-John Lindwürm went to the window and stopped beside Mayotte. 'What does a lobbyist accomplish, dare I question?' When he whispered the question, he ventured a little wink to the maid.

'I persuade influential people. For example, I talk to leaders, erm, politicians, officials, and other swayful members of society about *plans*...' bellowed Mrs. Oldcorne, raising her voice so that it extended across the room.

'I see. I guess your services might come in useful *one day*. What's your name again? I haven't seen a calling card.'

'I'm sorry. I'm Mrs. Oldcorne, from Priory Lodge. I assumed you would recognise me because my spouse is famous in town. We are the most prominent family in Staines Town. My husband is Henry Oldcorne. You *will* have heard of him. That's why I didn't offer a calling card.'

'No, I can't say that I have heard of Henry Coatworn.' Mr. Lind-würm touched Mayotte's sleeve, 'And you? What's *your* name? What are you doing with yourself these days? Are you also a lobbyist?'

With that question, Mrs. Oldcorne simply couldn't stand things any longer. She stood from her chair and banged her gloves against the backrest, causing a great snowstorm of dust to rise into the cold room. 'She's *just* a servant, sir. You *do not* ask her name. This really is quite extraordinary behaviour. It demonstrates the need for applicable instruction if you want to be accepted by civilised society. Furthermore, my name is Oldcorne, which is pronounced like a sheaf of the antique breadgrain, though with the flourish of an elegant *E*.'

'I see,' Asher-John Lindwürm said with a grin. 'Can you give me another example of what you can do for me and my business? Be quick, though, because I don't want *you* to be late for church. Your minister won't wait, will he?'

'He's a rector,' said Mrs. Oldcorne, with a snort of disgust. 'I can see you are too busy to entertain us this morning, so I will postpone our meeting-of-minds until you are of agreeable temperament and in a more pragmatic state of concentration.'

'Oh well, farewell then. Sorry, you couldn't stay any longer. Or perhaps you couldn't come up with *anything*. My man will see you out.'

'Come up with anything? Come up with? How rude! Who do you think you are talking to? We are the most prominent family in Staines Town.' Mrs. Oldcorne pulled her skirts free from the lacing on her boots and made for the door. With a swish of her sleeve, she stipu- lated: 'We are the *most* prominent.'

'Goodbye again,' said Mr. Lindwürm, with a twinkle in his eye.

'Logo...' offered Mayotte, as she stepped away from the window.

'What?' shouted Mrs. Oldcorne from the entrance hall. 'Don't spout Greek to the American gentleman dear. It's rude to make fun of him, just because he's a colonial. Furthermore, it's not your place to speak to your superiors...' She came back to poke her nose around the door, and to view Mr. Lindwürm. 'It's not her place, do you see? A servant must *never* be spoken to. A servant is here to be seen, though *never* to be heard. Please forgive her impudence.'

'No, *no*. I want to hear more. Did she say logo?'

'It doesn't matter.'

'What did you mean by that?' Mr. Lindwürm pressed Mayotte for an explanation. He touched the sleeve of her dress.

'You need to identify your products,' Mayotte told him, though she also gave a shy smile. 'You require an emblem. You're making automobile machines in your factory works, are you not?'

22

'I am.' Mr. Lindwürm returned the smile. 'How clever of you. How do you know about such things?'

'Have you heard of Daimler?'

'Yes, of course. I saw his new motor carriage at the Paris exhibition.'

'If he had a crest on his motors it would have protected his intellectual property...'

'Oh, I see. *I see.*' Mr. Lindwürm turned to Mrs. Oldcorne. 'You have a bright girl here, madam. She has a sharp mind. Keep her by your side. I'd wager she's your best asset...'

'Well, I'm sure. Though she's just a maid and has no place conversing with a gentleman of your rank. No place *at all*...'

'Why not? I'm just a regular workingman. I may have factories and own a heap of silver dollars, but I'm just an average guy from out in the weeds. Why shouldn't she talk to me?'

'Because, well, because it's *unnatural*. Such behaviour goes against the grain. She's a servant girl... and *worse*... look at her closer, don't you see? She has brown skin and exotic features... she ought *not* be conversing with a man of your breeding and wealth.'

Asher-John Lindwürm ignored the comment and returned his attention to Mayotte: 'Tell me more about this idea. How would I create a crest? How would I go about using such a thing?'

'I think the girl is talking about *heraldry*... a coat of arms and so forth,' interjected Mrs. Oldcorne. 'I'm also quite certain she doesn't know *what* she is talking about. She's quite a simple girl, of foreign blood, do you see? They're all quite maddening, aren't they? The darks? They're all filled with peculiar envisionings, aren't they? Leave her alone, *please*, Mr. Lindwürm.'

'Not so fast. Do you think I could get a crest?'

'Logo,' repeated Mayotte.

'Sorry, *logo*. Do you think I could get one? It would put me ahead of Daimler, wouldn't it? And Maybach too? It would put me ahead of other manufacturers, wouldn't it?' The industrialist peered into the distance for a moment. He then turned his focus back to his visitors: 'Yes, *both* of you are very welcome to drop by again *soon*. Um, Mrs. Oldcorne, be sure to bring *this* young lady with you when you next drop-by unannounced. If you visit upon an afternoon, I will show you my *garage*.'

'Oh, how splendid...' Mrs. Oldcorne articulated, in a tone that suggested mockery. 'I just can't wait to see your garage. That will undoubtedly be a true *delight*. Come on over, girl. We've stayed a little too long. *Now*, move quickly...'

They left the drawing room and pushed beyond the butler, who opened the door, with a sniff, as they approached. They stepped across a crumbled step and into fresh air.

'Come back soon,' Mr. Lindwürm yelled, from the porch.

'How crude,' muttered Mrs. Oldcorne. 'A stereotypical rough-billy with poor manners and low birth. He has no idea how to follow even the most *basic* moral guidelines. He doesn't understand the *first thing* about the simplest rules of conduct. *Garage*, I ask you? Regular *workingman*, I ask you? *Coatworn*, I ask you? *Daimler*, I ask you? Whatever next? Really, I have no idea why I bothered. And he's quite bizarre, don't you think? And you weren't much help, were you? What have I mentioned about speaking? *Don't* speak unless I expressly say that you may. *Never* do that again.'

'Sorry, Ma'am.'

In the kitchen pantry, back at Priory Lodge, the scullery girls undertook the labour of washing-up the kettles and basins they had utilized for supper. Everybody giggled as Mayotte told them about her early Sunday morning jaunt to see Mr. Asher-John Lindwürm.

'They claim he's very handsome... is he?' inquired a maid named Jean.

'He isn't as ugly as a bull, but I don't suppose I would describe him as handsome. He is *actually* fairly typical. Quite unremarkable. He has a short, square, and simple appearance. Although he had a weird eccentric *flow*, if you know what I mean by that?' explained Mayotte. All the young women gathered around to stare in increasing amazement into Mayotte's face as she spoke. Was this a fair appraisal of a mega-successful, spectacularly wealthy, industrialist?

'Did you see his cow-and-kisses?' asked the cook's assistant, an established girl named Mable.

'No, he spoke *about* his wife... but that's a matter that has puzzled me since our visit. The trouble-and-strife didn't come out to say *good morning*. Isn't that odd? And madam passed a disparaging remark about her in the carriage. Perhaps his wife was in her flea-pit when we got there. It was, after all, before ten. What wealthy wives get up before ten on a Sunday? Perhaps his cow-and-kisses had an acute case of morning pukes *too*... that would justify her absence.'

These words provoked much amusement around the big table. 'She's an Indian,' asserted someone at the back.

Several girls nodded their understanding, while others puckered their eyebrows or shook their heads. Mayotte said: 'Really? Are you having me on?'

'No, it's true, I swear,' extended Mable. She was considered to be the most astute of the servants at Priory Lodge. 'Someone knows the rural physician who was called to examine them when they first arrived here from overseas. And the doctor informed his assistant and now it's all over town. Lindwürm's wife is an Indian. The doctor's assistant swears it is true.'

'That can't be correct...' Mayotte bit the tip of her finger. 'Although, I suppose it would explain why Mr. Lindwürm didn't introduce us to her. It would also solve madam's off-the-cuff remark.'

'He's immensely rich,' interrupted Jean. 'They say he's so wealthy he could buy *everything* in this parish twice over...'

'Really?' said Mayotte. 'Is that so? Why didn't he buy himself a palace if he is so wealthy? How come he doesn't reside in Scotland? By the wide lakes and blue mountains? Why did he settle here in Staines Town? For what reason? To reside in a dilapidated neighbourhood? I didn't think much of his Chantry Manor residence; to be completely honest. I thought it was very ordinary. The parlour room was unheated. The thin and raspy drive had hardly enough room to turn a cabriolet, the front garden had almost no sculpture, and the hearth was unlit! What do you think of that? I'd venture to say that Chantry Manor is arguably the least majestic house I've ever been to. It doesn't seem appropriate for a multimillionaire inventor.'

'That is a result of him being an *outsider*, isn't it? explained Mable. 'Chantry Manor is all that he could get his mitts on. Large, impressive drums aren't typically sold to outsiders, are they? They are passed through family lines. Yup, good houses are passed from father to son. Without a bloodline, you cannot come across the Atlantic and purchase yourself a castle in Scotland. And, British ancestors live *forever*. So you can't wheedle sneak your way into their bloodline if you're a bloke. A woman can sneak herself in, through marriage, if she's crafty and resourceful... but *not* a bloke! So, what can a geezer do if he turns up in this country, a bloody foreigner, with a wodge of cash to his name but no lineage or breeding? Mr. Lindwürm might have pots and pans of gold, but he can only get what's available to him. And what's available to him, *round here*, ain't much...'

'I suppose you're right,' agreed Mayotte.

'And Mrs. Tight-blouse, the Indian wife... she's a factor, ain't she?' Jean suggested. 'Aren't I right though? Isn't that the truth?' Everyone sniggered. 'House agents don't offer castles to blokes who have an Indian as a missus do, they?'

'Really?' Mayotte asked. 'Is this all really true? Is it actually true that Mr. Lindwürm's wife is a *definite* Indian?'

'I sensed you knew. *Everyone else* is aware. It has been the main topic of conversation. It was hoped that the enigmatic Mr. Lindwürm was a respectable bachelor. But then it leaked all around town that he has a wife and he brought 'er with him. Girls all across town broke down in tears when they heard that the American geezer was already married. They claim that his trouble and strife is being held captive in that run-down house, like an ostrich. Nobody is permitted to see her, and she is not permitted to walk around our streets. Most girls think *phew* that was a lucky escape. *It could've been me.* Kept in imprisonment like an ostrich. All the girls have been tattling-on about 'is Indian wife for days. Have you not been following the scandal-mongering?'

'I choose not to listen to neighbourhood gossip,' Mayotte said, in a slightly prissy tone. She took a deep breath, 'Maybe I ought to listen in future.' She let out a hoot of laughter and everyone joined in with the fun. 'So, is she from Bombay or Madras? Is she from the Princely States? Is she, perchance, the daughter of a maharaja?'

'Not *that type* of Indian, you ignoramus...' said Mable. She poked her friend in the ribs.

Mayotte frowned, 'Ouch, that hurt. What kind of Indian is there? Is there *another* kind? Is there some kind of Indian I know nothing about? What type of Indian?'

'A real one,' offered Jean. 'You know, a native one. A primitive one. An American born one... you know!'

'Huh? A what?'

'Buffalos and tepees. Hides and loin-cloths. Bones and dust. Moccasins and feathers.'

'She's a savage?'

'Yes,' Mable nodded. 'She's a *savage*. Lindwürm married a savage. He got himself a squaw.'

4

Three days after they had thrust him into the edge of the workshop inside a sack, Stormbuckler was on the verge of clemency and discharge. The Reverend Burney returned to Staines parish poorhouse and headed for the oakum shop, to achieve what he construed as a 'solemn act of unpicking and unpacking' that would liberate Stormbuckler from solitary confinement. As before, the minister demanded that everybody should observe the ceremony. With an enormous pair of shears, the pastor nibbled the filaments and strands that kept the sac closed, then he loosened the twine-stitch ritualistically, to push-down the sacking material until it revealed the youth inside. Stormbuckler had imagined that his delivery into the light of day would be unduly harsh to bear, but in fact, the workplace was dull as a coal cellar when the sack was dragged from his face. The sky had lowered early, and the sun escaped behind globby clouds.

When Reverend Burney drew the sack down to Stormbuckler's knees and urged the boy to 'hop out', the youth wavered. To stop his precipitous tumble, the stout clergyman skewed forward to grab hold of the child's knees. Otherwise, he would have toppled. Once the cleric had righted himself, to accept the boy's hand and encourage him to step away from his dreadful quarantine, he had words for the matron's assistant. 'You, Seedpod, yes *you*. Bring the detainee a ladleful of water. Get it fast, because the captive is dry as a bone. I don't want him expiring on us.'

The instruction confused Seedpod, who provided Reverend Burney with a vacant look.

'Go then,' restated the cleric. 'Bring water.' Seedpod tugged at one ear and appeared to be unsure of his direction of travel. This was a curious and unexpected turn of events, since he had never before been asked to carry out a deed of simple charity.

After a short pause, the matron's favoured trustee headed in the direction of the pigsty. Once outside, he located the rainwater barrel and considered the dipper that hung by the tub. He gazed at the thing for a moment, then looked around, to check nobody was spying. Satisfied everyone was inside and still watching the unpacking, Seedpod tugged his dark-cotton trousers aside to pull his pecker from the folds — then he urinated into the scooped-end of the ladle. Once he had finished and the bowl was filled with warm and pungent liquid, he cautiously returned the workspace, where everyone waited, being sure not to spill a drop of amber liquid.

'Good lad,' said Reverend Burney. 'Come over and let the prisoner drink-up... let him *sip the nectar...*'

Seedpod came with the sour drink and Stormbuckler put his lips to the edge of the ladle and he tasted a mouthful. Stormbuckler stepped back and he grimaced.

'Drink,' shouted Reverend Burney.

But Stormbuckler would have *no more*. He turned his face away and locked his lips.

The cleric took the long-handled spoon from Seedpod's hand and gave it a long sniff: 'Did you piddle in this spoon?' he asked.

Seedpod rubbed his chin and looked to his feet for an explanation.

'Holy Joseph! Did you piddle in the prisoner's first splash? What kind of immorally wicked person are you, sir?'

'Me?' said Seedpod, with a distant smile. 'What did I do wrong?'

'Do not take that presumptuous line with me, sir. Don't become the innocent of innocence. Your behaviour is scandalous, sir. It is demonstrably unchristian of you, sir. You should be ashamed of yourself, sir. Someone *else*, bring *clean* water.'

A compassionate man afterwards handed Stormbuckler a beaker so he might have a hearty and healthier drink.

Stormbuckler wiped his mouth and spoke to the room: 'Thank you, to everyone, for your prayers.'

The audience cheered enthusiastically.

However, Seedpod exposed stained teeth and fixed Stormbuckler a cruel-hearted stare.

5

On a bleak, murky morning in fresh April, when the sun was practically a sickly, butter-disc in a stodgy sky, the collaborator, and co-supervisor of Mr. Lindwürm's industrial powerhouse, his teammate and aide-de-camp — a man identified as Ligore Lassiter — proceeded across the solemn and sodden moor to visit the doors of the Staines Town parish poorhouse.

The matron of the home found Mr. Lassiter at the front opening of the institution, by the hooded lychgate: 'Better come in,' she told her visitor, once he had dismounted. 'We have warm spiced rum to grant you. It's about to spittle-speck out there, so hasten inside. The sky is gloomy as an undertakers' blanket...'

Mrs. Pinsetter called for her trustee, Seedpod (who was never far away), to take hold of Lassister's pony. Once this was done, she escorted the important man inside.

'I shall *not* imbibe madam,' Lassiter told her, without offering any smile and only once they had stepped inside the dim hall. He removed a broad-brimmed hat that hid sly eyes. He placed the hat upon a peg. 'I will go directly to *chapel*.'

Mrs. Pinsetter narrowed her eyes, 'Chapel?'

'You have a chapel? I will pray before doing business...'

'Certainly, um, do you want someone to take care of you in the chapel? For example, I can get a buxom girl to come to sit by your side, to make your prayers *especially* enjoyable...'

'I'm not going to the chapel for amusement,' Lassiter retorted with a scowl. 'I'm going for *prayer*...' He gave another snort, then added, 'I won't be long. Afterwards, I have issues to discuss, so prepare an office for a conversation.'

'By all means, erm? It will be my distinct pleasure to entertain you in my parlour.'

Lassiter gave a half-hearted shrug.

'Will you take warm milk or minted water if you don't take brandy?'

'No, I will *not*,' he muttered.

Mr. Lindwürm's right-hand man discovered the matron's parlour without any help, and he entered without knocking after he had finished prayers in the chapel.

'It's good to meet you, sir,' Mrs. Pinsetter said as she stood up from her wicker chair and grinned. 'Welcome to our modest institution. Would you mind telling me how your boss, Mr. Lindwürm, is doing? I hope he is keeping well?'

'Mr. Lindwürm sends salutations, madam. He thinks highly of the good works you do here. You will find, in time, that Mr. Lindwürm is not merely an exceptionally wealthy man, but he's also a charitable pioneer and a merchant prince... The man I am honoured to call my best friend is an imaginative philanthropist.'

'I don't doubt it... are you sure you will not take a drink with me? Maybe I can tempt you with a mouthful of something sweet? Madeira wine, perhaps?'

'I will *not*, madam. I never allow the poison of alcohol to pass my lips. May I get to the point, dear lady?'

Mrs. Pinsetter tugged an ear, 'Why not sit down? I can offer you my own basket chair.'

'Ask your assistant to bring me a simple wooden pedestal if you insist that I must sit in your company. Though I am pleased to remain standing.'

Mrs. Pinsetter got her flabby frame up, to move to the door, and to call for Seedpod. The assistant attended right away. After whispered conversation, the trustee left to look for a carpenter's stool.

'Why not wait by the fire?' Mrs. Pinsetter offered, with a smile.

'I prefer the chill, if it's all the same. I find that a chilled room is better for a man's flow of circulation. Warm air from an open hearth makes a man dull-witted... Please, may we get underway?' He pulled his watch from his pocket, 'Time is short, dear woman.'

'Yes, sure. Um? Should my fire be extinguished? Would that make you feel more comfortable?'

'Oh, Mrs. Pinsetter, it doesn't matter about the fire, or a drink, or a chair. Please might we get started? I'm comfortable *enough*... I'm here to discuss an opening.' Lassiter said took a large breath and cleared his throat. 'There is a gap for one of your interns. I'm recruiting new workers for my division. My talents have been put to use at a new unit. After considerable prayer, it has come to me that giving such a magnificent chance to one of your inmates would be the most right-eous and Christian course of action.'

'That's very charitable of you, Mr. Lassiter. Very philanthropic. Mr. Lindwürm agrees, does he?'

'As I told you, my friend is a renowned philanthropist, and supports all of my initiatives.'

At that moment Seedpod stomped into the room carrying a foot-stool: 'Will this do?' he grunted.

'Place it by the wall, will you?' Lassiter said with a sullen glance. 'So, ma'am, what I need from you is a young Christian person who is willing, has a strong body, and is ready to work in the manufactory. The ideal applicant will be young and in good health, robust and hearty, and will be enthusiastic about his scriptures....'

'Most of our inmates meet those touchstones,' suggested Mrs. Pinsetter. 'Are you looking, particularly, for a boy?'

'Boy. He will be amply rewarded, of course, and will be housed and fed at our new steam shed. He'll be provided with work-boots and fresh work-clothes. So, you see, in other words, he will be off

33

your hands. Naturally, you will be financially remunerated for your good standing in the matter. You'll be rewarded for providing the perfect recruit. How does that sound?'

Mrs. Pinsetter's eyes twinkled, and she licked across her top lip. She clasped her hands to her chest and said, without thinking, 'Take Seedpod. He's my most reliable steward, aren't you my dear?' She nodded toward the adolescent who loitered by the parlour door. 'He's eager to begin and a very responsible young man, aren't you, my dear?'

Lassiter intervened: 'No, ma'am, I could never take your most reliable trustee. That would be totally unthinkable. No, I'm thinking of *someone else*. I am thinking of a person who has never been given the chance to advance above their current level of expectation. What is the best way to describe the person I'm looking for? — one who is adventurous. Yes, do you know anyone you'd characterise as intrepid? Do you know a boy like that? Someone who you might think is, how do I phrase this delicately, someone that you might deem, *expendable*?'

'Um, it's a golden opportunity, right? I wouldn't like to waste it. What do you think, Seedpod? Who would you recommend?'

Seedpod nodded, 'Instantly I would have to say the young Tom Bisbee comes to mind. He fits the bill admirably...'

'Does he? I don't know him,' mumbled the matron. 'Is the boy brave and sensible — and above all virtuous? Also, is he intrepid? And, *ahem*, is the boy expendable?'

'I think so, ma'am. Tom Bisbee is the constant companion of the deplorable cripple Stormbuckler. They sleep mat-to-mat, share mealtimes, gossip side-by-side, and pray together on the same pew. Separating them would be beneficial to both, wouldn't it? Being forced apart would make them grow stronger and teach them how to be independent. Tom would have a good opportunity, and Stormbuckler would learn how to stand on his own two feet. *Ha ha!* That's if he had two of the same!' Seedpod grinned at his own joke.

'Ah, is that the boy you mean? Stormbuckler's little friend? Yes, I think I know the lad you mean. Good thinking, Seedpod,' Mrs. Pinsetter gave Seedpod a smile. 'Two birds with one stone, eh?' She turned to Mr. Lassiter. 'Yes, as you heard, my trustee has reminded me that we have the perfect candidate for you. The boy in mind is totally trustworthy and is a tried-and-tested worker.'

'Good, that's settled. He'll win himself fifteen shillings bounty and will take accommodation and meals at steam shed 7 of Lindwürm's manufactory. Please have him delivered to Cromford Mill, by Two Rivers, on Monday next week. He should arrive washed and dressed. He'll start work right away. I am pleased to offer you a sovereign *now*, good lady, for your time and to serve as a search fee...' He took a shiny leather purse from his waistcoat pocket, 'And a shilling for your attendant...' he threw the silver coin to Seedpod, who caught it in his fist. 'Thanks for your help, lad.' Lassiter passed the matron a gold sovereign, then marched from the parlour without another word.

Mrs. Pinsetter put a hand on her wide hip and gave a sigh of satisfaction, 'What a truly excellent person. A true champion of men...'

'Yes,' Seedpod nodded, as he looked at his own coin, 'A true champion. That man is a saint. I better go help him with his ride... he might offer me another penny.'

After his time in the sack, Stormbuckler was allowed back to his place of employment, to sweat in the poorhouse piggery.

He enjoyed working with animals outside, so he reasoned that as part of his sentence, they might rob him of *that* precious enjoyment. But they hadn't, and he reasoned that was perhaps because *everyone else* imagined that working in the pigsty was *not* easy. But he had never disliked it. In fact, for Stormbuckler, it was an *ideal* occupation. He worked more-or-less unsupervised, and he was able to sketch out his plans and diagrams on gateposts and wood panels whenever he had some time.

It was true that working with hogs was physically taxing, and it was also true that Stormbuckler began and ended his working days earlier and later than *anyone* else. It was additionally true that he worked in *all weathers*, whether it was to dig solid earth when frost made the ground as hard as doorstones, or to fork-out fly-blown sties

35

in the skin-blistering heat of the mid-summer sun. But Stormbuckler never complained. Compared to being confined inside the oakum-picking shop, the piggery was very much his forechosen pick of employment.

Stormbuckler had worked in the poorhouse piggery since the age of twelve, helping old Mr. Jims, who had gained the status of trustee by taking responsibility for the animals. Mr. Jims had taught Stormbuckler how to prepare and serve the pigs their food, how to fork-over and replace their bedding straw, and how to get the mother pigs prepared for littering. He also taught Stormbuckler how to care for piglets once they arrived. And how to keep a boar away from a sow who sat *on heat*. These days, Mr. Jims would be found concealed from weather extremes in a dilapidated shed on the edge of the piggery. He typically kept his eyes closed and a pipe in his mouth. This was ideal for Stormbuckler because it meant he was essentially left in charge of his own affairs.

Stormbuckler spent most days washing and preparing the animals for market, or fixing their regular meals. In return for such labours, the pigs taught *him* lessons. Mr. Jims said it was important to talk to the pigs, 'Tell them what you're doing, or they'll not be happy. They're intelligent, do you see? You have to explain what's taking place, or they'll get anxious. Or *worse*, they'll get angry.' Stormbuckler understood this and talked to his animals all the time. 'You don't want an angry hog...' Mr. Jims would tell him, especially on the days when Stormbuckler was being closemouthed. 'An angry hog is the most dangerous animal in the world. An angry hog will kill a man with a single blow. Always talk to the hogs...'

So Stormbuckler talked to the animals and learned that each pig had his or her own unique personality. He eventually worked out what the assorted grunts, oinks, and the squeals meant, for example 'I'm cold' or 'I'm hungry' or 'I'm afraid.' After a while, he understood that, like humans, pigs had a social hierarchy and they fought to preserve it. Pigs were enthusiastically curious, and they loved to work things out. So, because of all this, Stormbuckler felt an affinity with the beasts. If two pigs had differences of opinion, Stormbuckler would ask them to talk it over. They normally settled disputes amicably, but if violence ensued, he withdrew to a safe distance and allowed them to sort things out without his interference. Stormbuckler also found that pigs could be loyal and comradely, and was immensely proud when his favourite sow, a medium-sized porker Mr. Jims had named Maxen, chased an intruder off one evening. Some guy had broken into the site to rob the poorhouse of its silver. But Maxen had broken down her fencing and charged at the villain. She had made such a rumpus that everyone came out and the constable got brought over from town to take the rascal away, in manacles. The man had cowered in a corner while Maxen puffed her snout at him. Stormbuckler liked to think that Maxen had been protecting *all of them*, but Mr. Jims said she doing what came naturally : 'defending her piglets and securing her stash of food.'

At around noon Stormbuckler heard one of his pigs make an alarm call, a series of grunting barks, which started all the other pigs *oinking*. Stormbuckler knew this was their signal that a stranger approached. He told the animals not to worry and explained he'd go and see who it was. A barrow-pig, a big lad that Mr. Jims had named Eglon, made a blowing *oof* that meant, 'Well, get on with it *then...*' So Stormbuckler vaulted over the hurdle to find out who was threatening to disrupt their peace.

As it happens, on this occasion, the stranger was his friend Tom Bisbee, who had come to visit him during a break.

'Are you well, mate?' Tom said. He had something held in his clenched fist that he wanted Stormbuckler to see. He extended his arm but kept his fingers closed.

'What have you got?' Stormbuckler asked, wrinkling his nose.

'I found it,' said his companion. 'I kept it till now. But you should have it back.' Tom Bisbee unscrewed his fingers to reveal a small cockleshell that sat in the hollow of his grubby palm.

'It's my beauty,' said Stormbuckler, with a wide grin. 'That's the shell I lost when they captured me. It fell out of my bag. Where did you get it? '

'It was in the same place you dropped it. I found it lay in the dunhouse dirt. I washed it with water then I sewed it into a corner of my blanket. Do you want it back?'

Stormbuckler made a downcast expression and rubbed his chin, 'Maybe it should go back in the ground. If they find it on me, I'm doomed...'

'Yeah, maybe you're right. That's why I didn't give it to you right away. But you can have it now if you want. It's up to you.'

'Can I ask you something?' Stormbuckler used hushed tones for what he was about to ask. 'How did they know about my bag? How did they know it was *me* who had put it there? I'd hidden it *well* in the ground. I have been thinking about that ever since they put me in the sack.'

'From what I heard, someone bleated. They ratted on you. Someone found the bag by accident when they poked about with a stick. They went to the matron, and they told her... the rest is history.'

'But how did matron know the bag belonged to me? It could've belonged to *anybody*. How did they know that I'd be in the lavvy?'

'Who else goes to the lavvy so early? Just you and Mr. Jims. You're up first because you start work at dawn with the pigs. Everyone knows that. And who else would keep bones and shells in a pig's bladder bag?' Tom Bisbee paused for a long while and, although he avoided eye contact.

Stormbuckler nodded.

So Tom said, 'Everyone knows you doodle-doo all day... Your *doodle-doos* are always of bones and shells.'

'Doodle-doo all day?' Stormbuckler repeated, feeling quite annoyed at this uncalled-for accusation. He crossed his arms over his chest. 'I don't *doodle do* all day...'

'What's that then?' Tom Bisbee pointed to numerous marks scribbled onto the lower barrier of the enclosure that separated the orchard from the garden. 'You did those drawings, didn't you?'

'Well, yes, *but* —' Stormbuckler examined the closest doodle-doo as if he'd never seen it before 'It doesn't prove I doodle all day... does it?'

'These drawings are of regular lines and curly shapes. Like they're supposed to represent bones and shells. Most folk, when they draw, do sketches of people... or trees. Nice things! But you scrawl bones and shells.'

38

'I see,' Stormbuckler said. He ducked his head and made a long sigh. 'The Reverend once told me that the shapes I draw are known as *geometric*.' He took a gulp of air, 'I draw them to get those shapes out of my head.' He reduced his voice to a whisper, 'These geometric forms chase me, in my dreams. The haunt my sleeping hours. It's the only way I can release the ghosts in my head. When I draw that kind of shape, I feel better. You think I'm mad, don't you?'

'Ghosts? You have ghosts in your head? Please don't ever-er tell anyone that, especially an adult... they will lock you up and throw away the keys...'

'I know it sounds crazy, *sorry*.'

'Why have you never told me this before?' Tom asked.

'I did not think you'd understand,' whispered Stormbuckler.

Both boys became silent. Tom Bisbee put a foot on the lower railing. Stormbuckler followed. He placed his stump on the rail. This simple act of unison eased the tension between them. 'I have something to tell you,' Tom announced. 'I'm bursting to tell you about my news. It's a secret, but I wanted *you* to be the first to know.'

Stormbuckler began to bounce his knee and put his shoulder close to his mate, 'What is it? My-oh-my what is it? Tell me, tell me.'

'I'm *going*...'

'Going? What do you mean going? Going where?'

'I'm leaving the poorhouse. They found me a job. A real job. A job in town. Down in town working in a new unit. Working in the manufactory. Working for a geezer they call Lassiter.'

'God, what a wonderful opportunity. This is miraculous news.'

'Yeah, I know. It is, isn't it? I shall be paid for my work too. And they will be bread. And clothes. And I will be boarded there. It's a dream come true...'

'It really is. I bet you cannot wait, right?'

'I can't. I'm so excited that my tummy hasn't stopped jumping about since they told me. I start work next Monday. That's when I say goodbye to this place forever and hello to my new life.'

'How amazing. God, you must be pleased. You have won this opportunity by being good and reliable. I am incredibly happy for you .'

'I'm glad you're happy. I'm glad you're fine with this news, my friend, because I was worried you might take it badly. More than anything I wanted *your* blessing...'

'And you *have* my blessing, mate. I'm going to say a special prayer of thanks tonight, a particular prayer of thanks for good news. *Such good news.*' And with those words, Stormbuckler did something he'd never done before — he gave his companion an embrace.

Tom Bisbee closed his eyes after their embrace, and he walked away. Stormbuckler noticed his pal's shaking legs, as he went. Tom turned around and said, '*Ooh*, I almost forgot this...' Tom tossed Stormbuckler the cockle shell.

Stormbuckler took possession of the shell without another word. He watched his friend wander into the main building. Stormbuckler looked at the shell, which was now wrapped so tightly into his fist that the sharp edges drew blood. He launched the shell as far as he could throw it. The shell shot into the air, to land somewhere far off. It landed, with a clomp, at least twenty steps from the pigs. 'Holy biscuits,' Stormbuckler said. 'What rotten news.' He heard barrow-pig Eglon give a loud grunt, so he pulled himself together: It was lunchtime for the animals. He knew he must feed the hogs. 'Coming,' he shouted. He flung his footless leg over the fence.

He returned to his essential work.

~

Priory Lodge had been buzzing with excitement and bustle ever since Mrs. Oldcorne announced she had asked the American magnate Asher-John Lindwürm to dinner... and he had accepted her invitation. She told everyone that it was most likely his *first social outing* in England, after arriving from the colonies. Their household had been fortunate enough to acquire the honour thanks to their mistress's ingenious, unblinking social gameplay. Mrs. Oldcorne had been astute enough to strike first, netting the county's most prestigious and prideworthy burbot.

So silverware had to be polished, lamps filled, grates cleared, and fireplaces scrubbed so they looked new. Carpets and curtains had to be swabbed, and furniture would have to be hand-buffed until mirror-polished. The gardens would have to be tip-top, the bulb plantations cut to perfection, the fountains repaired, the roses pruned, the hedges trimmed, the walls repainted, the containers freshened-up and all the vermin suitably controlled.

On the Wednesday before the millionaire-innovator's visit, Mrs. Oldcorne took the significant, and unusual, step of attending the basement of her own home to convey an informational address to her gathered domestic staff. Her ruffled bodice and lace-up collar sparkled superiorly in the muted pallor of this rarely visited down-stairs world. 'I do not need to tell you that the mechanical entrepreneur, Mr. Asher-John Lindwürm is coming to dinner *this Saturday.*' Everybody cheered. Some male attendants performed enthusiastic *huzzahs.* Mrs. Oldcorne allowed her staff to settle, then went on, 'I think Mr. Lindwürm's fortunes are inextricably linked to ours here in Staines Town. By stroke of chance — let's call it serendipity — the luminary industrialist has decided to settle in 'our neck of the woods,' which is a peculiar American expression that, based on my interpretation, means that he has entrenched himself within our vicinage. That means we will all reap the dividends of his successes. And I mean *all of us...*' Their mistress wavered, to consider her staff and offer each of them a smile of encouragement. 'I doubt that *anyone* in this town will remain unaltered by Mr. Lindwürm's operations in the community. The gentleman already retains and operates the largest of three mills and the manufacturing plant. He's opening another division this month and will procure the brew-house fields and the hop kilns...' This disclosure precipitated several footmen to carp and snort, because it might prompt alehouses to offer them fewer products. 'Whether we like it or not,' Mrs. Oldcorne added, as she lifted her voice above their grumbles, 'This American is here to stay. I predict his advent in our town will transform all our lives.'

'Ma'am?' asked the cook. 'I never catered for an American before... in twenty years as a domestic servant. Would you tell me what an American eats?'

'Good question, and thank you for it. It is my understanding that the average American consumes rare beef-steak and potato... these plain items are most often accompanied by a side-dish of mashed corm. I think the corn is made into fritters. Would you prepare something of that nature, to make Mr. Lindwürm feel at home?'

The cook tapped her pencil on her order book and frowned, 'Ma'am I was thinking, perhaps, of presenting a plate of roast beef with gravy and pudding, purees of vegetables with parcels of herbs, plus a second course of roasted poultry with bread-sauce. And a dressed trout as our centrepiece. With iced desserts...Also, a selection of spicy pastries...'

'That sounds admirable, would you be able to add beef steaks and mashed corn to your list?'

The cook opened her book to jot down notes, 'Ma'am, I ought to be able to get hold of the grill steaks, but I don't know where I'd get corn at this time of the year...'

'It does not matter, do the best you can.'

'What about wine?' asked the butler. 'I recommend a mature Cabernet Sauvignon to go with beef and a Burgundy for the poultry. Also, what's the man's main tipple? I understand that most American's enjoy a dram or two of best sipping whisky, although I have heard it's their unfortunate habit to adulterate the purity with ginger syrup...'

Everyone laughed at this ridiculous eccentricity and the butler smiled along. But Mayotte creased her brow and offered a suggestion from the back row: 'Mr. Lindwürm is a Wesleyan,' she shouted.

'I'm sorry dear,' cried Mrs. Oldcorne. 'The girl behind? The girl in the back row. Did you squeak something? We couldn't hear what you said...'

'It's me! My name is Mayotte...' The lady's maid pushed herself forward, 'I was suggesting that Mister Lindwürm is a Wesleyan...'

'Oh, it's *you*,' Mrs. Oldcorne crossed her arms and gave a hard smile: 'What does it matter what the man's religious views are? It makes no difference whether he's a Wesleyan or, I don't know, an oriental Buddhist, does it?'

Some of the staff chuckled, but the butler shook his head and frowned: 'If the young lady is correct in that assumption, and let us pray that she's not, but if she is... it leaves us with a complication, ma'am.'

'Does it?' Mrs. Oldcorne asked. 'What complication? Why do his religious observances have any?'

'Ma'am,' the butler said, using the most solemn tones he could muster, 'Members of the Wesleyan church are committed to total *abstinence...*'

'Abstinence?' Mrs. Oldcorne sent her most significant retainer a sceptical glance. 'Whatever do you mean by such a peculiar word? You don't mean temperance, do you? That cannot be right, surely, can it?'

'No, ma'am, I *don't* mean temperance ...'

'Thank goodness for that,' said Mrs. Oldcorne, allowing a relieved breath.

'I mean entire teetotalism.'

～

By Saturday, the luxurious house at Priory Lodge — the home of Henry Oldcorne and his ambitious wife — was in a state of commotion and agitation while the domestic staff conducted final preparations for the impending arrival of their most esteemed guest.

Mrs. Oldcorne sent-out two liveried servants to act as footmen and provisional ostlers for the American's carriage arrived when it *eventually* arrived. She'd also appointed her husband's best valet to act as provisional 'under butler' for the day and gave the man explicit instructions to wait outside, by the front gate, and be ready to welcome the rich industrialist into their home. And afterwards, the man should dedicate himself *exclusively* to the needs and require-ments of Mr. Lindwürm.

At roughly six o'clock, amidst feverish anticipation, Mr. Lind-würm's carriage had still *not* yet turned up. Mrs. Oldcorne paced up-and-down her entrance hall: 'Where is the man?' she asked as she ran a gloved finger across a silver-topped umbrella stand. 'He's about to become late...' She looked at the grandfather clock and said to nobody in particular, 'Is this accurate? Perhaps this clock is racing ahead.'

Her husband, always optimistic and jolly, grinned to his wife. Henry Oldcorne twistled the ends of his 'Imperial' moustache and provided the sagest opinion he could think-up on the spur of the moment: 'You should not worry, my lettuce. Colonial types *invariably* run late. It's in the juice of their forefathers, I think. Don't get your drawers in a tangle...'

'I need *you* to conduct yourself with poise, elegance, and *probity* when he arrives, sir. I do not want indecorous comments... like that one... while the American is *here* if you please, dear husband.'

'Yes, my lettuce.'

Mrs. Oldcorne absentmindedly played with a twig in the ornate floral display, then stepped to the open door to ensure everything looked tickety-boo for the hundredth time. She checked that her newly appointed *under-butler* stood in his allotted position. Her servant returned a disagreeable and uncouth 'thumbs-up' sign and she made a mental note to chastise him *later* about employing vulgar and familiar gestures. But, right then, with a cluster of tick-tocks, click-clacks, clink-clunks, and the most ear-splitting pops, an extraordinary contrivance turned the far corner of their long avenue and made its coughing-chattering way to the frontage of the Oldcorne's property. In a series of sharp chattering knocks, the entire screw-and-bolt mechanism came to a bizarre, wheezing, and snorting halt directly outside their front gates.

Mrs. Oldcorne had never seen anything like it in her life: the machine had a button-upholstered armchair attached to a spluttering engine. The chair was equipped with padded arms. A leather hood was applied over the lap of the passenger, who sat facing forwards, with a shiny brass repository and an assortment of glossy footplates below riding boots. Three cog-driven perambulator wheels supported the structure *upwards*, with a single trailing-wheel that crawled to the rear. Over the aft wheel sat another gentleman who wore a fisherman's coat and had been seated upon what looked like a child's high-chair. He wore a greasy cloth cap and held a set of silver handlebars in thickly gloved hands. His lengthy woollen scarf collapsed between the gap of his legs and looked as if it might get entangled in the gubbins below at any moment. The vehicle was completed with a briefcase knotted, apparently at random, on top of a cable package that hung, dangerously low, by a back tyre.

'There's two of them...' Mrs. Oldcorne shouted, hoping that at least one of her three servants might identify the 'correct' visitor. Both men on the peculiar, motorized tricycle looked similar, if not identical. They both wore tight goggles, both had bandanas strapped around their wind-chilled faces, and both wore riding boots with long raincoats. 'Which is the millionaire-inventor?' she shouted, hoping one of the servants might indicate. The temporary under-butler gave a shrug, and, after a short delay, the man went to help the front-seat passenger. He figured the man in the front, seated in the most comfortable of the armchairs on the contrivance, must be the principal and most notable traveller. So, he offered the man an arm so he might step from the dangerous contraption.

'Good evening, sir,' said the servant, using the script his mistress had drilled into him earlier, and that he had rehearsed several times over: 'Might I take your hat and cane? And, *um*, may I show you to the door while my colleague leads your horses to the stables... um?' The butler rubbed his chin and went blank because, of course, there were *no horses,* not was there any hat and cane to be taken.

The passenger removed a pair of goggles and pulled a kerchief down from his nose and chin, to reveal the extent of his face. While this was going on, the driver of the contraption, a shorter fellow, though dressed the same way, broke free of the metalwork and began to locomote himself, with some resolution, towards the front of the grand house.

'Um, sir...' yelled the under-butler, 'Might I stop you right there? You *can't* go in...'

The driver turned to gaze at the servant and to pull his driving gloves across the stretched joints of his knuckles: 'Whyever not?' the guest asked.

'Just to inform you, sir, and I'm sorry about this sir, but to inform you, sir, with greatest respect, that you must use the servant's entrance around the side. Would you please enter via the servants' side entrance? And please make way promptly there while I direct the principal guest into the lodge. Once I've delivered *your master*, I will arrange for someone to attend your needs in our basement...'

'Oh, it's fine...' said the tricycle driver. 'I'm sure we can *both* go inside...'

'Oh no, sir. You cannot. I must stop you.'

Then the temporarily appointed under-butler-for-the-day hurried towards the driver, though he also became aware that Mrs. Oldcorne motioned frantically *at him*, as if she was urgently seeking to gain his attention. At first, Mrs. Oldcorne indicated by waving her gloves in a gentle manner, but when her simple gesture failed, she began to gesticulate in a frenzied motion, as if she tried to bat away a queen hornet from her hair. Mrs. Oldcorne hopped from foot to foot, ten she glowered at her man in quite a fearsome manner.

'I'm sorry,' the servant said, 'My mistress wants me. She is indicating, quite wildly *actually*. Would you mind remaining here while I go see what she wants?'

The under-butler headed back towards the front door of the house, closely followed — footsteps behind — by the driver of the contraption and his passenger.

'What's wrong, ma'am?' queried the young servant, as he reached the elegant porch. Mrs. Oldcorne gave the servant the most peremptory shove — a push that almost completely toppled him off-balance — then she prepared her most irresistible smile for the two gentlemen who had trailed up the garden path, behind him. They'd raced on up.

The driver of the mechanized tricycle removed a cloth cap and said, 'Mrs. Oldcorne, it's a pleasure to see you *again*...'

'The pleasure is all mine,' she said, bending her knee in acquiescence.

'Can I present my best friend? He's the co-director of my company and has been in your country for the last months setting things up before my arrival onto these shores. He's my most trusted colleague, his name is Lassiter...'

'Good evening,' said the front seat passenger of the machine. He removed what appeared to be a smoking cap.

'I'm honoured, sir,' said Mrs. Oldcorne, giving the 'second in command' a small bow. 'I've heard good things.'

'Quite so,' said Lassiter. He made a growl-like sound before he returned a thin smile. He added: 'Would you do me the kind indulgence of keeping one of your trusted servants near our automobile during our visit? We have discovered, through painful experience, that our machine attracts a multitude of undesirable characters. They often chance to take-away a souvenir or two from our vehicle if we don't guard it...'

'Yes, of course. I shall post one of my most efficient men to guard-over your machine, *immediately*.' Mrs. Oldcorne shot a dirty look at her makeshift butler, 'See to it will you?' she instructed. Then she widened her arms and welcomed them both inside, 'Come inside. My husband is anxious to greet you.'

Mrs. Oldcorne guided the gentlemen into her lobby where her chief manservant extended his arm to remove their outer cloaks and gloves. The visitors passed-by the retainer without to stopping, and headed for the drawing room. Mrs. Oldcorne shook her head and looked daggers at the old butler, who remained rigid by the front door, his mouth agape and his arms held horizontally, waiting to take their non-existent capes and hats.

After a loud sigh, Mrs. Oldcorne raised her hands in a gesture of surrender and announced, 'Husband... he's here...' She had to do the butler's job for him, 'May I present the eminent American industrialist Mr. Asher-John Lindwürm and his co-director and companion, Mr. Lassiter.'

'Jolly good show,' bubbled the exuberantly whiskered Henry Oldcorne. He emerged from their best room and, as thoroughly rehearsed, he gave vent to a cheerfully prepared smile. He extended his arms fully, in an effort to formally receive his distinguished guests. Henry Oldcorne had dressed in respectable evening attire, with a dinner jacket adorned with glittering medals, and a pair of ironed trousers. Although Mrs. Oldcorne only saw his openly reddish face and recently wetted lips. Clearly, her husband had enjoyed one or two drinks while he waited. In fact, when she looked closer, she saw that Henry Oldcorne held a brandy balloon between pink fingers: 'What the heck is this? ' he blurted. His jaw dropped as he regarded the two men, His brandy-glass tilted at a perilous angle, almost spilling precious liquid. 'I mean, what in holy blazes?'

To ease the disgraciousness of her husband's impolite statement, Mrs. Oldcorne swiftly explained: 'The gentlemen arrived on motor transport, dear. Our guests arrived clothed in an entirely unusual manner, spouse, because they came by *mechanical* methods. Their machine, if you will, is situated stationary *outside*. Simply put, it is the most incredible device. Really extraordinary! So, dear husband, that is why they arrived at our door attired *thusly*.'

'Really?' said Henry Oldcorne. He offered the men a loud *harumph*. 'We expected you to arrive by carriage, didn't we lettuce?' He lifted the almost-empty brandy glass to his lips, then sneered. 'We expected you to be appropriately dressed for dinner. And, Mr. Lindwürm, sir, we expected you to arrive without company and to be here *bang-on-time*.'

'I'm sorry,' Lindwürm replied. 'I'd be pleased to offer an explanation: I brought my companion because I still feel ill at ease when I visit new people. I still feel out-of-water in this new country... new to me, that is. A fish, do you see? Do you understand? Possibly, no, you do *not*. Also, I find it easier to start my vehicle if there are two of us. The machine needs a push to get going, do you understand? And the reason for our lateness is due to poor navigation on my part... and for that, I apologise. If my travelling companion poses a difficulty for you, I can ask Lassiter to wait outside, if you'd like. Is that what you'd prefer?'

'Ha-ha! No, of course not. We don't want that, do we husband?' interjected Mrs. Oldcorne. She gave her spouse a theatrical smile. 'Mr. Lassiter is very welcome, isn't he dear? Yes, you are very welcome, very welcome *indeed*. Please come in, both, to the drawing room. Can we get you drinks? I think we *all need* drinks.' She glanced at her husband's empty brandy glass and whispered, 'Except, perhaps, *you*.'

The men strolled into the main room. 'My three wheeled riding car is a single cylinder model,' Mr. Lindwürm explained to Henry

Oldcorne, as he looked about their room. 'I have a twin cylinder riding car in development too,' he added.

'You don't say, old man! Good for you!' Henry Oldcorne played with the ends of his moustache and looked baffled. Nevertheless he soldiered on, as if he'd been propositioned by a visiting a princeling from Uttar Pradesh who posited a complex military conundrum at the Royal Military College. 'How utterly fascinating.'

'I have a four-wheel pre-production model *too*...'

'Good show, old man. Can I get you drinks? Best Scotch? Gin and bitters? Port wine?'

'Do you have mineral water?' Lassiter asked, on behalf of both. 'We'll take carbonated water.'

'Um? I think we have mineral water,' though Henry Oldcorne seemed mystified by the request. He hoped his butler would soon come out of hiding to help. 'Can you find carbonated water for our guests?' he shouted.

'Water, sir?' asked the retainer. He appeared at the door though remained rather flustered.

'Yes, *yes*, water. Surely it can't be too difficult.' Henry Oldcorne turned his attention back to his visitors, 'I'm sorry about my butler. He's most awfully ancient.'

'Not a problem,' said Asher-John Lindwürm. 'May we sit?'

'Of course, how rude of me. Sit ye down. *Sit ye down.*'

When the guests were led into the formal dining room for dinner, the strained and uncomfortable mood returned to the party. When they entered the room, Mr. Lassiter, who had been completely silent in the drawing room, as Mr. Lindwürm clarified that their motorised tricycle was propelled by *combustion* and not by 'steam' as Henry Oldcorne persisted in advocating, suddenly began to speak: 'Mr. Lindwürm and I refrain from consuming meat in any form,' he declared. 'It has to do with our religious moderation. We occasionally consume dairy and eggs. However, we never eat cooked or preserved beef.'

'Cooked or preserved, heh? So what about a juicy-red steak, leaking with fluids? I'll wager that's not out of the question is it, heh?' Henry Oldcorne gave the man nudge. 'Or a horse-meat tartare heh? That will go down a treat, what?'

Mr. Oldcorne beamed as he slapped Mr. Lassiter heartily on the back, causing the man to spill the glass of water he'd so carefully cradled all evening. The company-man frowned and replied, through *very* gritted teeth: 'We'll take a plate of vegetables, if you please. Would you ask your kitchen staff if your vegetables are contaminated with fats or meat sauces?'

'Contaminated? What? Our cook has been with us twenty years. She's a damn fine woman. She has never created a harmful dish in her life... The woman's a gifted chef de cuisine...'

'I'm sure she's excellent,' said Lassiter. 'But we find that vegetables are sometimes prepared by adding meat juices or animal fats to enhance their flavours, do you see? '

'Not really, old man. Why don't you lighten up? This is a dinner party, what?' I'm not hosting a meeting of the anti-vivisection league... Fill your chops with a big red steak, and grab a glass of claret, what? '

'Not now dear,' Mrs. Oldcorne said. She interposed herself between the quarrelling men, 'If our guests want to limit themselves to vegetables — that's entirely up to them. Please do not try to persuade them *otherwise*, dear husband.' She turned to address her principal guest, the millionaire Asher-John Lindwürm. 'I'll ask cook to come and explain what vegetables are unadulterated by juices and fats...'

'If you would, please. We would be most grateful. Thank you.'

'In my time, a companion ate what he was served in a hall... and he'd be grateful for it *too*,' mumbled Henry Oldcorne. 'I've eaten all sorts of repulsive horrors in my days, though I never uttered one single word of protest nor any snort of objection...Not one.'

'Not now, beloved, And, dear husband, we're not in your days any longer, thank goodness, and *this* isn't the Military Academy. These gentlemen have a perfect right to eat whatever they choose. They are guests in our home, so we must try our best to make them welcome.

And also, please, do not talk *sotto voce*, it's the very height of rudeness.'

'Sorry m'dear.'

~

After dinner, Henry Oldcorne hoped to lure the gentlemen into his smoking chamber, but neither guest smoked tobacco or swallowed alcohol, though he presented them with the choicest Dominican cigars and the brightest champagne-cognacs. Thus, Mrs. Oldcorne encouraged the guests to accompany her, instead, into the tapestry room. This was a fashionable living room that the lady of the house used infrequently to entertain her closer female friends.

Upon entering the room, Mr. Lindwürm marvelled at the splendid plaster-work ceilings, then reviewed the brilliantly sculpted chimneypiece. He completely discounted the rich draperies that embellished the walls. In fact, he relaxed with his back to her most prominent artwork, that of an intricate Flemish pastoral scene. Mr Lindwürm seemed entirely uninformed about quality textiles. 'Where is the lady with whom you came on your spontaneous visit to my house?' Mr. Lindwürm sought, as he sat back in her antique chair.

Henry Oldcorne grimaced, then he collapsed in a corner seat, to examine his high-gloss shoes.

'Do you mean my lady's maid?' Mrs. Oldcorne asked, offering a distant smile.

'I think I do,' returned Asher-John Lindwürm. 'I'm talking about the girl who accompanied you on the morning of your impromptu visit to my house... don't you remember?'

'I think you refer to my maid, sir,' Mrs. Oldcorne replied. 'She's performing other tasks tonight. She's probably busy in the scullery...'

'Get her up, would you?'

'I beg your pardon?' Mrs. Oldcorne clenched her jaw and crossed her arms over her plentiful chest. 'The maid is busy, sir. She's busy with *menials*. I shall *not* get her up. Whatever next?'

'I understand, madam. But, all the same, I should like to see her. Why won't you bring her up to see me?'

'Mr. Lindwürm would like to discuss things with the young woman,' Mr. Lassiter added. 'He asks, with due politeness, that you have your maid attend us. *Now*. Please...'

'They are guests in our home, and we must make them feel welcome...' mumbled Henry. He imitated the words used by his wife — against him— just hours earlier.

'Very well,' said Mrs. Oldcorne, in a thickened tone of voice. 'I'll ring for her... though the truth is... I'm not pleased.'

∿

After a while, Mayotte arrived at the tapestry room, led by a senior manservant who gave a condescending eye-roll before he closed the door. So the Oldcorne's maid stood by the entrance, smoothed her uniform skirt, then twisted her wrists. Mayotte wore a plain black work-dress, with a pure white apron attached to a bodice, with a small white cap upon glossy dark hair.

'This is the same lady that came to my house?' asked Mr. Lindwürm. He did not seem entirely *convinced*: 'Enter the light, my dear. Let us inspect you. Why is she dressed like this? She is dressed altogether *differently* than when I last saw her.'

Mayotte stepped into the centre of the room and stood on the Chinese silk carpet. She waited their scrutiny. She felt like a prize heifer on show at the Guildford stock market. 'Parade forwards please, and circle,' demanded Lassiter.

Mayotte stepped from the China-rug and strolled around the room in an aimless manner, while the men watched her movements. 'Good, *good*, you may stop,' announced Mr. Lindwürm. 'Would it be acceptable if I asked her to sit?'

'Um, I'm not sure that's entirely appropriate, sir. It's not tolerable, sir, with much respect. I might remind you that *this* is a simple servant girl and it's not her place to be sat in the presence of betters. Less still, to converse with the likes you.'

'It's fine with me," Asher-John Lindwürm said. 'I think I am what you might describe as one of her betters, indeed I have even been described as *exalted* in my time. And it's fine *with me*. How does it sit

52

with you, Lassiter? Will you allow this simple servant to sit and to talk with us?' His companion gave a vigorous nod. 'And what about you Henry? Is it alright with you if this girl sits in our presence?'

'I confess I'm not particularly committed either way... do whatever you want.' Henry Oldcorne leaned back in his chair and closed his eyes.

'That's settled,' said Mrs. Oldcorne, taking charge once more. 'Go grab a plain chair from the side and sit by the window,' she instructed.

Mayotte went to get herself a chair, but Mr. Lindwürm stopped her, 'Tell her to bring the chair here. To sit beside *me*. In the warm. I can't see her if she's sat all the way over by the window.'

'Bring it here, *bring it here...*' scolded Mrs. Oldcorne, as if Mayotte had done something wrong. The woman pointed at an empty space near Mr. Lindwürm, 'Here, *here*,' she repeated, before she released a *very* loud sigh.

Mayotte sat on the chair and tugged her clothing into place. She fiddled with her cuffs.

'Why is she wearing a uniform?' asked Mr. Lindwürm. 'She looked splendid in that chequered cornflower dress when she came to visit me...'

'It was not *she* who came to visit you...' Mrs. Oldcorne reminded the American. She gave a wave of her hand, then used a lower and more guttural tone, 'Oh, what's the use?' She rolled her eyes, then added: 'This girl is a *servant*, sir. It's a fact I have found myself repeating, though you continue to ignore words. The girl was dressed in blue when you last saw her because she had been accompanying me to church, don't you remember?'

'Ah, yes, *now* I do. Pray tell me, young lady, remind me again, what is your name?'

'Me sir? They call me Mayotte, sir.'

'Mayotte? That is French, is it not?'

Mayotte shrugged, 'How do I know? It's a name *they* gave me...'

'Who gave you?' asked Mr. Lindwürm. He focused on her face to examine her eyes.

'Them, they... these.' Mayotte smiled hesitantly towards her lady-mistress, Mrs. Oldcorne. '*They* gave me the name when they took me in, sir.' Then the maid diverted her gaze to Henry Oldcorne, who slumbered. 'They were good to me, sir, both of them. Exceptionally good to me. They clothed me, they fed me, and they gave me my name. They said my name ought to be Mayotte because it sounded sophisticated and continental — and the name suited my shadier skin, sir. They allowed me to work my way to temporary lady's maid...'

'Hold on,' said Asher-John Lindwürm. 'Let me get this straight. Are you telling me that you are the adopted daughter of Mr. and Mrs. Henry Oldcorne?'

'Yes, sir, I suppose I am, sir...' Mayotte seemed bashful. Her brown eyes became watery. 'I was an orphan, sir, before these Christians took me in. They have been exceptionally good to me... please, sir, I must stress that. I have been indentured since the day they found me.'

'This is quite extraordinary,' declared Mr. Lindwürm. 'You mean this girl, in every practical sense, is your adopted daughter, yet you indentured her?'

Mrs. Oldcorne crumpled her legs under the chair and dropped her chin: 'It's not what you think, Mr. Lindwürm. She hasn't lived a life of bondage, if that is what has been implied. Quite the opposite, let me make that most clear. We have fed and dressed the girl, and we spent our own good money upon her... we don't operate a charity. We adopted this girl out of Christian kindness... we have been caring to her. Yes, I suppose you might claim that she's *loosely* indentured to this household, but we have been substitute parents to her in every other regard... in fact we've been wholly generous... through-and-through.'

'You placed her into a life of servitude? Is that the action of a Christian parent?'

'As I said, Mr. Lindwürm, we don't run a charity. She is expected to earn her place in this world...'

'Quite so,' added Mr. Lassiter, with one of his trademark growls.

'Never mind,' said Lindwürm. He narrowed his eyes as he chose his next words cautiously, 'The young lady impressed me when she visited. She had bright ideas. Maybe we can do a trade?'

'Trade? What sort of trade?' asked Mrs. Oldcorne. She sat straighter to rearrange her necklace. She looked at her husband but noted that he still snoozed.

'Do you still want to be my lobbyist? Or have you rescinded your offer?'

'No, I'd like to do it,' Mrs. Oldcorne said, with a spark of interest. 'Is that what you are about to chat about?'

'Do you want to be kept on a retainer? Is that how things would work if I contracted you to be my lobbyist?'

'I suppose so. You would keep me on as an *influencer*, and I will hop-to-it whenever you needed expertise... there'd be a monthly retainment fee'.

'So, a guinea a month be an acceptable subscription, would it? Perhaps with extra fees and expenses to be paid when incurred?'

'That seems most generous,' agreed Mrs. Oldcorne.

'Very well. Mr. Lassiter here will fix-up a loose contract and he'll have it sent over. It will be lightly worded, of course, but even so you should ask a notary to review it if you have any concerns... But there's *something else* that I will need before I agree to the conditions.'

'Yes?'

'I need your girl, Mayotte.'

'Um, but sir, she's not for sale. As you know, she's precious to me and I'm training her. She's to be my mistress's maid, and she's very dear to me, isn't that right, my love?' Mrs. Oldcorne presented Mayotte with an overly charitable smile.

'Well, I think it's down to the girl *herself*. I realize this situation is a lot more complex than I expected at the beginning of our dinner party... especially since I now learn she is, to all intents and purposes, your daughter. Therefore, I can't expect you to part with your daughter *cheaply*...'

'Well, indeed,' Mrs. Oldcorne provided a nod and accompanying gulp. 'That's why I can't let her go...'

'No, I see that,' agreed Mr. Lindwürm. 'Of course, it puts the business agreements between us *on hold*. I will instruct Lassiter to delay, indefinitely, a contract for your lobby services.'

'Hold on, *hold on*,' shouted Mrs. Oldcorne. She gave both men a painful stare and rubbed the bristles on her chin. 'Let's not be hasty. I think we can negotiate something mutually advantageous. Why don't you keep hold of her for ninety days... to see if you can use her services during that time? If you have used-up all her abilities in ninety days you can send her back to me, no bill, no fees, and no questions asked. I'll lend her on *approval*. But if you think that she might still be utilized after a ninety-day trial period, perhaps we might come to a remunerative figure that I would view as properly adequate compensation for such a great loss? For example, I'd have to train another member of staff, wouldn't I? As you know, staff recruitment doesn't come cheap.'

'That's very clever of you, ma'am. I think it's a well-considered offer. And I accept. Have this young woman delivered to us at Cromford Mill, by the Two Rivers, on Monday *next*. Dress her in her smartest Sunday clothes. Will she stay with you during the trial period of ninety days?'

'Yes, she will stay *here* to take dinner with us and sleep in her quarters. And she will continue to act as my servant at busy times... but will be relieved of all other domestic duties during the ninety days test period. She'll be at your beck and call during her trial with you.'

'Excellent,' Asher-John Lindwürm said. He clapped his hands. 'In that case, our agreement for you to provide lobby services applies once more. Lassiter will have the contract brought over. I'm glad everything has been settled amicably.'

'Wonderful.' Mrs. Oldcorne sank into her chair with a lingering smile on her face.

'Should I go now?' asked Mayotte. She rubbed her forehead to look over to Mrs. Oldcorne.

'Don't ask me,' she replied, 'Ask *him*...' Mrs. Oldcorne pointed to Asher-John Lindwürm. 'He's your master now.'

6

On a sticky, stuffy morning, when the noxious odour from the pungent piggery steamed and sprouted so abundantly that the local people held their noses, Stormbuckler rose at daybreak to make his way to the vacant jerry-come-tumble and afterwards, to prepare for daily duties.

Having comforted himself, he sauntered to the slop pile and was astonished to discover that his wire-handled pail had been removed from the place he had last left it. 'Where did that get to?' he challenged the crow in the tree. 'Did you see who grabbed my bucket?' But the bird simply spread his wings, and neglected to answer the question. After scraping his ear, Stormbuckler heard a deliberate splashing clatter that developed from *inside* the animal enclosure. He jerked his bad leg over the hurdle to investigate the peculiar noise.

Bent, with one knee to the ground, and almost in religious deference to the beasts, a dark-haired fellow with a long, low face, broad eyebrows, tight eyes, and an unusually flattened nose, was busy sorting out the peels from the cores.

'What are you doing?' Stormbuckler shouted.

'What does it look like I'm doing?' the burly ruffian said, as he looked over. 'What do you want here, kid?'

'I can't find my swill bucket,' Stormbuckler explained. 'Did you take it, stranger?'

'Yeah! What's it to you? I already used the thing. I came to feed the hogs.'

'Why did you do such a thing?' demanded Stormbuckler. 'That's *my* job. I do the pigs. I get up early to feed them. I don't know who you are...'

'Well, I've done it already, haven't I? You are late. So be helpful and go fetch some water...'

'How?'

'Come and collect the bucket. Are you a bonehead or something?'

Stormbuckler toppled over the inner rail of the swine enclosure, in his typical shuffle-hobble fashion. Then he stumbled closer to the burly man. 'Is it here?' Stormbuckler asked. 'Is my bucket here? I can't readily see it.'

'What's the trouble with you? What's amiss with your leg?' The rough stranger stood full height. That's when Stormbuckler observed how broadly built the man was. The intruder was a behemoth.

'I ain't got no foot, nor ankle neither, on one of my legs...' Stormbuckler explained to the giant. 'On account of the fact that it went missing when I was born an infant.'

'Went missing? That's *inattentive* of you — why don't you try to cling onto your things? First, it's a foot, now it's a bucket. You seem to be very negligent with your accessories!'

'About the foot, Mister, I suppose I was too young to know any better... but about the bucket, I came looking for it, didn't I? And I ain't scared of you, no matter how looming you might look to be.'

'What's your name, lad?' The huge man tilted his head to assess the youth. 'You've a lot of gumption. I like a fellow who is prepared to stand and fight a corner...

'Stormbuckler... I don't have a first name on account of the fact that I lost that too! If you're totting-up all my relinquishments, you had better add *that one* to the list.'

'Well, Master Stormbuckler, my name is Kilda. I'm a travelling pugilist. I'm here to take care of the pigs.'

'Where is Mr. Jims? He's the swine-master. Mr. Jims is who I work for. I served with him for years, mister, no offence meant to you an' all, but I will *have to* correct this mistake with Mr. Jims...'

'Haven't you heard, kid? Your Mr. Jims has been carted to the infirmary on the moor. The shelter run by Servite sisters.'

'What's awry with him?'

'I don't know for sure. They just told me he had a fall. They told me he couldn't get a breath. Worried he might not live, so they carted him to the nuns. They left him there, to see if the sisters might restore his health.'

'I did not know about that. When did this happen?'

'*Yesterday*, lad. Maybe you were unavailable. Don't they tell you things?'

'No!' Stormbuckler returned a melancholy headshake and dropped his shoulders. 'I suppose they don't need to tell *me* anything...'

'Well, anyway...' Kilda the pugilist took a deep breath. 'I'm running things now. So you need to get that into your head. Get some water, then help freshen this place. It needs a rake-over...'

'Yes, sir.'

'Put your teeth into it...' suggested Kilda, the pugilist.

It was the third day that the newcomer had been in charge of the piggery and, already, the place looked ten times better than it had been before he commenced. Stormbuckler gave the man a bewildered smile. 'Teeth? How can I put teeth into drawing a rake?'

'You must put teeth and marrow into *all the things* that you do, if you crave success.'

'Marrow?'

'Of course, *marrow*. Advance with your bones, then drag the rake back with your blood...that's the marrow of this task.'

'Blood?'

'Here, let me show you how to *rake like a fighter*.' The barbarous man yanked the tool from Stormbuckler's grasp. It looked insignificant in his huge hands. Kilda drove the tines into the tilth with a

59

deliberate growl. After that, he ploughed a line of unmistakable furrows. Then he dragged the tool back with a handsome swish. He made raking look easy. Kilda the pugilist crossed the rake back to the lad, 'Now, settle with your legs apart, with the rake held steady in both your spitted palms, then raise it above your head...'

'Like this?' said Stormbuckler with a smile. He raised the rake until it was over his shoulders.

'That's the way — now hold it stable for at least ten jackety-jacks...'

'Jackety-jacks?'

'That's how we count intervals in the ring. One *jackety* amounts to a single second... so ten jackety-jacks equates to a knock-out. That's right, hold it steady...' After five seconds, Stormbuckler let the rake slip. The prongs bounced densely into the earth. Kilda, the pugilist, tut-tutted. 'You'll never get strong if you don't *try*,' he said. 'How will you be a fighter unless you throw all your teeth and marrow into things? Now try again. I'll count the seconds for you.' Stormbuckler struggled again, and this time managed seven jackety-jacks. 'That's a lot better. Practice every day...'

'But I do not want to be a *fighter*...' Stormbuckler groaned. 'I just want to take care of pigs.'

'Nonsense, that's shiftless talk...' snarled Kilda. 'We *all* have to fight. Each one of us. We must fight for things that make us strong. We must fight for things that make us better. For example, love is worth fighting for, isn't it? And so is friendship. Sometimes we fight for water. Sometimes we fight for bread. Often we fight for forgiveness. Someday, perhaps soon, we will have to fight for air. We are all fighters in the end...'

'I never thought of it like that.'

'One day, you will crave something with all your heart. And when that day arrives, you'll be glad I lectured you on how to be a competent fighter...'

~

Five days afterward, under Kilda's guidance, Stormbuckler sensed he became sharper, fresher and a lot more self-assured. Kilda the pugilist had presented loads of exercises that he could perform while he carried out his chores in the pig-pens. Stormbuckler guessed that each task he was taught could be energetically remodelled into what Kilda interpreted as: 'Blood-juice and grindstone *exercises* for blood-juice and grindstone *men*.'

After eating a lunch that consisted of beet-peelings, Kilda began to teach Stormbuckler how to pull his hamstrings on the pen hurdles. The big man paused his exertions just long enough to distinguish some of the charcoal sketches that the young man had etched onto the wooden boards during the preceding summer. 'You did those likenesses, right?' he asked.

'Yeah, um? How did you know it was me?'

'Well, it wasn't old Mr. Jims, was it? I doubt he could bring a straight line to a post even if his life rested upon it... with his throbbing bones, his jittery hands, and his failing eyesight... so, who else could have done it?'

Stormbuckler bounced on one foot and gulped. 'Sorry! Should we brush my drawings off?'

'Brush them off? *Why* would I want you to do that?'

'Um? I'm sorry. I expect you think they mess the place up!'

Kilda the pugilist slapped his thigh and let out a roar of amusement. 'That's a good one. Mess the place up! To think that etchings could mess-up a pig pokey! That's a corker, that is, ha! You are a notable jokester; did you know that?' But Kilda raised an eyebrow. 'It would be a sin to deny your talents. If your desires are to be expressed through drawings, so be it. It's part of your hidden nature.'

Nobody had spoken sympathetic words about Stormbuckler's illustrations before. Stormbuckler supposed that nobody liked his drawings much, which is why they never remarked upon them. 'God love you! Do you genuinely think I have talent?' he asked.

'Yes, I do. So what are they? This looks like a shell. And these are plumes. And that's the skeleton of a fish, is it?'

'That's right.'

'How is it accomplished?'

'With pieces of coal that I find here and around.'

Kilda the pugilist dropped his head to consider the radiating branches of what was undoubtedly a sea-urchin that sat upon the tentacles of a starfish. He puckered his nose. 'No, I mean, how do you get those shapes and lines? Do you reproduce them from a copy?'

'Just out of my mind, I suppose.' Stormbuckler brushed his ear with the back of his hand.

'But how?'

'I do not know how...' Though Stormbuckler *did* know how. But his friend, Tom Bisbee, had warned him that he should *never* tell anyone about the geometric forms that chase him in his dreams. 'I just *doodle*, and they appear like that.'

'Have you ever been to the sea? Have you seen these shells resting on a beach? Or a starfish in a pool?'

'No,' Stormbuckler allowed his arms to fall by his sides. 'I can't leave this place, can I?'

'Why can't you?'

Stormbuckler rocked from side to side, and he snorted, 'Well, they will not let me out of here, will they? And even if they did, how far would I get? How far can a lad go with only one foot?'

'That's defeatist talk, that is...' Kilda suggested. He frowned. 'You can choose to do whatever you want. Or you can choose nothing at all. It's completely up to you.' Kilda looked at the boy carefully, then he continued: 'You are a very individual person and sometimes you act strangely. They say, in the home, that you're an imbecile and you act like you have a monkey in your brain. I know you're disabled with that gammy leg, but I haven't seen the monkey in your brain. So I guess you can leave this place whenever *you want*. They can't force you to stay. I think you will just take off and go one day. This is not a Bridewell, lad. You have not been banged up by any courts. It's not your fault you're stuck in this place. Like everyone else in this dump, you suffered a run of bad luck, that's all. Sometimes they forget that this is a charitable institution and we have done *nothing* wrong. We can walk out of here when we are ready... I'm not saying we are ready today... we probably won't be ready tomorrow neither... but one day both you and I will walk out of this place.'

Stormbuckler shook his head. He did not believe *any* of this was true. And even if it was true, they wouldn't let him walk out, would they? He was a physically impaired nut-job, wasn't he? 'Anyway,' Stormbuckler said suddenly, 'If that's true, why are you here in this place, now?' He couldn't disguise a smirk. 'You could choose to swagger away now if you wanted to, so why don't you go?'

Kilda the pugilist let out a long breath and allowed his head to hang for a moment: 'I'll bide my time here, thanks. That's till I get myself strong and fit. Then I'll be out of this hole. Believe me.'

'Why don't you seek work in the town at the new manufactory? My friend went there. They will reward a hard-working man like you and will give you bread and board. Why doss here in this homeless shelter as if you're some kind of dependent?' Stormbuckler was going to add 'like me' but decided against it at the last moment.

'We all have our cross to bear, son. This is mine.' Kilda the pugilist slapped Stormbuckler between the shoulder blades. 'Besides, I could never work as a salaried slave in a manufactory. I am a free and independent man; I like to travel my own highways without a boss telling me where to go next. I will never tip a cap to a foreman.'

'Isn't the lonely path strewn with thorns?' asked Stormbuckler. 'Anyway, that's what they tell us in Chapel.'

'No, lad, the lonely path is strewn with *petals*.'

Both went silent while Kilda examined the skies. Then the pugilist grabbed Stormbuckler by the arm, 'Could you do *me* one of those?'

Stormbuckler rubbed his forehead, 'One of what?'

'Could you perhaps draw a symbol of defiance and rage for me? A skull and bones? Maybe inside a ring of rope, could you do that? For a patch? For a tattoo? With a skull like you've done here. Though not a man's skull... but a bull's skull, a bull's skull with the horns, inside a rope ring. That's a symbol that would characterise me. I want it to appear rough because I'm a scrapper. I know a scratcher, a tattoo artist, and I'd ask him to scratch your outline onto my right-hooker, what do you think? Would you do a design that the scratcher could copy? Would you agree to do it?'

Stormbuckler had never been happier om his life. His face broke into a clear smile, 'Yes, of course. But how would I do it? I could draw onto a gate post I suppose, but how would you take a gatepost to your scratcher?'

"I tell you what,' said Kilda. He relaxed his fighting arm and flexed his shoulder. 'I will bring a bit of rag. You will sketch an outline of the design onto the fabric, with charcoal. Then we'll get one of the girls to embroider around your contour. After that, I'll take the fragment to the scratcher, so he can copy it onto my arm. How does that sound?'

'Ruddy marvellous.'

Stormbuckler was not alone on the cold floor, that night, and for the first time since his friend Tom Bisbee had left the poorhouse. He didn't feel the usual sense of loneliness and desertion. After the last lamp had been extinguished by the matron, he became aware of a large, muscular presence that approached in the darkness. The large guy's bones laid on the wood shavings, with his foot-arches practically touching Stormbuckler's knees.

Stormbuckler felt unusually safe and well-protected. With a smile on his face, he drifted into deep sleep.

The following morning, Kilda the pugilist presented Stormbuckler with a blank, silvery square of beautifully woven material. Heaven knows where had pilfered a napkin of such superior quality, overnight: 'Here's the textile I promised. Will you squiggle-out the design onto it? Later, I will have your outline sewn with yarn. After that, I will take it to my scratcher so he can reproduce it on my arm...'

Stormbuckler glared at the portion of cloth as if it was a sullied arse-rag and he cleared his throat. 'Maybe you could ask your scratcher to compose something for you? You don't *need me*. Tattoo people can do that, can't they? If a tattooist can handle a needle, then surely he can pen a sketch too...'

'Why are you so reluctant *now*, lad? You sounded keen yester-day...' The big man folded the thieved napkin away.

Stormbuckler produced a slow sigh, 'It's just *that...*'

'It's just what? Yes, it's true, I can call for my tattoo parlour to devise a symbol, I suppose. But it won't be as good as what *you* would do. Nobody can do cartilages and rope the way you can. The inkers can be unreliable with their designs too... they're excellent with needles, but less good with artistry. I've watched them make dreadful foul-ups of a man's arm. That's generally because of the exceedingly strong grog they consume to give them courage to push *needle into skin*. It's always best to hand-over a design they can follow, rather than ask them to come-up with their own idea. I wish you would *reconsider...*'

Stormbuckler remained hunched. 'Thank you for your confi-dence in me. I hugely appreciate it... But *the thing is...*'

'What?'

'Um, if the matron finds me with a fragment of fine cotton in my possession, she will skin me alive. I am not allowed properties, do you see? I mustn't have belongings. Neither should you, by the way. If they discover this material on you, they'll reprimand you. They'll create a big scene and sling you out.... but me? They'll flay me... they'll murder me.'

'They won't touch a hair on your head with me around, kid. Haven't you noticed that the worthless louse Pea Pod is laying off? He hasn't troubled you since I have been around... has he?'

Stormbuckler produced a slow smile. 'Seedpod? Is that who you mean? He hasn't been around, has he? Yes, you are quite right.... what did you do?'

'I had a word in his shell, didn't I? I told the humgruffin to lay off... I told him that if he stirred even a single hair on your little head, he'd have to contend *with me...*'

'I see.' Stormbuckler nodded. He puckered his nose. Kilda's well-intentioned involvement might have reverberations, down-the-line, 'But Seedpod is a trustee, and he's the matron's favourite. He doesn't fear you or concern himself with what you might do...'

'Maybe, or maybe *not*,' Kilda the pugilist said, with a snort. He twisted his fist into a tough, bony ball, 'But the fellow won't take a chance. I've met his type a hundred times before. Actions speak louder than words... he won't risk getting a thump.'

Stormbuckler grinned and nodded.

'Look,' said Kilda, the pugilist. 'I don't want you to feel pressured into doing something you're not comfortable with. So I'll hold on to this snot-rag until you feel ready. Then, when there's nobody's about, I will pass it to you, and you can charcoal a design really quick. When it's finished, you can hand it back to me, right away. That way it *isn't* belonging... is it? It's just a bit of tatter that's being passed from mate to a mate. Got it?'

'I don't know... it doesn't look like *tatter* to me. It looks like a valuable piece of fabric. Where did you get it?' Stormbuckler gazed at the piece of fabric as if it was a portion from the holy shroud. Then he took a deep breath, 'Yes, of course, I can do it. I don't know what I was thinking... it will be fine.'

'That's more like it! That's the fighting spirit!' said Kilda. 'Later today I will pass it to you, and you will hide in Mr. Jim's box out the back and I'll keep watch. And you will do your charcoaling onto it, yes?'

'Yeah.'

'Let's get to work,' Kilda said, 'I'm glad you agreed.'

So, later in the day, as designed, the boxer stood guard while Stormbuckler entered Mr. Jims's shed and drew out an emblem onto the square of fabric he'd been given with a sharpened edge of coal. And when he'd finished the drawing, he carried it up to the afternoon light and appreciated the precise lines and pleasing curves he had laid down. He knew he had interpreted Kilda's wishes admirably. He had drawn a bull-headed skull, collected over crossed bones, set within a cable frame. Stormbuckler had finished the picture to the highest standards.

Kilda was beside himself with delight when he viewed the completed sketch. He folded the napkin delicately, then slid it beneath his underclothes. 'I'll have the girl embroider around the contours *tonight*,' he suggested with a grin.

'How will you get her to do that? What will you provide for her services? You don't possess a bean... What will you give her in return?'

'Don't trouble your mind with that, boy,' Kilda said with a full smirk and a twinkle in his eye. 'Don't worry about that *at all*. There are many ways to settle a debt with a woman... a fellow doesn't require diamonds or gold. Oft-times repayment can be satisfying for both parties, heh?'

Stormbuckler did not understand what Kilda meant by such inscrutable remarks, but nevertheless, he returned a contented grin. At least the pugilist considered his drawing to be solid enough to be preserved, retained, and commemorated in ink. Perhaps — in years to come — when a boxing opponent appreciated Kilda's tattoo, the prize fighter might point out that: 'Yes, I had it specially created by my friend, Master Stormbuckler of Staines Town...'

A week later, when a wicked wind blew in from the moor, clattering oak branches and frightening pigs, Stormbuckler arrived early for work and was shocked to find the drinking water was not ready, nor had the top-soil been turned-over.

Kilda, the pugilist, had disappeared.

The fighter had appeared from nowhere and now he vanished into *nothing*. Much like a rainbow, Kilda was only in attendance briefly. But was there long enough to brighten a downcast reality.

7

At some point during the morning, Stormbuckler was summoned to the matron's parlour. When he arrived, he found her sat in the wicker chair with globules of stickiness dangling from her fleshy jowls. With a butter-milk robe-cap pulled over her grey curls and layers of creamy tissue around her neck, the matron resembled an Egg Moon. Her head seemed ready to explode at any moment, to spill slippery brain-yolk over the floor.

'Where is the pugilist?' she demanded. She folded her arms and waited for his answer.

'Um, I do not know, how should I know? '

'Seedpod told me you had a *rapport* with the vicious thug. Didn't he tell you where he was going?'

'*Mmm* no, why would he?'

The matron gave the lad half-hearted shrug, 'I suppose you're right. Why waste words on a complete moron? I felt you might know, that's all.'

'I don't...'

'Well, don't waste more of my precious time, you bothersome shilly-shally... get going... get back to your pigs...'

'Sorry, Ma'am.'

'One thing before you go...'

'Yes, Ma'am?'

'Seedpod has enough to do without adding the piggery to his numerous sundry duties. But, obviously, in the light of the disappearance of the pugilist, you can't expect to assume responsibility for the pigs — with you being a useless cretin and so forth. So I asked Seedpod if he would temporarily oversee the piggery until we find a suitable adult who can perform as swine master in the absence of Mr. Jims. So, for now, Seedpod will be your superintendent. You must go to him if you need anything. But, remember, he has important duties elsewhere —stewarding duties — so he'll not be at your beck and call... and he will *not* be responsible for the husbandry of the animals, is that clear? He'll just be there to pilot and manage you when you most need it — with you being a simpleton, and a mindless juggins, and so forth. Got that?'

'Yes, Ma'am. Is there any news about Mr. Jims?'

'Mr. Jims? He was taken to the infirmary run by the Servite sisters, wasn't he?'

'Yes, I believe so,' mumbled Stormbuckler.

'Well, that's that *then*...'

That's that? Stormbuckler rubbed his chin and swallowed. He was not sure what her words meant, but they sounded *grim*; as if it was a final response 'He'll be recovered soon though won't he, Mum? No doubt he will be improving day-by-day, won't he?'

'Who? Mr. Jims? What scrattle are you prattling, boy? You really are a complete waste-of-air, aren't you? Of course, the old goat *won't* be improving. In fact, I shouldn't be at all surprised if he was stone-dead before his head hit their silent pillows. The chances of his survival were desperate even before he got carted to the nunnery... and a lot worse, once he arrived there! You really are a dribbling simpleton, aren't you?'

'Oh.' Stormbuckler swallowed hard and felt his eyes fill with water.

'Off with you. Back to your filthy animals. You stink-up my parlour with your malodorous presence, you detestable little mumpscab...'

'Yes, Ma'am.'

Once out of her room, Stormbuckler stroked his chin with his grimed fingers. At least Seedpod would only serve as his *temporary* manager while a replacement was sought. However, he was concerned for the wellbeing of Mr. Jims. He wished he had been able to see him before he had departed. He would have liked to inform him of the pigs' well-being. And to talk about earlier, happier, times. According to the matron's account, the elderly guy had apparently already passed away... but Stormbuckler refused to believe that could be true. He felt, in his heart, that Mr. Jims was hanging on. Perhaps there might be a chance to visit him before he made the journey into paradise? Stormbuckler hoped that would be so.

Just as he was about to step into open-air, Stormbuckler felt a pinch on his arm. He turned to see it was Seedpod who had grabbed him. The trustee approached his face, and Stormbuckler caught the aroma of pungent breath: 'I hope you are happy to hear I am your new *boss*,' whispered Seedpod. He gave Stormbuckler a yellowy grin. 'I expect the matron pointed out I'm *temporary*, and told you I'm only expected to provide casual and informal supervision, yes ?'

'Yes, Seedpod. *Ouch*, you're hurting my arm...'

'Well, she's wrong. I aim to be down the piggery *all hours*. I'll be watching you like a hawk. And you better get used to it — you scummy little shoat — because I am going to make your life a *living hell*. You had better believe it. It's best that you accept that your life is now over! I intend to exhaust you by staying on top of you day and night. You'll regret having been born. I see you for what you are—a worm turd—and I'll make you pay for everything you have done thus far in your pointless life. And what's this? It seems that your muscular co-worker is no longer there to save your neck. So, now you're all mine, ha ha!'

～

Soon after six in the late afternoon, while Stormbuckler stirred the peels and sloshes in the half-barrel, to feed his hungry pigs, he picked out what sounded like a hop, step, and a jump *coming-at-him* from behind. He turned his neck to see the shape of Seedpod leaping for him.

Stormbuckler didn't have time to ward off the sudden attack, he just enough ducked his head and jutted his elbows. Seedpod dropped on his back and employed all his bodyweight to pull Stormbuckler to the ground, crumpling the younger lad's knees beneath him. Stormbuckler caved under the strain of the attack, and hit his lip against the ledge of the pig's barrel, which caused it to bleed. He tasted sourness in his mouth.

'Sorry I haven't had time to come and boss you about,' hissed Seedpod. The matron's favourite trustee sniggered as he brought his mouth closer to Stormbuckler's ear, 'I been too busy ain't I? Never mind, I is here now, isn't I? I is here to give you *improvided* attention.'

Stormbuckler struggled to squirm free from Seedpod's tight hold, but found he could not move out of the body-lock that had been imposed upon him. He'd been captured between the crook of Seedpod's elbow and the boniness of a knee joint.

'Where are you trying to get to, my little worker? Why are you not being kind to your new boss? Come on, give me a kiss... give your new boss a kiss.'

Seedpod yanked-out his arm from behind, then screwed Stormbuckler's frame around so they gazed at one another. Once face-to-face, Seedpod spat squarely into Stormbuckler's lips. Stormbuckler turned his cheek and sought to bring his hands up, to wipe-away the gum, but his arms were captured behind his back.

'Why won't you give me a kiss?' Seedpod asked with a crazy, distorted smile. 'Don't you love me?'

Stormbuckler rattled his head, but felt too nervous to answer. 'What's wrong with your tongue, cripple boy? Doesn't it work? Can't you talk? Can't you kiss your boss?' Seedpod stretched a dirty hand, and drove his knuckles between Stormbuckler's red-raw gums: 'Open up, cripple-boy, open wide. Let your boss catch your tongue. Did you chomp your little flip-flap when you felled down? Is that what took place? *Oh dear.* Ooh, I can see red trickling from your mouth... Did you bite your flip-flap tongue off?'

Stormbuckler shook his head.

'*Open*,' demanded Seedpod, 'I won't ask nicely another time.' He pushed his bony knuckles hard into Stormbuckler's teeth. 'Let's see what's wrong with your flip-flap, shall we?'

Stormbuckler opened his jaws. What else could he do?

Seedpod pulled on the tip of his tongue with grubby, jagged fingernails, 'Huh? Wait, this tongue is intact... You've been lying to me, haven't you? The tongue is in good working order. It's slippery and disgusting, as I expected. Furthermore, it is entirely healthy. Why didn't you answer me when I asked you a question? Did you forget that I'm your boss and you're my subordinate? You must answer me when I am questioning you, heh?'

Stormbuckler tried to say, 'sorry,' but the word came out as: '*thorrly...*' because Seedpod grasped the end of his tongue and wouldn't let go. This amused Seedpod, so he convulsed with laughter. He leaned back and guffawed. As he did, he released the younger lad. The bully rested his haunches and let out a series of wild hoots!

Stormbuckler got to his feet to and brushed his sackcloth down, then flexed his bruised limbs. He looked round because he heard the barrow-pig named Eglon snort for attention. 'I'll bring your food in a moment,' he told the animal, as he wiped blood from his lips.

'You got to see the funny side though ain't you?' remarked Seedpod, as he pulled himself up.

'What?' Stormbuckler said, frowning.

'Funny isn't it? Real funny. Everybody hates *you*... you know that, don't you? That's why they put you in here with the swine... because you're a loser like those lazy fat beasts. But when someone shows you the slightest interest and asks for a kiss — you go all shy and untalkative, don't you?'

'I've got to feed the animals...'

Seedpod moved over: 'Let them wait. I'm your boss. Did you forget that already? I'll tell you when you are permitted to feed the animals... understand? I'm still talking. The animals will wait. Don't you understand a simple thing? You really are a cretin...'

'But they're ready for their scoff *now*... this is the time they have it.'

With that, Seedpod took a large dollop of pulp from the slurry-mix inside the barrel and squished it directly onto Stormbuckler's head. Stormbuckler heard the squelch when it landed on his skull, then felt the dribbles of slime as the slop oozed down his cheeks. 'Oh dear,' said Seedpod in a mocking tone, ' I guess you must have accidentally thrown some of that piggy-food on *your own* head... What a nincompoop you are? Oh dear, *oh dear*.'

Stormbuckler raised his arm to scrape the swill off, but Seedpod stopped him. 'No,' he yelled. 'Let the swine lick it off... let the hog do it.'

'What?' blurted Stormbuckler.

But Seedpod had already started to twist his limbs into an armlock. He pushed Stormbuckler's backbone beyond its normal limits and rotated him to the ground again. This time he dragged Stormbuckler towards Eglon's muddy muzzle, then pushed the lad's head against the pig's snout and he shouted, 'That's right, you filthy swine, lick it off the cretin's head... *lick it off the cretin's head*. Dirty filthy pig. *Dirty filthy pig*.'

Each day, for a full week, Stormbuckler prayed that Kilda the pugilist would come back to Staines Town poorhouse. But the prize-fighter never returned to save him from his tormentor. His torture extended each day. Stormbuckler was goaded, jabbed, booted, and throttled. Seedpod swamped his head into a barrel of water until he practically fainted. Seedpod spattered his face with animal defecate, then told Stormbuckler to *lick it off*. He was again-and-again pushed to the ground, and spat upon.

Frequently, Stormbuckler yearned to flee and hide, but was conscious of an obligation to his creatures. He knew that no one else would care for them; he was the only person at the poorhouse who would provide for their piggy needs.

On the eighth successive day, Seedpod came for him and snatched Stormbuckler by the hair. He flung him to the ground, then punted him in the face with his bony knee. Stormbuckler curled up so the teenager's boots presented no permanent damage. But Seedpod knelt on his midriff, making it difficult to breath: 'Cease struggling, beast,' Seedpod growled. He bent to prise Stormbuckler's single leather shoe from his remaining foot. 'You wretch. I always wanted to know how you'd handle having no shoe-leather at all.' He removed Stormbuckler's shoe, then he stood. He yelled, 'Get up onto your prickly toes, hah!'

Stormbuckler picked himself up but felt winded. 'Hey! Give me back my shoe,' he appealed.

'Go get it then... if you can...' Seedpod raised the shoe high above his head, then heaved it as far as it would travel. Stormbuckler watched the shoe skim through the air and out of sight. They both heard the object blast into bushes *outside* the boundary of the poorhouse grounds. It must have landed on wasteland, beyond their walls.

'Why did you do that?' snarled Stormbuckler. He couldn't conceal his temper.

Seedpod slapped him across the face. 'Don't come overbold with me, rascal. Don't forget, I am your boss, and you are my subordinate. I can do whatever I like to you. If you became defiant *again*, I declare I'll do better than merely slap you... I'll bring a knife and I will chop your fingers one-by-one... do you want me to do that?'

Stormbuckler looked to where the shoe might have landed. He felt slimy tears dribble down his cheeks: 'I cannot get another one. What have you done? I will get into deep trouble if matron finds I lost a shoe... they cost the poorhouse sixpence a pair. And she *hates* buying a pair when I only require one. She'll mince my guts to ribbons...'

'Animals do not require shoes,' Seedpod explained with a sneer. 'Do you see pigs wearing shoes on their trotters? No, you do not. Do you think you are better than pigs? No, you are no better! So *now* you can be just like your precious hog-friends, and you may trot around the slop in your bare feet... *Oink oink!* You should be happy! I've liberated your toes!'

And with that, Seedpod chuckled.

~

Stormbuckler employed himself, preparing the animal bedding. This involved forking heaps of dry straw onto a lining of sackcloth and hauling it over to the huts inside the animal enclosure. As he dragged the straw across the ooze towards the beasts, he heard his barefoot make suction and gushing noises in the soft, bubbly sludge. The goo festered across the animal yard. Liquefied excrement and other accumulations squelched between his toes, and the sensation was, to be honest, *pleasurable*, although he dared not glance down to see the type of muck he'd lumbered through. Meanwhile, his other 'foot' — the peg that was hidden in cloth — clomped as normal, to establish an occasional belch of its own as he trampled into the syrupiest parts.

Eglon, the medium-sized barrow pig, made a screech and greeted him with grateful eyes. Stormbuckler spread the bedding down but had to turn back toward the hurdles for a fork, because hauling the sack-cloth required two hands.

Eglon groaned, making a kind of griping puff, and looked at Stormbuckler as if he was asking: 'Where are you going? I need my food.'

'I'll be back in a flash, greedy-guts,' Stormbuckler declared.

Stormbuckler half-hobbled and half-squelched his way back to the tools, where he discovered Seedpod relaxed, with his scrawny backside leant against the timbers, gnawing on a shiny-red apple. Where had he found such a gleaming piece of fruit? Stormbuckler called for the bully to move aside so he could reach for the fork and continue his work. 'Want this?' taunted Seedpod. He took the fork by its long handle. 'I will prick you with the iron prongs if you get any closer...'

'But I need the fork for doing their bedding...'

'Let them do it for themselves...'

'The pigs? How can they do it for themselves?'

'Don't quarrel. I am the boss. You are my subordinate. They are beasts. They must learn to do things for themselves. You need to understand the hierarchy around this place.'

Stormbuckler produced a weary sigh. 'Very well then...' It wasn't worth debating with Seedpod when he was in this kind of mood. So Stormbuckler resolved to complete the routine task later — after he'd taken up roots and fishbones for the swine. Stormbuckler turned aside and painstakingly plodded towards the mash barrel. When he arrived, to lift the wooden scoop and fill the first slop bucket, he noticed that Seedpod drifted from his leaning-post and bumbled into the swine enclosure. Stormbuckler watched from the corner of his eye. The bully chewed on his fruit, and when he got closer to Eglon, he pushed the core of the apple close to the pig's snout and said, with a wide grin: 'Want this?' The pig made an earnest squeak and waved its corkscrew tail. 'Well, bad luck, friend, because you will not have it.' He swiped the fruit away before Eglon could snatch it. He held it way above the animal's head. Stormbuckler spotted, even from a distance, that the soot-black eyes of the pig followed the core. 'Want it?' said Seedpod again, as he lowered the fruit. The pig advanced, rolling his shoulders. 'No...' Seedpod raised the fruit higher. He did this twice more before the beast became disinterested and squatted back on its bacon. 'You don't want it then?' Seedpod shrieked. He flung the unfinished fruit out of the yard, into far bushes. 'Pity...' he told the animal. The apple had looked juicy and sweet.

Seedpod returned to the edge of the compound to investigate what Stormbuckler had been working on while he'd been away, irritating the pigs. The teen smirked as he regarded the other youngster fill a pail with pig slop. When the moment came, Seedpod announced: 'Here, let me *help you* with that heavy load...' Seedpod came over, to place his hand tightly around Stormbuckler's fingers, covering the handle of the bucket with his own grip.

'Do you want to help me bring the animal feed to them?' Stormbuckler asked, slightly unsure of the lad's motives.

'Yes, why shouldn't I? I'm the boss, aren't I? I can do what I please, can't I?'

'It's better if I do it *on my own*...' Stormbuckler declared. 'You do *not know* —' Stormbuckler broke off from what he was about to say.

'I do not know *what*? Come on: out with it. You were about to tell me something I didn't know... it must be something of great importance... This ought to be good... A bit like a worm telling a shark how to cut his teeth...'

'I was *just* going to say...' Stormbuckler took a wide breath and braced himself for the clout that would inevitably follow. 'I was merely going to say that you need to talk to the beasts when you bring their food to them. So they know what to expect... You must tell them what you're doing, so they don't become too anxious.'

'Do what?' Seedpod sank the bucket with his muscled arm and pushed his face until it was just inches from Stormbuckler's ear. 'I'm sorry, did I hear you correctly?'

Stormbuckler acknowledged the question with a nod, though carried his head low and held his lips tight, as he prepared himself for punishment.

'You might communicate with swine, cretin, but I belong to a superior species,' explained Seedpod. 'I'm a member of mankind. God gave mankind dominion over all that creeps on the earth. And that includes *you*, maggot breath.'

'I retract my suggestion,' Stormbuckler murmured. 'I did not mean to offend you. ' But Seedpod kept hold of the food-bucket and wrested it away from Stormbuckler's puny grip with one giant wrench. He returned the slop into the collection barrel, where it came from, and dropped the container with a noisy splatter.

'What did you do *that* for?' grumbled Stormbuckler. 'I was just about to satisfy them. The beasts are hungry.'

Seedpod wrenched his arm and slapped the kid's face with the back of his hand. The swift blow made a thud that struck Stormbuckler's mouth like a wet hammer. It was a slap that induced a passion of pain. The pain jarred the depths of Stormbuckler's sinews. The blow was so loud the hogs heard it. They started to *oink* frantically.

'Get this bucket over to the water barrel...' hollered Seedpod.

'Water?'

'Yes, *water*. Did you hear of it? It's the liquid stuff that falls from the sky. Go over and get me a bucketful of the stuff...'

Stormbuckler faltered. 'Why? What are you going to do with the water?' Stormbuckler was sure he was in for a giant soaking.

'*You'll see.* Go get a bucket of water for me. Make certain it's a full bucket. I can't hold here all day waiting, so hurry. I've got other obligations to attend. The matron calls for me to attend her at around this hour.'

So Stormbuckler sloped off to fetch a full pail of water.

When he came back, Seedpod snatched the handle and said, 'Give me...'

Stormbuckler hesitantly surrendered his control of the bucket and waited. But Seedpod didn't tip the water over his head — as expected — instead, the bully mooched carelessly across the pen enclosure, bucket in hand, until he arrived at the bundle of dry bedding that Stormbuckler had already spread-out for the animals. The bully turned to wink and smile, then dumped the entire liquid contents over the air-dried straw.

'They won't appreciate that...' Stormbuckler grumbled under his breath. 'That's the last of their bed-straw. The swine won't like that one bit. He should have spoken to them. He should have explained.'

Seedpod sauntered back and dumped the bucket by Stormbuckler's naked toes. The cold, harsh-metal rim missed his leading toenail by a hair's breadth. 'I've got to get going,' Seedpod announced. His face was a picture of self-contented complacency. '*You* do the rest...'

So, Seedpod left Stormbuckler to resolve things with the pigs.

Stormbuckler spent hours sweeping the pig's bed in an effort to dry it. The animals surrounded him and appeared increasingly disturbed by his efforts. He tried to settle them by making soothing sounds — *oohs and aahs* — but knew it wouldn't really help. The animals seemed ruffled because that idiot Seedpod had jumbled their routine. They felt great confusion and, quite literally, they felt higgledy-piggledy.

After doing everything possible to dry their bedding, he went to feed and water his grumbling beasts. Stormbuckler delayed by their swill feeder to be sure his swine ate appreciatively. The larger pigs showed up first, grunting and snorting, wagging their ears and tails, and puffing eagerly. Next came the minor beasts, who snorted and staggered, shrieked, and jostled, as they pushed ever-closer to the food. Stormbuckler lingered by the feeder for them to finish. While they ate, he spoke comforting words, and gave soothing strokes and reassuring neck-rubs to his animals. And once their eager meal-time was over, and the last of the beasts had twisted in the dry bedstraw, Stormbuckler prepared for the morning. He withdrew from the pigpen to return to the fodder trays in the yard. He searched around for his tools and supposed he had thirty minutes of pale light left in his day. Suddenly he thought: *should I take this opportunity to find my lost shoe?* It was heaved a long way off by that scalawag Seedpod. It might be worth seeking the shoe before dusk settled in and while that rascal wasn't about. If he didn't find it, the matron would lash his bare skin and blame him for losing such a valuable item.

Stormbuckler limped off, in an uncertain direction. He hoped that he headed towards the place he saw his single shoe being tossed by Seedpod. Soon, he arrived at a low-lying hedge, then a clump of tall weeds, and finally a large shrub that was dressed in spiny bristles. He trod carefully over these hazards —toes first, peg after — then staggered closer to the boundary wall of his prison-home. Storm-buckler had seldom been so close to this physical barrier with 'the outside world.' In fact, Stormbuckler had only left the Staines Town poorhouse twice in his young life. Once, when all the inmates had been delivered into town to chant carols at a special service held in the parish church. That expedition was two years ago, and it remained a fond remembrance of better times. He often thought about how the event had happened. He remembered that they had practiced for days, out in the frosty cold of the poorhouse yard, learning to sing carols in perfect harmony. Then they had been taken into town on the back of a rattling, wonky-wheeled wain. And had been washed and dressed, to look like fine. To resemble upstanding citizens. Even though they were not! And he remembered how the elegant upper-crust Staines Town parishioners clapped good-heart-edly at their singing. And he recalled that each of the poorhouse children had been given a shiny apple, as a reward.

When he was five years old, poorhouse children were required to march to the High Street to wave flags in support of a less important monarch who was passing over the town bridge. This was the only other occasion he had left the boundaries of his institution. He remembered that it had rained, and he had shivered in the cold without a coat or hat. While other town residents took advantage of free eggs, cherries, and ale, the poorhouse children were instructed to march home after the spectacle was over. So Stormbuckler and the other child-inmates had marched back to the institution, in single file. He recalled shivering in the biting rain and leaving the flag-draped streets empty-handed of those promised eggs and cherries. The same pitiful kids who had lined the street with waves and smiles were put to work inside the house, by lunchtime, as if it had been any other day.

Stormbuckler sighed as he viewed the boundary wall. He regarded the steep, slippery-looking, sides and the high top-plate — fitted with battlements. It was as if the poorhouse was a castle and the boundary walls were ramparts.

Then he remembered why he had come this far away from the piggery and cursed himself for not focusing on the task at hand. *Where was that shoe?* It must have landed here some place. The idiot couldn't conceivably have hurled it over the tall wall, *could he?* Stormbuckler moved to the bushes to investigate various round shapes that may (or may not) have been a missing shoe. One shape moved with a snort. Stormbuckler supposed it must be a hedgehog. He picked up a stick to puncture the next brown shape that he saw. It felt mushy and exuded a nasty smell. When he stepped back, he trod on a spiny holly leaf and the spike sent a shot of pain through his good foot and through his ankle and into his knee bone, 'Oh my good gad...' he said with a grimace. 'That bleedin' hurt like crazy.' And that was when he heard the lumbering sound.

Whatever came his way was moving terribly slow, heavily, and awkwardly. He remained silent and concentrated on the steps that arrived closer. It didn't sound like Seedpod — much bulkier. Unless the bully was japing around. And even matron wasn't that ungainly when she strode around the grounds on her rolling-pin, legs. Who could it be? For a moment he believed it to be Kilda the pugilist. Perhaps Kilda had returned to save him from daily mistreatment. Stormbuckler's heart skipped a beat. But then he remembered that Kilda *lurked* like a cat; he was a wiry fighter, a scavenger, and a thief — he would *never* make a blundering clatter like that.

80

Stormbuckler took a gulp just as the thing appeared. At first, he couldn't quite believe it. He rubbed his eyes with his fists. Then blinked as his mouth dropped open. He contemplated the madness before him: 'How did you get here?' he heard himself saying. He stared, with astonished eyes, at the immense bulk that stood brazenly in the clearing. Gazing back, with a conscience-stricken expression on a piggy face, was Maxen, his favourite sow. She seemed embarrassed and perhaps almost repentant. 'How did you get out of your compound? What did you do? Did you break a fence down?' The pig moved closer and brushed her cheek against Stormbuckler's leg. Then she bobbed her colossal head to sniff at his bare toes. 'You shouldn't be here. You know that, don't you? I've got to get you back to your pen. Where did I drop that stick?' He recalled that Mr. Jims once told him that if a pig was to escape, the only way to get him or her back into their pen was to prod them gently, with a stick up the bum. And, while prodding, make mollifying noises. According to Mr. Jims, that was the only way to persuade a pig to move. Although, to be honest, it didn't look like Maxen was going anywhere, stick-up-bum, or otherwise. In fact, she by-passed Stormbuckler and collapsed her weight against the boundary wall.

Stormbuckler went to her and said, 'Stop mucking about Maxen. You cannot sleep here. Go back to your pen. It's a big problem for me if you don't go back...' But the pig made a small croak, yawned, then closed her eyes. 'Please, I beg you. Help me out. You should go back, Maxen. I will be in big trouble if you don't return. You've gotta help me. I don't know how you got out of your enclosure, but they'll blame me if they find you have escaped. They will flay the skin from my backside.'

Maxen completely ignored his pleading and started to snore.

'Holy biscuits,' Stormbuckler whispered. 'Don't go to sleep, Maxen. They will boil me alive for this...' He collapsed on the soft earth and listened, for a while, to the pig's heavy breathing. The sky turned dusky grey as the sun set beneath a distant horizon. *Distant horizon?*

He considered Maxen's buxom brown rump, and he kissed it. She presented freedom. She'd offered liberty with that wonderful, fat, posterior of hers. Indeed, she'd moved tighter to the wall, to suggest that he could get onto her back and employ her hind-quarters as a step towards deliverance.

'You don't you mind if I step on you?' he asked, tactfully. Maxen produced one of her characteristic squawks and waggled her ears. So Stormbuckler leaned on his healthy leg, established his stump on the rear of the pig, and adjusted his balance so his shoulders were propped against the moss-carpeted wall. After this, he employed the flexibility of his 'good leg' to heave himself as high as he might, in an energetic bounce, to launch himself from the pig's fleshy haunch. She was the most convenient height to become a useful 'step-up' that he could use to scale over the wall. When Stormbuckler reached the top of the 'battlements', he hesitated for a moment, and wobbled haphazardly. But then he slipped down the opposite side of the wall, scraping and ripping his hands over stone and lime, as he tumbled. He touched down in a heap of nettles at the bottom of the wall. Stormbuckler rested in their stings for a moment, to clear his head. As he lingered, he thought he heard a set of bulky and inelegant vibrations. It meant that Maxen lumbered away. She'd served her purpose, he supposed. He hoped she now trudged back to her pen. He smiled widely: 'What a girl!' He stared across the starkness of the moor towards the darkest part of the purple sky. A band of jackdaws flapped excitedly in the wind, then they headed west. He determined he should follow where they were off to.

Stormbuckler did not know where he was going — but one thing was for sure: he knew he would never go back.

Stormbuckler did not know which way to head, but heard a heron produce a rambunctious shriek as it raised blue-grey wings to lift off into the velvet dirty sky. He understood that the bird would now retire to its resting place, since its hunting day was over, and perhaps the bird would find a roosting place in a thicket of trees. So he determined to follow the bird. Perhaps it might lead him to a healthier place. The moor menaced in its despair and soaking shades. Stormbuckler reasoned he had to leave behind this bleakness promptly if he was to endure. A clump of shrubs would afford him warmth and shelter, if only temporarily, if he could find them. But on the moor, there was *no* shelter. Of course, his peg foot, shrouded in fabric, delayed him; the damned thing kept becoming clogged in pockets of mud. But, oddly, his other foot being unshod seemed to help. He discovered he could dig his heels or bare toes into the heavy mud to advance himself and release the maimed leg. Perhaps Seedpod had done him a favour, by flinging away that shoe.

The heron dissolved into the gloom, but when it did, Stormbuckler renewed his intention to ultimately arrive at the outer limits of the moor, where parish boundary stones marked the meeting place between fierce wildishness and respectable civilised culture. He recalled, in an indistinct manner, that the march back to the poorhouse, after singing those carols at Christmastime, had taken half a day. So he guessed the town might sensibly be presumed to be five miles away. Though, was that where he headed? He didn't know, for sure, which direction the bird had taken him. He had no plan. He carried a muddle-headed notion that he might undertake to meet Kilda the pugilist. Or maybe he could seek to contact his friend Tom Bisbee, who now worked at the Staines Town manufactory. Beyond that, Stormbuckler did not know what to do next.

He felt that the night air would smother him. It was as if it stood by to blanket out the final wan moments of his existence. It felt as if the night air encompassed his shuddering shoulders. The air dragged him down, as his frail and uncertain totter turned weaker. The inmates of the poorhouse regularly talked about consumption and chronic cough being precipitated by being outdoors in damp air. It was generally acknowledged that exposure to the elements provoked fatal illnesses. Stormbuckler had no coat, nor hat. He only possessed the rags he stumbled in, fading and battered. Soon, it would be awfully dark. Too dark to see where he headed, and the clouded sky offered no hint of starlight. So it was obvious that he'd succumb to consumption. Yet Stormbuckler bumbled on. He clumsily moved into the dangerous air that turned ever colder and threatened to take him into its eternal embrace.

At first, he was not sure if he could see a brief contour of timbers in the distance, but when he got closer, he became sure he *discovered it*. A circle of largish trees stood tall and steep, and they had what looked like enormous bread baskets at the absolute tops of their bare branches. It was the heron colony. It meant that following the gigantic bird had been worth it all along, and he hadn't gone around in an almighty circle, to return to where he'd started. But what would he do now? What path might he take, next? He did not know which way the town could be — for all he knew, he'd wandered away from settlement and drifted into the wider heaths that lay to the east, well beyond food and shelter. He hesitated by the trunk of one of the broader trees and noticed that the ground under his bare toes was rugged and stony. Obviously, he couldn't turn back, but he didn't want to stick around in this place either. It was raw, and it was desperately lonely. Should he go straight, or left, or right? The decision was his. 'What do you want to do?' he asked himself. He felt the answer in his fingers, and upon his breath. He knew he must rest. Later, once he'd restored his exhausted bones, he'd find water and food. So Stormbuckler determined, forthwith, to fold himself into an uncomfortable, but tight, ball under the king heron's perch. And once he'd done that, he slipped into a dark and heavy sleep.

Stormbuckler dreamed that a terrible silvery bird was trying to get his attention. The bird called a name: 'Frank...' The bird yelled the name over-and-over. 'Frank. Frank. *Fraaank*.'

'I'm not Frank,' he told the stupid bird. 'Cease calling me by that name...' He put his fingers in his ears to stop the screaming. 'I do not know any person named Frank. Leave me alone!'

The bird stuck out a long tongue and refused to stop shrieking. It jabbed him in the face with a long brick-coloured beak. The poke it gave him hurt like billy-hoo. Then the bird flicked his face with angry ash-grey feathers and gazed at him long and hard with its mean, yellow eyes. 'Stop staring at me that way. I don't know who Frank is. Leave me alone.' But the bird shook its head, and the black crest shone like polished coal. The bird opened its bill again, 'Frank, *Fraaank...*'

Stormbuckler woke up with clicking and crashing all around and a high scream that sounded similar to '*Schaah...*' above his head. For a moment, he didn't know where he was. Then, a twig fell down from high above and hit him in the face. The sting transported him back to reality, and he recalled what he'd accomplished the previous day and remembered how he'd arrived at this lonely place — a hole under a tree, in the midst of nowhere at all. He rubbed-away an indentation in his skin with filthy fingers as he took stock of his plight. He was in a peculiar little woodland and a glimmer of sunlight crisscrossed a broad canopy of skeletal branches to brighten his resting place. At the tops of those high trees thrashed immense birds. Each bird vigorously spread out a long neck and flailed a wide set of wings. *These* must have been the strange noises that woke him.

Directly, he was seized by an inescapable sense of coldness. The chill extended savagely across his bones, and he shuddered. 'God, I'm frozen...' He pulled himself up. He felt woozy and his good-limb was sore, so he was unbalanced. What was the line that Kilda used on a cold morning? It made him smile, even though he didn't altogether understand it: '*It's bleaker than a brothel-keeper's heart...*' The recollection generated a smile that flickered across Stormbuckler's face as he wiped fingers through his hair to get rid of fragments of twig and leaves. Then he stretched his muscles and headed west.

The march was painful going across hidden pockets of sticky clay that lay between knee-high tussocks of thick grass. Every step was a challenge. He contemplated turning back and seeking another route, but come what may, he ploughed forward, although he didn't know why. At last the day grew lighter, and he was immensely glad he hadn't tried this route during the night because it was a trickier challenge than the one he'd faced the previous evening... he had been sensible to delay this march until dawn.

After what seemed like an hour had passed, although the sun's movement indicated it was probably only forty minutes, he heard a faint bell ringing in the distance. He initially questioned whether he'd imagined the sound. But no, there was a distinctly regular chime, carried on the breeze. Stormbuckler decided to take a short detour in order to examine the source of the sound, so he moved somewhat north-westward. After half a furlong of stumbling and plodding, he finally identified the location of the bell's ringing: he saw a long configuration of ashen buildings on the immediate horizon. He felt uplifted by this sight of settlement because the buildings meant *food and water*, so picked-up-pace and he aimed straight for them. Agonizingly, he found he had to skirt around a long soggy area — it looked as if a stream had broken its banks — and this redirected him *away* from the set of buildings. But he soon re-guided himself back on-track. Promptly enough, he reached the outer walls of the structures.

Initially, Stormbuckler assumed he'd turned up at *another* poorhouse because it looked the same as his own institution. There were several tell-tale clues that this was an establishment analogous to the one he'd left behind. First, there was the bell. The bell clanged with fretful earnestness, requiring bodies to pick themselves up and begin production. Then there was the towering boundary wall — the administrators of this place did not call for anyone to enter or leave. Then there was the architecture: the main house was something like a shrine, without being absolutely committed to worship. So, there were church-like towers and church-like domes, and church-like pointed arches, and lots of other ecclesiastical features, but the layout looked prosaic rather than spiritual, with a group of conjoined bulky buildings, all with chimneys, and a stable-yard, a group of barns, and separate wooden structures.

Stormbuckler wandered around one-half of the boundary and planted himself at the imposing entrance. It had tall pillars, a deserted guard-box, and an iron grate to stop livestock infiltrating the grounds. It amazed him to discover that the double-gates had been left wide-open. How odd? Why establish a tall wall around an institute, then allow the gates to be left open, so anyone might enter? That suggested madness. Yet, the arrangement suited him well. He cruised through the gateway, across the iron grate, and entered into their hallowed grounds.

Within the grounds, the place seemed forsaken. Stormbuckler was instinctively drawn to an ornate stone-worked arch that squatted over a main entrance. There were religious emblems sculpted into the rock above twin oak doors. After wavering, he pushed at the left door with an unsure shove. It surprised him to discover that it opened with a sigh, sounding like a doleful spectral spirit woken from slumber. He strode inside. Stormbuckler took-in the bouquet of spiced carbolic soap and coal tar. There were numerous passages running from a large hallway. A wooden table had been set aside, but the attending chair was vacant. He lingered and listened. The bell halted, so the place became uncannily silent. He shuffled down the immediate corridor to determine where it might draw him.

The place had a sense of purity and zeal about it, yet also seemed haunted by a saddening ambience. *Where was everybody?* Stormbuckler made a series of ungainly one-foot steps down the passageway and acknowledged that the clomp of his peg-foot grew louder-and-louder in the comfortless echoes. Each step that he took reflected on the flat stone walls and the chilled tiles, so his echoing stomps extended the length of the corridor, declaring his arrival better than if he'd shouted: '*Oi-oi*. Anyone at home?'

He passed several sealed doors and didn't have the nerve to try any of them, but then he showed up at a wider entranceway where the double-doors had been left wide open, so he snooped inside. Along the borders of a large room, Stormbuckler saw rows of simple beds. Someone had made-up each bed with spreads and blankets. Most of the beds were empty, but he spied at least two beds that had lumpy forms in them, sheltered beneath covers. 'What kind of place is this?' he whispered. 'What kind of poorhouse where residents are permitted to sleep beyond daybreak?'

He nervously entered the wide room and made his way towards the brightest edge. He counted twelve beds on each side. As he guessed, only two beds had sleepers. He paused to examine a bed by the far wall. The individual in the bed had been dressed, head to toe, in cream-coloured bandages. The figure reminded him of the character referred to in the Holy Bible as Lazarus of Bethany. Stormbuckler had often heard the story of Lazarus in the poorhouse chapel. He recalled that Christ had called on Mary and Martha and had restored their brother Lazarus to life after the sisters had given up on him. In fact, they had even wrapped his broken body in grave clothes.

'May I help you?' came a feeble voice from the dark. Stormbuckler turned around, because the speech seemed close. The voice appeared from *nowhere*.

He assumed that whoever had asked those words must be near *or by* the figure of Lazarus in the bed. Stormbuckler gulped, then leaned-in to examine the figure's face. He was at once taken aback, then horrified and confused by what he saw. Because the face he saw belonged to someone *he knew*. He recognised the sleeper with those bandages. Was this a nightmare? Was he still living inside a bad dream? Stormbuckler's heart rate hastened, while his skin moistened. He felt an almost overwhelming sense of bewilderment.

'What is this place?' he heard himself say.

'You are with the Mother of Sorrows,' returned the hidden voice.

'*What* do you mean?' Stormbuckler searched around because the voice seemed even closer. He trod toward the sound.

'This is our foundation,' the voice responded. 'Why are you here?'

'Where is everybody?'

'Those who cannot be carried remain rested. Others are performing the Rosary of Seven Sorrows...'

'Performing?'

A small-boned woman appeared from behind the bed. She had been kneeling beside the bandaged figure of Lazarus. The woman had silvery hair and an oval face. She wore a pale apron over a darkened gown. A stone crucifix swung from a rope around her midriff. 'All the others are at *matins*. May I request your name?'

'Me lady? *Um*, they call me Stormbuckler at home.' He sighed self-indulgently, perhaps pleased to be alive in this place of nightmares.

'Do you want to sit, Stormbuckler?' The lady asked. 'You look fit to dop. Come, sit on the bed.'

He did her bidding and sat where she pointed. The mattress felt soft and nothing like he'd experienced in the poorhouse. 'You must be extremely wealthy,' he pointed out, 'To live as nobles in a magnificent palace like this and to languish on mattresses filled with bedstraw and topped with blankets *all day*...'

The lady smiled. She rested beside him. 'What is your full name? Why are you here, Stormbuckler?'

'Um? My full name? They call me Stormbuckler because I shuffle clumsy, and I fuss and bungle on one foot. I don't have a *proper* name. I have no family and I wasn't christened. Would you mind explaining who lives in a grand palace like this?' He bit his lip and glanced around the vast space with nervous eyes.

'There is no need to be apprehensive,' the lady responded, in soft tones. 'You are in a safe place. This is a caring society. I am Sister Mary Paul. We serve the sick. Are you sick?'

'Um? I don't think so.' Stormbuckler's eyes darted left and right. 'Is this an infirmary?'

The Sister smiled, 'Yes, Master Stormbuckler, this is an infirmary. A Servite institution. Have you come to visit a patient?'

Stormbuckler frowned and studied his foot. He wiggled his bare toes before he drew a deeper breath. 'In fact, yes, it's true, I have. My friend is in this place. His name is Mr. Jims. I came to visit him.'

'Do you know the gentleman's first name?' sought Sister Mary Paul. She offered a sympathetic smile. 'I do not know the name you offered...'

The question puzzled him. 'Um?' Stormbuckler rubbed his grubby fingers across a bewildered brow; if Mr. Jims ever had a first name, he never used it. 'It's Mr. Jims the swine keeper,' he said.

'No matter,' declared the Sister. 'You seem to have bedded down in a ditch last night, by the look of you...' she considered his threadbare work-clothes. 'Where did you sleep last night?'

'Me lady? I fell asleep in a hole under trees.'

'A hole?' her face lit up. 'How desperately early-Christian of you, master Stormbuckler. May I ask if you ate this morning?'

'No, I don't think I did.'

'Why don't you remain here? I will see if I can locate some gruel. Would you appreciate something to eat? '

'Yes, *I would*. Yet I would not choose to charge upon your hospitality. I'm certain it would lead to great inconvenience. And anyhow, I do not have a single penny to repay for your kindness...'

'Nonsense,' answered Sister Mary Paul. She placed a palm on his arm and held it for a moment. 'Promise to remain here. I'll look for porridge... it'll take a few minutes... we seek no payment.'

'Are you positive that I'm not putting you to too much trouble? I'm sorry to be an intruder. Please forgive my trespasses.'

'Do not worry, Master Stormbuckler. Stay here, repeat your prayers. I shall be back in a moment with a warming dish.'

The Sister rose, so Stormbuckler joined her. But she forced him down onto the mattress with a certain hand placed upon his shoulder. He searched into her eyes. He said: 'Before you take off, might I ask a question?'

'What is it, my pilgrim friend?'

'Who is the fellow knotted to this bed? The man wrapped in binding strips? The man dressed as if he were Lazarus? I think I recognize his face.'

'That gentleman is Bisbee. Mister Tom Bisbee.'

'My God,' Stormbuckler whispered. 'How did my good acquaintance, Tom, land himself in a place like this?'

Sister Mary Paul came back soon with a pot of steamed porridge and a portion of hard, sour bread. Stormbuckler accepted the food and gobbled it promptly.

'Do you want more?'

Stormbuckler rocked his head. 'Do you mind if I ask about Tom Bisbee?'

'What do you wish to know?'

'How long has Tom been in this place, in this — well, you know — in this state?'

'Mr. Bisbee was brought to us yesterday... He had suffered most dreadfully...'

'What took place? I mean, what happened to him? Was it consumption? I ain't never seen an individual swathed head-to-foot for a malady before...'

'It's not *malady*. Tom Bisbee had been very severely burned...'

'Burned? How did Tom get burned? I don't understand...'

'Neither do we, for certain. The factory delivered him to us in this state. They informed us he had been involved in a works accident. They didn't expand upon things. That's absolutely their right, of course. We don't ask too many questions. So the factory guards dropped him here and offered a generous contribution to cover the cost of his confinement and our caregiving. When we examined the gentleman, we discovered he had been scorched along one side of his entire body...'

'Mercy! How? Why?'

'An occurrence, the factory guards said. A works *accident*. That's the way of things in a town manufactory. He's not the first to be brought here *in this state*...'

'An accident? Well, I never! He's not the first? Is that what you said? There have been others like him, brought here like this?'

The Sister expressed a tolerant smile: 'Are you certain you do not want more porridge?'

Stormbuckler rattled his head: 'Would you permit me to stay with Tom? *Here*, I mean? Can he talk?'

'He's been given a draught to dispose of his terrible pain. I'm afraid he won't be able to talk... but you may settle with him if you'd like.'

'Can Tom hear me? If I tell him my tales? Will he be able to attend my stories if I whisper them softly?'

'Perhaps he will. I don't know.'

'I will not get in the way, I promise. It's just that I'd like to stay here to tell him all my exploits....'

'I'll bring a stool, and fetch some more bread. But I must caution you...'

'Caution me?'

'Yes, I'm sorry to tell you this, but a priest has been sent for. He'll perform the last rites. I'm afraid your friend Tom Bisbee will not last.'

'Will not last?'

'Your companion will be raised to glory very shortly. I'm sorry.' Sister Mary Paul received Stormbuckler's hand in her own. 'I'm genuinely sorry.'

8

Mrs. Oldcorne insisted she would prepare the lady's maid known as Mayotte for her first day working for Mr. Asher-John Lindwürm at his Cromford Mill works in Staines Town. 'You must get into something plain and unfashionable,' advised Mrs. Oldcorne as she selected two of her most modest dresses from an immense wardrobe. She held the grey dress to the light. 'This one is penny plain without elaboration or frills...'

'As you wish, Ma'am...' responded Mayotte. She dropped her head and bent one knee. 'It's very good of you to lend me your outfit.'

'Yes, I'm sure it is. But I don't want a gal of mine to be turned out like a tramp... *or worse...*'

'Worse?'

'I don't want a girl of mine to be dressed like a hussy.'

'Quite, Madam. That outfit looks *unhussylike...* did you wear it?'

Mrs. Oldcorne overlooked the veiled insolence and bought the garment against her maid's slim body. 'Of course, you're skinnier. And a good deal — shall we say — a good deal *less* well-developed?'

'Let's say that, shall we?'

'Get into this frock while I find you a pair of my dullest shoes and the simplest of all bags to go with it.'

'You are exceedingly kind,' said the girl.

So, once she'd drawn the frock over her chemise and drawers, Mrs. Oldcorne motioned Mayotte to sit by the light. 'I want to brush out your semi-ferocious hair,' explained the lady of the house. 'While I do that, I will offer advice about how to present and conduct yourself...'

'Of course, Ma'am.'

'First, do not forget you're representing me and your master, so you must be on your best behaviour at all times. And never forget that, although he's moneyed, Mr. Lindwürm is simply a common colonial. He's not a sober Englishman like your master, my beloved husband. So you might encounter manners that seem swinelike and uncultured. For example, he won't have any moral code of conduct or possess respectable manners... but that's to be expected from someone who is not far removed from being, *himself*, savage. Also, never forget you represent *not just me* but our entire social class. You represent our Empire. And our sovereign Lady, the Empress. Is that clear? Don't allow this brockish American brute to take advantage of you, bodily, I mean, girl. Most importantly, never let your civilised standards slip. Am I understood?'

'Yes, Ma'am. May I ask what social class I should endeavour to represent?'

'Don't get funny with me, girl. You know very well which class you are from. Although you are, of course, drug up from peculiar and exotic blood and were raised from the lowest underclass of any society on earth, you *now* portray the British Imperial middle class...'

'Me Ma'am? I'm a modest working girl? How can I —'

Mrs. Oldcorne cut Mayotte off half-sentence. She yanked on her maid's hair so roughly it caused the girl to sneeze. 'Yes, I declare it will be difficult for you, my dear. I concede I had my uncertainties about this transaction... but Mr. Lindwürm determined to settle upon *you*. For some reason. And he is not the type of fellow who takes *no* for an answer. I just wish he'd singled out someone else to play his Galatea, but there we are... we're stuck with things now...so all we can do is profit from things.'

'Yes, Ma'am.'

'So, mind your habits, be on your best behaviour and act as lady-like as you can manage. No profanity, no lolling, and please struggle as best as you can to be humble and subordinate in your enterprises with him, yes?'

'Yes, Ma'am.'

Mrs. Oldcorne raked a comb through the maid's unruly hair. 'And now for the important part of my guidance...'

'You have my fullest attention, Ma'am...'

'I require you to be my *eyes and ears*...'

'What does that mean?'

'Don't ever forget you represent me and your master. So be watchful. We call for you to report back any odd comings-and-goings, business dealings, hushed discussions, any odd remarks, and so forth...'

'How will I identify if these comings-and-goings and remarks are odd?'

'Anything that seems curious to you must be reported. Anything you think is irregular must be shared. Anything you think is contrary to the common rules of decency should be presented back to us. In fact anything the American asks you to do that dances upon your conscience must be delivered back to us... Am I making myself clear?'

'Yes, I think so, Madam.'

Mrs. Oldcorne smoothed-down the second-hand gown and installed an insincere palm on the girl's young shoulder: 'Inform us Mayotte, of what you see. Report what you hear. Learn everything you can about this ghastly colonial... the most insignificant thing might be the most vital. So listen well to exchanges, gossip to other workers when you can, read his plans and look at his strategies... be certain to report *everything* back.'

'I think you're proposing I should be your spy...'

'Nonsense, dear. Spy is such a murky word! Of course, we do not want that. You must be *yourself*...'

'But you call for me to sniff and snoop around?'

'Snoop? I never said the word snoop! I never advocated such a filthy thing! Nobody likes a ferret, Mayotte. All we propose is that you are inquisitive. And analytical. Keep your wits about you and be my eyes and ears.'

'I think I understand,' said Mayotte. She lifted from the dresser.

'Good girl. Let's look at you. There you are. A picture. Non-remarkable and unassuming. Plain as a pikestaff... that's the fashion I was reaching for when I dressed you.'

'I can't thank you enough,' said Mayotte, offering a curtsey.

Oh, I know,' said Mrs. Oldcorne.

~

The Technical Director looked up and sighed, 'I don't know what I'm supposed to do with you, um, miss? My employer, Mr. Lindwürm, didn't say what he wanted with you. I have no idea what he has planned. I have no experience whatsoever with, um, women. There is no place for, erm, females, within manufacturing. Um? Mr. Lind-würm merely told me you were arriving today. He didn't expand further on it. Other than to say you were, um, an individual of distinctly female persuasion. As I can see *now* for myself.'

Mayotte examined the man at the desk. He was aged about forty, had grey hair and little round glasses ledged balconylike over pincoffin eyes. He seemed shorter than most of the fellows she'd worked with at the Oldcorne residence. She eyed him, unsurely.

'Most of our workers come in two distinctly different flavours...' the campion-eyed man continued. 'There are the able. And there are the *not so able*. The incompetents heave, push, lug and pull stuff about. They're retained for their bullish strength, their muscular tenacity, and their capacity to keep their mouths locked shut even while they haul kit around that's often twice their weight and size. The able and skilled workers, meanwhile, will deliver certificates when they arrive, and I identify appropriate positions for them within our company based upon experience, accomplishments, and competencies. Thus, our employees are regarded by us as either assets or implementers. Which are you?'

'An investment, sir...' she replied.

'Well, that's a confident answer, I suppose. Though your purpose doesn't fit the pattern I just explained. So it leaves me exactly where I was two minutes ago: None the ruddy wiser.' He stared unblinking at her neckline. 'I wish Mr. Lindwürm were here so he could explain the

96

validity of his ideas in relation to your hiring and could enlighten me with his brilliance. I'm not a prejudicative man, and I'm sure there must be a valid reason for it, but I can't figure out why you, a woman, are here in my presence. Maybe you might yet become useful, though I can't see how that would *possibly* be! Have you had any prior experience?

'Experience? Doing what?'

The man rubbed his fingers and gave Mayotte a disapproving look, 'Exactly. *Exactly.*'

'When will Mr. Lindwürm be here?' she asked. 'Perhaps he can explain to us what he expects...' Mayotte provided a helpful smile.

'It is unlikely he will be in today. Nor tomorrow. He spends a lot of time in his private garage. He occupies his valuable time on his numerous inventions. He leaves everyday operations to me.'

'Well, um, what is done here?'

'You don't even know that?' The Technical Director gave a snort. 'You're testing the absolute limit of my patience, young woman! He sends me a young female who doesn't know the first thing about anything. Why?'

'I think he wants me to offer suggestions...'

'Suggestions? Is that what you think? Since when do we require suggestions from a trifle like you? I'm sorry to dishearten you, dear. I venture to guess that Mr. Lindwürm wanted you here for an ankle...'

'Ankle?'

'I don't wish to put finer point on it. I merely suggest that Mr. Lindwürm is partial to a well-formed ankle. What other reason could he have for enticing you here? It's the only reason I can think of for recruiting a —' the Director made a hacking sound in the back of his throat because the next word he'd utter would be a vile profanity.

But Mayotte cut in: 'Well I'm here! Whatcha gonna do?'

The Technical Director shuddered at her words. He stared at her with a horrified expression: 'What did you say?'

'You heard. I don't mean to be pushy, mister, but you're making me feel undesirable and unwelcome, aren't you? What's your name, so I can report back?'

'Mr. Siebert. Mister James Owen Siebert.' The lenses on his wire-framed spectacles steamed-up as he gazed in bewilderment at this forward young woman, who didn't seem *in the slight* overawed in his managerial presence. He shifted his feet under the heavy desk. 'I don't think I've ever met a woman who comes across as confident and self-possessed as you. What's your name again?'

'Mayotte, if you please. Those were flattering words, in my opinion. I'm not afraid to voice my ideas; was that the reason he hired me?'

'Maybe now I can see what attracted him...' Mr. Siebert stood from his desk but indicated she ought to remain seated. He was about to do his routine speech: 'We create machinery. We produce a variety of vehicles, including steam vehicles, pedal-powered vehicles, and combustion vehicles. We design and create motorized transport, steam yachts, bicycle gears, and other experimental engines. And we're experimenting with a galvanic gondola that we hope will power a ballonet airlifter. We produce every component ourselves, and we ship our equipment all over the world. There are four parts to our enterprise: our mill, which I opened myself and operated before Mr. Lindwürm came to these shores; our manufactory, where most employee's toil; our new steam-house where yachts are created and launched and, finally, our latest project that we house in a place we call Steam Shed 7. It is run by Mr. Lindwürm's trusted friend —Ligore Lassiter...'

'Oh, I've met him...'

James Owen Siebert grimaced and put up a hand to stop her senseless chitter-chat, 'Let me finish. We have over a hundred employees in our plant and none... *not one*... is a woman. You are, in every sense of the word, *the first*.'

'Really? I'm your Eve?'

'Hmm... please Miss, let me continue without constant interruption... so being the first and only woman here, I am sure you can imagine that there will be certain, *ahem*, shall we say complications? Impediments that you will have to overcome on a daily basis! The first, probably the first of many, is that you will no doubt get unwanted attention, perhaps even affectionate advances, from our male workers. Can you handle that?'

'Handle advances? Yes, I certainly *can*... I will bat them away...'

'Really?' James Owen Siebert cleared his throat, making a loud, guttural noise that sounded like a hornet had been trapped in a jar of treacle: 'And there will be other sources of irritation. More than I can calculate at the current moment... but am I making myself clear?'

'Not exactly glass-like, *mush*, if I'm being honest. But I get your general gist. What you're saying is that, because I'm the only girl at your plant, the men will exploit my weaknesses and impose themselves upon my bones... is that about it?'

'I couldn't have put it better...'

'Yeah, I know.' Mayotte gave a sweet smile. 'I think I should start with a goosey-gander. Will you show me around your facilities?'

'Um? Yes, I guess I can. Do you have any other questions at this stage, though?'

'Actually, there is one thing I should like to know right off, *mush*. Who designs all your — you know — gubbins?'

Mayotte watched Mr. Siebert silently mouth the word *gubbins*, before he spluttered a reply: 'I assume you mean the machine parts? The wheels, the axles, the cranks, the chains, the bearings, and the gears? Mr. Lindwürm's elaborates each conception himself, although at the early stage it is a mental image. But a team of top engineers and technicians are then entrusted with the task of turning his mental concepts into reality...'

'I see,' said Mayotte. 'Then I would like to start my tour by visiting those top engineers and technicians.'

'Well, you'll need to wait because I need to complete my documentation. After that I'll take you on a tour of the manufactory.' James Owen Siebert shook his head slowly as Mayotte stood to leave. She was sure she heard him murmur: 'Extraordinary, really *extraordinary*...' as she tip-toed from his office.

After a while, James Owen Siebert left his chamber, looking irritable in a leather apron knotted over a baize waistcoat, dusty breeches, and thick paddock boots. He produced a lengthy guttural growl as he gestured Mayotte to *come along*.

Almost at once, there was a sharp and pungent smell of soap and lubricant in the air, and she could pick up high-pitched whining sounds that reminded her of packs of impassioned wild dogs wailing their hearts out, at a greasy moon. She supposed these awful sounds came from some unseen, but ghastly, machine.

Siebert led her to the primary space, a gigantic cathedral of turbulence and smog. There, Siebert raised his tone over the clamour of grind and grumble. He shouted precisely into her ear: 'This is where we do our ironwork and forging. The mill is principally an hydraulically powered undertaking, but we also have two engines of steam.'

She remained close to him as they marched towards the shop-floor, 'We have a pudding-coal furnace outside, but otherwise, we accomplish most of the processes *inside* this single building.' She shuffled past musty sacks of charcoal, sulphuric pulverizing machines that sounded like rows of children screaking in an empty church, then rows of agitating pots, vociferously rotating press-wheels that made sounds like hail-stones flung against chapel walls. There were scraping mills that sounded like mothers weeping at infant gravesides. There were lines of simmering wood-kegs and ugly rolling machines that lolled-out products that resembled blueish calf tongues. There were a noisy steam hammers that thrust gases high into the air and created walloping blows and deadly counter-blows with iron fists. There was an engine that looked like a horned demon and possessed a set of evil claws. There were vast cogwheel mechanisms that shot sparks of fury into the air, and beyond those, there were flaming furnaces that fumed mountains of chaff. Workers had littered *all* the floors with spokes, spurs, and dagger-heads of jagged metal. There were boiling kettles of tar *everywhere*. One man lifted a flaming rod and plunged it into hissing liquids, creating frying spasms of smoke and fire. What came out of the liquid resembled spectres rising from a baptismal font. Then Mayotte figured-out why the workers were *all* dressed as if about to embark on a fox-hunt: it was to defend themselves from the gases, the sparks, and the lethal-looking metal darts that flew out *everywhere*. Yes, they had furnished almost every inch of this place with clanking, pointy, and burning *death*.

~

Mr. Siebert took her into the fresh air, and she took a lungful of coolness, then choked forthwith, and became unsteady on her feet. She felt she might throw-up. 'Are you all right, miss?' he asked, proffering a smug smile. 'You've gone green. I wouldn't go onto the shop floor in *those*.' They both looked at the soft pull-on slippers her mistress had chosen for her to wear on her first day. 'You'll need to change into clogs *anyway*, when we go into the powder rooms.'

He took her into the first of three smaller buildings, where pairs of stout wooden clogs were racked against a wall. He stopped to pull his riding-boots from thick hairy ankles, using a bootjack. As he hauled his smelly leathers away, Mr. Siebert made a series of grumpy huffs. She watched all this, then peeled away her mockworthy brocaded slip-ons from dainty bare feet, though she was careful not to disturb the puttees she'd wound around her ankles. Mr. Siebert watched her movements, and licked his bottom lip, although he made no comment. He passed a pair of wooden clogs, taken from a pigeon-hole in the rack. She put them on. She abandoned her slippers on the ground.

They strolled through the airless, parched-dry atmosphere of the first powder-room where she viewed containers of salts and grains stored in racks, rolling, and pressing mills, and sifters. Then outside, and right-away, into a similar room, and then into a third. In the last two rooms, she witnessed labourers heaving, turning, and pushing large barrels around. She assumed these barrels contained powders and chemicals.

Once outside, Mr. Siebert told her they must now go to the draughting office. They reached it via a tall wooden staircase that felt slippery and looked thoroughly unsafe. At the top of the rickety flight, through a stable-door, they entered the relative peace of an office-space fitted with windows and with oil-lamps suspended over inclined desks.

'Welcome to our draught office,' Mr. Siebert said. 'We have a dozen schematic and drafting technicians here... their job is to capture the geometric features of each product or component that we hope to manufacture, and create for it a technical diagram.' He took her along a row of drawing boards, while men, most of them hunched and spectacled, leaned hollow-eyed over drawings that had been sketched onto vast sheets of paper. She stopped by one diagram and admired the man's neat pen-lines.

'Did you say you were creating a steam yacht?' she asked. 'I should like to see a picture of *that*...'

'Um, yes. One of you, yes *you*, the lad with the black hair, get this young lady the set of schematics for the steam-puffer Spry Shimmerfly...'

While the clerk hurried off to find the drawing, Mr. Siebert explained what she would see next: 'The Spry Shimmerfly is a little water puffer that we are putting together on the banks of the river. At this stage, she's just a prototype. But we think she'll be an energetic little whizzer when she becomes fully operational.'

The clerk brought over a huge file of documents. Some papers were as large as yellow pillowcases. Mr. Siebert laid these documents out, one-by-one, onto the only flat-surface in the room, a polished table by the largest window. 'As you can see,' he resumed, 'She's a lighter with a boiler behind, a castle for four men and a derrick. Also, as you can see from this diagram, she has a water-butt and a pan-loaf set mid-central. She carries a cargo of gravel or coal and she's powered by an engine that is designed and manufactured *here*. The vessel is not elegant, but she's dapper.'

Mayotte admired the thin lines, the neat curves, and the splendid arcs with interest. But the drawing didn't represent a yacht *to her*. 'I asked for a picture. Not a diagram. Where is the completed vessel?'

'What? Well, the vessel is not completed, is it? We are still working on her at the steam-house, down by the river. I have already told you that. So we don't have an image of the completed vessel yet, just plans.'

'But I mean, I need to see the picture of the finished product so I can properly appreciate it. I can't visualize the Spry Shimmerfly from dry-as-dust ink-plans, can I? I should like to see her coursing through the choppy water.'

Mr. Siebert folded the papers away and gave her a surly look. 'Well, that's because you don't have a technical mind, do you, dear? These are specialised diagrams, drawn to scale. You need to have a different mindset to appreciate what we're doing here. You need a man's mind to absorb *this*. As a female, you haven't got what it takes...'

'I see,' Mayotte said. 'May I ask you another question before you file those drawings away?'

'I suppose so.' Though he knocked his knuckles along the table in a cantankerous manner.

'Is the Spry Shimmerfly understood to be a commercial venture?'

'Commercial? Well, yes, *of course it is*. I presuppose that Mr. Lindwürm's inclination is to make several similar vessels and sell them to waterways and boat-houses across the world. Why? Why do you ask? What has that got to do with anything?'

'How will the prospective purchasers understand what they're getting if they can't visualize the commodity?'

'They can see the prototype for themselves at our steam-house, can't they? I don't know what you're getting at...'

'I thought you suggested that the vessel wasn't completed yet...'

'I think the lady is proposing that she'd like to see a model of our puffer...' responded the black-haired junior clerk, who had brought the schematics over for Mayotte's inspection.

'Oh, right. We have a scale-model by the river. Therefore, a prospective purchaser might look at that.'

'You told me earlier that you send machines around the world? But now it seems you're suggesting that customers must come here to view scale-models or to witness half-finished constructions... which is it? You are not making any sense!'

'Well, it's more than half-finished...' said Mr. Siebert, though she sensed he spoke through gritted teeth, 'And I genuinely don't understand what your banging-on about...'

'Do you have a pamphlet?'

'Pamphlet? What do you mean, pamphlet?'

'Something to send to a future customer. A booklet with a picture of the completed steam-yacht depicted on the cover. I should like to see a pamphlet for your Spry Shimmerfly...'

'Well, so you might, dear. But our customers don't need to see such a silly thing... Now, if we might move on...'

'Don't they? How do you know?' Mayotte drew her fingers through her hair. 'Do you have a picture of the completed steam-yacht, sat on blue water, puffing flawless cotton-ball clouds into a perfect sky?'

Mr. Siebert looked annoyed, 'Well, of course, *we don't*. We don't make whimsical picture postcards here, my dear; nor do we construct fancy carton tops. We are machinists. This is an industrialized plant...'

'That's where you're going wrong...'

'I beg your pardon? What impudence! How dare you indicate that we are going wrong... on your first day? I'll have you know that we are a remarkably *successful* manufactory. We offer superior products within a specialised field of enterprises...'

'Barely a household name, though, are you? What's your brand? What mark do you work under? What's the proprietary name for the products you assemble?'

'Well, that's completely unrelated. We produce top-quality machines and we're proud of what we achieve. That's *all* that matters...'

'But couldn't you accomplish more? That's all I'm recommending. Where is your promotional information?'

'I don't even know what that term means. Though it rings like silly vaporescence to me! Feminine piffle-puff. What are you blathering about, young woman?'

The clerk with the black hair intervened, before attitudes between them reached boiling point: 'Perhaps the lady is right, sir. It's true that we don't offer our clients a picture of an ultimate product, do we? Wouldn't it be beneficial to present future buyers with an image of what we aim to achieve?'

'What a lot of bother that would be!' suggested Mr. Siebert. 'I'm confident we can proceed, gladly, with *no* picture postcards... and *no* piffle-puff!'

'As your young man has responded, it would be an agreeable thing though, wouldn't it? To show a client? Or perhaps persuade a client's wife? If I might be audacious again, sir, I think what you require is a design illustrator: someone who can produce a detailed impression of a completed product...'

'Can't one of our planning technicians do that?'

'Why don't we ask them?' Mayotte glanced around the draught office. A few men rattled their heads. Others blatantly ignored her. All of them pressed their noses to their blueprints. 'I guess we have the answer,' Mayotte announced with a smile.

9

Back at Priory Lodge, on the evening of her first day at the manufactory, Mrs. Oldcorne raked through Mayotte's hair with a bone-handled comb: 'So, what did you observe for me?' she asked.

'Well, for a start I discovered this outfit you lent me is *not* satisfactory...'

'Not satisfactory?' Mrs. Oldcorne let out a tiny yelp. 'But that's very ungrateful *of you*. I allowed you one of my old frocks and that's all you have to say? It is plain but elegant. It is simple but decorative... what was wrong with it?'

'Ma'am, please believe I am grateful to you. But the fellows that work on the manufactory floor are out-fitted as if they're about to go horse riding. They bear brown leather blacksmith's aprons over tweed, farrier's gloves, tight breeches, traveling boots, and collar-scarves. The only feature that's missing from their get-up is a sturdy riding crop...and I shouldn't be surprised if they were equipped with those, too!'

'Even Lindwürm?' Mrs. Oldcorne spotted her own eyes in the dressing mirror, so scanned her reflection. 'Mind you, he carried positively atrocious pantaloons when he showed up here for dinner here, didn't he? And he'd knotted an altogether tasteless neckerchief around his throat, so maybe you're right...'

'I didn't see Mr. Lindwürm at the plant.'

'Why ever not, dear? That's the reason you're there, isn't it, to interact with the millionaire? Why didn't you see him?'

Mayotte threw a wave with her fingers: 'Because he didn't show up for work...'

'He didn't? Do you have any idea where he might have been? Was he gadding about conducting business deals? Did he meet, perhaps, some mysterious third party?' Mrs. Oldcorne ceased combing and gripped Mayotte's shoulder. 'I shall want to know who he is meeting, even when he is not as his place of business. Do you understand that, girl? And also where he goes. Do you follow what I am saying? You'll have to ask around. Or find some other way of invading his privacy. For example, will you have access to his diary?'

'Diary? I have no knowledge of any diary, let alone where it might be kept. I don't think I am engaged at the manufactory as some kind of administrative assistant... if that's what you thought.'

'Aren't you, dear? Isn't that why he called for you? I thought he recruited you to be a source of feminine sunlight in the otherwise shaded realm of dry masculine mechanicals. I thought he took you on to become an object of pleasant natural grace among the many stone-faced, downright dreary, cock-a-doodle-dandy's that besiege his daily routines.'

'What? Like the dour Mr. Lassiter, do you mean?'

'That's squarely who I mean...'

'I never saw him neither...'

'That's irremediably un-syntactic of you, girl...' Mrs. Oldcorne tutted. She tugged a portion of her maid's haircut, just above the ear, to cause her to flinch, inflicting a stinging lesson in diction: 'Try not to speak like a fisherman's daughter in the presence of your betters, dear. It establishes you as... well, it establishes you as puerile and vulgar.'

'Sorry, Ma'am...'

'So, where was Lindwürm? Did you identify his whereabouts? You did not tell me the rest of the story...'

'In his garage. I understand he took the entire day off. By the sound of it, I think he regularly takes days off — to stay at home. He prefers to stay at home and toy about with his engineering.'

'At home, huh? I will require you to call on him again... while he is at home... to discover what he's up to...'

'Ma'am?' Mayotte bit her lip.

'Yes. Prepare an excuse to withdraw from the manufactory, so you might visit his home. You know where his home is, don't you? So go see what he does in this garage...'

'It seems I have to account for my movements to an old gentleman named Mr. James Owen Siebert. He's an austere-speaking fellow they call the 'technical director.' He's the fellow I work under. I judge, and this next comment is between you and me Ma'am, I judge that this Mr. Siebert runs the place. He's the proper boss. The other two are absentee proprietors.'

'However, it's not this Mister 'Sea Bright' I prefer you to focus your time and attention on, right? He's a passing captain on the choppy waves of fortune. No! I require you to focus your pistol-sights on the grandest grandee of them all that, our Mr. Lindwürm. D'you see?'

'Yes, Ma'am.'

'So, as soon as you can please, I require you to establish an excuse to leave the manufactory and travel to the home of Asher-John Lind-würm, and see what he's up to.'

Mayotte nodded.

'Get yourself over to his horrid abode and slink around. Have a good sniff into his corners and crannies and try to find what's going on, will you? Report all your findings back to me, yes?'

'Yes, Ma'am.'

Stormbuckler had been told that Tom Bisbee, his bandaged friend, would *not* endure the day. Though Tom had been given medication to diminish the agonizing torment he suffered. So Stormbuckler lingered by his friend's bedside in a calm state of mind. As he waited,

Stormbuckler confided stories about the poorhouse and his antics up to that moment.

Stormbuckler told Tom that Mr. Jims had been taken ill. He told Tom about Kilda the pugilist showing up at the institution and taking over Mr. Jim's duties. He told Tom about the exercises that Kilda had taught him so he might become stronger and more confident, like the big man himself. He told Tom that Kilda had asked him to draw a skull and bones for a tattoo he planned. Then Stormbuckler told Tom about how Kilda disappeared one day and had been replaced by Seedpod. And he told Tom that Seedpod had made his life a misery. And, finally, he told Tom about how a pig helped him depart the poorhouse and how he happened to be here at this Servite infirmary, searching for Mr. Jims, but instead stumbling upon his best friend.

After a while, some of the walking patients returned to their beds, shuffling clumsily, slipping under bed-blankets, quietly closing their eyes. Stormbuckler supposed they had returned from a chapel some-place where they had performed the mysterious thing called the Rosary of the Seven Sorrows. After these shamblers and stumblers entered the ward, a line of stretchers was brought in, one after another, carried by Sisters dressed in the same way as Sister Mary Paul. Each of the stretchered patients was turned over to a separate bed. Soon, the ward was fully occupied again. But even though it was filled, there was still a hush about the place — a sense of peace. As Stormbuckler observed the last stretcher return to the ward, he figured out how very sorely ill his friend Tom must be. Everybody was required to go to the chapel for worship, no matter how poorly they were. That is, everyone but Tom and the other bandaged soul across the room. These patients could not be moved!

Regularly, during the long day, Sister Mary Paul would appear to pull covers or establish a tender palm on the only part of Tom's body that had not been swathed in white material. She brought a cold cloth to his bandaged forehead, or touched the fingers of his left hand; the tips of the fingers jutted from the wrappers. Sometimes Sister Mary Paul pressed a dampened sponge between Tom's cracked lips. When she did these things, she spoke a virtually imperceptible prayer.

She smiled each time she passed Stormbuckler. Towards the mid-point of the day, she brought in another hunk of bread — this time more mealy crust than flesh — but Stormbuckler crunched it down appreciatively.

'The priest will be here soon...' Sister Mary Paul declared. 'Sister Margaret Gregory, the hospital administrator, will complete an *evaluation*.'

A little while after these remarks were spoken, there was an atmosphere of alertness in the ward. Several supplementary nuns arrived at Tom's bedside and busied themselves, preparing bolsters, tidying pans of liquid, and wiping down the bed-spread. After this, and with insufficient forewarning, a stout woman entered the space. She wore the same grey duty apron as other nuns, over a dark smock, but although she looked the same as the others, this woman possessed an air of leadership. Faltering a few steps behind her was a lanky, white-haired man with arms as narrow as hay-hooks.

The influential woman paused momentarily by a bed near the entrance because an inmate had raised a weakened head to ask her a question. She responded, so the thin man white-haired man waited behind, and bit his fingernails.

'That's Sister Margaret Gregory,' confided Mary Paul. 'She is here to make a judgment...'

'Do I have to leave?'

'No, stay here. I'll explain who you are.'

After the short delay, the superintending nun approached Tom's bed. Stormbuckler could tell from the unrelenting expression on her face that Sister Margaret Gregory called for high standards. Sister Mary Paul briefed the hospital administrator in hushed tones. The two women glanced at Stormbuckler during their conversation, so he supposed they discussed his presence. Then Sister Margaret Gregory went to Tom and touched his skin, just above an eye. She pushed her ear against Tom's rib cage, then she tugged his bandaged wrist and held it for several minutes. The senior nun removed the top blanket to unmask Tom's cold feet, then held his toes and felt along Tom's shins and ankles. After this, she established an impassive expression, but invited the thin white-haired man to come by Tom's bed. She pulled the thin white-haired man nearer. They both considered Tom's face. Then Sister Margaret Gregory peered Stormbuckler's way, and threw him a deadpan look.

Stormbuckler watched Sister Margaret Gregory withdraw to an arm's length, while the thin, white-haired man remained bowed over Tom's body. The man dabbed something onto his friend's forehead. Stormbuckler heard strange words being uttered, something like: '*Misericordiam adiuvet te per Dominum, ut gratiam Spiritus Sancti...*' Though he couldn't hear all the words, they sounded like a weird incantation. After these words, the thin white-haired man did something particularly odd: he kissed Tom's bandages, and then he kissed all over Tom's face, and he kissed Tom's chest. He made a gesture of the cross over Tom's heart. Next, the thin white-haired man took a miniature book from an inside pocket and began to read. As he did this reading, Sister Mary Paul and Sister Margaret Gregory knelt by Tom's bedside, bent their heads, and crossed their hearts. Stormbuckler didn't know if he was presumed to kneel *also*, but before he had made any decision, the women got themselves up, and Sister Margaret Gregory marched elsewhere. She left the thin, white-haired man at Tom's bedside. The fellow tucked-away his items, his pocket-sized book, a crucifix, and a tiny water bottle. Then he spread his arms above Tom's bed.

'Let me introduce you,' suggested Sister Mary Paul. 'This is Tom's best friend, Master Stormbuckler.'

'How are you, fellah? I am Father Felim O'Divilly...' The thin white-haired man stopped what he was doing over Tom's bed and presented Stormbuckler with a merry smile. He extended a thin hand to stroke Stormbuckler's shoulder. 'So, here's a thought for thee, young fellah: I'll be headed back into town *right now*. So I was wondering if ye'd be requiring a lift in my gig? I have an empty seat if you want a share of my ride? How does that suit thee, fellah?'

'Um? Me sir? No, I can't go. I must wait here with my friend...'

As Stormbuckler mumbled those words, he saw Sister Mary Paul fold some bandages over Tom's eyes. And that's when dreadful melancholy seized his heart — it felt as if a lance had passed through his body. He had been punctured. Pierced by sudden sorrow. Stormbuckler gasped because the air was taken from him... the grief was so unforeseen that it became *excruciating*.

But Stormbuckler sensed Father Felim's tender palm upon his shoulder. 'That's why we must be off, do you see? The Sister has other duties to perform. So back to town we must tootle lee loo. Are you joining with me, or are ye not? It will be company for me along the boreen, so I should prefer thee to come along.'

'Um? I do not have coin to offer you in return for such a ride.'

'Coin? I would not take brass from thee, Master. Not upon a day like this. No, young sir, let's be off.'

Stormbuckler looked towards Mary Paul: 'I must say goodbye to the Sister. She has been kind...'

'She hasn't time to talk, she's too busy, *too busy*... Don't delay her with your heartaches, young fellah: the sands of time run swift, *fugit irreparable tempus*.' Father Felim O'Divilly possessed an esoteric twinkle in his grey eyes. 'She'll wish us well on our way, of that I'm sure. She has a good heart filled with Christ's sweet mercy. Sister Mary Paul desires the sweet graces of heaven, for thee and for me, but *only* if we make haste from this place... we must away *at once*.'

With a firm fist pushed against his back, Stormbuckler found himself steered from the Servite infirmary and into the blinking light of day. From the entrance, Father Felim O'Divilly drew him to a single, black-polished horse that had been tackled to a ramshackle gig, arranged by a block of stone. The priest encouraged Stormbuckler to step into the carriage and so he landed himself upon a springy seat. The priest unhitched his animal, raised himself alongside, then took the reins. Soon they rumbled down a track and into the moor.

They drove for the town.

~

They steadily clip-clopped along the highway, and Stormbuckler wondered whether he ought to tell his companion that he'd never met a Roman Catholic cleric before. But the Father *tooralood* and *tooralayed* to himself and seemed entirely immersed in his *Roman* thoughts. Earlier than perhaps he had forecast, Stormbuckler saw they passed the parish boundary stone. Then he spotted the first traces of settlement. A flock of chickens on a green, a stoic scarecrow leant indifferently against a pole, a hoary dog yapping at a grain barn, and tufts of smoke lifting from straw rooftops.

'Do you have a place to be dropped?' asked Father O'Divilly.

'Me sir? No, sir. *I'm —*'

The priest reached out a steadying hand and patted Stormbuckler on the shoulder. 'You feel lost, don't you, son? I appreciate how you feel. Bless you, my son. But the bewilderment will lift in time. I'm going to say a prayer for you tonight. So that tomorrow you will feel fresh and light as summer rain.'

Stormbuckler didn't fathom why the priest had declared such oddly curious words, he nodded his thanks anyway, and said: 'Thank you for your prayers... I can pick up bread and board at the manufactory. Would you dump me there please? It's where my friend Tom Bisbee formerly worked...'

'The chap I just delivered last rites to?' muttered the priest.

'Um? Yes, *the same...*'

'Are you certain you want to go to the manufactory? I mean, why would you choose such a frightful place? You saw what befell that poor young fellah!'

'That's *why* I want to go there. I want to find out what happened to Tom. I want to find out *for myself.*'

The wheels of the gig run onto rutted ground as they approached the centre of town. Stormbuckler sniffed cabbage and tallow, apple cores and mutton-bones, mud, and black-water — the bouquets of life in a riverside town. They turned a corner to travel at a slower pace by the riverfront, then came to a halt by a darkening pier by one of the highest residences that cast a shadow, as if it were in a line of top hats.

'There you are, young fellah,' said the priest. He held a tone of climax in his voice.

'Is this the end of the road?' Stormbuckler asked.

'Roads have no real ending, young fellah. All of us are presented with life's empty highways, though occasionally we arrive at a location that disrupts our narrative. But in the end, we must travel where our empty pathway take us.'

'But I alight here for the manufactory, right?'

'Aye, that's what you do, son. Peace be with you when you take your leave.'

Stormbuckler dropped into gooey-splashy puddles. The priest made a series of clicking noises, then he tugged at the reins to get himself underway.

The priest left Stormbuckler alone and unsettled for several moments. The buggy drove into the drab distance. But Stormbuckler gathered his fortitude and ambled along the riverbank to inspect the structures that he passed.

A sour-looking thug paced beside a wall at the entrance of one riverbank building. Stormbuckler announced, 'I'm searching for employment.'

The man gave him a dubious look.

'In the factory,' Stormbuckler added.

'What's your experience, mate?'

'Me? I work with pigs.'

The man let out a hoot and smoothed his stubbled chin with brown-stained fingers. 'There's a mash-yard along the towpath, just by the wharf. They might employ your talents...' The man gave Stormbuckler a rum-eyed glance. 'Whatever *they might be.*'

'Do they need a livestock man?' Stormbuckler asked.

'Hah! No mate. Nobody needs a flaming' livestock man down here by the water. But they might call for a barrel roller, huh? Could you offer your back to a barrel?'

'Maybe I could. Thank you, sir.'

'Whatever steadies your soul, mate...' said the man. He ducked inside his workplace.

Stormbuckler left in the direction the man had revealed, along the Thames waterfront. He searched for a 'boatyard' which he assumed would be discernible when he happened across it. Perhaps he'd encounter the adjacent mash-yard (whatever that was) close-by. After a few hundred yards of dither and pootle, he showed up at what was doubtless the 'new' boatyard. Stormbuckler identified the smell of fresh-brushed shave-wood, as well as the fragrance of varnish and soap and some lighter aromas that probably included embers and fats, machine oils, and lubricants. Once outside the building, he spotted metal-forged objects shrouded in sacks of cloth. Now and then, laborers left the main building to fetch parts for their store. Next to the boathouse, sharing the same shoreline, was a thinner and significantly lower building that had a wide cobbled entrance-way. Stormbuckler assumed this must be the mashing plant. The yard contained a large shed, with haylofts on an upper floor, and a scattering of auxiliary buildings. There were further moorings on the edge of the river for the kegs. He noticed that the mashing plant presented a pleasing fragrance that hinted of fruit berry sweetness and malted generosity. Stormbuckler raised his nose to the air and said, aloud, *this will do*.

He loitered near the central door of the mash-yard and shilly-shallied around as other workers emerged. These workers lugged bulky containers. Stormbuckler gained the attention of the man he supposed must be the *bloke in charge*. This older man retained an elegant moustache. 'Do you require a barrel roller?' Stormbuckler yelled.

The moustached guy returned Stormbuckler a sceptical eye, 'It so happens you're in luck, son. Our best lug did not come to work today; the fool got drunk and lobbed himself into the river. Are you a companion of his? You don't look much like a toiler to me. If anything, you look like you have a hint of the namby-pambies about you... Are you sickly?'

'I can work.'

'I suppose you can, my son. But can you work *vigorously*? Our last lug toiled harder than most, do you see? He strove like an ox. But the fool run a barrel over his foot. Broke his toes clear away, so he did. Crushed his ligamentous pinions with the merciless rim of that there tub. These colossal casks are lethal, my son. The knife-blade barrel-edge will cut three toes from your foot as quick as lightning will spark away clouds on a summer day. You won't see it come, neither. The lip on that there tub cruxated his phalanges to blessed-thuggery, no word of a lie. God comfort him. What did he do? The lug gulped a gallon of malt beer then threw himself face-first into the black water. Why? No use to anyone no more, was he? Not without his toes. Poor fellah!'

'Really?' said Stormbuckler, open-mouthed. 'Well, the same *cannot* happen to me...'

'Why not?' challenged the charge-hand. He gave a frown.

'Cos I previously lost my pinions. In fact, my phalanges got cruxated to thuggery before I could crawl!' Stormbuckler adjusted his stance to lift his 'bad' leg so he might display his defect to the man.

'Getaway,' responded the chargehand. He approached Stormbuckler for a better look. 'Clean off? Sliced clean off, was it? I've never seen anything like it in my life. Gone to thuggery, has it? Good grief.' The man gazed into Stormbuckler's naïve eyes and decided to make a snap evaluation. Stormbuckler returned a fixed gawp and nodded. 'You seem like a bright young man, and you have fire inside your scalp,' the chargehand suggested. 'You must be as brave as a bear to be amputated in that way, to lose a foot in a barrel roll, yet come back for more suffering. You're the bloke we need.' The chargehand threw Stormbuckler a hearty whack across his shoulders. 'Come in! I'll show you what we do. Welcome to our team.'

In the course of her second week at the Asher-John Lindwürm works, Mayotte established a better understanding of what might be the best workwear for a young woman who functions in a manufacturing environment. She knotted her hair tight in a bun; she wrapped bandages around her legs, from ankle to hip, and she borrowed a leather smock from Henry Oldcorne's man-servant (he used it when he polished pots.) Mayotte even cajoled her mistress into lending her an expensive tweed, a fancy Norfolk jacket, with leather patches on the elbows, that she wore under the smock. Mayotte also became better acquainted with her surroundings, yet still had no clear understanding of what her obligations and responsibilities involved.

She invested a lot of time with the drawing technicians, mainly because their office was the sole place she found peace from the relentless hum and ferocious exhalations of the manufacturing plant. She took a shine to one of the gentler lads in the office, a meek young man named Larkin Eaglehurst. He was a nervous character, with dark velvety hair, tiny eyes, and girlish fingers. The chap reminded her, somewhat, of a 'mouldy-warp' — yes, Eaglehurst was a mole-like fellow. 'How long have you worked for Mr. Lindwürm?' she had asked him one morning.

'Just over twelve months,' Master Eaglehurst had told her. Though he dared not look openly into her face. She spotted he shifted his legs awkwardly under his drawing board.

'How did you get this assignment?' she'd asked.

'My mother saw an advert in the gazette. A draughtsman needed for a busy office.'

'You don't come from this town?'

'I come from Dartford. It's at least a day's ride from here...'

'So you abide hereabouts?'

'Yes, the pay is very satisfactory, so I can afford a modest lodging upstairs from the Thames Brewery. Further, I put a few pennies aside each week for my mother...'

'Aren't you a good lad?' Mayotte said. Then she nudged him and thought about ruffling his hair, but concluded that such an impulsive display of enthusiasm might confuse the innocent young bachelor. Instead, Mayotte grinned. Master Eaglehurst returned her gaze, though his ears reddened. 'Have you ever made friends with a girl before? ' she enquired.

'Um, *no*. I encountered daughters of my own age in church. That's when I sang in the choir. But I never schooled with females. To be honest, I never expected to work in a place where females were considered equal to males...'

'Do you believe me to be your equal?'

'Um... I think so, *yes*. You're in the building with us. You seem to be a representative of the non-industrial workforce, although I cannot pretend to understand your role. What is your specialization? What is your proficiency? Nobody seems to know what you are doing here...'

'Can't you guess?' she had whispered.

Master Eaglehurst had scrunched his light brown eyebrows and had touched his pink nose with the blunt end of an ink pen. 'No, I really cannot guess. What can it be?'

'My field of expertise is asking lots of irritating questions...' she had told him. The answer made him smile. She had almost cracked him.

～

At noon, James Owen Siebert came to the draughting office to talk to several of the youthful draughtsmen about plans for the steam-yacht: Spry Shimmerfly. Mayotte sensed they planned to launch the steam-puffer quite soon. It seemed that Mr. Siebert wanted to check over plans to be sure everything had been completed satisfactorily.

'Will this take long?' she asked.

Mr. Siebert snorted and raised his eyebrow: 'As long as it's necessary, miss. Why don't you do something mindless, huh? Some senseless *anything* that would keep a female of the species amused for a while? This is *men's* work...'

Master Larkin Eaglehurst produced a bashful smile. Mayotte bowed to both fellows and she said, 'Well, yes *I will*. I'll catch you brain workers later. *Toodle-pip.*'

Mr. Siebert sputtered something in a low voice that she didn't overhear, then he focused his *proper* male mind on the plans for the steam-boat. Mayotte skulked from the office, like a house cat with a stolen chicken-bone between her teeth. She slunk from the main buildings *too*, then outside onto the riverbank path. In the air, she skipped to the main road, where she knew she'd be able to engage a hansom cab.

At the municipal water-trough, by the Town Hall, she spotted a vacant two-wheel cab, so she got in. The driver glowered through the hatch.

'What do you want?' the guy shouted.

'Take me to Chantry Manor, the villa of Asher-John Lindwürm,' she directed.

'It's eightpence a mile, love. Do you have one-and-fourpence hidden in your knickerbockers? Because, if you don't, you may as well unfold your scabby limbs from this carriage and go bubble your skull in a mash barrel.'

'Do you want to see silver? Is that what you suggest?'

'Sorry, love, but I've been 'ad over by young slips like you before. It doesn't look like you have a farthing to your name, let alone two bob.'

Mayotte sniffed and turned-out her little brown purse from the pocket of her borrowed Norfolk jacket. 'There,' she said. She held two silver shillings aloft, so the fellow might see her fare. She turned the coins in the window-light so they would glint. 'Will this satisfy?'

And with those words, the hansom jerked from the stand, to rattle towards Kingston Road, and then further, onto Chantry Manor.

Mayotte tapped the hatch to get the cabbie's attention as they hurried into the track that led to Chantry Manor. 'Stop *here* will you driver...'

'Whoa now! Are you sure, miss? Only we ain't arrived at the American's gaff yet.'

'However, I would like to be settled here, driver. Is that permitted?'

'Very well.'

Mayotte held up the two shilling pieces and considered, for a moment, to ask the driver for change. After all, the fellow had been disrespectful to begin with, and was disinclined to take her when she'd first danced into his conveyance. On the other hand... she might call for his services in the future. So she decided to tip him: 'Keep the change...' she muttered.

'Do you want me to wait here, miss?' he said, grabbing her coins.

'No, thank you. You may hasten back to town and await your next fare... I'm done with you.'

'Very well, miss.'

She left the carriage and looked up. The cab driver extended a lifted cap, then turned his cab around in the narrow space, to trot off, back to town.

Mayotte paced to the home of Asher-John Lindwürm, drawing long strides, and swinging her arms with an air of natural confidence.

At the address, she sidestepped the noisy crumblestone path by preferring to walk along the grass verge instead. Using this approach, she shuffled towards twin architectural pineapples, sculpted in stone, positioned at the end of a remarkably short driveway. Mayotte contemplated beating upon the giant door, but did not want to warn any servants of her uninvited arrival. So she strolled abstractedly around one side of the main building as if she was engrossed in a world of her own. If anyone had stopped her, she decided she'd tell them she had become disorientated. She followed a set of ruts that promptly led to a triple-door facade and, later, onto a tall hardwood construction that Mayotte decided must be Mr. Lindwürm's famous garage. She picked up high-pitched scraping noises coming from within, so assumed Mr. Lindwürm must be hard at work, tuning-up one of his devilish contraptions. 'Good,' she said, quite loudly, 'Keep at it...'

She twirled on a toe, like a ballet dancer might pirouette at Sadler's Wells, to examine the principle residence. An unlatched side-door suggested an invitation. So Mayotte headed towards it. After a glance across her left shoulder, she stole herself inside.

Having lived and functioned as a servant all her life, Mayotte knew that the finest way to navigate a manor like this one was to exploit the 'back stairs.' Of course, it would be more likely she'd bump into one of the household staff as they darted from chore-to-chore if she used this route, but it was better than trudging up a grand staircase to be detected by the proprietor's butler. *No, that would be unacceptable.* So she soft-shoed to a narrow door that she spotted by the boot-rack, pulled the door open, and considered the pantry staircase that rose ahead. She passed through the door and ascended the staircase with a devil-may-care attitude.

Mayotte did not see anybody on the staircase, so she emerged, secretly, on the upper level of the main residence, just under the attics. She found herself upon a spacious landing, fed by the principal staircase, with the secret flight of servant's stairs hidden behind a casing behind her, next to a walnut cabinet. Mayotte got her bearings, and guessed the two front bedrooms were retained for houseguests, while the two side rooms were antechambers, probably sitting rooms or dressing rooms. This meant the remaining large doors — the two found at the rear of the property — *must* open into the master bedroom and its associated suite. One of these two doors seemed somewhat more freshly painted than the other, with polished brass handles, so Mayotte guessed *this* was the main door that the primary resident would use. Therefore, she went to the *other one,* the servant's door, and she pressed upon it with her shoulder, then unlatched it with a click, and she moved inside.

The chamber was softly lit by sunshine that drained through floor-to-ceiling windows, covered with a semi-transparent, organza-style fabric. Heavier curtains had been drawn and now they hung under an imposing, embroidered-silk pelmet. There was a slim side-door just to the right of a hollow fireplace, and Mayotte guessed it probably led to a robing room with a corner window. She admired the crystal chandelier that dangled from the opulent plasterwork, and she trod across bare wooden boards that were topped with a velvety duck-egg-blue carpet. Mayotte admired a freestanding armoire wardrobe, a dressing table, a grand chest of drawers and, tucked away in a special alcove, an enormous four-poster bed. They had *not* fitted the posts with a tester or curtains. Without these normal hangings, the bed looked strangely cold and utterly angular. It reminded her of the perpendicular white-stone bones one might erect around a family interment-vault. Mayotte presumed that, without posts and curtains, this bed would be very cheerless at night.

~

Mayotte rubbed her eyes to gain an unobstructed view — at first she thought she was imagining what she saw. But it was genuine: she observed a languishing woman on the bed. The woman was attired in 'lounging clothes,' which comprised floppy leggings, a delicate top, and a silvery scarf. The lolling image haunted Mayotte, for several seconds, so splendidly vulnerable and practically supernatural was she. The woman roused from her slumber suddenly, with no obvious external sounds to startle her. 'What? Who? 'Who are you?' inquired the fascinating woman, evidently disconcerted by the presence of an intruder in her room.

'I'm sorry ma'am...' said Mayotte, thinking hurriedly. 'I entered into the wrong room *by accident*; I'm trying to locate Mr. Lindwürm.'

'My husband?' the woman asked. She rubbed her cheeks. Then she sat up to stretch out skinny arms. Mayotte guessed the lady must be about forty summers, though with her exotic skin and glistening black hair, her body seemed younger, as if it belonged to a twenty-year-old. The woman's hairstyle was lengthy enough to run down her back and might even extend to a waistband, if she wore a dress.

'Sorry, ma'am. I didn't mean to wake you...'

'I had a dream... the crow lifted mourning into the sky...'

'The crow, ma'am?'

The woman ceased her stretching, to put her legs on the tip of the bed. 'What is your name? I don't recognise your face... Are you new here?'

'Yes, *I am,* my lady. I'm Mayotte. Your husband hired me for his manufactory in town... I'm not one of your domestic servants.'

'He engaged a girl?'

'Yes, he *did*, Ma'am. I came to see him today, to see what he wants done. I'm still waiting for his instructions.'

'Do you know anything about dreams? Here, come sit by me. Your eyes are brown, and your skin is hazel. Do you dream? Do you still understand the messages that dreams bring?'

Mayotte moved to the bed with a bewildered look and sat upon the soft mattress: 'I have nightmares, ma'am.,' she disclosed. 'I'm sure *everybody* does. Is that what woke you up, my lady, an unpalatable dream?'

'What do you know about crows? Some say they bring bad luck...'

'I don't know. Did you dream of a crow?'

The woman studied Mayotte's eyes: 'After the great flood, the Creator delivered a rainbow arc across the sky, a sign of the new covenant. Then he sent an emissary from heaven to tell man to send a trusted bird high into the cloud to pick up the colours. So man did as he was told by the sky-god and shot his favourite bird, a crow, into the sky. Since then, until today, the crow is the sole multi-coloured bird in creation.'

'I thought that a crow was *black*...black as night!'

'Not actually... No, *not black* at all. If you stare with your eyes and you see things with your true heart and if you observe creation the way our Creator has taught, you will learn that a crow is a million hues and a thousand pigments... the crow is genuinely the rainbow bird...'

'Is this what you dreamed?'

'No,' the woman sobbed, becoming tearful.

'Was the was the crow flying?' Mayotte asked. 'Flying to the rainbow?' She put a palm on the woman's sleeve to comfort her.

'No, the crow was grounded. The crow feasted. The crow consumed all that the man worked so hard to achieve. Everything that had been sown. Everything that had been carried to fruition. The crow dined on man's boldest endeavours...'

'What you require, ma'am, if I might be so bold as to make this suggestion, is a ruddy great scarecrow...I'd stick a scarecrow into the middle of your dreams if I were you...'

'Really?'

'That'll stop the colourful little blighter...'

The woman smiled: 'Maybe we can talk a little more, some other time. But now I need to be dressed and bathed, so I will call my housemaid. Do you know where my husband is?'

'Um, *no*...' Mayotte lied.

'You'll find him in the garage. With his engines...'

'Ma'am, before I leave you, can I ask you something? It's somewhat personal, but I'm burning to ask...'

'What is it?'

'Are you *truly* what people say you are? Are you *genuinely* an Indian? Are you *actually* a primitive?'

'Since you ask so bluntly, I will tell you what you need to know. My name is Arrow-Miaow. I'm from a tribe known in your language as the Leni-Lenape people. And you?'

'I am Mayotte.'

'Are you French?'

'I don't know...'

'Don't you know which tribe you belong to?'

'Mmm? No, I never thought of such a thing. Why? Do you think I ought to know?'

'Why, *yes*, of course.'

On the following morning, James Owen Siebert advanced from his office in a thundering, rumbling mood. He jabbed a packing case clear as bull-dozed himself straight for Mayotte: 'Mr. Asher-John Lindwürm demands to see you,' he bellowed.

'Yes, *yes*, very good. Keep your wig on, cock. You'll do yourself a jolly mischief by getting hot and bothered like that...' suggested Mayotte. She remained calm but appreciated the truth had come out. Lindwürm had discovered she had slipped to the tycoon's home without approval. 'So when does he want this quiet word with me?'

'He requires seeing you *now*...' Mr. Siebert growled.

'Now?' Mayotte asked. She nibbled her bottom lip. Her eyes expanded. 'So soon? Where is he?'

'In my flipping office. Sat in my chair. He cussed and darned at me as if he was an unlucky prospector toiling miserable fields... You've bloody-well done it *this time* missy... the fellow is *crazy-mad* with you...'

Mayotte clumsily brushed down her leather apron, inspected her borrowed tweed jacket for loose filaments, rolled her shoulders, then said: 'Right then, let's get it over with...'

Mayotte meandered into Mr. Siebert's office as if she didn't have a care in the world. She even gave the technical director a relaxed nod as she went in.

Inside Mr. Siebert's office, sure enough, she found Asher-John Lindwürm at the desk. He wore a grey tie, a wing-collared shirt, a pearl-coloured suit, and his pomaded hair glistened in the morning light. 'Ah, here she is,' he said. 'Come in. Take a pew, my dear.' The millionaire-inventor pointed to a padded seat that had been planted below a row of framed certificates.

'Good morning...' Mayotte said, as she sat.

'Now, you are known for your plain-speaking, right? Yes? So I'll come right out with it... as plain as can be. Is it true you came to my home yesterday? You came without bidding or petition from me?'

'Um, yes. *I came —*'

Mr. Lindwürm held up a palm to discontinue any hurried excuse she might offer. 'If your virtues and capacities did not attract me, my dear, I would discharge you on the spot. Do you hear? But because of other factors, I am forced to re-evaluate *that* position...'

'Sir?'

'Is it true you met my wife?'

'I did. I'm sorry, I think I went into the incorrect bedroom by accident...'

'Never mind. But my wife seems to have taken a shine to you. She wants me to give you a chance to meet her again. In fact, my wife told me to pass an invitation that you should call upon her, quite soon, to take afternoon tea. Will you do that?'

Mayotte forced a sigh of relief and let her wrists loosen in her lap. 'Yes, I would love to...' she smiled.

Asher-John Lindwürm pushed his brows together to make himself look fiercer. He readjusted his jaw to make it stiffer, then presented a piercing stare, 'Now attend me *closely*.' The American lifted himself from the chair and pushed closer. He allowed his rump to rest on the edge of Mr. Siebert's desk: 'Now you've met my wife, I request you do *not* run your mouth off all around town—' Mr. Lindwürm cleared his throat before he resumed, 'About her, um, *shortfalls—*'

'Run my mouth off?' Mayotte interrupted. She scrunched her brows. 'Shortfalls? What does that mean?'

'I don't want you to blab about her limitations... I don't want you to talk about her shortcomings. I don't want you to be indiscreet about the *details*...'

'Indiscreet? Details? Me? Never! I wouldn't...'

'Now, listen,' Lindwürm said, vigorously: 'If I find you have run your mouth off, I will pummel you into the ground like a cockroach. You *comprende*?'

Mayotte understood the threat in the man's eyes and watched as he clenched his fists into shapes that were quite capable of hammering a young woman's skull into mush. 'Yes, sir. I have it.'

'Good.' Asher-John Lindwürm gave an indistinct smile, 'Anyway, now that matter is concluded, lets speak about *other* things. What have you been doing with yourself?'

'Um? That's why I came over to your place, *actually*...' Mayotte checked the American's face to see if this would be an appropriate moment to plead her case. She found herself shaking. She rubbed her hands on her knees: 'I have seen most of your manufactory and have met most of your workers...' she went on. 'But, *so far,* I do not seem to have any role here — nobody knows what I'm presumed to be doing in this place. I hoped you might shed some light on my duties. What do you expect of me?'

'Logo...' he said. 'That's why you're here.'

'Logo?' Mayotte returned a confused look.

'You told me I should get a logo to protect my intellectual property... don't you remember?'

'Oh, yes...' Mayotte understood what he meant. 'When we came to your gaff on that Sunday morning, me and Mrs. Oldcorne, I think I blurted something about a logo, didn't I?'

'Yes,' said Asher-John Lindwürm, with a grin, 'You told me I should have one. Although Mrs. Oldcorne wasn't best pleased with your advice, if I remember correctly. But your suggestion got me thinking. I want one. I was impressed by your imaginative faculty. That's why I hired you.'

'I see.'

'So, have you started on it?'

'What? The logo?'

'Of course, *the logo.*'

'I suppose so, in fact...' Mayotte squirmed in her seat, pleased to feel a little bolder, but still not entirely confident: 'I have quite a lot of ideas. But, to be honest, your diagram-drawers in the draughting office are *not* up to the task... *sorry.*'

Asher-John Lindwürm looked-up at the rafters and he slowly whistled, 'Yes, I can see that,' he whispered. 'Their job is to create technical plans for precise engineering purposes. They can't dream up artistic ideas because they're not, with due respect to their technical skills, they're *not* aesthetic types. They are mechanical people with mathematical minds and algebraic hearts...'

'Anyway, where do we go from here?'

'We?' asked Asher-John Lindwürm. 'How should I know?' That's why I recruited *you*; I have no time for *minutiae.* Just get it done.'

'Me? Get it done?'

'Yep. You can do it, can't you?' He glared at her and started to roll his fists again.

'Of course I can do it, Mr. Lindwürm. Leave it with me. No problems. I'm great with minutiae.'

'Good! Very good.' He lifted his butt from the rim of the desk and headed for the door. He motioned for her to get up, too. 'I need to get on with my day. So do you! I'm off to an important meeting. Tell Siebert, on your way out, he can come back into his office. I will *send word* to you...'

'Send word?'

'About coming to take tea with my wife, yes?'

'Oh, yes. I nearly forgot.'

'Well, do not forget, miss. And do not forget what I told you earlier: reveal nothing about her. Do not breathe a word about her ailment; do not tell another soul in town... Got me?'

'Yes, I got you, Mr. Lindwürm,' said Mayotte, though she offered another puzzled look. *What ailment?*

'Very well, then. Good day.'

10

For several days, Mayotte had pestered Master Larkin Eaglehurst to 'escort her on a pleasant walk at lunchtime.' So that same Tuesday, she concluded the day had arrived for their romantic walk. 'Put on your smart tunic,' she told him. 'I will wear short boots and a bonnet. And you shall accompany me along the wharf-side.'

'What else do I need?' Master Eaglehurst inquired, with puppy-ish, ever-trusting eyes and a simple smile.

Mayotte had acquired a fondness for the little dimples his face established when Eaglehurst offered an uncomplicated grin. 'You'll simply need to bring natural grace... and that amiable smile of yours.' She nudged him in the ribs.

So, at noon, she coaxed Master Eaglehurst to accompany her for a stroll along the riverbank. She met him, with a parasol under her arm and a beribboned bonnet relaxed softly upon her head. The other draughtsmen ignored what they observed. So the couple went into the mottled noontime light, and Mayotte said: 'We will walk along the side of the wharf, and you will entertain me with your wit and cleverness.' And with those words, she advanced an arm under the crook of Eaglehurst's elbow, so they would become associated as one, if other's saw them. They walked arm in arm along the shore.

She was sure his ears had turned pink, so she pulled Master

Eaglehurst closer and rested her cheek against his shoulder. 'You're a good one,' she said. 'You know that?'

'Thanks for saying-so. Do you genuinely think that? I'm not entirely sure you are being honest with me.'

'Let's head to the boathouse. To see if we can get a view of the Spry Shimmerfly...' she suggested, turning them around.

'We can go that way if you prefer,' he told her. 'But the Spry Shimmerfly will still be inside her house. They're making final adjustments before the big launch day.'

'I can't wait,' Mayotte told him, giving a little wriggle. 'I predict it will be the occasion of the year. Everyone will be there...'

'Yes! Mr. Lindwürm invited lots of dignitaries. He even persuaded the Lord-lieutenant of the County along.'

'How grand,' she said. 'But I don't know if I'm invited... am I?'

'Of course you are. You must come along to the launch because everybody from the manufactory will be there. It's a works day out. They have given our office a half-day off. The entire works will be turned-out.'

They walked in silence for a bit until they arrived at the boathouse. 'It smells of pine and pistachio...' Mayotte said, lifting her nose to the air and grinning. 'Quite nice...'

'That's the boat varnish they use to brush the hull. It keeps the timber from rotting...'

'You know *everything*,' she whispered confidentially, into his ear. Mayotte gave the lad a playful jab in the ribs. 'You are so clever.'

'Well, I do not know,' he said, presenting a shy smile.

'Tell me,' she continued. 'What is developing in steam shed 7? Only, that place is a bit of a mystery. I never got to see it when they took me on my tour, on the first day. They never trusted me, I suppose...'

'Steam shed 7? Um, that's Mr. Lassiter's province. I have nothing to do with steam shed 7.'

'But doesn't Mr. Lassiter have plans and diagrams that need to be drawn? I'd love to see those plans...'

'I suppose he does. He must have schematics. But we don't do them. Not in our office. I've never considered it before, but since you mention it, I suppose he has his own people working on his plans and charts...'

'Wow! Are you proposing there's another draughting office in town somewhere? A place I haven't visited yet?'

'I suppose there must be,' proposed Master Eaglehurst. 'I guess Lassiter must have his own technical drawing people over at steam shed 7.'

'I'm sure you have been to steam shed 7 yourself, haven't you? You looked around the place, yes? I am sure you would have spotted a back office if you went in, wouldn't you? What's Lassiter doing over there?'

Master Eaglehurst shrugged, 'I do not know. I've never been there, actually. Furthermore, I don't know anyone who has. I don't know who works there. It's a very hush-hush project. I know it's some kind of construction plant... but honestly, that's all I know. I don't think you should ask too many questions about the place. If you want my heartfelt advice I wouldn't mention it again...'

'Why not?'

'You met Mr. Lassiter, didn't you? He's the oldest companion of Asher-John Lindwürm, *and*...'

'*And* he's formidable?'

'Hah, yes. I was going to say he's intimidating. But you know precisely what I mean.'

'Yes, I met him once. I found him unapproachable.'

'Unapproachable? I'd say he's *unnerving*...'

'I know.'

They came to a halt in front of a building just beyond the boathouse. And here Mayotte became interested in something that sat a dark nook, so she asked Master Eaglehurst to accompany her to explore what the thing was. When they got there, the discovered the nature of the shape. It was a young man, scarcely much older than Mayotte, and he was sat on a half-barrel, busy with a slice of charcoal in his hand. The young man sketched the shape of a bone onto a piece of old tree bark with zeal.

Mayotte and Eaglehurst moved forward, slowly, arm in arm, and saw the young man's intense focus. Mayotte noticed that he had a steady hand as he traced the fine contours over flat bark.

'What is it?' Mayotte burst forth.

The young man with the charcoal pencil physically recoiled and he almost tipped from his makeshift stool.

'My, oh, my, I sincerely apologise, my dear. I didn't mean to startle you,' she exclaimed.

'Righty-ho miss,' responded the young fellow. He put the coal to the floor to regard them. 'I was distracted by my sketch. Tis' why I did not notice your approach. I didn't suppose anyone would try to sneak up on me.'

'Do you work at the boathouse?' Mayotte enquired.

'No, miss. I'm a barrel roller at *this* mash-yard.

'This is their land...' declared Master Eaglehurst. 'We have stridden, accidentally I think, onto the frontage of the mashing sheds.'

'Oh, I see. In that case, I'm sorry to intrude. I did not realize we had passed across our own curtilage. Are we trespassing? In which case, should we go?'

'I'm sure it's not a problem,' the young man told her. 'And I'm sure nobody cares.'

'So what are you drawing?'

'Oh, yes, well, um... it's a group of feathers and bones... I hope it might one day become a tattoo on the arm of a prizefighter.'

'May I see?' Mayotte pushed closer and took a glance. 'Good... isn't it Larkin?'

'I suppose so,' Master Eaglehurst offered, doing his best to keep on the girl's better side.

'Well, there you are then...' Mayotte said, with conviction. 'My boyfriend should know, shouldn't he? ' She secretly pinched Master Eaglehurst's arm because it was the first time she had used the term *boyfriend*. 'He's the best drawing expert at Lindwürm's plant... aren't you, my dear? He's one of their finest draughtsmen, aren't you, my dear?'

'If you say so.' Master Eaglehurst turned bright pink. 'I'm sure I don't deserve such high praise. Not me.'

'So what do you think, dear? The lad is a good sketch artist, isn't he?' Mayotte squeezed Master Eaglehurst's arm to gain his agreement. 'Tell the lad what you think.'

Larkin Eaglehurst peered at the charcoal sketch, rubbed his chin, and said, 'Yes, it's particularly good. A quite accurate depiction. Very thin sketching. Exceptionally fine work.'

'There you are,' said Mayotte, giving the lad with the charcoal a broad smile. 'Did you hear? You have genuine talent. That's what the principal draughtsman for Mr. Asher-John Lindwürm has said. And he should know. What is your name?'

'My name is Stormbuckler,' replied the lad.

Mrs. Oldcorne clanged her bell for Mayotte to appear at her parlour and attend to her needs: 'Ah, there you are, girl. Where have you been?'

'Sorry, ma'am,' offered Mayotte, yielding a knee. 'I have been clearing away my work-clothes and adjusting my hair into a sensible bun... to begin my domestic duties.'

'Good. So tell me *what you know...*'

'What I know, ma'am?'

'Yes, what you've picked up at the manufactory? You've been eavesdropping for me, I assume?'

'Oh yes, of course, madam. I found out that a steam-cutter is about to be launched on the river.'

'That sounds perfectly tedious,' Mrs. Oldcorne gave a sniff. She considered her nails and rolled her eyes. 'I hope you have something more *noteworthy* than that!'

'All the privileged, wealthy, and elite will be at the launch. The whole factory will turn out for it. It's going to be a grand affair. And Mr. Lindwürm invited the Lord Lieutenant of the County...'

'Did he now? Really?' Mrs. Oldcorne perked-up upon hearing that portion of news. 'I'm sure the Lord-Lieutenant is the Viscount Eudicot — if I'm not very much mistaken—he's a privy counsellor *too*... Good! I will sit him to the right of Asher-John Lindwürm, with myself seated on the Viscount's left...'

'And Mr. Lassiter? Where will you park him?'

'Who dear?'

'The best friend, the confidant and the right-hand man of Mr. Lindwürm.'

'Oh, him! That horridly *plain* man! Yes, I suppose he can sit behind. The chums generally sit *behind* the mains...'

'I see.'

'Get me an invitation, will you? I'll do the rest...'

'Hasn't Mr. Lindwürm invited you and Mr. Oldcorne yet? I am surprised to hear such news. All the other big-wigs have been sent their invites...'

'No dear. Quite possibly, ours got lost in the post. Make sure our invitation gets re-sent, will you, girl?'

'Yes of course, ma'am.'

Occupying a privileged spot on the dock were the firemen, stevedores, and water-tenders who formed a long line on the water's edge, and readied themselves, caps in hand, to wave-off the Spry Shimmerfly. Mayotte distinguished a lot of blocks and rigging, ropes and cables, and contrivances of all sorts that looked like groups of miniature see-saws, all with jibs and turnstiles, ramps and wheels, and larger lumps of timber that Master Eaglehurst had described as '*temporary cribbing.*' The upper part of the ceremonial area was a parade of colourful garlands. But the lower part, down on the greasy cobblestones, was an imbroglio of obstacles and palisades.

The boat ramp had been buttered with whale-oil, and most of the thin panel-walls of the boathouse had been cleared away so the public could admire the magnificent steam yacht, sitting there *dry* on her haunches. She was bolstered by a long series of monstrous oak struts, and she was trimmed light green and gold, with ivory details, painted especially for the occasion. It seemed as if the vessel *popped* with shackled energy.

'Typically it would be a folly to launch a vessel of her weight perpendicular to the shoreline...' Asher-John Lindwürm had told the most distinguished guests that sat around him on the upper tier of the timber grandstand. 'But she has no fuel, the engine is not running, there is no cargo, almost the entire superstructure has been taken out, and she has no water. Therefore, we have the Shimmerfly down to her bare-bones. I'm sure she'll splosh into the Thames like a gudgeon dropped into a fish kettle...' Everyone around him chuckled at this announcement.

'She'll go in arse about-face, will she, Lindwürm?' Viscount Eudicot asked.

'Yes, sir, she has her stern facing the water, as you can see. It might be a bu=it late to turn her around *now*...' Mr. Lindwürm quipped.

The Viscount seemed unamused by this remark, so most of the hangers-on muffled their sniggers and placed gloved-hands across smirks.

'Is there any danger of her tipping and capsizing?' asked Mrs. Oldcorne, sensing the Viscount's displeasure as she attempted to ease the situation with a question of her own.

'There is *always* the potential for misfortune,' admitted Asher-John Lindwürm. 'Launching a vessel, even one as conceptually advanced as the Spry Shimmerfly, can *never* be taken for granted. Why, several factors must be considered: water depth, stability, and weight relationships. But our engineers are fully aware of these dangers, and have pre-planned for *any* contingency... My only worry is that she might collide with the riverbank on the way down, and such a collision might cause a little damage. We'll see. Are you ready to play your part, my Lord?'

The Viscount made an emphatic *harrumph* which Mr. Lindwürm took as a sign of agreement. So the American said: 'Come along with me to the temporary pier, sir. You'll name her the Spry Shimmerfly and thereafter you'll break the sacrificial bottle across her bow.'

'Yes, I'm ready to go...'

'Will you join us, your excellency?'

The suffragan bishop of Dorking took up his crosier and silk gloves.

'The Bishop will say a prayer just before the christening. Then we'll come back to the tiered benches, to view her slide into the river.

After that, the band will play and provide for the good health of the boat and crew. The ceremony will last about twenty minutes, no more. Then we will retire to The Feathers Inn, where I have secured an upstairs room for luncheon. How does that sound?'

'Utterly wonderful...' said the bishop. Several of the entourage applauded enthusiastically at the prospect of free lunch.

Mr. Lindwürm took the Lord Lieutenant of the County, and the Bishop, and they went to the launching pier and after they arrived, the atmosphere became muted. The three men gazed up to the three tiers of benches where the great and the good of Staines had been seated. The bottom row of benches comprised the attendants and assorted equerries, who were told to bow their heads so their 'betters' could see what was happening. But the second line of big-wigs consisted of senior members of the manufactory personnel, including Mayotte and Master Eaglehurst. Lindwürm's general employees, the labourers, machine operators, mill-workers, cladders, framers, joiners, mill-wrights, and all the ordinary fixers, were restrained behind substantial barriers on ground level, though each man was given a flask of ale 'to shut him up'.

Most of the manufactory's iron-workers were engaged on ropes and chains on the slipway. These men were told they'd earn themselves a full jug of grog if they performed well.

On the launching pier, Asher-John Lindwürm pulled a yellow scarf from his inside pocket and held it aloft. He waved it around so the crowd on the benches could see. This caused a stir, and several spectators applauded. Then Mr. Lindwürm dropped the scarf, and the wispy fabric flittered and danced in the air. This was the signal that the iron-workers had waited for.

'Pull the hog chains...' the lead loading-hand shouted. Teams of muscular men took the slack of the rope-ends and hauled vast chains.

'That's it...' said Mr. Lindwürm. 'She's about to get going. Excellency, please give your prayer...'

'Almighty God,' shouted the old Bishop. The audience closed eyes, many put hands together to bow heads in prayer. 'You who guided Noah in the structure of the Ark, and who soothed furious seas to bring salvation to the fishers of Christ, Almighty God we invite your blessings on this vessel. We ask you to provide kind protection to your servants who will serve upon her... Please listen to us now, and save us, so we do not perish in the waters...'

'Your turn, my Lord,' prompted Asher-John Lindwürm.

The Viscount cleared his throat and pulled back the jeroboam of Laurent-Perrier, a container four times larger than any normal champagne bottle. 'I name this vessel the Spry Shimmerfly. May God bless her and all who sail on her...' Then the Viscount let the bottle spin and watched it bounce against the hull. It cracked upon impact, and everyone applauded.

'Excellent,' said Mr. Lindwürm. 'Let's go back to the ladies, shall we? That's where we'll view the fun as she crashes into the water, and you fellows will share a toast with me.

The Viscount and Bishop nodded their agreement.

But that was when everybody heard the frightful *scream*.

Mayotte had watched the entire episode unfold and, perhaps because things became so dramatic, she experienced the incident slower, and in more detail, than if she had experienced it in *ordinary* time: she had observed James Owen Siebert go onto the dockside to supervise the launch. She'd seen her boss step around the ropes and tackle; she'd seen, more than once, that he tripped over lumps of wood as he shouted instructions or checked notes. And when Asher-John Lindwürm dropped his bright yellow scarf to start the procedure, Mr. Siebert had taken his watch from a waistcoat pocket to verify the appointed time. Mayotte had averted her eyes from Mr. Siebert for a fleeting moment, because everyone in the grandstand had *oohed* in open-mouthed excitement as the steam-yacht faltered and wobbled on its belly, like a slobbish sea lion about to slither from a perch.

When she had glanced back to view Mr. Siebert, she saw him proceeding to scrutinize his pocket-watch. It seemed he was about to bark an order, though his left leg had been entangled in a noose of rope that he'd stepped upon, probably mistakenly. Mayotte guessed he tried to think-fast about his predicament. Should he drop the timepiece and unravel the rope? Or should he hop free from the coil and save his expensive timepiece? Any reasonable person would have dropped the watch, but Mr. Siebert was notoriously thick-headed and famed for his deliberative reasoning.

Mayotte heard whistling, and handclaps from the crowd so knew the posh-nob ecclesiastic, in his fancy robes, had uttered a prayer, though she couldn't tear her eyes away from the unfolding spectacle by the launch-pad. She saw that Mr. Siebert had not untangled himself from the rope. Instead, far from that, he became more entangled. Mr. Siebert still had his watch in his hand, though his wire-framed spectacles came unbalanced and slid from the tip of his nose.

The Spry Shimmerfly glided graciously towards the cold black waters, like a mother hippopotamus about to wallow, bum-first, in cooling *mud*. But that was when Mr. Siebert's enmeshed snag changed from being a bout of silly japery and threatened to become an all-out calamity. Mayotte saw that the loop of rope had tightened around the man's ankle, so now he became caught in a man-trap of stiffened rope and restraining cord. The cable had been connected to weighty timber blocks, and those blocks were now being sucked down the slipway by the heavy steam-yacht.

Suddenly Mr. Siebert was yanked from his feet by the whip-lash motion of the runaway rope... and with a great jolt, his body was dragged upside-down, to slide along the well-oiled surface, towards the river. For the first time, others around Mayotte saw his predicament. One girl screamed. Within seconds, just a moment after the steam-yacht made a satisfying splash in icy waters, Mr. Siebert trawled into the same water, headfirst, to be tugged under by rope-work. As he tumbled into the water, the massive blocks followed. Mayotte watched in horror as Mr. Siebert became dragged into the depths.

Mayotte stood to wave for the awareness of one of the big men who tugged on the ropes... but all were busy with their functions. So she looked at Master Eaglehurst and screamed, 'Did you see that?' But he replied, with a ridiculous grin on his face: 'Yes, she slipped in smooth, right? Very magnificent.'

So Mayotte stood, and against the instructions she'd been given, she dashed from the seated area. She tripped down the steps then ran across the work-space towards the river. That's when she spotted the lad on his barrel. At first, she did *not* remember the youth. He seemed vaguely familiar (though she didn't know why). The youth had elevated himself onto a hogshead keg, perhaps to gain a better view of the Shimmerfly launch. Mayotte wondered why the youth wasn't behind the large barriers where the other workers had assembled. But then she comprehended that he *wasn't* one of Lindwürm's workers. No, this man worked in a *different* yard. That's when she recalled where she had seen him before: the lad was a tub roller at the mash-shop.

The tub roller pranced from his elevated observation point, with long, springy steps. He dashed from land to the riverside in a fraction of a moment, without thinking twice. He threw himself headlong into the wintry river. By then Mayotte was about half-way across the yard-space. The lad evaporated into muddy gloom. 'Oh, my God,' she murmured as she reached the shoreline. 'Someone, anybody, *help!* Please help.' Several stevedores and water-tenders had lined-up for the launch, so they eyed her with suspicion... though not one of them moved a muscle. 'Please, help, ' she shouted. 'Someone, *please* help.'

She heard a gurgle and a soft sucking sound and noticed the head of the tub roller appeared from the murky depths. He seemed to struggle with something heavy that became wrapped around his leg. The youth kept looking down and gurgling while he wrestled with something that snatched at his limbs. At last, and just in time, one of the biggest dock workers saw that someone had fallen in the drink, so the man dashed over to extend a hand — to grab the boy from immersion. As the giant dock-worker yanked on the lad's arm, he learned that, actually, the youth was trying to save *someone else*, who he held with his other arm. So the dock-worker yelled, 'Oi, you lot, don't loiter like a row of geese, give us a hand...'

Two other dockers came over, and together the three men hauled the tub roller from the deadly water and, with him, Mr. Siebert. They laid their rescued, soaking bodies onto the port wall and one man, a man who'd probably seen this type of thing before, knelt beside Mr. Siebert and pushed large hands onto the gaffer's stomach. The technical director spewed-up a potful of mud and water. The experienced dockworker then put the gaffer onto his side and rubbed along the length of his spine with oily hands. Meanwhile, the tub roller improved promptly and was about to get up and move away.

'Where are you going?' Mayotte shouted.

'Me?' said the youth. 'I need to get back to my work; my rest-break is over.'

'No,' she hollered. 'You cannot go, not now! You saved a life. You're a hero. Look at you; you're soaked to the skin...'

'It's fine, miss...' the barrel-boy said. 'I need to return to my job.'

After the rescue, Mayotte grabbed the tub roller by the arm and pulled him toward the bigwig's seating area. As they approached, Mr. Lindwürm rounded-up his most important guests, to usher them from the viewing platform and towards the drinks reception. He'd extended his arm across the Lord Lieutenant of the County when Mayotte grabbed the tycoon by the arm. 'Mr. Lindwürm, I want you to meet Stormbuckler. This is the lad who just saved Mr. Siebert's life.'

'Oh, good. I'll see we reward him...' Mr. Lindwürm muttered. He gave a weak smile. But then looked along the line of important dignitaries who seemed bothered by this common girl's discourteous intrusion. Mrs. Oldcorne gave her maid a singular wince of displeasure. Mr. Lindwürm was about to dismiss them both when Mayotte stomped her feet hard onto the boards. She crossed her arms with a frown. 'Don't you understand? This lad saved your topman's life. The lad is a hero. A lifesaver. And also, this is a truly fortunate moment. Very fortunate indeed. It is serendipity. Because this lad is also a graphic artist.'

'Is he? How smart of him,' commented Mr. Lindwürm. 'He's no doubt a clever lad, but certainly I must move on. I cannot expect these good people to wait in the cold while —'

'Don't you get it? ' Mayotte shouted, 'This fellow is precisely who you are looking for. This lad, this hero, could work on your logo...'

'Oh, I see. Do you think we ought to take the youth on? To work on drawings and so forth? As an expression of our gratitude?'

'Don't you? I do. He's a perfect fit. Heroic and talented.'

'Well, you better see to it. Put the lad on a retainer to start with. Sixpence a day? How does that sound, young man?' Mr. Lindwürm's observed the lad's eyes light up immediately. 'See he gets lodging nearby, too. Can you fix that?'

'Yes, Mr. Lindwürm, I can fix it,' Mayotte said.

'I'm sorry to be brief with you, but I have honoured guests waiting. I will leave the minutiae to you, my dear. Will you get things done?'

'Yes sir, I'll organize things, I'm sorry to disturb you...' she offered her best curtsey to the nobs, 'My Lord, *Madam*...'

Asher-John Lindwürm extended his hand towards Master Storm-buckler, who was so surprised by everything that had happened that his mouth *dropped* open. 'Good to have you on board, old chap,' added the millionaire-inventor, as he shook the lad's fingers. 'Now, run-along please both of you. I'm sure you have lots to do. ' Mayotte nodded thanks and dragged Stormbuckler away.

11

Mayotte appeared early for work at Cromford Mill the next day and was astonished to discover that Mr. James Owen Siebert was not yet occupying his office. It was the first time she'd turned up before the head guy. She headed into his office anyhow with a cheery grin upon her face and a shrug that betrayed a devil-may-care attitude. 'He's doubtless convalescing from his tip in the water... the poor old goat...' she mumbled. She drifted to the old guy's desk to finger through his paperwork, hoping to find something that might catch her eye. While she leafed through a great wodge of invoices, she heard a loud *cough* from the door. She glanced around to see a snake-hipped man dressed in jet black. He appeared to be dressed in the Spanish-style, with a wide-brimmed hat, a knee-length jacket, black breeches, and riding boots. A crinkled dress shirt was visible under an elegantly embellished vest. Mayotte noticed a gold-linked watch-chain attached to a broad leather belly band.

She brought the sheaf of papers to her chest and squinted at the man. She promptly recognised him to be Ligore Lassiter, the partner of Asher-John Lindwürm.

'What are you doing here?' the man whispered.

Mayotte withdrew from Mr. Siebert's desk. 'Um, I came to find the gaffer. But he ain't here.'

'Give me *those*...' Lassiter ordered. He approached with a snarled expression on a reddened face. A glint of determination stretched across his lip. He extended a gloved hand, 'What are you doing with those documents? Why are you looking at his papers?'

'These do you mean? They were on his desk; they must have dropped. I was taking them over to where they belong... I was about to put them away in his cabinet.'

Lassiter tore the papers from her grasp and contemplated the topmost invoice. He let out an exasperated sigh. 'Who are you? What are you doing here?'

'Me, sir? I am Mayotte, sir. Don't you recall? Mr. Lindwürm. took me on...'

Lassiter threw her a withering glare, then swayed his head from side-to-side, 'Oh, yes, you're the servant in the guardianship of the Oldcorne family. I remember you *now*. Though *today* you look different...'

Mayotte grinned anxiously and fidgeted with her cuffs, 'It might be the work-attire, sir, that fooled you. I am turned out in a leather apron and tweed jacket because I find it's more satisfactory for the manufacturing environment...'

'Nevertheless,' continued Lassiter, as he returned an even trickier look, 'It does not explain your presence in this office. This room belongs to the technical director, James Siebert —'

'Can I cut in?' interrupted Mayotte. 'I know this office belongs to him, sir, but by habit I typically pop in here when I arrive for work, do you see? To present my salutations to the old gaffer and see if he demands anything from me...'

'Do you? How irregular. Such behaviour is unacceptable and will cease forthwith. Do you understand? You are *never* to enter this office without express invitation or unless bidden by a superior, do you hear?'

'Yeah, I got that. It's as clear as crystal, *mush*...'

'What did you say?' snarled Lassiter. He strode nearer. 'Did you call me mush? Did you?' He shifted so close she could detect the stench of fishpaste on his lips.

Mayotte smoothed the skin on the back of her hand with a fingernail. 'Sorry, boss, I didn't mean to offend you... but honestly the word is a term of endearment here in Blighty.'

'Do not get over-familiar with me, young woman. Who do you think you are? You will adopt a strict formal style when you address me. Is that clear? You might get away with injudicious terminology in the Oldcorne household, but you'd be ill-advised to try it here.' Lassiter lifted a hand to grab her chin with his gloved fingers. She felt the cold leather tighten around her bones as he doubled his grip. 'I want to stress the next point that I make: if you *ever* talk to me in that same overly defiant way again — I will jab your eyes out of their sockets with a rusted screwdriver. Do we understand each other?'

'Yes, mister... I mean, yes sir.' Mayotte gulped hard. Her legs shuddered. 'I understand you perfectly well... Um, actually you are hurting me...'

Lassiter surrendered his grip. 'Right, get to work...'

Mayotte bent her knee and pushed away, to escape.

'Oh, there is one *other* thing before you go....' Lassiter added.

'Yes, sir?' she said. She bobbed her head.

'While Mr. Siebert is unavailable, recovering from his tumble into the black water, I will be the jurisdiction around here. So you will take orders from me. Me alone. Here's my first direction You will find a young fellow outside by the shard bins... I instructed him to leave the building right away, but he seems to be loitering about for some reason— it seems he's got an idiotic notion that we offered him a job... he looks like a vagabond to me. I don't want *his sort* around here.'

'A-ha! That must be Stormbuckler, sir. I told the young fellow to come here. He's the hero who rescued Mr. Siebert from the dunking. After his act of bravery, Mr. Lindwürm kindly offered the lad a role. As a designer — '

Lassiter raised his gloved hand: 'I don't want to hear another word. Get him off of our land *this instant*... We are not managing a shelter for the homeless; this is a place of industry. If the lad is insolvent and *you* feel sorry for him, give him some pennies from your own purse and point him in the direction of the church... It's *their* job to provide alms, *not* ours...'

'Yes, sir,' said Mayotte. She offered another curtsy. 'I'll do that right away.'

~

Outside, by the huge bins where the workers disposed of broken bolts, bent pins, and ironwork shavings, Mayotte found the lad they called Stormbuckler. She grabbed his arm to tug him away, to get him moving expeditiously from the main building. She said, 'Morning fellah. Sorry about the rush, but there's a bigwig in there that already took a dislike to you. Maybe I will explain about *him* some other time. Right now, though, we're going to get you to the draughting office. That's where we'll find a safe space to *hide* you...' She guided Stormbuckler in silence until they reached the high and slippery staircase that led to the plan-drawing office where they'd find the line of drafting technicians lent over drawing boards.

Once inside the large office space, Mayotte uncovered a half-concealed location behind a wooden cabinet, where the lad might sit and gaze at the other workers. 'Would you require a desk?' she asked. 'Only there's not enough space... yet. But we can see how things go later, yes?'

Stormbuckler raised an eyebrow and looked around the office wonder, 'Are all these characters drawing?' he asked.

'Yep, that's what they do. They draw plans of boats and engines, and *suchlike*.'

'I never dreamt I would be in such a place. This is genuinely astounding...'

'Yes, I suppose it is...' mumbled Mayotte, somewhat preoccupied by other thoughts. She looked back at the lad and cheered up, 'Ah, here he is. Here's Larkin...'

A young man with velvety dark hair and tiny mole-like eyes came to join them. 'Do you remember Master Eaglehurst? You met him one lunchtime?' she asked, clutching the young man's arm.

Stormbuckler looked at the elegant gentleman, dressed in a fine suit, with a silk tie around a stiff collar, and with a gold watch held on a long chain that hung from a snakeskin belt, and he said, 'Your boyfriend?'

Mayotte rubbed the back of her neck and wrinkled her fingers. 'There's not a clear commitment; at this stage, we're not serious-minded about any relationship. It's developing. I think Larkin is still trying to decide whether he hates me, or not! Aren't you, my dear?' The junior drawing-clerk shuffled and offered a nervous smile. 'Anyway, Larkin, my precious, do you remember when we went for our delightful walk that single lunchtime? Do you remember seeing this young lad, Stormbuckler, working on a charcoal sketch? We discovered him near the slipway of the Shimmerfly. You must remember him, my dear. Of course, back then the youth was a barrel-roller at the mash-yard... now he's *with us*... He'll be sketching our logo. Isn't that nice?'

'I think I *almost* remember,' offered Master Eaglehurst. He studied Stormbuckler's face. 'Does the fellow still draw?'

'Yes, of course, he does. That's why he's here...' declared Mayotte. 'This is the best place to install him, right? Tucked out of the way in a dark corner? Don't you think?'

'Well, of course. We would be happy to accommodate him; we have papers, pencils, pens, inks... everything is here.'

'Wonderful, can I leave the youth with you? Under your light supervision? That's not much to ask, is it, Larkin? Tell me if I make too many demands on you, won't you, my precious?'

'No, this is fine. Everything is *fine*...' Master Eaglehurst edged closer, and allowed his sleeve to brush Mayotte's shoulder.

Mayotte turned to gaze into his dark little eyes. 'I will make it up to you my dear, I promise. We'll go out one night, on the town! How do you fancy a good meal and a bottle of the best wine? Is that a pleasant prospect?'

'It sounds first-rate...'

'Keep this *hush-hush,* please, Larkin... an arrangement between ourselves, yeah? It wouldn't do any good to blather about Mr Stormbuckler all around the shop, yeah? His presence here is kind of sensitive... *on account of...* on account of, *well...*' Mayotte whispered into Master Eaglehurst's ear, 'Mr. Lassiter is not happy that he's here...'

'Oh I see,' said Larkin. 'Say no more...' He placed a finger over his lips.

'Um? Can I ask you both a question?' Stormbuckler spouted.

They both turned to examine the youth, who sat with his lousy foot wrapped in bandages, sporting the shabbiest clothes they had ever seen. His face was a mess of boils, his neck was a broth of pimples, his hands were covered in scars, and his arms were maps of burns and sores. 'Take him out this lunchtime,' offered Mayotte. 'Make him wash. Buy him new threads. Get him cleaned. He looks like a vagrant we found under a hedge.'

'I'll do that,' Master Eaglehurst agreed. 'There's a gentleman's outfitter on the corner of Kingston Road...'

'Will a half-crown cover it?' asked Mayotte. She fiddled with her purse to find a large silver coin.

'I should say so... but I have five guineas if we overspend.'

'*Please!*' interrupted Stormbuckler, this time *yelling*. 'Why is everyone talking over my head as if I'm not here? I want to ask something...something important!'

'Sorry, my dear,' Mayotte said. She tugged at her lapel. 'We're trying to help you. Don't you see? I'm organising things here, trying to get you fixed-up, that's all...'

'Where is Kilda?'

'What?' Mayotte offered a blank expression. 'What was the word you said?' They both gave Stormbuckler a series of puzzled expressions.

'Kilda? Kilda the pugilist. I should like to see him. Where is he located? May I see him?'

'I'm sorry dear, we're baffled. The name is not familiar not us — who are you looking for?'

'Kilda. Kilda the pugilist.'

Master Eaglehurst shook his head and Mayotte shrugged: 'We're none the wiser, dear... who or what is Kilda?'

'That is *his*...' Stormbuckler exclaimed, unexpectedly. He stood to shamble across their office, to a pin-board on the other wall. From the board, he took away a square of exquisitely woven cloth. Then he hobbled back to them: 'This cloth belongs to Kilda. How did you get it?'

Mayotte looked at Master Eaglehurst, and the young man gazed back. They both rubbed their necks. 'It's an embroidery I found,' Mayotte explained. 'I brought it here to show Larkin and the other sketchers. I showed it to them as an example of the type of design I want for our logo. I found this portion of fabric by the side of steam shed 7.'

'It's not *yours*...' Stormbuckler snapped. 'You stole it.' He glared at Mayotte. She gasped because he started to bare brown teeth and he looked barbarous and feral. 'Kilda would *never* have given this keepsake away... he valued it... this sketch was precious to him...'

'Um? I'm sorry dear, we're as confused as you seem to be. Also, if you don't mind me saying so, we're getting somewhat bothered by your increasingly hostile manner. Why are you getting so hot and bothered by a silly handkerchief? I found it lying on cobblestones and I brought it here to show Master Eaglehurst. He pinned it onto the board. That's all there is to it.'

'Why am I getting hot and bothered? I'll tell you why I'm getting hot and bothered, lady... it's because I made *that drawing* for my friend... It's *not* yours and you had no right to keep it. You ought to have it returned it to the rightful owner. I did that sketch for my friend. My friend named Kilda. It's my link with him... so I ask you, once again, where is Kilda? '

'We do not know of anyone by that name, do we?'

Master Eaglehurst shook his head.

'He's a huge, sturdy man. You can't have missed him. He's a giant. He has enormous fists. He has rare muscularity... you *must* know him. You'd know Kilda if you saw him...'

'No,' Mayotte and Master Eaglehurst had blank eyes. They shook their heads.

Mayotte studied the design: 'You did not do this though, right? With respect, my dear, a girl does embroidery like this. This kerchief has been accomplished with neat stitches... a girl's small-fingered stitches...'

'Look attentively,' submitted Stormbuckler. 'Under the stitchery, you will see my *original* design... I sketched it in charcoal.' He held the cloth to the light for their inspection.

'You did this?' Mayotte cried. 'You? *You* did this?'

'Yes, so where is the owner? Where is my friend Kilda? I should like to return this fabric to him.'

'This is marvellous. Splendid. I told you our meeting was serendipitous, didn't I? Somehow, I do not know how, but somehow, we have found the *exact* designer I want for the company logo. This is undeniably, *genuinely* incredible...'

But Stormbuckler did *not* look enthusiastic. Quite the opposite! He rubbed his forearms and drew his eyebrows together: 'I want *nothing to do* with either of you. Not unless you explain what happened to my friend, Kilda. Come to think of it; you also need to explain what happened to Tom. You ought to provide an account of how Tom Bisbee got those terrible burns. This place is evil and you're hiding dark secrets... You are dishonourable, and I think you have sinister motives. I don't want any part of this.'

Mayotte knew she had to make a sensible decision in a difficult circumstance — she had to *think fast.* Thinking-on-her-feet was her speciality, a rare talent, though she knew that this puzzle would take singular cleverness to solve: 'Look,' she said, as she cast docile eyes toward Stormbuckler, 'I understand your doubts... believe me, I *genuinely* do. I would never dare to prevail on you or urge you to do something you felt uncomfortable with... but I ask you to allow Master Eaglehurst to get you some clobber and take you out for a bite to eat, yes? I don't want there to be any problems between us — you, me, or Larkin. You can say 'no' if you wish, and you can walk away *right now* if you must— or at any time in the future... but please give us a chance to prove we're not as despicable as you might think we are...'

Stormbuckler rubbed his jaw and nodded.

'Larkin will take you to an outfitter that he knows.' Mayotte's request took her young boyfriend by surprise, so he jolted. Then he ran his fingers through his hair. She gazed at him, but continued. 'Afterwards, Larkin will take you to a lodging where you can get scrubbed-up and take a rest. Perhaps you'd secure a room for him at the Swan Inn?'

'Now?' Larkin Eaglehurst asked, his eyes growing wider. His gaping mouth suggested he'd been taken by surprise by such her requests. It was *still* early morning, and the workday had not officially begun.

'Yes, *now*, because Stormbuckler can't stay in this place a moment longer, can he? Not with a cloud of suspicion hanging in the air and Lassiter on the prowl. It's best he escapes the environment right away, don't you think?'

'Will you square it with Mr. Siebert, then? He'll wonder where I have got to...' offered Larkin Eaglehurst, with a gulp.

'He's not here today, dear. He's still recuperating. There's nothing to worry about. But if there's any repercussion, any at all, I will take the blame.'

'Thank you...'

Stormbuckler scratched his arm and said, 'Why are you being so kind? I think something dishonest is happening here... but I can't be sure. Where I come from, they had a saying: *If you smell a rat, there's generally a rat about...*'

'Nothing bad will happen. We are not being dishonest... we are not being *ratty*, honest! How can I make you believe? Please *trust me*. I promise I will find out what happened to this character Kilda, I swear it...'

'You do? You swear it? And you'll see about Tom Bisbee's accident too? Will you find out exactly what happened to my friends? If you find out, you will earn my trust...'

'Yes, I promise. I would never force you to do anything you felt uncomfortable with. I understand you have doubts and fears about your destiny and the fate of your friends. We absolutely want you to work with us on the logo for the company... That's why we want you to trust us...'

'I'll think about it,' Stormbuckler said, gazing at Kilda's hand-kerchief.

'That's all I ask,' Mayotte said. 'Just think about things. And, thank you for being patient with us.'

Once Master Eaglehurst had taken Stormbuckler away to be cleaned-up, Mayotte rubbed the base of her neck and approached the most senior plan-drawer in the office, 'Sorry to disturb you, sir,' she said gingerly, with fingers pressed against her waist to accentuate her curves, 'Do you know where I might find a tally of all the company employees...'

'Tally? Do you mean a list?' asked the man. He paused, briefly, to look up from his drawing board.

'There must be some accounting records...' Mayotte clarified. 'For example, who keeps a record of the salary that's paid to employees?'

The guy shrugged. 'Who knows? Probably the account practitioners? Our accountants are down by the Town Hall, I understand...'

'Thanks.'

The man wiped a dewdrop from his nose, then pushed his pen back to the paper. He ignored her swinging hips as she stomped out of the office.

Mayotte rushed into the centre of town in a state of confounded uneasiness.

For the first time, in a long while, she felt a burgeoning sense of disorientation. The intimidating threats given by Mr. Lassiter had caused her a grand fit of the nerves, and his mishandling of Stormbuckler's induction had thrown her plans into disarray.

Mayotte arrived at the market square to view the flock of make-do stalls huddled under the protective shadow of Staines Town Hall. She wore factory-grade breeches, puttees, an apron, and boots. She was indebted to her factory-wear now, because she stepped across horse-dung, dog-wee, cabbage slop, meat seepage and slippery fish-scales. The ooze slipped and squelched from hand carts, barrows, and tabletops. The leakage dribbled across cobbles and made even careful walking risky. So Mayotte slowed her pace, heedful not to tip into slurry, as she tried to walk along edges and close to stone walls. This way, she'd hoped to avoid the huckster's eyes and the general ruckus of the crowd. Mayotte marched along a line of imposing entrances until she found the one she sought. She stopped at a brass plaque that read: Malachy Mahogany and Sons, Society of Accountants, England.

She stepped through the baroque entrance, took a quick look at the clamour and confusion in the street, then retreated into the serene, almost sanctified, atmosphere of the accountant's chambers. The rooms weren't large, but didn't feel cramped, either. The brown walls were lit by pale lanterns. A junior employee sat by a desk at one end of a long room. The youth had a broad forehead, snowy-white papery skin, and agile-looking, ivory, fingers. He wore a pair of tie bands around his neck that lent him an almost ecclesiastical guise. 'Are you Mister Mahogany?' she asked, with an accompanying curve of her knee.

'Ha! No of course not, miss, you must go through *there...*' The clerk sniffed and waved a slender finger towards a heavy door at the far end of the reception-office. Mayotte murmured her *thanks* and pushed deeper into the darkness. Venturing further into chambers, she discovered fragrances of wax and lacquer, mould, and bark. She passed through another door and into a room of scrolls, then into another one, filled with ledgers. This room was followed by a space that had been filled entirely with locked metal boxes. Finally, she stepped into a trifling room, furnished with a smooth table, and a chair for writing, plus a simple bookcase. At a broad table sat a plumpish man with receding hair. He sported a faint wisp of moustache and held a pair of teary eyes: 'I'm here to find Mr. Mahogany...' she uttered, 'Are you he?'

'Yes, miss. How can I help?' The man didn't get up.

'I'm Mayotte,' she said, bending her knee. 'You might have heard of me. I'm the girl who works at the manufactural enterprises of the American inventor, Mr. Lindwürm. He newly hired me as a temporary consultant... I'm on their books.'

'Ah, yes...' said the man. He brought a pair of tortoiseshell pince-nez to his nose to squint at her. 'How is it to be the only girl in a machinofacturing plant?'

'Oh, I don't get any trouble, guv'nor. I possess plenty of grit and gristle. I give as good as I take.'

'Quite.' Mr. Mahogany took a long sniff, then dropped his glasses onto his papers. 'How can I help?'

'Well, sir, they sent me from Mr. Siebert's office, didn't they? Do you know Mr. Siebert?'

The accountant nodded and interlocked his fingers.

Mayotte continued: 'Mr. Siebert wanted me to locate an employee, an employee named Kilda...'

'Locate, did you say? Has James Siebert lost a member of staff? That's awfully neglectful of him...' The man offered a smile.

'The employee is absent, rather than misplaced, sir. We also want to review an employee by the name of Bisbee. A Master Thomas Bisbee. Does that name mean anything to you? Do you have records?'

'Records?' The man furrowed his brows. 'What do you mean, records?'

'Well, uh...' Mayotte looked around the room to take time to consider her next sentence: 'Um? Do you possess a current list of Mr. Lindwürm's employees? The amounts we pay them, et cetera? For example, do you have a record of who I am and when and how I'm paid?'

'Do you mean a payroll ledger?'

'Yes, I suppose I do. Is that a comprehensive list of employees?'

'A payroll ledger is a precise record of salary and so forth,' Mr. Mahogany explained. 'Although I'm surprised that Mr. Siebert sent you for that. He ought to have known better!' Mr. Mahogany took the pince-nez glasses into his hands again, as if he was about to find-out the records. But he stopped, '*You see...*'

'Yes...' Mayotte prepared herself for an inevitable comment: something like you *wouldn't understand* you are just a girl, or it would be *too complicated* for a feminine mind. But instead, the man took a deep breath and announced, 'I don't have the payroll ledger... we don't keep it.'

Mayotte rubbed her head and gave Mr. Mahogany a puzzled. look, 'Did you say you don't have it? Is that what I heard? It seems odd. Are you not our accountant?'

'You heard correctly; but we don't keep the ledger here.'

'Well, where the heck is it?'

'Mr. Lassiter brings the books over once a week, Thursday morning, actually. Then he takes them away again, back to his residence, right after we've done our work on them and we've totted things up. I suppose he keeps them under lock and key. Miss, I warn you, Mr. Lassiter is protective about the company's transactions, expenses, assets, liabilities, revenues, and suchlike. Perhaps that's why he doesn't trust us with the storage...also, he won't like it that you've been asking about them!'

'But you work on the accounts?'

'Yes, once a week. Like I said. When he brings them.'

'Christ alive!'

'Now, please, miss, I must protest over your *terminology*. Please carry in mind that my sons and I do not enjoy blasphemy. We are representatives of the Society of Friends.'

'Sorry, sir, I did not mean to offend, but the announcement you gave is bothersome... don't you have *any* employee records for Mr. Lindwürm's works? Any at all?'

'*None*. Come back on Thursday. We can look into it, *thus*.'

'Maybe I will.'

'Or you could ask Mr. Lassiter for the information you require. Why don't you see him about it? It seems the most straightforward step, if you don't mind me expressing it...'

'Of course, Mr. Mahogany. That's how I will accomplish this task. Splendid advice! You've been a great help. I'm sorry to have taken up your valuable time.'

'No, not a problem at all,' the bookkeeper said. Although he also presented a snort that probably meant the *opposite*. 'I'll have to *declare* this, of course.'

'Declare?' Mayotte flipped the fringe of her hair. 'What do you mean, declare? *Declare* what?'

'I'll have to report your visit to our premises. Mr. Lassiter is clear about that. He instructed me to *declare* any unexpected visits or enquiries that are not of the usual kind. He also warned me that someone might seek to ask uncustomary questions about his employees.'

'But I'm an established member of his staff! Nevertheless, of course, yes I see, and that's *fine*.' Mayotte bit her top lip. 'I have the full and express approval of Mr. Lassiter. And, more notably, of Mr. Lindwürm himself...'

'In such case, you have naught to fear when I declare your visit, miss.'

Mayotte turned from his presence in an ostentatious manner. She escaped the office looking both relaxed and fully gathered-together. But inside, she boiled a broth of bubbling consternation.

In the ante-room, she neared the table of the junior accounting clerk, the young man who had the same bleached paper-bark skin as an aging silverwood tree: 'Hello again,' she declared, giving the youth a cheery smile. 'I've come from Mr. Mahogany's office...' Mayotte drew a gulp of air and glanced into the young man's sad little eyes, 'He gave me instructions to speak with *Mr. Lassiter*....' The clerk nodded his understanding, 'Mr. Ligore Lassiter? You don't know where he lives do you? Only, I've forgotten. Mr. Mahogany advised me to go to his residence to get what I needed. '

'The Red House on Spriggs Lane. I thought everybody knew...'

'Oh, *of course*, I'm sorry. My mind went blank. I'm clueless today, thanks for prompting me. I'm a scatter-brained girl, d'you see? Thanks for nudging my recollection.'

The clerk produced an indifferent shrug.

Mayotte strode away from his desk, to leave the suffocating stuffiness of their chambers, and to tread lightly into the outside world — or more precisely, into the malodorous chaos of the Staines open market.

At the front door of the accountant's building, she settled on the stone step to witness the lifting brick chimneys of Lindwürm's manufacturing activities. She observed the spouts that belched clogging spirals of effluvium into the cloudy atmosphere.

Then Mayotte drew-in her elbows, gulped some turbid air, and set-off on the next part of her quest.

～

After Mayotte had left Malachy Mahogany's chambers, she made immediately for the municipal water-trough where she hoped to find the same hansom cab that she'd used before, when she had visited the home of Mr. Asher-John Lindwürm. She'd already described the two-wheeled carriage, to herself, as 'lucky', so was contented to see 'her' taxi as it waited at the stand, unoccupied. She lifted herself onto the footplate and entered. The driver glared at her, like before, looking daggers from the hatch in the roof. 'Where do you want?' he snapped.

'Do you know the Red House on Spriggs Lane?'

'Of course, I *bloody* do... why?'

'Do you know the dwelling that is two doors along from the Red House? Yes or no?'

'Do you mean the house of Archibald Whipple?'

'That's the *exact* one...' Mayotte said, giving the man a nod and cunning grin.

'That will be eight pennies... Have you the coin? Because I'll not let you inside 'ere unless you have!'

Mayotte held up a piece of silver to confirm she was worth the ride. With that, the hatch smashed down and the Hansom cab shook-off in the direction of the causeway, on the south side of the river.

Within minutes, the cab arrived at a dilapidated building that was, presumably, owned by a bankrupt older geezer named Archibald Whipple. The building stood two buildings beyond the Red House.

'Thanks, driver,' Mayotte said.

The cabbie opened the hatch, so she raised her coin, and the man snatched it away with blistered, leathery-smelling fingers.

'Keep the change...' she suggested.

'Thanks miss. Do you want me to wait?'

'It's unnecessary. See you again.'

Mayotte trod off the footplate and, forthwith, sank into a puddle of semi-liquid gloop that sloshed across the frills of her work-boots and almost arrived at the cloth-strips that she'd laboriously wound around her ankles. Still, she pretended it didn't matter. She began to walk nonchalantly towards Archibald Whipple's entrance. Though, once she heard the cab turn around and trot off, she deviated from the provisional course and, as an alternative, headed back along Spriggs Lane to find the Red House — which was her *legitimate* destination *all along*.

After an abbreviated totter, Mayotte reached a magnificent red-brick country house, set back from the road, and endowed with a long driveway. They had installed a collection of finely cut ornamental trees on an island in the centre of a magnificent courtyard. There were eight rectangular windows on the dwelling, all set above a handsome porch, with six more windows by the main door. Mayotte supposed the home must accommodate at least five double bedrooms, upstairs, with perhaps four large reception rooms on the ground, plus space in the attic for twelve servants. The place was much bigger — and to be frank, much *loftier* — than Asher-John Lindwürm's dreadful pile; the mediocre house she had visited that Sunday morning with Mrs. Oldcorne. Mayotte wondered how Lassiter had acquired a *far more* lavish place than his boss? She settled on the thought that Mr. Lindwürm preferred to exhibit fewer trappings of unmistakable wealth. *That must be it,* she said, softly. However, one thing was sure: it would not be easy to enter the Red House without drawing attention from the occupants, much less search a mansion of this one's super-imposing size. Taking a deep breath, Mayotte walked to the far edge of the long driveway, where a dark hedge formed a boundary to Lassiter's land. She assumed that, by using this troublesome route, the servants would not see her approach from the windows of the redbrick house.

At the margin of the property, she skirted the far side of slab stone walls, masked under the shadow of a fine-looking maple. Then she brushed below an assortment of yew branches that extended fingers across her scalp to scrape her hair, then she advanced ever-closer to a glistening bull-bay hedge. Yet again, she was pleased she had put on factory clothes, because the hedge prickled and tore at her tweed. After pressing through a deadwood screen and lots more branching sprigs, she spied a side-door that seemed to be the servant's service entrance. It had shabby lintels, worn panels, and gallery smells leaked through loose doorjambs. A cooking pan had been left behind, by the sidestep; and a traditional hawthorn besom was propped by a wall, nearby. She took these discarded articles to be evidence that the lower classes periodically exploited this door. It would accommodate her purposes admirably.

~

Mayotte sidled to this service-door and nosed her way inside. She was glad that her sense of smell was so acutely honed that she could distinguish cooking smells, the bouquets and odours of scullery soaps, and the exact brands of washing detergents. These aromas came from the left, so Mayotte presumed the servants were busy laundering in an adjoining wing.

Mayotte headed right. She sidestepped a sizeable pewter-cupboard, then passed foodstuffs that had been left out to cool. She drew a sharp left that found her facing a servants' staircase which, she supposed, led directly to the servant's chambers in the upper body of the house; presumably via a service-door that opened to the first floor. This was *precisely* what she used herself to attend Mr. and Mrs. Oldcorne in their house.

Mayotte knew that the fortunate classes created ingenious methodologies, especially in grand houses, to be sure their basement workforce remained 'invisible' to their upper-class guests. The servers, of course, were supposed to attend masters and mistresses at a moment's notice, yet were confined to windowless basements or remote attics. To move around, unseen, the servants used hideaway stairs and narrow passages. They navigated labyrinthine networks to *service* a grand house like this. In most great houses, through such hidden passageways and covert stairwells, servants entered and left rooms — their movements unseen by the *upstairs* residents.

Mayotte employed the spindly back staircase to obtain access to the upper part of the house. Once out of the staircase, she hustled her way down a cramped corridor until she happened across a light-weight door that, she knew from experience, would shift easily, probably with a touch of her shoulder, to take her out onto a landing.

Once out, overlooking a magnificent lobby, she supposed the two main bed-chambers lay at the back of the house, so they had windows overlooking the landscaped gardens. That meant there were probably *other* guest bedrooms situated at the front of the property, with windows that looked onto Spriggs Lane. Mayotte supposed these guest chambers were seldom used... from what she knew of Ligore Lassiter, she suspected he was not the type of person to be neighbourly and accommodating. *So where was his study?* He wouldn't keep records and ledgers down with the servants, would he? No, she was reminded of Malachy Mahogany's words: 'Mr. Lassiter is very protective of the company's financial transactions...' The corporation books were probably in his boudoir, and his boudoir *must* be attached to a master bedroom. But which chamber would it be? He'd prefer the morning sun, wouldn't he? So perhaps his bedroom was on the east side? Mayotte had to single out one of the two king-rooms, so she studied the rugs. One entranceway had a rug that was a bit more worn than the other. Mayotte plumped for the bedchamber *with the worn rug.*

She took a moment to listen for sounds, then slipped to the bedroom door and turned the handle. The door opened promptly. Immediately, her eyes settled on an elaborate marble-topped wash-stand with a jug. When she inspected these items, she discovered the bowl contained warm water. The revelation convinced her she had made a wise decision. *This was, indeed, Lassiter's room.*

The main windows had been opened to allow fresh air to circu-late, and long gilded-yellow curtains had been pulled-back, though not yet fastened. *This is it,* she whispered. This is where Lassiter slept last night. She inched past a night table where a set of cufflinks had been laid. She'd have to be circumspect from now on, she decided, because Mr. Lassiter would no doubt employ a gentleman's valet, and the manservant might still be around finishing general tasks. She listened once more, but all she heard was the heavy tick-tocking that came from some place *near*. She heard an associated crackling sound too, and it was apparent these noises came from a substantial pendulum clock that, she assumed, must be concealed behind a chiffonier or armoire. Mayotte took a few deliberate steps towards a large piece of furniture, careful not to creak on the wooden floorboards, but then spotted a recessed entrance that led to a private room. She lingered for a moment, drew a deeper breath, then changed course, to tread lightly into this smaller studio-room.

Inside, Mayotte saw the source of the tick-tocking: it came from a delightful, long-case clock. The handsome timepiece produced deliciously resonant 'beats,' and she felt unmistakably calmed by the steady rotations of the wheels, the twists of the cable units, and the regular *clonk-clank* of the long pulleys. For a moment she became fascinated, perhaps even hypnotised, by the rhythms. The vibratory motions of the pendulum lulled her into a false sense of security. Mayotte knew she needed to *snap* herself out of it, so she wrenched her eyes away from the clockface to survey the inconsequential study-room. It had been simply equipped, with a writing desk set as close as it could be to the natural light from a distant window. And there was a book-shelf that contained a single leather-bound notepad. Mayotte flipped through the pages of the pad and found *all of them* to be empty.

She saw a chair with red cushions, but otherwise, the room looked empty: there were no pictures, no embroideries, no ornamental fabrics, no flowers. This was a man's room. And, explicitly, the owner of *this* study was a sober and moderate person, with regular habits. But where did he keep his accounting books? She needed to see the payroll that Mr. Mahogany, the accountant, had suggested Lassiter kept under lock and key. She wanted to study this ledger to try and find-out more about the characters Bisbee and Kilda that the new lad had mentioned. But where was his secret payroll? Mayotte decided it must be hidden in a strongbox, and Lassiter's box must be tucked-away somewhere in *this* study, perhaps deposited in a hole. She gazed around the room *again*, but shook her head. There was nowhere to hide a large ledger book.

Mayotte assumed the ledger must be capable of being lifted

because Lassiter transported it to-and-from Mr. Mahogany's office, every Thursday. Equally, she figured it must be fixed and sealed, so perhaps bolted away somewhere. She guessed she sought some kind of solidly built box... but where would such a receptacle be stashed? She knew that Mr. Oldcorne's safe had been tucked away behind a painting in his library, but this room contained no wall hangings of any type. On her first inspection, the room had no place to hide a lock-box.

Mayotte shuffled closer to the bureau and explored the drawers, but none of them was large enough to contain a ledger. She offered one side a tentative tug... but the drawer had been locked. Lassiter must take the key with him. But where was his hiding place? Where was his casket?

Tick-tock. She contemplated the room again. From skirting board to plinth, from crown moulding to cornice... the room was *empty* of decoration. Tick-tock. Except... *except*. Mayotte felt her heartbeat quicken as she turned toward the grandfather clock. Why keep a big, noisy gadget next to a bedroom? She'd seen their butler clean-out the Oldcorne's clock, and had watched the repairman work on the time-piece when he visited once a year to adjust the inner workings. Hence, Mayotte knew that the base of a long-clock contained a miniature cupboard, below the gubbins. It was in *this* miniature cupboard, always found beneath a long case clock, that a repairer would store his cogs, his screws, his little screwdrivers, and his brass oddments. Tick-tock.

She crouched down by the side of Mr. Lassiter's clock-case and, indeed, she found a brass handle located in the centre of a glossy hatch, low, by the base of the mechanism. The repairer's cupboard was wide enough to accommodate a strong-box.

'My! What an excellent place to hide one's secrets,' she whispered.

However, the low cupboard was difficult to access. Mayotte had to buckle onto all-fours, just to get close enough to pluck at the handle with the extreme tips of her fingers.

That's when he *charged* at her.

12

Mayotte floundered.

Whoever had struck her had dashed into the studio, silently and swiftly. Like a white owl in the night. She hadn't even noticed his approach because she had been focused on the *tick-tocking*. Mayotte was hunched by the clock and unprepared for his attack. She had no idea what was going to happen, and didn't have sufficient time to react. Her attacker came-at her with a bedsheet. And he smothered her with it!

Mayotte brandished her hands, not seeing her attacker, but attempting to scratch-out his eyes or slash eagerly at his limbs. However, her opponent was more powerful and *far* more agile. For a moment, she relaxed her muscles and smelled his breath next to her ear. She tasted blood in her mouth. And heard him make a *shush!* sound. The man clasped her jaw between powerful thumbs, and Mayotte felt the warmth of his body crush *close* to hers. She made another spring for it once she regained sufficient strength. This time, she kicked out with her knees, ramming the bony parts as hard as she could into the softer sections of the man's body. Mayotte heard the *tick-tock* from the grandfather clock, and this sound gave her the strength and motivation to make this one last attempt to shake him off while she still possessed the muscle. But the man stood firm and he clutched her even *tighter*, in an unwavering embrace.

Subsequently, and with a groan of surrender, Mayotte crumbled into his arms, while her foe stood above and carried her in a firm embrace. Then she heard him whisper, 'Do not speak. Keep still. Your silence is *essential*. We must go. The bad man comes.'

'Let me see... *let me see...*' she hissed. Mayotte shook her head with such spirited insistence that her assailant couldn't ignore her protests for much longer.

'Fine,' he said, 'But you must *shush...*' He drew her up on her toes, then displayed her head from beneath the bed-sheet, like an inept tomb-looter might untangle a mummified body — with ham-fisted fingers and a pair of butter-thumbs. As the sheeting pulled away from her eyes, she kept still so she could take stock of the situation and see who'd violated her and figure out how she might escape. She was *not* prepared for what she saw once he had discharged her head from the tangle. She swivelled her neck to eyeball her assailant and was astounded! The guy was no whipper-snapper, not by a long chalk. When she scanned his dark brown eyes, she calculated he must be at least *sixty summers old*. His hair was white as chalk, though lengthy. It hung across his shoulders like the shroud of a bride. His white hair tumbled like spillage from a cream churn... yet seemed well-brushed, with sealed ends dipped in tallow. The man's cheekbones were high, his lips were wide, and his forehead was sagacious. Any indignation and displeasure she bore in her chest soon melted when she studied this old man's ancient and enlightened face. So she became *compliant*.

'We have move quick,' the old man told her.

Mayotte nodded as he nudged her from the studio and into the main body of the bedroom as if she were a bolt of fabric and he, a costumier, was moving a roll. He manoeuvred her to the long curtains that hung in the corner and ordered her to stand completely still. Mayotte intuitively recognized it was *essential* she did as he said.

She now realised why the aging guy had suppressed her voice and movements in such a firm way. A dubious-looking man entered the room. The fellow was young, maybe twenty, with wavy black hair, an ugly mashed nose, cauliflower ears, and broad hands. She could see his movements through the gauzy fringe of the curtain fabric. He was dressed formally, in a long black jacket over dusty breeches, a silver waistcoat, and a silk tie on a stiff white collar. He could have been one of Mr. Lassiter's business associates if she hadn't spotted one thing: the tell-tale contour of a timber stock, tucked under his right arm. The man came armed. Lassiter wouldn't have armed associates, would he? The guy was equipped with a vicious-looking, long-barrelled shotgun and, as Mayotte squinted through the fabric, she *also* noticed a gun belt tied around his waist, and a holstered-pistol.

The gunslinger didn't seem bothered to take a proper look around the room... perhaps he *played it cool*.

The guy sauntered into Lassiter's studio, where the big clock was located, and a little later, he emerged with an amused smirk on his face. He ambled across the bedchamber as if he had all the time in the world. Then the guy hesitated, hardly four feet from their place of concealment. He moved his shotgun, so the stock rested on an upper arm joint, then patted his nose with a free hand while Mayotte held her breath and prayed her heart would stop *thumping* in her chest. For one terrifying, hair-raising, moment the gunslinger glanced directly at their hiding place. He even took a tentative step towards the outline of their bodies, buried behind the draperies. That was the moment that Mayotte felt sure their time was up. But, as luck would have it, and with a startling din, the grandfather clock marked time with a clatter. It didn't ring; it *madly* clicked. Lassiter's clock whirred and cackled unequivocally — the gubbins smashed against metal and oak hardness —so the clacking became so loud the gunman became agitated.

Perhaps the gong had been disengaged, Mayotte assumed. Luckily, after the smash and jangle from the clock, the gunslinger shifted his position, this time to withdraw from the room altogether. He held the same satisfied smirk on his face as he departed their company.

They stuck around for many deep breaths, hidden behind the shelter of the curtain, before they *dared* move. When they did advance, the old guy shifted behind Mayotte to extract her entirely from the constrictive bedsheet he'd used to confine her: 'Come,' he said, patiently. 'We have to take the hidden stair to escape... while we still have a chance.'

Mayotte nodded her understanding, so they made off the way she had come up, *via* the servant's passage, and out through the side door.

Outdoors, in the garden, Mayotte took a sweet sip of air. But the old man hurried her away from the house. He shoved her towards the end of the lawn.

'I came from *that* lane...' Mayotte told him. She pointed in the opposite direction. 'Why shouldn't we go that way?'

'No, *that way* is foolish. *That way* is bad. *That way* is not safe.' Then the old man growled. 'Wicked men are out the front.'

'How did you know the gunslinger would come into the room?' she asked.

'The dangerous man?'

'Yeah, the bad man. How did you know he'd come into our room? He didn't hear me clumping around, did he?'

The old man tugged on her arm, to pull her beneath an over-hanging bush, then he pressed her head low to move around a rift in the hedgerow. 'The bad man comes into the house each quarter-day. And he does the same thing when he arrives. He is a smooth-running instrument. I observe the man's movements for a long while...'

'Oh, I see. But you saw me sneak into the house and you recognized I'd be in danger because I hadn't gotten out before his appointed visiting time? Is that it?'

The old man grunted as he shifted Mayotte in front of him. She noticed a sketchy path ahead that ran to open land and, in the distance, a saturated meadow. 'Let's go to my camp...' the old man told her.

'Can I ask what *you* were doing there?' she countered. 'Why have you been watching the Red House?'

'Me? I seek someone... I wait for *someone*.'

'Seek? Wait? Whom?'

The old man puffed, then he tugged on her shoulder to wrench her around, so that they faced each other. When they stood head-on, the old man gave Mayotte a scrutinizing stare. It was as if he strove to read her mind. Once he'd finished focussing on her brain, he raised an eyebrow. He said: 'It might be *you* that I waited for.'

'Me? What do you mean me? Am I the one you seek? Me? How can it be me? I don't even know who you are. How did you know I would arrive at that place? Not even I knew I'd go there, until, well, *until I got there...* so how could you have known?'

'Come,' said the white-haired old man. He gripped her elbow. 'We must keep moving.'

13

The ancient man, with snowy-white hair, took Mayotte through a tangle of thickets, then beyond a pocket of spiny furze-bushes. He picked at some yellow petals as he trod, 'Good food,' he suggested. He placed a flower onto his tongue, and she watched him chew it.

Then, in a hazy clearing, she noticed his camp. It had been tucked away near a thin, scaly-barked tree, and had been decorated with beautiful, bronze-green leaves. She viewed an angular structure that had been wrapped in rough-cut animal skins. She suspected the hides formerly belonged to deer. Five skins covered a roof, while lower walls were constructed of sheaves of stacked straw. In the centre of the structure, she glimpsed a square portal. 'I camp overnight here,' he told her. He motioned that she should enter.

Mayotte lowered her head to pass through the entrance and grimaced because she expected to be met by an unpleasant odour. But when she sniffed, she found the hideout to be genuinely nice. It smelled of freshly cut meadow grass on a summer morning.

The old man immediately dropped onto an animal skin. He sat in a cross-legged position, with his back to a cushion of shaggy fleece. He invited her to join him on the ground, to sit cross-legged opposite. So Mayotte sank to her knees, then adjusted herself, with her feet on a mat made of woven fibres. She let herself sink back against her own soft cushion of sheepskin.

'How long have you lived here?' she asked, blinking because her eyes had not yet adjusted to the shade.

'I stay in this place for a short while. Until I finish my task. I am a hunting man. A tracking man. Once I'm done with my hunt, I move on.'

'Who are you?' she asked.

'You may call me Toad Blackwing...'

After he'd uttered his name, there came a period of lengthy silence. Mayotte tried to make sense of everything. But the old man closed his eyes. She had a hundred questions for the old-timer, but felt uncomfortable about asking them out loud now he dozed. Eventually, after a long silence, Mayotte muttered: 'May I ask you something. How old are you? '

'You waited all this time to ask *that*?' the old gentleman whispered. 'Was it your finest question? I expected better *from you*. For instance, I hoped you would ask me something of value. Try again. Prepare an improved opening question. Do you want to learn? Do you want revelation?'

Mayotte took a deep breath and tried again. 'Why were you there in that house?'

'I look for him.'

'Who?' Mayotte tilted her body towards Mister Blackwing and she allowed her lips to part a little.

'I look for the man who stole my daughter.'

'Stole your daughter?

'He stole her from me. *They* stole her from me.'

'Who, *who*?'

'The white man. He arrived at our territory. He kidnapped my daughter. The white man carried her back to his nation, across the winter sea.'

Mayotte assimilated his words. Then she said: 'Are you, um, are you an Indian?'

'I am from the Leni-Lenape people...'

'In America?'

'Yes, Abooksigun, in the place *you* call America. I crossed the winter sea to be in this salty place. I seek a daughter and I hunt the man who took her from me.'

'When did this happen? When did this bloke kidnap your girl?'

'Many years have passed.'

'Erm?' That didn't seem to be the answer she required, so Mayotte tried another path: 'Why did you come to this salty place now?'

'The one who cries the most is with our Creator, the skygod. My beloved Awèna — the girl's mother — rests in paradise. So I'm free to track my prey...'

'How did you learn English?'

'The white man taught my people many useful things. How to shoot a rifle, how to steal from another man's garden, how to wager on a game of chance, and how to drink fire-liquid that kills a person's soul. At first, the white man spoke a language that we heard but did not understand. But my people are skilful with lips... we sing, we recite poetry, we tell tales... so it became easy for us to chew upon the white man's simple words and learn his straightforward language. Ku uwatu Lënapei lixsëwakàn.'

Mayotte swallowed, then rubbed the back of her neck. 'If I told you I knew where your daughter was being held, would you believe me? Would you then trust that the person you seek is not me?'

Now it was Toad Blackwing's turn to be surprised. He inclined his body forward, to listen more keenly, 'You have met my daughter, Abooksigun? '

Mayotte swallowed and nodded. 'I think I may have met her. There cannot be more than one, surely? Not around these parts. The woman I met, she's an Indian. I think she said she came from the same tribe as you. That can't be a fluke, can it? I know they hold her in a rich man's house. And the rich man came from America too. So it all fits. Everything I've told you might be coincidence, but what if it's not? Furthermore, and with respect to you, but it seemed to me that you are old enough to be the woman's father...'

'Where is she? Where is my daughter? Tomorrow I will reclaim her. I must prepare...' Toad Blackwing clasped his hands together.

'Um, it's not as easy as that, erm... it's *complicated*...'

'I thought as much, Abooksigun. Like all white people, you twist and turn like a maggot on a line when you are faced with the consequences of dishonesty...'

'Um, you do not have to be horrible to me...' Mayotte squeezed her hands into her lap and looked down. 'I wasn't being dishonest; I just didn't want to raise your hopes. Getting her out is not going to be easy. Don't you understand that? It will take some, er, well let's just say it will take some preparation and plotting. What I'm trying to tell you is that releasing your daughter is not going to be trouble-free...'

'When can it be done?' Toad Blackwing asked. 'When will you take me to my daughter, Abooksigun?' The old man raised his head skyward in prayer. 'This is why I came to this salty place. My journey is over. This is where my life leads... I have tracked, I have trailed, I have shadowed... now I complete my final hunt. The quarry brings Toad Blackwing here, to a damp nation. You must take me to her — so I might complete my hunt.'

'Would you give me a few days? I need that long to make all the arrangements...'

'A few days, a few hours, but no more.' Toad Blackwing crossed his arms and narrowed his eyes. 'My hunt is almost done. I cannot linger in this soggy place any longer. I desire to finish what the universe started...'

'Yes, I understand. I'll make the arrangements, I promise.'

'A white person says one thing yet does another. Why should I trust you, Abooksigun?'

'Um?' Mayotte looked at the old guy and she brought her knees to her chest. 'I'm sitting here with you, in your tent, right?' She looked around the canopy and turned up her nose. 'Do I believe *everything* you tell me? Er, *no*. Do I think you're insane and live in a bizarre make-believe world? Er, *yes*. Did you surprise me in the Red House and try to suffocate me with a sheet? Yes, *you did*. So maybe you're as untrustworthy as I am. Just a thought: isn't it possible for us to share a cautious trust?'

'Fine words, Abooksigun. I'll give you two days, then you will take me to my daughter.'

'Why do you call me Abooksigun? It's not my name. My name is *Mayotte*...'

'Mayotte is not yours to keep. It is not fitting. It is a name given by a dominant individual. Abooksigun is appropriate... You have a host of spirits within you, girl. You have wildness within your temperament that reminds me of my offspring. Therefore I name you: Abooksigun.'

She nodded, her eyes aglow, then she whispered: 'Thank you...' She didn't know why she appreciated what the old man had said, but she *did*. It was a rare moment of value.

'Abooksigun, may I ask you a question, my turn now? Why were you in the Red House? Why did you steal into that place of badness and danger? I have watched that place for many days. I'm sure my daughter is *not* there... though I waited, hopeful they might bring her. But they have not brought her. I witnessed wicked men coming and going...but they never brought my daughter.'

'Your daughter is *not there*. She's being kept at a less grand place, a few miles away. I will show you where — and, cross-my-heart, I will help you. To answer your question, I went to the Red House to look for records, written records in a ledger, records about some lost workmates... I was doing it for a friend.'

'We're both seeking something,' Toad Blackwing declared.

Mayotte nodded, 'Maybe so.'

'And, Abooksigun, this friend of yours, the one you did your dangerous mission for, where is *he* now?'

'How did you guess it was a man?' Mayotte shrugged. 'But anyway, yes, you're right, he is. Um, he's back in the manufactory, down by the river.'

'You left your friend, this man, in the dark place by murky water? That place is a bad dish... a *bad dish* indeed. Most foul. You must ask your friend to leave that place behind. He must flee that terrible place, *depart*...'

'I don't know,' Mayotte said, with a wave of her hand. 'It seems a genuine opportunity for him...' Then she broke-off because she recognized she had been talking, the whole while, about Stormbuckler — and not about Master Eaglehurst who was her current boyfriend. 'Anyway, I suppose working in the plant will give him a chance to make a name for himself...'

Toad Blackwing said nothing. He rolled his shoulders, folded his hands into his lap and he sat *utterly* still. Mayotte didn't know what she ought to do next, so she waited and regulated her breathing. She counted to a hundred then rubbed her thumbs together. She was about to ask permission to leave when Blackwing took a prolonged breath, leaned forward, and spoke once more, though this time in a whisper: 'Tomorrow I will continue to hunt for the thief who stole my daughter. Two nights after that you will return here You will take me to her. That is our agreement.'

'Shall I go now?'

'Yes.'

14

Once Mayotte had left Toad Blackwing's camp, it became apparent she didn't know precisely where she was. She resolved not to bother him again but instead to struggle to find her own way home, to pursue the path she'd taken to his hideaway. But the going was difficult and, perhaps predictably, she became lost after cutting across the sodden meadow. The sun had already dipped behind the clouds when she spotted a place to rest. She delayed forty minutes, maybe longer, until the sun crept westward across the heavens. Mayotte used her instinct to suppose she had to walk northeast to get back to town; because the cab had drawn her south of the river, and she had wandered at least a mile westward from Spriggs Lane. She appreciated it would be a painful slog but trudged homewards anyway with an odd sense of composure, as if, somehow, she'd been offered inner peace by the wise, but crazy, old man.

It was after six when she turned up at the Oldcorne's mansion, bone-weary from her exertions. She lugged herself up the servant's back-stairs to her garret but was too exhausted to do anything but topple onto her wood-framed bed. She closed her eyes for mere minutes before the laundry maid named Jean burst through the door to tap her on the shoulder. 'What, what?' Can't you see I am asleep?' Mayotte whined.

'You still have your boots on, silly...'

'Have I?' Mayotte pulled herself up and rubbed her bleary eyes. 'Oh, gosh, I'm a mess, aren't I?'

'Get your uniform on, *quick*...'

'Hmm? Why? I've finished my day...' Mayotte fell back onto her blanket. 'I'm exhausted. Done in. Can't you leave me be?'

'No, you must hurry. Get your uniform on quick. Get washed. I'll bring a basin. I'll help you brush your hair. Madam wants to see you *at once*. She rang down. She wants you right away...'

'Good grief, now? Now? Why now? Hell, what a day this has been! What does she want?'

'Come on, lazybones. Get yourself up.'

Mayotte got washed and presentable, put on her black dress, white cap, and apron, and thus submitted herself to Mrs. Oldcorne's drawing-room where she yielded a knee at the door and was prompted to come into the light — to settle by Mrs. Oldcorne's favourite armchair.

'Ah, there you are, girl. Where have you been? I've been waiting earnestly to see you.'

'I'm sorry, ma'am,' Mayotte said. She clasped her hands by her apron. 'I arrived late from the manufactory...'

'Indeed? Well, that's what I wanted to talk to you about...'

'Oh?'

'Yes,' Mrs. Oldcorne smoothed her skirt before she continued, 'Certain knowledge has been revealed to me... Certain discoveries have come to light and so forth... Certain conclusions have been made by a dependable source...' The lady of the house stared solidly into Mayotte's eyes as if she was ready to accuse the girl of something shameful, 'Well, after hearing this information, I have made a disagreeable resolution, and it is this: You must break off your employment with Mr. Lindwürm. Your suspension takes immediate effect.'

Mayotte brought her hand to her heart, then swallowed.

'There, I said it, girl. It's my decision. And it's definite. You will return to your obligations in this house and, erm, we'll say no more about it. Put that experience behind you. That's my advice. And look to the future.'

'Um, ma'am, did I do something wrong? Some mistake I might remedy? '

'No, nothing like that,' Mrs. Oldcorne said. She dismissed the notion with a swing of her Lorgnette spectacles. 'It's not that you haven't made several mistakes during your life. Of course, you have, you make mistakes as regularly as a fat man breaks wind... but on this occasion, it has nothing to do with you. You are not to blame. And, anyhow, that's not the point, silly girl. The point I am making is that you will no longer be in Asher-John Lindwürm's employment. My decision is final. You *must not* return to his plant. Is that clear?'

'May I ask why not?'

'No, of course you may not. How dare you? What a grand opinion you have of yourself, girl, to question me in such a direct and provocative manner!'

'But *please*, ma'am, this places me in a very awkward position. I have several liabilities at the factory. I've started an attachment with suitor... I've made other alliances. I cannot break things off now, can I?'

'An attachment with a suitor? Well, in that case, it's your own silly fault! Whatever were you thinking? And, *yes*, you must do squarely that! You must break-off this so-called attachment and those alliances *right now* if you recognize what's good for you. You will also ignore any assignments that Mr. Lindwürm gave you. Is that clear? Break it all off *now*.'

'But, ma'am... You were very keen on me going to the manufactory, weren't you? I'm halfway through —' Mayotte leaned closer to her employer, to whisper her next words, 'I'm halfway through discovering the American's secrets... the mysteries you ordered me to spy-out...'

'Shhh!' hissed Mrs. Oldcorne. 'Enough of *that* talk, girl, and stand back from me. I do not know what you're talking about. I do not know what you mean by those words. It is claptrap. I will deny everything. Do you hear? I will deny it all.'

'But ma'am, will not you be penalized by Mr. Lindwürm? I understood you had entered into contractual agreement with the American? Some kind of bond?'

'Contracts can be broken; agreements can be retracted. It's for the best... We'll discuss this some other time...'

Mayotte went quiet and stared blankly into the distance.

'Didn't you hear me, girl? I said we'd debate it some other time... off with you.'

Mayotte tugged her ear and narrowed her eyes. 'Is this only provisional? Subject to confirmation? Only, madam, I'd like to extend my contract with Mr. Lindwürm's plant. Would you allow me to continue at his manufactory for just a little while longer? Please reconsider! Might I be permitted to go back... um, I don't know, after you've calmed down a bit...'

'Calmed down?' Mrs. Oldcorne shot a fierce glance at her maid, and carried her chin higher. 'How dare you? It's not your place to question your betters or explore a better's motives. It is definitely not your place to produce impertinent remarks about a better's mental state.'

'I'm sorry, ma'am,' Mayotte bobbed her head and dipped a knee. 'It's just that this announcement has come as a bit of a shock.'

'Yes, well I'm sure it has...' Mrs. Oldcorne pinched her spectacles back into their leather case. 'It was also a shock to me when I heard what I heard. Be that's as maybe — I warned you before about being opinionated with superiors. In the future, please credit me with a bit of common sense, will you, yes? This decision is for your own good!'

'Yes, madam.'

'Good. Off you go.'

15

Master Eaglehurst drew Stormbuckler to his favourite local tailors: Messrs. Whipwell and Troon, Gentlemen's Outfitters of Distinction, in Kingston Road. There, he chose some contemporary clothes for Stormbuckler: a pair of grey worsted trousers equipped with quarter top pockets, a morning jacket, a white shirt, collars and cuffs, a pair of braces to go under a charcoal vest, a carton of tacks, and a silk tie.

A proficient alterationist came to administer the purchases while another placed the clothes in packages, wrapped them in brown paper, and tied them with twine. When they'd finished, Master Eaglehurst helped carry a box as they strayed into the High Street in search of more possessions. They were like a pair of King's Scholars on the tug, with full smiles and an abundance of blustery attitude. Stormbuckler peered at his bandaged stump and didn't have the heart to tell his new gentleman companion that he had no boots or socks to go with these splendid new threads... perhaps it was better not to say nothing at all. He did not want Master Eaglehurst to become embarrassed about the impediment, and it would have been cruelly ungrateful of Stormbuckler to mention it now.

Master Eaglehurst led Stormbuckler through the port ware-houses, then beyond a row of cheerful red-tile cottages, each with a modest black cowl over the front door that made the little buildings look like a row of crouching Cistercian nuns. Then to the Swan Inn's immaculate porch, a venerable construction that clung to the muddy edge of the riverbed like a clothespin might fasten onto a grandmother's sleeve. Stormbuckler was shaken up by the experiences of the day and felt uneasy about accepting charity from a fellow he hardly knew, so he wasn't altogether disappointed when their half-day excursion was almost over, and they stepped across the threshold of the riverfront inn.

Although Master Eaglehurst had been merry enough, and helpful too, during the day, he had seldom talked much about himself. Eaglehurst seemed to be a singularly modest character. Yet, he enjoyed Stormbuckler's tales and notably appreciated the story about quitting the poorhouse via a pig's rump. He became especially amused when Stormbuckler told him he had traded his life in a poorhouse for a new life in a duck house. 'What's a duck-house?' Master Eaglehurst had asked, providing a pertinent *hoot* at such a ridiculous notion.

'It's like a hencoop, but for aquatics. I discovered the little place by the river, behind a shed. It's where I live. I like to think of it as my primary dwelling, although it's also used by several ducks.'

After a squawk of mirth, Master Eaglehurst replied: 'Are you serious? Oh my gosh, you *are serious*, aren't you? What must it be like to live in a duck coop? Heavens, what must it be like?'

'It's not so bad,' Stormbuckler had told him, with a straight face. 'The ducks don't barge in on me when I'm changing. The ducks don't punch me in the ribs when I'm slumbering. The ducks don't shove me in a sack and prick me with pins when I have done something wrong. I've found that ducks can be very reasonable co-tenants and are not *nearly* as disagreeable as humans...'

Master Eaglehurst had laughed-and-laughed at this observation.

At the Swan Inn, Master Eaglehurst went to the reception counter and struck up a restrained engagement with the owner. Stormbuckler presumed that Master Eaglehurst then passed an abundance of high-value coins to the landlord, because the licensee expressed amazement at the quality of the treasure he'd been given, then stuck the coins into the front pocket of his tattered apron. After this transaction, the elegant Master Eaglehurst returned to Stormbuckler and said, 'Look, old friend, I have got to get back to the office. I arranged for food to be delivered to you, and a bath to be poured. I also paid for your lodging for a week, in advance. You'll be brought to your room by the inn-keeper or his servant. And, um, someone will be along later to see that you've settled in. Perhaps it will be Mayotte, or more likely me. And at that stage we can enlighten you... um, what I mean by that is, um, we can advise you further, erm, to put you in the picture, so to speak... and so forth. Does any of this make any sense?'

'Not really,' admitted Stormbuckler. 'But it's good of you to take care of me today. You've been exceedingly kind. I appreciate everything you have done.'

'Look, old man, I know it's not the best start. I wish I could offer you more. I really do! You know, I don't know what Mayotte has planned for you... she's an organizer, isn't she? But, erm, I'm positive you'll benefit from her wisdom... I'm sure we all will... you, me, everybody. Because the one thing I can say about Mayotte, without expecting any contradiction, is that she's thoroughly and absolutely reliable. Don't you think? Well, you would assert such a thing if you knew her like I do. Um? Look, old man, accept these...' Master Eaglehurst squeezed two large coins into Stormbuckler's grubby palm. 'Just in case there are extra disbursements I haven't thought of.'

'Thanks again,' said Stormbuckler. He glanced down at the coins.' You don't have to do this.'

'I feel that I do. I'll show up later to see how you've settled in...'

'Maybe we can have a drink at the bar?'

'A fine idea.'

∽

When Master Eaglehurst left the inn, the licensee took Stormbuckler to a sumptuous room that nestled below wooden timbers and overlooked the bustling towpath. The chamber came equipped with a bed that had a candock, and a cotton pallet. Stormbuckler also discovered a chest, a wardrobe, a basin stand, a rush recliner sat in a recess, and a wooden slipper-tub concealed behind a screen. It was, quite simply, the most splendid room Stormbuckler had *ever seen.* When the proprietor handed him the big-key for the door, he didn't know whether to hug the fellow, or weep!

Thereafter, while he reclined in his room, Stormbuckler considered the elegant Master Eaglehurst and the young woman named Mayotte. The young gentleman had been upright and genuine, if a little shy. Stormbuckler ruled that the gentleman was a good fellow. The girl, on the other hand, was a cunning, scheming, and devious little fox; he saw she was repeatedly chewing on her lip, as if she was always *about to* develop a diabolical plan. He had no faith in her. The girl appeared insincere. She was condescending, too. He had no taste for her company. Stormbuckler was still determined to find out what had happened to Tom Bisbee and, apparently, Kilda as well. And the girl suggested she might be able to solve the puzzle about their fates. Accordingly, Stormbuckler resolved that he must *try* to maintain a cordial relationship with the girl, regardless of his personal opinions about her, especially if he wanted to investigate his friend's disappearance and Tom's terrible accident.

Stormbuckler rested on his bed and contemplated the offer that the Mayotte girl had made. 'He'll be sketching for us...' she declared, when she introduced him to Eaglehurst. Wouldn't that be prodigious? If he had a job in a pleasant office, and could work as an artist? *Wouldn't that be a dream?* Just as he grinned at the thought, there was a hammer at the door and a liveried servant allowed himself in, bearing a platter of cold meats, cheeses, and pickles. 'Here you are mate...' said the servant. As the fellow placed the platter on one side, he glared at Stormbuckler's club foot. 'The best you can do is eat while you can, mate... whilst there's still cash in the kitty, huh?'

'What do you mean?' Stormbuckler withdrew his troublesome leg from the mattress and watched as the man re-arranged the slices of meat and cheese, fanning them out to produce a better display for the plate.

'I mean what I said, mate. You're not fit to be here, are you? We've had a wager, me, and the other pot-boys; we figure you'll be gone in three days. Wednesday. That's what I reckon. I placed my sixpence on Wednesday: I bet you'll be gone by then.'

'Why? Why would I be going *anywhere*?'

'Your gallant benefactor put two guineas in the kitty, didn't he? We think you'll spend the entirety of it by Wednesday. Our cook, the soppy old cow, thinks you might eek it out till Friday, so she offered sixpence on the last day of the week... but there again, she ain't seen the state of you, has she? She doesn't know about your gammy leg, does she? Or the fact you're red-raw and lousy under the skin.'

'Don't you think I'm fit to be here?'

'Look, this is the best place in town. It's not a doss house for down 'n' outs is it? Look at you — you're a vagabond in rags, with a pathetic foot, and you've been out in the town gathering alms, haven't you? That's why the Christian gentleman has felt sorry for you, isn't it? Because you're a pauper... a parish derelict... I can smell poverty a mile off... I can smell that you're *nothing but a derelict*... that's what you'll *always be,* mate. Mark my words...'

'Why are you being so mean?'

'Mean? Because I don't appreciate attending good-for-nothings, that's why.' The servant moved to the door and glanced around the room. 'Eat up, mate. Bath water's coming next... it will be the first wash you've had in months! Still, at least you will get a decent night's sleep here. Though, if it were up to me, I'd boot your arse out in the morning and keep the money. But it ain't up to me, is it pal? Your fancy man put eight-and-a-half crowns into the kitty, in advance, didn't he? And our landlord is an honest Christian, ain't he? Let's see how long you take to spend it all up! Good night... *sir*.'

Stormbuckler was taken aback by the servant's mean and hurtful assertions. But he also saw what the scoundrel had in mind: He *was* a poor man. He still *is* a poor man. He always *would be* a poor man. And these facts made him an inappropriate person in a dignified setting. Though Stormbuckler took heart once he'd taken his first taste of the softest gammon in the world. 'I should have told him I'm a technical artist,' he muttered between mouthfuls. 'I should have told him I work for a millionaire inventor. I should have told him I am employed in an art studio... I should have told him he ought to treat me with respect. Ha! I should have told him to bring mustard.'

When Stormbuckler woke from his first slumber in a proper bed, he had a wide smile upon his face: in the looking-glass, he saw that he resembled a frog who'd eaten a sausage, *sideways*. He pulled his bad leg toward the window, to watch wherry-men scull their skiffs across light waves, to avoid a regatta of royal swans. Then he wrestled with the harsh realities of his situation: Stormbuckler was not a brainbox, no one could accuse him of that, but even *he* could deduce that if he earned sixpence a day in the technical drawing department of Lindwürm's works, it would provide him with a weekly income that amounted to half-a-crown. If he could somehow keep his barrel-rolling job too, he'd earn an additional threepence a day, thus his salary for an *entire* week of work would be less than four shillings. Master Eaglehurst had supplied the innkeeper with two guineas to cover a full week of board. On Stormbuckler's rough reckoning, he'd have to earn a further *thirty-eight* shillings a week if he wanted to live in the same kind of style for the rest of his days. And that sum that didn't consider his repayment of debt to Eaglehurst. With an irritable expression fresh on his face, Stormbuckler understood why the servant had told him: *you're not fit to be here...*

A maid brought warm water for a basin and removed the chamber pot. She even supplied a fresh warm towel. 'Gaw, I could get used to this, though...' he muttered. After his wash, Stormbuckler dressed in his new clothes, using the peacock mirror that hung on the wall. It took effort and clumsy fumbling to balance his one good foot while he attempted to put the new clothes upon his body in the correct order. When he decided it was the best he could accomplish, he stopped to glance at the reflection in the mirror. He looked *inconsistent* — mismatched. He resembled a bear wearing a frock to a monkey's wedding. Despite the fact that he looked out of place, despite *everything*, he left his room, locked the door, and went downstairs wearing his new suit, to find a place at the far end of the main bar where he would wait, in peaceful silence, for Master Eaglehurst to arrive. Or perhaps Mayotte.

At ten-past-nine, a maid traipsed over to ask if he required anything. 'Like what?' he replied.

'Drink? Porridge? Fish?'

'Yes, I *would*...'

'Well, what then?' the girl grunted. She provided a grumpy squint.

'Porridge, please.'

'To drink?'

'Water.'

'Are you sure? Most people want light beer; it's far better for you...'

'Yes, I will have what most people want,' he told her.

She gave an indifferent shrug and tootled off.

A little while later, the server brought porridge. It tasted so good he nearly wept with pleasure. The oatmeal had been stewed in milk, *not* in cold water. And the meal *hadn't* been swelled with wood shavings, which was how they did it at the poorhouse to make it go further. It oozed cream and sweetness. Also, it did *not* contain a tablespoonful of salt. He had become accustomed to all these adaptations to the recipe, while he lived at the institution. But *this* was how porridge *should* taste!

Stormbuckler took a sip of the warm beer and waited. A large clock in the lobby suggested it had gone past ten. When the maid came to collect his oatmeal dish, he asked if the lobby-clock was accurate. She returned a contemptuous sneer that suggested it certainly *was*.

At eleven o'clock, Stormbuckler felt uneasy and fidgety. The maid brought another beer and told him they'd be serving the lunchtime menu *soon*. He thanked her, but shook his head. She marched-off in a fit of grim humour, as if she'd been told she reeked of a nanny-goat's back-passage. He hadn't upset her deliberately; so he guessed she was just being a bit snippy *with him*.

It was gone midday when Master Eaglehurst stumbled in. He looked positively distracted and off-balance. He came at once to Stormbuckler's table, although he surveyed the bar the entire time. 'Have you seen her?'

'Who?' asked Stormbuckler, open-mouthed. He might have

offered a welcoming smile too, but Eaglehurst would have been oblivious to it, if he had. The young gentleman's mind was elsewhere. His eyes were fretful. He scratched the back of his hands with a broken fingernail. 'Mayotte? ' he snapped. 'Have you seen her? Has she been here? I don't know where she is...'

'Nope. I waited here all morning. No sign of her. I'm glad to see you —'

'Where could she be?'

'I don't know. Didn't she come to work?'

'No, she has not come in today. I don't think anyone noticed her absence or cares much, but she's, well, she's — '

'Totally reliable?'

'Yes, of course. I know I said *that* about her yesterday afternoon... Look, old friend, I'd better ask around to see if anyone saw her or spoke to her. I won't be long.' Eaglehurst stormed away to speak to the staff and management.

A little later, Eaglehurst came back and looked more worried than before.

'Why don't you take a seat?' Stormbuckler offered.

'Yes,' said the young man. He swung a seat around. 'This is most out of character for her. I wonder where she got to? I'm worried sick...'

'Don't you want a drink to calm your nerves?'

'No, I'd better not. I need to find her. Look, old man, I'm going to leave now. I'll go back to the works and have a scout around. But if she shows up here, be a splendid fellow, will you, and bring her back to the drawing office? There's a wonderful chap...'

'You want me to stay here and wait?'

'Would you do that? I'd be exceedingly grateful.'

'It's not a problem... How long should I stay?'

'As long as it takes, old boy, *as long as it takes.*'

And with those words, Master Eaglehurst rushed away.

The complete day passed, evening drew-in but Mayotte never appeared at the Swan Inn. Master Eaglehurst did not return, either.

Stormbuckler went to his bedchamber, and the same servant came by, as before, to bring cold meat, cheeses, and pickles. 'There's still plenty of cash in the kitty, mate. Eat up. Do you want a bottle of fine port wine brought up too? The best there is...'

'No, thank you,' said Stormbuckler.

'Wednesday. That's what I reckon. Is my wager still safe?'

'I'll let you know...'

'Yeah, you do that mate, *hah*...' The servant gave a wink. 'The bath water will be brought along presently. Have a nice evening... sir.'

The next day, Stormbuckler repeated the same pattern of behaviour as before. He rose at first light, checked the view from his window, performed his ablutions, and dressed for a day at the office.

At ten past nine, in the bar, he ordered porridge; and at eleven, another jug of warm beer. Just after one o'clock, Master Eaglehurst shuffled into the bar-room, looking flustered. He gave Stormbuckler a pained stare and said, 'Still no sign of her?'

'No. What about your end?'

Eaglehurst's eyes darted left and the right, 'Nothing. Nobody has seen or heard from her.'

'What are we going to do?'

'I honestly don't know. I'm willing to do anything.' Master Eaglehurst rubbed his windpipe with damp fingers. 'Could I prevail upon you, do you think?'

'Me?' Stormbuckler swallowed. 'What can I do?'

'While I'm waiting in the factory, waiting for her to show up, would you do me a big favour? Would you go to her home to see if she turned up there?'

'Of course, anything to help. Where does she live?'

'That's the thing, old boy, nobody seems to know... Mr. Lassiter keeps the staff records in a safe, in his stronghold...'

'Let's go there and ask him...'

Master Eaglehurst moved closer to whisper into Stormbuckler's ear, 'Mr. Lassiter is especially unfavourable to employees. He is a stone-hearted chap and adopts a rather unpleasant outlook...'

'I see. *I think.* What about Mr. Lindwürm? Doesn't Mr. Lindwürm know where she lives? Surely, he must know?'

'I suppose you're right. Either we ask him, or we try Lassiter. I know which one of I'd prefer to go to with this question...'

'I don't know *either* of them, so I can't measure their differences...' Stormbuckler admitted, 'But I guess we should see Mr. Lindwürm...'

'We? I can't see him, old boy. I just can't... No, it has to be you.'

'Me? Why me? Why can't *you* do it? It would be better if the enquiry came from someone of your importance and standing, surely? As I told you, I do not know the man, and he doesn't know me... I only saw him one time, and that was for seconds...'

'Look, old chap, and I wouldn't prevail if there were a better way. But Mr. Siebert is back at work now, and he's a hard taskmaster. He expects me to have my nose on the drawing board eight hours a day. He doesn't even allow me to slip out for lunch. My job is at stake here, don't you see that? I can't shilly-shally all over the shop, trying to hunt her down. I'll be honest, old friend, they have already bitten me in the ear for this whole thing. Mr. Siebert is not happy that Mayotte hasn't shown up for work. I'm getting the blame! He already gave me a final warning about it. I have got to get back quick now because he's thinking of firing me. He's suggesting that I was influential in her decision to stay away from the place. So you'll do it, won't you? Please say that you will...'

Stormbuckler gave a quick smile, then wrinkled his forehead, 'I'm still not entirely sure what you want me to do...'

Master Eaglehurst looked around, and smoothed his sleeves. 'Get yourself over to Mr. Lindwürm's mansion. Ask him if he knows where Mayotte might be. If he doesn't, get him to provide a home address for her. Then check the address he gives you... I'll give you two florins, one for each ride.'

Stormbuckler rubbed his cheek. 'Where does Asher-John Lind-würm live? I don't even know that. '

'Here,' Master Eaglehurst took two florins from his waistcoat pocket. 'Go to the cabs in the market square and ask one take you to his pile... that's all you need do.'

Stormbuckler looked at the coins. 'Are you sure Mr. Lindwürm will see me? Let alone converse with me? He's a millionaire-inventor. I'm just a pathetic — *I'm just...*'

Master Eaglehurst considered Stormbuckler and smiled, 'You are his most trusted employee, aren't you? You are the hero who saved his technical director's life. And look at you... you are every inch the perfect gentleman now. *Every inch*. Of course, he will see you. He will be happy to see you.'

Stormbuckler shifted in his seat and pushed his bandaged stump against the shoeless sole of his better leg. *Every inch?* 'I wish I could be so sure,' he mumbled. 'Anyway, after I've been to see him, what then? Do I go to her house and ask her where she's been? What do I do next?'

'Yes, please, I beg you, bring her back to me. At least return with good news. I'm counting on you. I'll stay in the office until you return with good news. I will stay late.'

'Excellent, I will see later, then, to provide an update.'

'My prayers are with you...' said Master Eaglehurst. Then the young man dashed off.

Once Master Eaglehurst had left the Swan Inn, Stormbuckler stomped back to his room, to change out of the blasted monkey-suit they'd given him — to get himself back into the more comfortable down-and-out threads he was accustomed to. He decided the rags were much more practical to walk around town in, without getting noticed. No one saw a rough sleeper. Vagrants were invisible. In a monkey-suit, he looked as visible as a donkey invited to a duchess's christening party. But out of the stupid suit, he was what-he-was: A pauper. And, *anyway*, the monkey-suit was an absurd outfit... it looked idiotic the way he wore it, with tousled hair and *without* shoes and stockings. So Stormbuckler took off the foolish attire and found-out his trusty, bedraggled, remnants from below the bed, where he'd stuffed them on his first night at The Swan. *Belongings!* What was the point of them?

~

Stormbuckler met the truculent servant on his way down the creaky stairs to the exit. 'Are you going now, sir?' asked the man. He gave Stormbuckler the once-over. 'Had enough? Not leaving for good, are you, sir? There's still cash in the kitty... Will you not come back for more?'

'I'm out for a short while...' Stormbuckler told him. 'I'll be back.'

'You'd better be, mate...' The servant held his nose because of the pong emanating from Stormbuckler's threads. 'And it's not Wednesday yet! I will lose my tanner if you go today. My wages are riding on your back.'

'See you later,' said Stormbuckler.

'Oh yeah, very likely...' said the servant. He returned a mocking sneer.

~

Stormbuckler limped into the marketplace and dodged merchants and swarms of customers. The redbrick chimneys of the Lindwürm factories loomed over the space, looking like pustules that discharged blackened suppurations into the air. However, horse droppings, dog-piddle, cabbage slop, slimy fish, and all the other excretions that came from the colourful handcarts that huddled around the square seemed more harmful than any fumes from the manufactory smoke-stacks. Stormbuckler smiled because the effluence of the market reminded him of home — the stench reminded him of his poorhouse piggery.

By the water trough, he located an empty two-wheel cab and looked up at the driver. The driver returned a glare. 'What do you want?' shouted the cabbie. 'Get away from here, you filthy wretch. Keep moving, or I'll take my whip to your hind. Do you hear?'

'I need to go to the home of Mr. Asher-John Lindwürm,' Storm-buckler shouted. 'Will you take me?'

'No, I bloody won't. Sod off. I'll bash your brains in if you get any closer...'

Stormbuckler held out one of the two florins that Master Eagle-hurst had given him for the ride. He took it from his grubby mitts. His pockets had fallen out months ago.

'It's eightpence a mile, mate,' said the driver, when he saw the glint of silver. 'That's one and four pennies in total. Are you willing to spend that much on a ride?'

'Yes, sir. *I am.*'

'Get yourself a square-meal and a bath with those coins. That's my advice. Get some clobber from a rag trader... don't waste money on a ride!'

'No, sir, I really *do* need to take this ride. Please let me in...'

The driver took a deep breath, then looked around the plaza as if he half-expected to see a well-to-do stockbroker approaching his carriage, or maybe a banker, or even a parson: just *any fare* that was better than a pauper. But all he saw were bargain-hunters and coster-mongers. 'Yeah, all right, pal. Quick then. Be sure nobody sees you step up. But pass me the silver before we go... pass it *now* through the hatch. I've been bilked before by thieving hedgehogs like you... It won't happen again...'

Stormbuckler stepped in and handed a florin through the hatch. The driver inspected the coin as if he expected it to be made of plaster. He bit it with his front teeth, then stuffed it into a pouch. The driver tugged twice at the reins, and they pulled away with a jolt that knocked Stormbuckler into the wet-leather seat. And they were off.

∾

The hansom soon arrived at a large Regency-style home. Despite the fact that Stormbuckler had never been educated about architecture, he could see that the place was practically in ruins. Plaster had dropped from the walls, disclosing spotty pink blotches that resembled welts caused by a colossal cane, and paint on the front door had collapsed, dripping away like rotten skin on the rump of a sick sow. Stormbuckler assumed the edge of the grass lawn hadn't been scythed for several months because the stone path was strewn with dandelions and stinging nettles. One of two architectural pineapples at the porch had seen better days. The stone fruit looked as if it might topple from its plinth at any moment. 'You sure this is the place?' Stormbuckler yelled. 'It looks like a battered dirt-box to me...' He narrowed his eyes and gazed at the driver through the hatch, 'I might be pauperised, guv'nor, but I ain't a complete fool. This is not the home of a prosperous industrialist, is it? It's the home of a down-at-heel curmudgeon. I demand to be taken to the millionaire's *palace*, not this chaotic ruin. Take me to the precise place I asked for...'

'Believe me, friend, this is the precise place you asked for. I vow, on my mother's grave, heaven celebrate her memory... that this is the address you begged me to brung you— *this* is the home of the American industrialist.'

Stormbuckler shook his head and threw a grumpy scowl at the man. He shoved the side door and pitched his bad leg out of the carriage.

'Do you want your change?' shouted the driver.

'Keep hold of it. *Wait here,*' Stormbuckler instructed. He resolved to look around the place first, before he'd return to the carriage and angrily express his opinion of the driver.

Meanwhile, the cabbie glanced at the two threepenny bits he was about to hand-over as short-change, and he said: 'Erm? I can't wait forever, mate. I'll be honest; this change won't provide for a trip back to town.'

'I have another,' declared Stormbuckler. He held his second florin aloft for the fellow to see. 'Will you wait?'

'I suppose so,' responded the driver, although he extended a lengthy sigh. 'But not all day, right? Don't be long... I have more suitable customers waiting for me back in the square. Just dash up to the door, grab your alms, and dart back here. Hurry!'

Stormbuckler nodded, fully supposing the hansom cab would turn around and rattle-away the instant he turned his back. But he staggered along the untidy drive, anyway, heading for the tatty front door of the rundown mansion. But then, curiously, Stormbuckler crouched to one side. He found an inconspicuous place to duck, under the shade of a dim hedge. *What am I thinking?* he mused. Even the cab driver assumed he was a filthy hobo, so the household employees would *certainly* be sceptical... they'd see him as an unsavoury down-and-out who came to solicit handouts. He anticipated they'd chase him away. They might even take a broomstick to his behind — or set the hounds on him. The prospect made him shiver. So, instead of thumping on their front door, as he had originally planned, Stormbuckler chose to take a more circumspect approach to the property. He scurried around the border of the building and searched for a servant's entrance, where he hoped he might present himself to a sympathetic scullery-maid who would take pity on him, and perhaps allow him inside.

Stormbuckler adhered to a set of deep cart-ruts that brought him to three tall doors that were attached on the front of a large out-building. He lingered by this odd-looking building for some time, and rolled his shoulders. He was about to proceed again when a hand snatched out from the darkness and dragged him by the scruff of the neck. The abrupt jerk surprised him so much he almost hopped out of his skin. 'What the fox — ' he blurted. He craned his neck to see who had stolen up behind and attacked him in such a harsh manner. His encroacher turned out to be *even more* astonished than he was! Her eyes were full as saucers, and her jaw sank low, allowing her face to take an oddly fishy appearance.

'It's *you...*' she suggested, drawing her snatching fingers away from his neck, 'What the holy heck are *you* doing here?'

Stormbuckler rubbed his shoulder and frowned. His attacker was the girl named Mayotte. 'I could charge you with the same question,' he grunted. 'Everybody's seeking you... why are you hiding here? What are you up to?' He gave an irritated snarl.

'I can explain, ' whispered the girl. 'But not now, because it's complicated. Come into the hedges and duck-down.'

Stormbuckler produced a blank look and moved away.

'Get back over here...' she urged. She extended her arm again, this time to snag his elbow and to lug him into shadows. Once they were submerged into darkness, Mayotte drew a protracted breath before she spoke again: 'Actually, you're the last character I expected. What are you doing here?'

'Um?' Stormbuckler scraped his head. 'I came to find *you*. But now I've found you. So I'll be off. Bye!'

'Hold on, *hold on*. Why did you come *here*, exactly? That's what I'm asking. What made you think I'd be *here*? More to the point, *who else* knows I am here? '

'Well,' Stormbuckler proceeded to scratch his head faster. 'To be honest, I don't think anybody knows you're here; nobody would have guessed it. Would they? You're not presumed to be here, actually, right?'

'Well, no,' Mayotte shrugged. 'But neither are you. But you are here... so that thinking explains nothing...'

'Erm? Master Eaglehurst... his gut is tied into knots over you... he's worried sick because he thinks you walked out on him. The man is overwrought. He's beside himself with apprehension...'

'Is he?' Mayotte presented a little grin. 'The poor little hart....'

'You've been leading him on. Haven't you? And that ain't right, is it? But who am I to get involved? *Anyhow*, the kind young gentleman handed me some coins and instructed me to come out to *this place*.'

'Why? Why didn't he come here himself to get me? I still don't understand! Why did he send you? *You*, of all people? Why?'

'Stop charging a million and one questions at me!' snapped Stormbuckler. He gave a petulant pout. 'The young gentleman says he's in trouble with Mr. Siebert. He claims he isn't allowed out of the office. I got bored waiting at the inn. So I didn't mind coming to find you.'

'Why *here* though... of all places?'

'To ask Mr. Lindwürm if he'd seen you or heard from you... since you had been missing for days... Master Eaglehurst reckoned that even if Mr. Lindwürm didn't know where you were right now, at least he could provide an address we might check.'

'I see,' said Mayotte. She nibbled her bottom lip. 'That makes sense. The puppy is in love with me, isn't he? He's doing his best to find me. I suppose that was a legitimate way to go about things.'

'Come back with me,' jabbered Stormbuckler. 'Master Eaglehurst is depressed. You must come back and settle this.'

Mayotte dismissed the thought with a shake of her hand, then she tweaked his shoulder. 'How did you get here?' She studied his eyes.

Stormbuckler recoiled from her fingers. 'I came by hansom...'

'Where is the carriage now?'

'Stood in the lane, opposite, I suppose.'

'Clumsy,' she responded. She tapped her thumbs together.

'Why?' Stormbuckler threw a black look. 'What do you mean: *clumsy*. And another thing: you've no right to handle me. Stop grabbing at me! I hardly know you. So keep your deceitful hands to yourself.'

Mayotte ignored the tone of his disapproval: 'You must send the cab elsewhere right now... someone will notice it standing there and we can't take that risk.'

'Aren't you coming?'

She picked at her earlobe, then shook her head, 'No. I must stay here. I'm waiting for someone.'

'Who? I'm baffled... ' offered Stormbuckler. 'I was told you were missing, but now I have found you. Though you are skulking about Mr. Lindwürm's private yard, for some peculiar reason. And you inform me that you will wait. Yet Master Eaglehurst has searched high-and-low for you. And, what's more, I've been expecting to start my new life. But in the meantime, the whole world has paused for you... When will you allow us to begin? Who the hell are you to keep us all holding on? Why have you been missing this while?'

'Missing? Well, I haven't been missing! I have been here. It's a bit too complicated to explain...'

'I see.' Stormbuckler gave a heavy sigh and rolled his eyes.

'What does that expression mean?' she asked. 'Why do you look at me with such disapproval all the time?'

'I think you know why...'

Mayotte stamped her foot, 'If I knew why, I wouldn't have asked you, would I? Dimwit.'

'Dimwit, am I? Yes, I suppose I *must be*. I suppose Master Eaglehurst is a dimwit *too*. For falling in love with you. So is everyone. We're *all* dimwits. Everyone and anyone who ever worried about you. Everyone and anyone who was ever persuaded by your conniving. Everyone and anyone who stupidly took what you said to be true. We're *all* dimwits! You are just an artful, opportunistic, devious, Janus, aren't you?'

'How dare you...' Mayotte prepared slap him across the face, but held her temper: 'This is crazy! It is total madness. I barely know you, yet we seem to fight like leverets.'

'I agree,' mumbled Stormbuckler. 'If you're not coming back, what do I tell Master Eaglehurst? What explanation could I offer?'

'Erm, do not tell him anything... not yet. I have another important and desperate problem to deal with. It's critical in fact, possibly a matter of life and death.'

'Oh?' Stormbuckler wrinkled his nose as if he detected another bad pong, another of her outrageous lies. 'Go on,' he muttered, 'You may as well indulge me...'

Mayotte crossed her arms and inclined her head. She was at the point of telling him about Toad Blackwing, but his last remark prevented her telling the entire story. Why should she tell him anything? He was a total stranger. She owed him no loyalty, and he owed her none in return. She decided she did not need to tell him the complete story, not yet: just the little he needed to know at this stage. Mayotte chose her next words carefully: 'You could do me a favour — a huge favour — it needs to be done. And it needs to be done *now*. I think you are the best person for the task. Once it's done, I'll go back to Master Eaglehurst. I will make it up to him, I promise. I'll compensate you too. If that's your worry. It is my commitment. You have my word on it.'

Stormbuckler rubbed his neck, then wrinkled his brows: 'Go on then. What is it this time?'

'Go back to your hansom and ask the driver to take you to the Red House on Spriggs Lane. Do you have cash? I can give you a florin.' She took a silver coin from a broad pocket on her apron. Stormbuckler gaped at her garb and saw she was dressed as a maid, this time, in a servant's uniform. And this was not her normal get-up. Before, each time he'd seen her, she'd been dressed as a rich lady.

'Why are you dressed *like that*?' Stormbuckler asked. He tilted his head to one side and gave a probing look.

'It's a complicated story,' Mayotte said, with a shrug. 'Another long story I don't have time to explain right now...'

'I believed you were a senior person in Mr. Lindwürm's organization...' hissed Stormbuckler. 'I believed you were a boss-lady. But all this while you have been a maid-servant?'

'Yes, and well, *no*. I don't know. Maybe. Er? Perhaps it's both. Actually, I'm as confused as you. Appearances can be deceptive, can't they?'

'I should say-so...' Stormbuckler huffed. 'I'm starting to think you misled me *all along...*'

'Look,' Mayotte said, with a frown. 'I know how this looks. I know it's confusing —I know you are disconcerted — but things will get resolved, trust me. You'll get your job at the plant. I'll get hitched to Master Eaglehurst. Mrs. Oldcorne, my employer, will be compensated for her efforts. And Mr. Lassiter will get his comeuppance... and, *well*, everything will turn out for the best. Trust me! After all, you are a talented artist, aren't you? I managed to get you a job, didn't I?'

'Yeah, you said all those things before. Yet, look at me now: I'm sneaking around someone's grounds, hiding in rags, and I'm being continually prodded by a sharp-practising *mountebank*.'

'Is that what you *really* think of me?'

'Here we go again...' said Stormbuckler, he rubbed his neck. 'Boxing like a pair of leverets.'

'I'm sorry. Yes, I guess that, from your perspective, things are a bit muddled...'

'A *bit* muddled? Hah! That's an understatement.'

'Let me finish... if you do this assignment for me, everything will work out fine. I'm sure of it. Will you do it?'

'Go on then, what must I do *this time*?'

'Take your cab to the Red House on Spriggs Lane, yes? Once there, go to the side door... see if *he* will come in with you... *he* won't be inside, though... *he'll* be waiting in the back plot. I'm sure *he'll* come, though, and when he does, *he'll* grab you. Once you contact him, bring him here. Bring him *here* to me.'

'Who?' Stormbuckler asked.

Mayotte stamped her foot as she felt suddenly unable to utter his name. 'When *he* comes just give a keyword...' she continued. 'Can you remember a word?'

'Of course I can remember a bloody word,' Stormbuckler clenched his fist. 'I'm not a half-wit. You may not believe this, but I have a brain inside this skull.'

'It's a difficult word,' she said, trying to calm his temper, but getting him even more vexed.

'Try me... for goodness sake, *try me.*'

'When *he* comes to grab you, tell him *this* keyword. Tell him: Abooksigun. Say the keyword exactly that same way. After you say the keyword, tell him Abooksigun needs to see him here urgently. He'll understand what it all means. And why he must come. Bring him *directly* here.'

'A-book-sigun?' repeated Stormbuckler.

'Yes, that's it,' she raised an eyebrow as if amazed by Stormbuckler's unexpected powers of recall.

'I think I can handle it,' Stormbuckler growled. He gave a look of sourness. 'But who is this strange person who has no name? Why won't you tell me? Do you know how super-annoying you can be at times?'

Mayotte eliminated his question by pushing up her nose. Instead, of answering, she said, 'He might not come right away. But please be sure he'll find you sooner or later, so you might need to dash around the side, like you have here, to conceal yourself by a side door. Just like *this*. But when *he* comes, tell him the keyword precisely. Then make sure you bring him directly. Do you have all that?'

'Yes, I have all that. And when this is over, you will tell me who this guy is... right?'

Mayotte gave a little nod: 'Yeah, of course I will. Why are you so doubting? Right off you go. See you later? Yes?'

'What will you be doing while I'm off on this errand?'

'I expect Mr. Lindwürm will leave his house and go into the garage workshop. And that's when I hope to sneak inside to visit his wife...'

'Will you be *outside* when I get back, though?'

'Probably,' Mayotte said. She turned away. 'Off you go, dear. I'll see you later.'

Stormbuckler hurried back to the hansom cab that waited outside the home of Mr. Asher-John Lindwürm. He lifted a bright florin, but the driver shook his head and said, 'Jump on mate, let's settle the other end.'

Once inside the carriage, Stormbuckler hit the roof of the hatch with his bare knuckles.

'What is it?' the driver yelled.

'I need the Red House; do you know it? On Spriggs Lane?'

'Yes, I know the place... I'll do the ride for that two bob. But I ain't giving you more than fourpence change on the grounds you kept me hanging for ten minutes. Is that fair?'

'Fair enough,' said Stormbuckler. 'Let's move.'

16

After an energetic trot, Stormbuckler's hansom carriage arrived at Spriggs Lane to find the Red House. They drew up alongside the residence and Stormbuckler passed the driver a florin before he trod down from the carriage. 'Do you want the pennies I owe?' asked the man.

'Keep them,' replied Stormbuckler.

'Blimey, thanks,' said the driver. 'It proves you can't judge a man by his tatty image... don't it? Gaw' bless you, mate.' He raised his crop, and the cab trundled away.

Across the lane, Stormbuckler viewed a splendid carmine-coloured Georgian country house established a little way from the road and appointed with a stately entrance. A group of delicately chopped lollipop trees had been planted in a separate bed that had been situated inside a fancy courtyard. An opulent-looking set of oblong windows sat in a row above a splendid portico. Each window in this line was framed with a luxurious drape, with each drape pulled back to reveal its golden interior. The panes reminded Stormbuckler of the rectangular slit-pupils that the goats at the poorhouse had for eyes. There were six other 'goat's eyes' on the ground floor. Stormbuckler could tell, right away, that this place was far more remarkable than the tumble-down lodge he'd called upon earlier —

whoever occupied this manor-house was wealthier than Asher-John Lindwürm.

~

Stormbuckler took a long breath, then headed for the house. He lurched along the furthest edge of the driveway, where he discovered a gloomy, olive-brown hedgerow served as a boundary. He drifted along this hedge since he assumed an unorthodox approach to the house would be prudent under the circumstances. Then they might not set their hounds upon him.

As Stormbuckler arrived at the walls of the Red House, he skirted the frontage of the property, to creep around the side edge, hidden by the shade of a maple. He scrabbled under a cluster of stalks, then dragged himself against the crumpled bark of a bay tree. He glanced down at his tired shreds and he smiled; the branches had tugged and yanked at the cloth, and crust from silvery boughs had scattered flecks of powder across the shoulders. He felt pleased he'd changed into rags!

After forcing his way through a thicket, Stormbuckler noticed a side-door. He assumed this must be the servant's entrance. He'd located it: the side door she had mentioned. The door had worn-out frames, clapped-out door boards, and peculiar cooking odours that spilled from the cracks. 'Well, this is it,' he whispered to himself. 'When will the stranger show up?'

Stormbuckler struggled to recall Mayotte's words: *He might not come right away...* that's what she had said. Also: *You'll need to hide by the side door.* He resolved to take this opportunity to rehearse the keyword she'd given him: A-book-sign. Yes, that was it! Stormbuckler uttered the word over-and-over in practice. He could see the side door from his sheltering place... would the forecast stranger come from that door? Or would he come from another direction? Maybe he should get closer to the building? To sit by the rainwater pipe?

Stormbuckler chose to proceed from his well-concealed position to take-up a fresh hiding-place, crammed tight against the rainwater pipe, pushed low, and squashed against a dirty stain that he saw on the wall. So he crept out and found his next waiting spot. In the dirty, worn-out shreds, he became practically invisible against the wall. Once he'd settled into a ball, he closed his eyes and daydreamed of being back in his room at the Swan Inn. He imagined chewing soft slices of pink ham; washed down with malted beer.

∽

Stormbuckler guessed he must have dozed because he felt cold. Further, he became aware it had had turned distinctly murky. He sniffed moisture in the air, so it seemed probable that a remote rumble of thunder had wakened him from his slumber.

He felt along his good shin to notice it tingled, so he stretched-out his good knee, heard the joint click, then rolled his shoulders because they'd gone stiff. It was no good sitting in this damp place for much longer, he decided. His bones had hardened, and he needed to limber his joints; otherwise, he wouldn't be able to spring into action if-and-when this stranger ever arrived. He looked over at the bushes and reckoned it would be drier under the leaves when the storm came. So, with a hefty push, he got himself onto his good leg, shifted his gammy leg around, then rubbed grit from his backside. He was about to move to the shelter offered by the leaves when he heard the first undeniable clap of thunder. The sound splintered the sky, an impressive boom that sent furious thumping echoes across the heavens. Although Stormbuckler couldn't think of anything he might have done to deserve a *reckoning*, looming clouds appeared to portend some sort of punishment.

Stormbuckler pondered the furious sky, then moved his head to take stock of the bushes that would offer some protection from a rainstorm. The leaves narrowed as they prepared to be routed by a brutal wind that boiled above. The branches trembled and squinched.

That's when *he* appeared. The stranger stepped from the side door. For a moment, they stood *face-to-face*.

Stormbuckler regarded a young man, presumably in his mid-twenties. The fellow had jet black hair, a modest nose, mutilated ears, and wide shoulders. The stranger sported a long overcoat worn over bluish breeches, with a silvery vest, and collar and tie. Under normal circumstances, Stormbuckler would have cowered from such a knavish-looking individual. So, for a split second, Stormbuckler contemplated running into the nearby bushes. But, instead, and possibly *against* his better judgment, he caused himself to look bigger by stretching-out both arms. Then he carried his chin high, and thrust-out his chest. Stormbuckler did all these things to offer the man an aspect of supreme confidence. While he did these movements, Stormbuckler yelled the word: 'A-book-sign.'

The man approached with determination, and Stormbuckler learned, in the fateful second that followed, that the man was armed with a long-barrelled gun. The stranger twisted his arm in a smooth, well-practiced motion, striking Stormbuckler in the face with the weapon's butt. Stormbuckler was knocked to the ground instantaneously because the hit was so quick and precise. He heard the bone in his nose splinter, tasted blood in his mouth, and then felt woozy.

Stormbuckler passed out.

17

Stormbuckler became aware that a gang of men had seized him and were lugging his body somewhere. He surmised from the voices that there were three of them. Not just the one who had appeared from the door. He presumed the fellow who came out of the house was their boss, because he yelled the orders. The other voices sounded subordinate.

'Who is he?' one assistant asked.

'Looks like a wretched vagabond,' said another.

'A vagrant trying his luck...' declared the boss. 'A foreigner. He used a foreign word when he *came at me...*'

'Came at you? This urchin? This foreign muck? He came at you?'

Stormbuckler felt a boot slam into his ribs.

'Yeah. Aggressive he was, *too...*'

'Well, they are, aren't they? These foreigns are always aggressive, ain't they? It's in their blood, ain't it? This one looks to be Ottoman, or perhaps Persian.' Stormbuckler was awarded another kick, this time in the groin, for *looking* Ottoman or Persian. 'Take him to the back and *finish him...*'

'*Finish* him?' queried the youngest voice.

'Yes, you heard. Bang *bang!* Nobody is going to miss a derelict, are they? We're doing society a service... disposing of unwanted vermin.'

Stormbuckler heard snickering all round, while the youngest one said, 'Yes, well, when you look at it like that it makes sense...'

'Can you imagine what Lassiter would do if he heard we freed an Ottoman interloper who had charged one of his guards? He'd go raving hysterical...'

'Yeah, he'd go altogether a-poppy-lectic!' the other voice announced. 'He'd roast our nuts.'

'He'd boil our skulls,' admitted the youngest.

'So let's be smart, yeah? Let's take the Osmani round the back and finish him, yeah?'

～

After the discussion, Stormbuckler felt his limbs wrenched and twisted, as he became dragged along hard ground. Then he was hauled onto his back, so cold rain splashed across his blood-soaked face. It was as if heaven wept with compassion. As they pulled him down a garden step, he felt his spine slip along the gravel, then his head hit a hefty object. For a brief while, the three males lowered his limbs, as if they braced to do something. Stormbuckler drew a deep breath and listened for any sign, any inkling, that would alert him to what might follow. He identified the odour of tobacco in the air, revealing that whatever the gang was planning, it could be suspended for a smoking break. This postponement offered Stormbuckler some optimism and time to recuperate. He tried everything he could to revitalize his fighting spirit or, at least, strengthen his flight response.

His heart rate strengthened, his sphincter relaxed, and his temple throbbed. He began to sweat and, though he wasn't notably hot, he was comforted by the big raindrops on his face.

～

Once they'd finished their smoke, the men returned attention to Stormbuckler's broken body. They grabbed him under the armpits, and he heard one man hiss: 'Don't get too close...'

His teammate said: 'Yeah, his type carries parasites... crab and lice... He doubtless *peached his pants*, the dirty sultan.'

'That's foul,' said another man, so hammered a knee into Stormbuckler's groin. 'What a revolting waste of space...'

'Indeed! let's push him against the wall and give him all the barrels at once...'

'What? Like a firing squad?'

'Yes, it will be fun, right?'

'Yes. But how will we get the maggot to stand up straight?'

'Lean him against the wall...it doesn't matter if he *sags* a bit.'

'Don't we blindfold him?'

'Nah! They only blindfold the honourable ones. Scum like this one doesn't deserve privileges.'

'How do you know all this stuff?'

'I'm interested in killing, ain't I?'

So the men propped Stormbuckler up against what felt like a stone wall, and despite his knees cracking and hips swaying, he discovered that his bad foot had been twisted in such a way that it stuck under his good leg, so he stood in more-or-less a vertical position. So, almost steady on his own two legs for the *first time* in his pathetic life, their wretched prisoner now faced an impromptu firing squad.

Stormbuckler attempted to open his eyes, but found they were clogged with blood and salty tears. The gangsters had left his arms dangling, so he drew up a limp fist and he rubbed a damaged knuckle against his brow. It took a lot of effort, but it was useful because, when he opened an injured eye, he saw his attackers. Two young lads were about fifteen paces away. Both had their rifles pointed at his heart. Stormbuckler mumbled, 'Abooksigun.'

Then there was a colossal boom.

∿

Stormbuckler heard the massive crash from his side.

'What are you doing?' he heard the boss man yell. It seemed the man in charge had returned from whatever he'd been previously doing, and he'd fired a warning shot at *his own men*.

The boss-man seemed maddened by his underlings, 'What do you think you two are bloody-well doing? Have you both gone flaming mad?' There was a momentary pause in proceedings as Stormbuckler listened to sounds of angry shoving. 'Not here, *not here!* Did you two took leave of yo' senses? What's wrong with you boneheads? Can you imagine what Lassiter would say if he saw a scattering of shotgun holes in *the walls* of his fine house? Are you both nuts? What did I tell you? I said *take him down the back*, didn't I?' the boss-man shouted.

'Sorry,' came the youngest of the guys.

'Carry him *right* to the back — right to the end bit of Lassiter's land, where you're not overlooked, where people can't see from the road. Good Claude! You don't have a working brain 'tween you, do you? Once you have him down the *far end*, way out of sight, get him onto his knees and *pop-pop* into the brainbox. That's how to whack someone! Nice and simple, *pop-pop*. Do I have to supervise the whole time? Do I have to think of everything? After you've done the deed, find a sack, put the bones in the sack, then throw the sack in the river.'

'I'm sorry,' said the other thug. 'We'll do that directly.'

'I'll stay here to be sure no one else comes by. What jokers you turned out to be...'

Stormbuckler found himself half lifted, half dragged, and drawn from the wall, to be hauled across the garden lawn, his toes dragging in the turf, to the end of Lassiter's land. He did his best to see where he was being brought, though his eyes kept giving out, and the storm clouds overhead blackened the sky and made it troublesome to see. Eventually, after lots of snorts and bellyaches, the two subordinate henchmen delivered Stormbuckler's body to the far end of the land, where trees and shrubs reached out to create a natural boundary to the property. 'Here?' The younger one asked.

It seemed the other one glanced back towards the house to get guidance from his boss, though it was too dark to see him. 'I presume,' he replied, 'Let's get him further into the bushes. Out of sight. Under those rugged branches...'

'Righty ho...'

They mauled Stormbuckler's body down a modest dip, where he felt twigs scrape his head.

'Here?'

'Yes, this will work. Boy! I'm totally exhausted by all this lugging. I didn't expect him to be so heavy. I'll have a smoke first. Get my breath. This Osmani is weightier than a sack of corn.'

'Yes, *he is...*' responded the first. He kicked Stormbuckler in the shins for *being too heavy.*

'Let's get him on his knees before we have our smoke. I'm still wild as a wet hen over this hog-pickle... I need a smoke to steady my hand. Look, now it's started to rain harder and the baccy'll get wet! I need to grab me a drink at the tavern and wash me ruddy hands.'

'Me too.'

'Let's have a quick smoke, then get it over with.'

They shifted Stormbuckler onto his knees and he felt a hand snatch at his hair and shove his head down hard. He submitted, to put himself into prayerful position. 'Look, the Ottomani is appealing to his foreign god...'

'Ha-hah.'

It was then that the creature rushed from the undergrowth. The predator moved as quickly as the wind, as suddenly as a panther, and as quietly as a nighthawk.

The creature flew at thugs with unstoppable fury. Like a hot-blooded timber-wolf with a score to settle.

∽

The attack on the two henchmen was swift and lethal. It was over in the glint of a razor-sharp knife-blade. And, after it was done, Stormbuckler's limp body was lifted from the ground by the half-man creature, to be hauled over a wide shoulder and then carried away from the blood-soaked madness.

When Stormbuckler was dragged onto the wild thing's back, he saw a hatchet-like weapon in the scary creature's hands, and glimpsed a bloodied knife that the creature returned to a belt loop. 'Abooksigun?' he asked.

'Where is she?' demanded the half-man creature.

Stormbuckler opened his eyes to see the wounded attackers' bodies, now shattered and sprawling in the mud. Rain pelted their battered bodies.

The half-man moved skilfully through thick under-growth, taking Stormbuckler's shattered body *away* from Lassiter's land. They pushed deep into dense woodland.

'Abooksigun...' Stormbuckler muttered again. He hung limp over the shoulders of his half-man rescuer.

'Where is she?' the half-man asked. 'Do you know where Abooksigun is?'

'The girl?' muttered Stormbuckler. 'Mayotte?'

'Yes, the girl. I expected her to come. Not you. Who are you? Why did you come in her place?'

'We have to go back to her,' Stormbuckler replied. 'She may be in danger. We have to get back *now*. Back to the place where she waits...'

'Not that way...' the half-man said. 'The lane leads to murder. I know how to circle around the big Red House. Then you will guide me to her...'

'Yes, we must get back,' Stormbuckler sobbed.

'Patience, chipmunk,' chuckled the half-man. 'I have you safe now, Tònikwsëma.'

Somehow, the half-man, half-creature found a tangled route that led them back to the causeway and then onto a cobbled road that Stormbuckler hoped would bring them back to town. In the poorhouse they said: 'fortune favours the plucky,' so Stormbuckler thumped his knuckles on his saviour's shoulders and shouted, 'Let me down, let me fall.'

The half-man twisted his back to unload Stormbuckler's body by the side of the road. He collapsed into a clumsy sprawl, then rolled headlong into a muddy ditch. 'Thanks,' he murmured through clenched teeth. 'We need to get a cab.' And, with those simple words of resolution, Stormbuckler staggered into the centre of the pitted road like a jaded billy-goat. He stood in one of the muddy ruts and wobbled on his feeble legs.

A carriage approached, veered left and right, then lunged *towards him*, rushing to the Abbey River. The driver didn't stop or even attempt to slow, but instead he shouted: 'Get out of my way, drunken fool.'

After the near-miss, Stormbuckler looked at the half-man, half-creature and both realised they were as bedraggled as each other. Now that he studied the half-creature more closely, he saw that he wasn't a wolfman or half panther *at all*... but just an elderly man. The more Stormbuckler scrutinised the fellow, the more he realised his rescuer was quite old. His skin had wrinkled, his eyes had sunken into his head, and his long white hair had fallen like snow sheets across skeletal shoulders. He was also dressed *unusually*. Patchwork textiles were haphazardly sewn onto fibrous leather stripes. The man wore two belts around his waist, one equipped with a sheath that held the brutal knife that he'd wielded during the rescue, and the other took an axe.

'If anyone stops to pick us up, they'll need their brains testing,' mumbled Stormbuckler, though he remained fixed in the centre of the road, fists clenched, with his chin lifted. He tried again.

The next carriage was about to launch precisely at him, just the way the earlier one had, but, at the last moment, he heard the driver shout, 'Whoa there!' The driver brought the transport to a muddy stop. 'Did you hail?'

'Yes, we must go to Asher-John Lindwürm's house. Do you know it?'

'Two of you?'

'That's correct.'

'Two bob, mate. You got that?'

'Yes.'

Stormbuckler gestured for the old man to come out of the ditch. Once the old man arrived, Stormbuckler pushed him up the doorstep, bundled him inside, then forced his hips onto the wet leather seat. Afterwards, Stormbuckler fell in, bad leg first, and he bounced alongside.

'It's a good job it's *you*....' remarked the cab-man. 'I recognized you from before, mate... Otherwise I would never have stopped. Not in this weather, not with you looking like *that*. Gad, it's lashing out there. I almost didn't see you. You look like you've been through the Battle of Balaclava.'

'I have,' Stormbuckler told him. 'And thanks for stopping.'

'Who's your new partner?' The driver looked through the hatch. 'He seems distant. Like he's not all there.'

'They call me Blackwing,' replied the old man. 'Toad Blackwing. Of the Leni-Lenape nation ...'

'I never heard of it, pal. Right, hold on to your braces, let's be off...' And with those words, the hansom pitched away.

18

By the time they arrived at Mr. Lindwürm's rag-stone manor, the rain had ceased peppering the roof of the hansom and the storm-clouds had parted to leave a velvety, navy-blue glow in the cold air. Stormbuckler passed his last florin through the hatch to the driver, and Toad Blackwing opened the side door and left the cab, followed by Stormbuckler. As the hansom pulled away, the old man said, 'When will I see Abooksigun, chipmunk?'

'She's here,' he said. He ushered the elderly man across the muddy track to the front of Mr. Lindwürm's residence.

'She is inside?'

'Not that easy. She's around the back, by the side. We have to be furtive. We must sneak around the edge.'

Toad Blackwing seemed oddly satisfied when he heard this news. He grinned: 'Well, I can be sneaky.'

So they broke through a hole they found in the perimeter fence, then approached the house, using the far edge for cover. After that, they followed the cart-ruts that coursed toward the front doors of the tall building that Stormbuckler had supposed Mr. Lindwürm used as his carriage shed. Stormbuckler took Toad Blackwing into the darkness, along the far-side of the wooden structure.

'*Over here...*' came a female voice from the shadows. They

followed the sound and located Mayotte. She hunched under the leaves of a laurel. Although she had found refuge from the storm, her maid's uniform was saturated by the rain. 'Where have you been?' she complained. 'I'm soaked to the bone... What took you so long?' But then she spied Toad Blackwing behind, she said, 'Thank goodness you found him. I've been quite worried about him.'

'Will you take me to my daughter, Abooksigun?' asked the old man. 'I am eager to see her.'

'Yes, I know. But *not yet...*'

'Why not? When? I am impatient to see her...'

'Daughter?' asked Stormbuckler. 'What's all this about a daughter? You said nothing about a daughter.'

'Good heavens, grant me patience,' whispered Mayotte. She gazed at the youth: 'What have you been doing?' She examined Stormbuckler's hair. It was matted with blood; his eyes were half-closed, and his nose looked as if it had been smashed by a cricket bat. 'You look as if you've been brutalized in a dog-pit.'

'Yes, I disagreed with some guys at the Red House... and it's all your fault...'

'*Silence*,' snapped Toad Blackwing. 'I sense movement...'

Everyone held their breath and remained still as the side door of the house opened and a man stepped out. He checked the air by holding out a palm. When he seemed satisfied the rain had ceased, he bent to pull on a pair of work-shoes left by the step.

'Who is that?' whispered Toad Blackwing. They observed an unremarkable man, perhaps in his mid-thirties. He had short black hair and rolled-up sleeves.

'That is the famous Mr. Lindwürm,' Mayotte suggested. 'He's the owner of the place. He caused my delay. Once he goes into his garage, we can sneak into the house...'

'Then you will take me to my daughter?'

'That's the plan...'

'Is she expecting me?'

'Um? Not exactly. In fact, I don't suppose she's expecting anyone. That's why we must be cunning.'

'Oh, good,' said Toad Blackwing, 'I can be cunning.'

'Does anyone want to explain to me what is going on? This is all *news to me...*' muttered Stormbuckler. He threw a frown.

'Shh!' Mayotte banged him on the shoulder. 'Wait here...'

'Here?'

'Yes, of course wait here! You must keep watch on the garage, to be sure Lindwürm stays inside.'

'And if he comes out?'

'Um, I don't know... erm? Think of something to delay him, obstruct him if you can, make a huge din, make a racket, make a big noise that will alert us... create a diversion so we can make a break for it...'

'I assume, in that case, that he won't be over-pleased to find you've broken into his gaff?'

'Not over-pleased, you're right. He keeps her, his wife, he keeps her a prisoner... she's a prisoner up there...' Mayotte pointed to an upper window.

'A prisoner?' asked Stormbuckler, gazing at the window that a back light had illuminated.

'I'm sorry — there's no time to explain. Are you ready?' Mayotte threw a hand onto Toad Blackwing's shoulder.

'Yes, I am ready to sneak,' replied the old man.

'Good, and you know what you're doing?' she asked Stormbuckler.

'Yes, I am instructed to wait here and watch the garage... And I'm supposed to make an immense hullabaloo if it looks like Lindwürm is heading indoors. '

'Perfect, good. Everyone knows they're part. Let's move out. Good luck, people.'

Stormbuckler discovered a better vantage point, facing Mr. Lindwürm's garage, after Mayotte and Toad Blackwing had gone to crawl into the main house using the servant's entrance. He rested with his back against a crisp tree and his buttocks on a bed of pine needles that had been dumped by an inept gardener. He licked his wounds, both literally and metaphorically, once he settled. As he wiped away the dried blood from his face, he relived the ghastly events that had just taken place. It wasn't just the physical anguish of the attack he had to deal with. He also had to grapple with the mental and horrifying image of those ruined and destroyed bodies sprawling in the mud following Toad Blackwing's intervention. In Stormbucklers's mind, the encounter was already becoming a nightmare-*like* memory, a fragment of texture that became practically imaginary. Stormbuckler accepted that the rainstorm, coupled with his fatigue, increased this dreamlike impression of events. However, when he tasted blood on his fingertips and felt along his cracked ribcage, he realised his experiences were not just genuine, but also eclipsed any other sensations he had felt in his life. They say you're never more alive than when you have faced death, And likewise they say that an end is also a beginning, and he now started to guess this meant when a person had defrauded death. So, at that moment, young Stormbuckler felt like as if was at the advent of something new and amazing: at a strange equinox between chapters in life. He didn't feel wiser, or more certain, or even better blessed than he'd been before. Stormbuckler just felt changed. He also felt lucky! But, then again, he *always* felt lucky... this sensation wasn't new to him. They'd lecture about *being lucky* in the poorhouse. Their slogans included things like: don't prepare for something you may never receive; focus on what you might *give* — not on what you might take; the key to endurance is hope; and Stormbuckler's favourite poorhouse slogan of all: find gladness in invisible things because only those things bring legitimate fortune.

19

Mayotte advanced stealthily up the servant's staircase. She heard soft squeaks and padding sounds made by the leather sandals of Toad Blackwing, who followed right behind.

She surfaced by a casing and adjacent to a cabinet, on the upper level of the house, then crept out onto the spacious landing that was fed by the principal staircase. She turned to see if the old man had climbed the stairs without difficulty and was surprised to find that he was right behind her. He was a very *sprightly* old man! Mayotte located the master bedroom and its associated suite and selected the service door, to open it. But before entering, she stopped to whisper something to Mr. Blackwing. 'Tuck yourself inside here, so you're not seen by servants on the landing. It's a changing room. I'll go to see if your daughter is there, and I'll try to explain what we're doing in her house. Do you mind waiting for a moment? We cannot just break in and alarm her, can we? I need you to be tactful. Can you behave? I don't want to panic her... do you see? We need to be cautious.'

'Very well, Abooksigun.'

With those words, Mayotte left the elderly-man in the ante-room. She tiptoed into the main part of the bedchamber, to locate the hidden, special alcove, that she knew contained Mrs Lindwürm's enormous four-poster bed.

Mayotte approached the alcove and discovered what she thought was a sleeping woman on a mattress. The figure lay spread-eagled on the silky sheet, dressed in the same 'lounging clothes' that Mayotte had seen on her first visit— loose-fitting slacks, a satiny blouse, and a silvery turban. Mayotte was completely fascinated by the motionless figure, who seemed so exquisitely acquiescent in her wonderfully angelic repose, that for several seconds she couldn't speak. So it was a surprise when the reclining figure spoke first. 'Is that you?' the slumbering angel asked.

'Um? I'm sorry, Ma'am, it's not your maid. And it's not your husband, it's *me...*'

The woman wakened from her doze to stretch her shoulders and take note. 'Isn't it Mayotte?' The lady raised her head. Her black hair glistened as she shook it away from her face. 'It must be you, isn't it? 'Please come closer so I can see your face...'

'Madam, please do not be alarmed,' Mayotte inched towards the bed. 'I have someone with me who is anxious to see you...'

'Yes, I was expecting you to come-by. My husband told me that he asked you to visit. Call me Arrow-Miaow, please. Madam is too formal. Did you say you brought someone?'

'Thanks *ma* — I'm sorry — aero-miaow-rah,' Mayotte tried to draw her tongue around the peculiar name. 'You don't mind, do you?'

'Mind what, my dear?'

'That I brought someone...'

'Who is it?

Toad Blackwing entered the room at that same moment. The woman was taken aback by his appearance. It was as if she saw a ghost. A ghost that had returned from a different time. Her eyes widened as she took a long breath. Arrow-Miaow put her palm to her breast, and stated: 'Eche tamwe, Sakimawo? Ahinu-kuk kitakimaike. Amànkamèkòk ëkèk aone...'

The old man went to the bed and sat by the woman. She looked into his eyes, and they held hands, his in hers. Mayotte restrained herself, aware that she should not interfere in this affectionate *reunion*. So, while Toad Blackwing and Arrow-Miaow gazed into each other's eyes, demonstrating recognition and appreciation, Mayotte looked-on politely.

Eventually, after a lengthy silence, Toad Blackwing turned his head to speak to Mayotte. 'This is not my daughter, Abooksigun...' He seemed displeased. 'You have made false representations about this woman. Nothing is more sinful than honeyed words that sow the distortions of deception.'

At first Mayotte smiled, thinking the old man must be joking. But Blackwing's eyes remained clear. His expression was unshakable. She frowned, scratched an ear, then said, 'You're kidding, right?'

'This female is Aluns Pushish-Mèlimwis...' Blackwing offered these confusing words as if they would clear the matter up. 'This is *not* my daughter. Thus, you have perpetrated a seducement.'

'But? How can that be? I don't understand... Of course this is her!'

'He describes you as a wildcat...' interjected Arrow-Miaow. 'I'm sure he sees you as powerful, yet gentle. Actually, although he uses harsh words *now*, deep down I think he trusts you. I'm sure you had good intentions, but he says he can't be sure what your intentions *are*. Though he wants you to know I am *not* the one he seeks.'

'But who are you? You seem to know each other... I mean, you both speak the same language, don't you? I do not mean to be presumptuous, but don't you think one of you has made a mistake? Many years have passed, perhaps, you don't recognise each other?'

'Oh, I recognize her,' Toad Blackwing observed.

'Yes, he recognizes me,' Arrow-Miaow confirmed.

'I'm confused. If this woman is not your daughter, who is she?'

Arrow-Miaow laughed at the comment. She raised an eyebrow and said: 'He recalls my face from an exceedingly long time ago. From a day that has now passed into the shadows of time. He once visited my village to examine a sick child. I don't know if he told you this, perhaps he didn't because he is modest and lacks pretension... but this gentleman is *our chief*. He's the head of our people. He's grand-ruler of the Leni-Lenape nation.'

Toad Blackwing pulled Mrs. Lindwürm closer and whispered something into her ear. She nodded and said, 'He wants me to tell you he crossed the winter sea to be in this salty place you call home...'

'Yes, yes. I know all those things... we've *already* had that!' Mayotte felt herself getting cross, so banged her fist against her chin, 'I hoped this unification would bring everything *back together*... yet it appears I have provided another dead end... and the story has *uncoiled* itself.'

Chief Toad Blackwing spoke into Arrow-Miaow's ear. The angelic woman brought her hands together then pushed her chin up. 'He asks me to explain why I am here. He wants me to tell you who I am...'

'Go on then...'

'I am unique among my people,' Arrow-Miaow said with a grin. 'That is why the chief remembers my face. My people place great significance on hunting, fishing, tracking, and outdoor activities of all kinds. When I was in the springtime of my life, very young, my elders noticed I was uncommon among children. I have a malady, do you see? I had a disease that could neither be cured nor understood....'

'What is it?'

'I am unique among my people,' she repeated. 'The elders said I was 'a prisoner of my choosing.' They said my condition condemned me to a life of exclusion...'

'Why? What is the illness?' asked Mayotte.

'I have an extreme fear of open spaces. Even abandoning the safety of my bed makes me feel sick, palpably sick. If I am asked to leave my place of refuge, I become gravely infirm.'

'My heavens! That must be terrible for a person of *your*... well, you know, your tradition and heritage...' Mayotte lowered her gaze to take a gulp of air, 'So that's why you don't go out? That's why you're confined to this room?'

'A prisoner of my own choosing...'

'But I thought, *I thought*...' Mayotte allowed her arms to drop by her sides. 'I believed your husband had imprisoned you here. I assumed Lindwürm had confined you to this place...'

'Lindwürm? No, not him, not the great white man. If anything, he has been my best protector. He's been my brave rescuer. A great champion. One winter, he passed through our village, and heard of my plight. He sought me out: he discovered me laid on a bed, inside a shelter. The great white man saw my predicament, and there-and-then he offered to rescue me, to free me... to take me across the salty sea to a better place, a new land where I might stay out of the sun. Where I could remain a recluse. And one day I might be cured by a new type of electric medicine that is not known by *my* people. Of course, our elders were grateful to him because I was a great encumbrance upon them. Moreover, my disadvantage brought ignominy to my parents and shame to my tribe. So, they were pleased to let me go. They allowed me to leave with the white man. He gave me a special sleeping drug so I could make the long sea crossing. And he learned how to feed me with a dripping bag. So we travelled across the salty sea, together. Yes, Lindwürm rescued me... now I am here. I live here with him, so we tell people that we are married, and perhaps we are in some eyes, but most people don't understand our connection ... but we have *never* been intimate. We are not in any typical couple-hood. Our partnership is one of mutual co-existence. That's all. But you may call him my husband, if it helps. And I, his wife.'

'There's no need for you to concern yourself, Abooksigun...' Toad Blackwing said with an air of calm confidence. He rose from the bed.

Meanwhile, Mayotte remained motionless. She gaped at the half-stretched Miaow Arrow lying on the bed.

'You can't address all the world's problems,' the old man added softly. 'And you can't accomplish everything by yourself. I apologise for growling at you. Please accept my apologies. You had no idea what you were doing. I see that now.'

Mayotte listened to the old man's words, but she felt totally incapacitated. She had supposed, wrongly, that this angelic woman had been kidnapped and was held prisoner. But she hadn't. She had supposed, wrongly, that the woman was Lindwürm's wife. But she wasn't. She had supposed, wrongly, that Lindwürm had been a monster to her, and he incarcerated her against her will. But he *hadn't*. And she had supposed, wrongly, that the old man was a crazy geriatric: though now she learned he was a king. How much more had she got wrong? How had she formed all these erroneous notions? Where had all these false theories and perceptions come from? What was wrong with her?

'You will help you find my daughter...' the tribal chief continued. 'I know she must be somewhere on this island. You will help me find her. And the male youth too, the chipmunk, he will also help us. I am certain of these things... The search is not yet over.' Mayotte wanted to agree, and she wanted to shout yes, *yes, yes,* but she was stunned — transfixed — *amazed* by something she had seen on the bed. Whatever it was, the sight made her tremble.

'What is it?' asked Blackwing. Something in her eyes suggested things were wrong. He took her hand. 'What is it that has stupefied you so, Abooksigun? The old man looked into her wide, astonished eyes and he whispered: 'What's got into you? What's wrong? What have you seen?'

Mayotte lifted, unstable, and gazed open-mouthed at something on the bedsheet. She even raised a finger to point at whatever it was that she'd seen, by what had alarmed her so much, but then, at that exact moment, the entire house became inundated by an enormous vortex of buzzing, whirring, and astonishing resonance. All three instantly put their hands over their ears, to protect themselves from the dreadful din caused by spinning, clacking, and spitting sounds.

'My heavens! It's Stormbuckler. It's the hullabaloo,' shrieked Mayotte. 'Stormbuckler has created his commotion...that's what I told *him* to do. It's the signal. It's the signal that Mr. Lindwürm is coming back indoors.'

'Hub-a-lub-boo-boo?' questioned Toad Blackwing, now with equally anxious eyes. 'What is Hub-a-lub-boo-boo?'

'No time to explain, chief, but we must dash...'

Mayotte pulled the old man's arm to get him away from Miaow Arrow's bed.

'See you another time,' declared the angelic woman, in a surprisingly placid tone, given the increasing racket from outside. 'Please call again soon.'

Then, even with the terrible noise going on outside, she dropped backwards onto her sheets and fell into a deep sleep.

20

Stormbuckler became utterly rigid when he heard creaking and grinding noises coming from the large garage doors. *Was Lindwürm on the move?* Stormbuckler felt his pulse quicken and suffered a quiver in his stomach. The American's silhouette appeared near the garage entrance. The figure didn't seem to move towards the house, but vacillated and fumbled around in an almost ambivalent manner. *What was he doing? Dammit!* Stormbuckler expressed his frustration by kicking at the earth with his pegged-leg. The clouds gathered again, and now he saw that the unmistakably dodgy Lindwürm began a new and unexplained activity near the giant doors of his garage. Nothing was going the way Stormbuckler wanted today. He took a deep breath and moved from his safe position to get a better vantage point, though he knew he was *less well* hidden, and had to stretch his neck in the gloom to see what was happening. He felt sploshes of rain hit his head and acknowledged he'd have to think up, fast, some kind of way to hold Lindwürm back if the man made a sudden bolt for the side-door of his house. What had the Mayotte girl told him? *Make a hullabaloo?* Isn't that what she had instructed? He'd have to think about how to do such a thing. Stormbuckler looked to the earth, thinking it possible, though improbable, that a negligent gardener had dumped a large handbell or a functioning policeman's rattle thereabouts. He frowned when all he saw were leaves and lumps of mud. *Maybe he could throw stones at the top window?* Would that be enough to warn them? He looked at the window and thought he glimpsed shapes in the soft light thrown through the drapes, though he couldn't be sure. Besides, there was now a *new* set of sounds — a series of shrieking graunches — and these fresh sounds came from inside from the garage. When Stormbuckler looked anew at the work shed, Lindwürm began opening it up, to reveal a grotesque and ghastly machine that had previously been hidden in the shadowy space within.

Stormbuckler felt a sour taste in his mouth and a sense of dizziness overcame him as an enormous clatter began. It sounded as if a huge, evil beast had come alive inside the garage. The whirring, birring noises began as wild moans but rapidly developed into a clamour of distorted mangles and mechanical blunder. And then the machine itself rumbled out, into nightfall, on countless little wheels of its own: like a crab fish might crawl on its belly, though this crab fish was a decidedly atrophied and mutilated version. Stormbuckler calculated that the base-part of the machine was larger than three altar-tables strapped together, although the motorized creature had a hump. A repulsive hump. Lindwürm sat on this hump, an outgrowth of deformed vertebra, and played with various controls; his protective gloves manipulating gears and silver handles. The driver manoeuvred the blustering contrivance out of the garage and into half-light thrown by the windows from the house. Seen from Stormbuckler's point of view, the machine had the body of a deer-beetle and the tail of a rain-worm, with serrated teeth along the length of its head, and a tusk protruding from one side. The carapace of the beetle was iridescent bronze, with streaks of glossy copper and shiny violet. And the beetle dragged its posterior behind it, like an afterthought. Furious gases expelled into the air from this trailing posterior. As the machine approached Stormbuckler's position, the noise became unbearable. 'Holy armpits! What in heavenly-heavens is *that*?' he gasped. Yet the ghastly contraption had yet to show-off its most extraordinary capability: because as Stormbuckler watched in fear and wonder, the entire hump, that's the bucket shaped bit where the driver sat, *rose* from the beetle's carapace, like the head of a cobra might rise in anger from a snake-charmer's basket. And then it magically twisted and turned like a python's would do. So the driver *rose up* from the base of the machine. The man levitated. Yes, Lindwürm climbed higher, though he remained sat-upon the deformed and monstrous hump. And soon the man was twice as high as the contraption itself and he began weaving and worming on the control-seat, like a mouse sat upon the head of a hooded snake. Stormbuckler could see the arteries and capillaries that led from the base-part of the machine, and upwards, to the elevating hump-part and he guessed these tubes fed the control levers at the very top. Soon enough, Lindwürm sat upon this extraordinary, elevating throne, and reached a point that was higher than a tree. In fact, he reached the same level as the upper windows of his house and Stormbuckler feared he'd be able to see through the windows and glimpse the Mayotte girl *inside*. But the entire contraption set-off again, under its own steam, and propelled itself with blundering blindness along the bumpy tracks that led from the garage doors to the corner of his house.

Once they heard the racket, Mayotte and Toad Blackwing escaped from the house, using the *main* staircase. They left through the *front door*. Mayotte was surprised they didn't meet any serving staff on their way out, but was glad their escape went without a hitch. Once they arrived on the front porch of the property, they caught their breath, then began to dash along Lindwürm's worn-out drive-way and into the lane, where they paused to see an immense beetle-like machine blast around the corner of the house, followed by a shockwave of engine-noise and a great flurry of sparks and steam.

'Is that the hub-a-lub-boo-boo?' asked chief Blackwing, his eyes swollen like a frog. He put a trembling hand on Mayotte's shoulder. 'The monster grunts like a bear and stands tall as willow...'

Mayotte gulped. She said, 'Holy hawkbits... I don't know what that hell-beast is, but it is horrorously scaresome, ain't it? And *yes*, it really does make a hub-a-lub-boo-boo!'

'Should we wait for chipmunk?'

'I don't think so,' Mayotte replied, already breaking into a sprint. 'The monster looks like it's coming straight for us...'

The Chief didn't wait to be convinced. He moved quicker. The old man soon out-paced her. 'Murder and dread...' he shouted. '*Murder and dread.*'

They collapsed in a ditch near the graves at Laleham, and Toad Blackwing pulled Mayotte close. He'd seen many disturbing things in his long life: a lone wolf murdered by a family of raccoons, a wolverine that had become trapped on the fork of a tree and was devoured, breathing, by a troop of skunks; and a bear that took the head off a man with a single, powerful blow. He had crossed the winter sea in an iron ship and seen how ghostly messages could be sent under the waves by asking the words to crawl through an underwater pipe. He'd even seen how a steam locomotive could throw up its own rain-clouds. He'd seen all these things, but never had he dreamed of the hellish things he'd witnessed that evening. 'In all my days — in all my nightmares,' he told Mayotte. 'I observed nothing so diabolical as the things I have seen today.'

'I know,' Mayotte said, still gasping. 'I'm still literally shaking.'

They waited in the ditch until both recovered their courage and vitality. Then Toad Blackwing said, 'What did you see in the bedchamber, Abooksigun? Something scared you... what was it?'

'Earlier?'

'Yes, when we were in Miaow Arrow's room... It was something you saw, something that paralyzed you. But the terrible noise came, so we ran.'

'Oh? Yes, it intrigued me, but it didn't scare me.'

Toad Blackwing searched her face: 'What did you see?'

'When she was laid on the bed, you know, with her pyjama-leg rolled back, Miaow Arrow revealed a mark on her ankle.'

'Did it look like a branding mark?' he asked.

'Yes, I suppose it did. Though I've never seen a branding mark myself, so I can't be sure. But we asked Stormbuckler to create a branding mark for Lindwürm's business ventures, so I'm familiar with the concept. It was more like a tattoo. Like the ink that sailors wear on their muscles. But I've never seen a tattoo upon a woman's body before...'

'Ah-ha,' Toad Blackwing gave a playful smile, 'The *ikto* ...'

'Ikto? What do you mean? Do you know what it is?'

'Yes, the ikto is the sign of the Leni-Lenape people. It's our emblem, if you like. Each of our relatives... all our living blood, all our family, all our relations... *everyone* is marked the same way: with the symbol of the ikto.' Then the old man unwound the long strip of cloth that had been coiled around his lower leg this whole time, to show Mayotte his *own* skin-mark. 'Is this what you saw on Miaow Arrow's ankle?'

Mayotte glanced at the mark, but she wasn't sure. The old-man's tattoo had faded. Also, it looked much smaller than the one she'd seen on the woman's ankle. Besides, it was too dark to distinguish it properly. '*Probably*,' she mumbled. 'When did you get it done?'

'They put an ikto into our skin when we are very young. Beyond our second summer, but before our third.'

'And what is it? Mayotte asked with a grimace. 'It looks awful... *hideous*... like a rock crab with a copper heart.'

Toad Blackwing chuckled at her remark and gave her a playful prod. 'It's the ikto,' he said, 'That's what she looks like to us. The ikto is our symbol of patience. And also our symbol of creativity and flexibility. She reminds us that we have a shadow-being that resides in our depths... a darker side to our personality. The ikto reminds us that we have hidden aspects we dare not think about. We all possess malevolent characteristics and she, our ikto, teaches us we must learn to understand the shadow-being that lurks *inside*. Our ikto reminds us we must control our desires if we want to succeed... The ikto is the one who weaves life. The ikto is the one who teaches tolerance... yet the ikto *also* shows us how to gather the elements, the good, the bad, and even the disconcerting, like the things we witnessed tonight, she teaches us to gather our experiences together so we might create a perfect, albeit delicate, *integrity of being...*'

'Is she a spider?'

'Ha!' Toad Blackwing gave a wink. 'Yes, perhaps she is... I don't know! She's the ikto.'

'Why does she have six legs?'

'Can you count six legs in this light, Abooksigun? If you can, you must have better eyes than me. In fact, you must have better eyes than a woodchuck...' He gave another wink, then wound the cloth back around his ankle.

Mayotte brought her knees together and rubbed the folds of her apron. 'My heavens, I must look an awful mess. I'm wet and covered in grime. My mistress will go mad when she sees me like this. I'll need to go back and rinse this out, and wash —'

'Shush!' he pulled her arm. 'Do you hear that?'

'I hear nothing,' said Mayotte.

'*Exactly*. The sound has stopped. Perhaps the mechanical beast has been conquered by the chipmunk. Or it has exhausted itself?'

'Maybe...'

'We must rescue the chipmunk...'

Mayotte pulled her brows together. 'Must we?' She seemed unsure.

'We cannot abandon him now, can we? But how can we help him?'

'I suppose we can rescue him,' she agreed. She gave a hesitant smile. 'But I'm afraid to go back there...'

'Come, Abooksigun, we must withdraw to my secret hideout. That's where we will plan our next move. Also, I need to demystify Leni-Lenape thought-crafting and talk more about the ikto. Will you come with me to help devise a plan to save chipmunk and locate my daughter?'

'Can the ikto help?'

'Yes, in fact, I think the ikto is the only power that can save our chipmunk now.'

'I did not know things were so serious! Is his life in danger?'

'Not just his life, but *all existence* is in danger if we don't save him. Yes, this is a catastrophic turn of events. If we're not careful, his denial of metaphysical power and lust for mechanical power will unbalance the universe and cause ruin, destruction, and calamity.'

Mayotte's eyes widened as they began their long trek back to town. 'How do you know all these things?' she asked.

The chief smiled. I know *nothing*. My ikto knows it all.'

21

At his angular structure, covered in rough-cut animal skins, concealed behind hedges on the south side of the river, Mayotte lowered her head to pass through the entrance and she sniffed the delightful smell of fresh cut meadow grasses and crunchy reeds.

The old man immediately sat in a cross-legged position, with his back to a cushion made of shaggy fleece. Mayotte sank to the ground opposite. She kicked off her light shoes and allowed her bare toes to knead the fibres of a mat the old man had woven pink sedges. She allowed herself to sink into a soft cushion sheepskin.

'What do you want from the universe, Abooksigun?' Toad Black-wing asked. He didn't look into, or even glance at her face. His eyes remained steadfastly *closed*, as if any response she might provide would be transmitted *via* some unseen medium rather than be articulated by words or gestures.

With a quickness she could not have foreseen, Mayotte felt awkward and silly. 'Um? Me? Just the same as everybody, I suppose. I want to be wealthy, healthy, happy, and successful.' Though even as she uttered these words, Mayotte felt embarrassed and uncomfortable because she *knew* her answer was inadequate. Those words were trite and meaningless. Those silly thoughts carried little emotional weight.

'Are you able to chart your own course freely?' he asked.

'I suppose *not*,' she whispered. She sniffed and rubbed her chin with a knuckle.

'Has the universe given you the freedom to define yourself?'

'I suppose not.'

'How do you balance what you *want* out of life with what you *need* out of life?'

'I thought both were the same thing. Aren't they?'

Toad Blackwing did not answer. He quietly rocked on his knees, very lightly, though he remained thoroughly shut-eyed. He seemed to absorb something that she couldn't puzzle out. *Something* that he tapped into. If pressured to explain his state of being to another person, (was it a quality of being?) she'd speculate he was replenishing his life-force by exploiting an undetectable vein of *innerness*.

Then he said, 'What is the chipmunk, Tònikwsëma, to you? Why do you want to help the youth?'

Mayotte squeezed her brows and bit her lip. 'Um? I don't *actually* know. We seem to be connected, but I don't understand how we can be. Does that make any sense? Our paths appear to be linked. But how? I can't understand why I think that.'

'Yes, your fortunes are interwoven,' commented the old man. 'So perhaps if you help the chipmunk, you help yourself...'

'I hadn't thought of it like that, but now you've said it...'

'What else do you desire? What about the other young man?'

'Master Eaglehurst? Erm? Is that who you mean? If I'm honest, I'm going off him. Is that wrong of me? Oh God! Why am I so pathetically shallow? You must think I'm a useless featherbrain!'

'And what do you owe your bond-mistress?'

'Bond-mistress! Is that what Mrs. Oldcorne is to me?'

'You are her servant. She is your shackler. She coerces you. She is your subjugator, isn't she?'

'I'd never thought of her in that way.'

'Well, is she?'

'Now you have put those thoughts into words, I suppose she is.'

'What do you owe her?'

'Um? I owe her nothing. I have been faithful, constant, and true-hearted for many years. I have laboriously served her all my life. I paid my debt. I owe her *nothing*.'

'So, let me be bold and let me ask my question again,' Toad Black-wing relaxed before he spoke again. 'What do you want from the universe, Abooksigun?'

This time, she didn't hurry to answer. Mayotte closed her eyes, like he did. She rocked her head, like he did. She rolled her fists, like he did. Progressively, a mist cleared from her mind; she saw her aspirations in finer detail. 'I want to chart my course. I want to be freed from indenture. I want to understand myself better. And I want to save the chipmunk named Stormbuckler because his potential and mine are, somehow, connected.'

'Good, Abooksigun. *Very good.* Those are dignified ambitions. I'm proud of you.'

'Um? But how does that help you? Erm? What do you want from the universe, Mister Blackwing?'

'I have completed almost everything I set out to achieve. But one thing remains. I must rescue my daughter from the evil one. That is why I crossed the winter sea to be in this salty place. It is my ultimate purpose.'

'But how can *my* motives and desires help *you* achieve *yours*?'

'Ah, Abooksigun! You presume our fortunes do not overlap... but they do! Oh *yes*, our destinies fold together like paperbark on maple. Our lives are inseparable. Our interlacement is as intricate as any spider web. But *now* I want to speak about how my people consider the universe. I'd like you to try *thought-crafting...*'

Mayotte pressed her eyelids tighter and rocked quicker.

'To a being who expects to interact with the universe in a concrete, physical, and a dynamical way, the fabric of the universe may *appear* mechanical. That is how most pale-faced men see the universe. As a mechanical place. But what if it's not? What if the universe is *not* mechanical? What if the universe is an organic structure that never changes? What if the universe is intangible? What if the universe is indescribable? What if the universe is impalpable?

Every day, we (all of us) get up, intending to complete our mundane tasks that are essential for survival. But what if the most *critical* tasks do not require force or movement? What if the most *critical* tasks involve self-awareness, imagination, and volition? What are the tools we need for such tasks? Yes, physical necessities propel us: we seek water, food, shelter, sleep, and hygiene. We require security. We require a sense of social belonging. That is why I built this shelter. Because, like you, like all humans, I am a chemical being. But what about my spiritual needs? Can water, food, or shelter satisfy those parts of my being? Or must those parts be neglected, or made subservient, by physical requirements? It concerns me that modern man, people like your chipmunk, Tònikwsëma, with his appetite for mechanical systems, might fail to interact with the *unknowable* universe! Because, beyond his chemical requirements, he will also require self-esteem. He will require foresight. He will require curiosity about the things that he cannot easily sense. He will require beauty, both within and without. He will require a sense of motiva-tion. Can the machines that begin to dictate and control his life also help him to achieve and access these barely perceptible things? My people, the Leni-Lenape people, we think not.'

Mayotte rocked, with her eyes closed.

The old man continued: 'My people seek to achieve their goals by pushing past the universe's physical restraints.'

Mayotte breathed deeply.

'My people are willing to take on this daily challenge because we are aware of other options. We attempt to interact with the universe in a way the sky-god intended. Because potentiality — the actions we take that lead to success — potentiality does not need to be concrete or physical. Potentiality does not have to have any physical existence to be of value. Potentiality is an unseen substance. For you to achieve your ambitions, my dear Abooksigun, you must learn and practice *thought-crafting*. Because thought-crafting develops potentiality. And we will begin right away. Here is my next question for you, Abooksi-gun: what is the unsettled mystery? What is the key to this puzzle?'

'Steam shed 7,' Mayotte mumbled.

'You have the answer *already*?' asked Toad Blackwing.

'I do,' she said. Mayotte nodded her head with absolute certainty. 'The key to all this is what they're doing in Steam shed 7.'

'We shall go there tomorrow. That is our way post. You came to it through thought-crafting. I am proud of you, Abooksigun. I'm *enormously proud.*'

22

Mayotte scurried home, her head a fluttering flurry of possibilities.

When she reached the corner of Bridge House, in Clarence Street, a powerful arm wrested her into an alcove. Her cheeks were crushed, her lips squeezed, and her mouth clasped by a man's fingers in black gloves. When she figured out she couldn't scream, or even deliver a whimper, she sought to thresh her arms and waggle her legs in defiance, but the tall man had clenched her into a merciless embrace. When he was fully certain she presented no more struggle, the man very gradually discharged his arrest upon her. As he granted her some movement, Mayotte guessed that any passers-by might assume that what they saw in the alcove was just *another* drunken sailor canoodling with just *another* housemaid outside just *another* tavern. It was a typical sight in a riverside town, and would be unworthy of closer investigation.

Mayotte took a breath once the fellow released his palms from her mouth. 'How dare you lay a finger on me, you dirty hound! I'll see you in the dock for this outrage. I'll have you in shackles for this assault upon my person,' she breathed. She looked up and into the man's face. And although his eyes were obscured by the shadow cast by a wide-brimmed fedora, she spat into his face. Then she hissed like a house cat. The man wore a black coat, fastened by a single white-metal brooch. She saw that his left cheek bore a lone scar, perhaps earned during a duel, but otherwise the man was clean-shaven. Her spittle dribbled down to his lips. The fellow looked to be about forty years old.

'Let me present myself, young lady,' responded the man. He discharged his hold a bit more, but she was still not free to run because he now clamped his knees close to her legs. She struggled but found she couldn't kick out at him. Also, his grip was ready to be clamped across her face anew, if called for. 'My name is Major Taber-nacle Lipsniffle. You may call me Tab. I am sorry to have had to engage you in this undoubtedly discourteous and ill-bred fashion, but we must be on our guard and your wellbeing is my paramount priority. Let me be hastened with my explanation please, dear woman, and straightforward in my advice. My warning is this: please do not attend Lindwürm's steam shed 7.'

'How do you know about that place?' Mayotte demanded, tugging her wrists free. She was surprised that he allowed her fists to be released so easily, so gnawed an index finger.

'Ah! We at the Intelligence Department of the War Office know many things, young lady. We have been watching your progress with interest.'

'You have been watching me?' she asked. 'You filthy hound. I shall report you to the Magistrate.'

'Purely observations, my dear. Nothing improper or voyeuristic, I assure you. But we know that Mrs. Oldcorne asked you to *look into* Lindwürm's activities...'

'How could you *possibly* know that?'

'Erm? She's an unwitting intelligence component in this equation. Put simply, my dear, Mrs. Oldcorne acts as what we call, in this profession, an *inadvertent factor* — that's a person who arranges to look into things for the War Office — but mistakenly assumes she performs some other graceful service. Of course, in her own way, *she does*. We don't tell her everything, naturally. I'm sure she's uniformly circumspect *with us*. But Mrs. Oldcorne has been providing us with information about Lindwürm's activities for several months. We have long suspected that her information is being developed from an insider, a person we would define in this business as an *infiltrant*, because we are quite sure she has not embedded herself into Lindwürm's machinofacturing works under her own false cloak. So we know she must have solicited an aid to do the snooping for her: it didn't take us long to see *your* comings-and-goings and draw straightforward conclusions about your locomotions. And, now, we fear for your safety, young woman, because a whistle-blower has forewarned us of a grave threat, a very *grave* threat, to the Empire. It's a threat that has been wrapped in secrecy in Lindwürm's steam shed 7. So this is a time for pistols and daggers, miss, and not a time for feminine wiles, dainty seductions, and your pretty sophistries, my dear. The time has come for intervention and face-to-face confrontation. Accordingly we must ask you to tiptoe aside from your activities at the works, young lady, and let *us* take over.'

'If all this is true, and you're not merely toying with me, what do you know about steam shed 7? What are they doing there?'

Major Tabernacle Lipsniffle removed a large leather-bound wallet from the inside pocket of his cloak, unfolded it, and presented her with a silvery badge which read Corps of Royal Engineers above a splendid royal cypher. The words 'Sacred Duty' were written underneath, as a motto. By the side of the insignia was a simple white card that read: Major Tabernacle Lipsniffle (RE) is authorised by the Intelligence Department to fulfil the duties of Assistant-Director of Domestic Intelligence for the War Office.

'Doctor Fleetwood-Pinch of the British Association for the Advancement of Esoteric Technosciences gave a report on a technique he called "Bradiant Induction" at last year's Spectral Triggering conference. Fleetwood-Pinch advocated for the technique of transmitting an immensely powerful flame through the luminous substance of an object to promote its intense deflagration in his paper to the B.A.A.E.T. He asserted that this results in instantaneous scintillation and a detonation. Fleetwood-Pinch has since warned the Crown that Lindwürm is attempting to replicate his experiments at steam shed 7. He fears that individuals, perhaps many individuals, will become mortally wounded in these experiments.'

'Oh God!' whispered Mayotte. She shuddered and grew breathy.

'So, I repeat my warning: please do not attend Lindwürm's steam shed 7.'

'Does this mean my employment with Lindwürm is over?' she asked. 'I'm sorry to be thinking about myself at this time. You must think I'm a decidedly shallow person, but I thought I was doing well in the manufactory and this would be my big break!'

'I'm concerned about your safety, my dear. Those men are beasts, and I highly recommend that you sever all connections with Lindwürm and his henchmen. Erm, we might extend you some alternative employment... if you'd be interested.'

'Alternative?'

Major Tabernacle Lipsniffle smiled a jolly grin and dropped his arm from across her shoulders.

Mayotte glanced at his loosened embrace in a doubtful manner. 'What do you mean, *alternative?*'

'Something dignified. Something befitting. Something appropriate.'

'Like what?'

'Your information gathering skills have impressed us. And likewise, we have admired the high-quality material you have collected and communicated back to Mrs. Oldcorne. Do you think you'd be able to provide misinformation to a third party... as well as accurately and effectively retrieve details from them? Would you be able to do both if we were to deploy you into an alternative organisation or household?'

'You want me to spy for you?'

'Why not? You seem proficient at the task... I'd even say you're adept. And we'd provide you with generous allowances. Best of all, you'd be carrying out a Sacred Duty for the Crown.'

'Would I get one of those?' Mayotte asked, pointing a finger at Tab's silver token.

'Let's talk about this job offer some other time. But for now, please observe my warning. Don't go to steam shed 7. I must bid you farewell, but we will meet again. Soon.'

And with those terms, Major Tabernacle Lipsniffle relinquished his embrace on her body and he side-stepped into the shadows. He evaporated into the depths of the night in the twinkle-of-an-eye.

23

Upon the break of day, and following a fretful and troubled night, Mayotte slithered from her garret at the Oldcorne residence, and she very cautiously inched down the servant's back stairs to arrive at the pantry-kitchen. Two domestic workers already toiled at the counter-tops, even though it was so *painfully* early. They strove to get the breakfast trays prepared. Mayotte greeted them with a silent nod, but pressed beyond their sweating limbs to make for the service entrance. She brought a finger to her lips to beseech her colleagues to be reticent about her movements. Then Mayotte unlatched the back door, dragged the hood of her shawl over her head, and tiptoed into the drizzly morning air.

She hastened across the bridge towards Toad Blackwing's camp. Her conversation the preceding evening with Tab, the gentleman from the War Office, had consumed her mind and his comments had been deeply disquieting. But what most troubled her, the thing that unnerved her the most, was something that Toad Blackwing had proclaimed: *We shall go there tomorrow*, he had declared. And he was talking about *steam shed 7*. As a matter of fact, she had proposed as much to the old man. And today she fretted that the silly old fool might decide to proceed there, *alone*. Even though the man from the War Office had been particularly persistent in his warning: *Please do not attend Lindwürm's steam shed 7,* he had urged. 'This is a time for pistols and daggers,' the fellow had added.

Once over the bridge, Mayotte made her way along the causeway to the ditch she knew she had to cross, and then out onto open fields that ran adjacent to Mead Lake ditch.

Eventually, she skirted a wide thicket of elderberries, and rubbed a long cobweb from her face as she reached the old man's encampment. Almost immediately, she knew something was amiss. She sniffed ash and wood-smoke in the air and thought she picked up the sound of a man's voice. So she hesitated, hunched beneath wet branches. Thus, on her knees, she clambered forwards in soggy mud.

Lingering by what was once Toad Blackwing's camp, were two men. Both sported yellowish brown straw hats. Both wore black tunics furnished with wide lapels. Both were dressed in grey stocking with black riding boots. Both were lightly bearded, and both grew their head-hair so long it reached their collars. Both men wore gun belts, clipped slackly around thin waists. These two men looked so remarkably *similar* that Mayotte guessed they were born twins, from the same mother. One of the identical brothers kicked up ash from Blackwing's burned down construction. 'Heavens!' whispered Mayotte. 'They ignited his shelter!' She didn't want to make a noise, crack a twig, or cause a bird to lift, so stayed as still as she could and watched for several minutes. It seemed the ruffians had recently burned the old man's tent down, because it smouldered in increasing drizzle. But it also seemed that Blackwing had *not* been at home when they'd shown-up to do their torching. The twins looked frustrated by this turn of events.

'He'll have our marbles *for this,*' said one. 'He'll dangle us from a lamppost if he discovers the old man got away.'

'What if we *don't* tell him?' said the other.

'What are you saying?' returned the first.

'I'm recommending that we tell the boss we *did the deed...* we *accomplished* what he asked...'

'And if he requires proof?' asked the wavering brother.

The other bent into the ash and dragged a bunch of sullied feathers from the ash. The feathers were stuck to what looked like, from the distance, a long pipe. She guessed they'd rescued old man's playing pipe, not his smoking pipe. She saw fingerholes in the tube.

'We bring the boss *this*. It's indisputable proof he was boiled in the bonfire, ain't it? He'd never have let go his peace pipe, would he? They *never* let go of their pipe when they're about to enter their pagan heaven, do they? Even if you stab them in the heart, they won't let go. Everyone knows that.'

'Do you think the boss will believe us?'

The other brother shrugged. 'Why not? It's plausible, ain't it?'

'I hope you're right.'

Mayotte edged away, moving as stealthily as a wildcat would track a goose. And once she was a healthy hundred paces from the two thugs, she tore across the meads, splashing and crashing by ditches, nettles, and tripping over hummocks. She was in a mighty hurry: because if Toad Blackwing was *not* in his encampment when the marauders had ransacked it at first light, then she knew, with utmost certainty, where the old man *would be* right now: he'd be at steam shed 7!

Steam shed 7 was located north-west of town, not overlooked by residences, but instead bordered by lost paddocks and forgotten wildlands. Steam shed 7 was situated along the little-used Yeoveney branch line, which connected to the Colne freight line. The nearest structure was a pound mill, although even that building was downstream and perhaps three furlongs away. The elongated brick steam shed had a row of eight oval windows on one side and another eight down the opposite length, but those far windows were twice as large as the others, and were designed to allow the waning afternoon sunshine into the catacombic interior. However, all of those windows were blackwashed and shuttered, as though someone had gone to great lengths to ensure that no passer-by could ever peer inside. The only windows that allowed light to enter the huge building were six ventilations, no more than slits really, and these were positioned very high up, in fact just under the gables. Mayotte guessed there were another six ventilations on the other side. She supposed they were designed to allow steams and gases to escape into the fresh air.

The 'front' end of the building, like most steam sheds, incorporated outsized and monumental cathedrallike doors, but the rail entrances at Shed 7 were not only unwelcoming and unattractive but also unserviceable because, despite being supplied with two internal roads, with a coaling road branching off outside, the lines were now rusted and degraded. Therefore, the doors were sealed tightly *shut*. Some said that the Yeoveney branch line, which began as a horse-drawn operation before being converted to steam, was never profitable. So when Lindwürm found an opportunity to buy the steam shed for a low price, he jumped at it. Workers had told her that at the further end of the shed was an office, workshop, and forge, as well as a store. But she didn't know much more about the place.

The building's most notable feature, the distinguishing trait that marked out this steam shed from *all others*, was its amazing height. Why had they built such an unusually tall steam shed? Did they expect towering locomotives? The black slate roof of the steam shed was at least as tall as St Mary's church tower, if not taller, and the common wisdom held that the significant height of the building permitted engines to 'steam off,' that is, to release their pent-up and ferocious energies in a harmless and discrete manner. As Mayotte drew closer to this uniquely *high-level* shed, she realised she had a gigantic problem: if all the windows were shuttered and the main doors were barricaded, how was she supposed to get inside and save Toad Blackwing? She'd approached the steam shed with the pallid morning light rising behind her back, hoping for at least some cover... because there were no natural impediments, no trees, walls, or hedgerows to hide behind, so it was difficult to approach the structure without being seen. It appeared as if the new owners had cleared the surrounding land to ensure that no one could sneak up on them unnoticed. So now she lay flat in the mud and waited. She dared to raise her head slightly to check for any signs of activity. If she was lucky, Toad Blackwing — the old fool — will have turned up at the place and broken in before anyone had arrived. That would be the best option because she'd be able to free him before the 'heavies' showed. But while she laid there watching the place, she was disheartened by what she observed. Uncomfortable fear crept into her guts and began to buzz around her insides like a thousand moths. Mayotte noticed what appeared to be a horseless vehicle at one of the structure's corners. It was a small unroofed motorised autocar with four wheels, a wide footplate, a rudder handle, and associated chains and levers. This motor-landaulet was parked near where she had, only once, dared venture before, some several weeks earlier: it was parked at the corner of the steam shed where she had discovered Kilda's fragment of cloth, dropped into the mud. On *that* occasion, an armed patrolman had turned a corner and shouted at her and lifted his rifle. So she had run away, holding her skirts between her legs, and had sprinted until her breath was exhausted. On that occasion, when she had finally turned her head to look around, the building was just a small cigar-box in the distance. But *today* she discovered she could move gently forward from her flat position on the earth, utilising her knees and toes to improve her snakely progress. She grazed her knees, scuffed her elbows, and wounded her hips as she went, but she didn't dare to rise, or her silhouette would've revealed her existence immediately. She hauled herself near enough to sniff the coal-tars and lubricating oils from the horseless carriage, but only after a very long and painful drag across splinters and sharp gravels. But then she also detected *another* aroma: a more common odour: the fruity foamy pungency of horses. She wriggled a little further to her left, to see two horses, both tacked though unsaddled, fastened onto hoops on the steam shed wall. Reflexively, almost without conscious any thought, she felt disappointed and discouraged. At least three workers had already arrived! It meant they had either run across Toad Blackwing *already* or, perhaps worse, he was yet to cause his disruption, probably breaking stuff and causing general mayhem, so she'd be too late to stop him. If it was the first, if they'd discovered him and apprehended him, she might *still* stand a chance to intercede and broker his release. She might be able to negotiate on behalf of the old man, perhaps by appealing to their mercy and explaining he's a just muddle-headed old fool who doesn't mean any trouble. *Yes*, she decided, bringing herself to her knees, *it was the only way to proceed.*

She'd *have to* go in there and talk terms with *them*. But how would she get in? How did the workers gain access to this impenetrable shed?

Mayotte edged around the corner and glimpsed a slim wooden side-door, no wider than her shoulders. The doorway was painted the same colour as the brickwork, and she wouldn't have noticed it if she hadn't seen mud and scuff marks near the threshold. *Aha!* The door had been amazingly concealed. That must be how *they* ventured into their lair! She looked around to make sure no one approached, and when she was positive she wouldn't be seen or caught, she elbowed the cunningly concealed door and forced herself inside.

The abdominal cavity of the main space resembled Mayotte's vision of a great abbey. There was an immeasurable vastness, a hollow depthless magnificence, and a blank echoing grandness to the huge expanse. But it was also a longitudinal space and so there was a sense of confinement and locked-in narrowness that made her feel uneasy. She glanced up to see the structural framework of timbers, the heavy joists, and massive beams, all the woodwork that kept the impressive roof from falling in. In many regards, steam shed 7 was a breath-taking constructional marvel. But it *also* felt nightmarish.

Mayotte edged a corner and came face-to-face with *him*. She came face-to-face with Ligore Lassiter. His eyes filled with blazing danger. Ready to do harm and injury. 'You!' he hissed.

'Um, yes, me! Actually I came to see *you*. I have some important information to impart, *erm...*'

But Lassiter slapped her across the mouth. The *thwack* caused her to shriek. She fell backwards.

'Intruder!' Lassiter shouted. 'Will someone deal with this intruder? We have an invader on the premises. *Intruder!* Do I have to do everything myself?' He put Mayotte into a headlock, using his elbow to constrain her airway so she couldn't easily breathe. He pulled her up, so she stood on the tips of her toes. Then he dragged her brutally towards a large brown door. He kicked the door open with a booted foot, then dragged her inside.

'Did nobody hear me shout?' he growled.

'Sorry boss,' said one goon, his cowboy boots still up on the desk. The others stood to see what happened.

'Don't just hold there like a family of gibbering bullfrogs. *Someone* get a length of whipping tape so we can rope her...'

One guy pulled his collars together and said, 'I'll go...' He headed out of the office.

Lassiter hurled Mayotte by the door, then stepped over to her collapsed body. He trampled his boot-heel into her shin. 'Ow! That's hurting' me really bad, mister...' she whimpered. 'It's me? It's Mayotte. I work with you. I'm *not* an intruder. You're frightening me, Mister. I came here to tell you something. I have vital information. Important information.'

'Shouldn't we hear her out, boss?' asked a shorter man. This man had hidden himself in the furthest corner, but now came forward to make his thoughts heard. He seemed less chunky, less sturdy, and less shabby than the others. In fact, this one had dressed himself fancier, with a red bow-tie and purple braces. He looked wealthier too, with a well-ironed dress-shirt that covered a stout stomach. He didn't wear cowboy boots, either. Mayotte gazed at tis guy's spherical face and his ovoid spectacles and she decided he *wasn't* one of the regular thugs. She guessed he must be one of their *technical* guys.

'I've heard it *out* many times before. I've lost patience with it. This one is always nosing about, and I've had enough of it. Rummaging into places it ought not be. Forever peeking, forever probing, and forever ferreting. It's an earwig, this one. It can't be trusted, neither. A lying, crawling, stinking, ferret. So, when he gets back with the whipping tape I want one of you to tie it to the test post and we'll use it for our next recap procedure.'

Some henchmen sniggered when they heard this news. Some licked their top lips. One crony salivated so much that Mayotte saw a blob of saliva dribble from the corner of his mouth.

But the fancy guy with the red bow tie came-over all uneasy or disturbed by his boss's comment. 'Hey Lassiter, you can't do that... well it's obvious *you can't*... she's a... well it's obvious isn't it? She's a woman...'

Ligore Lassiter turned and faced the man, convulsing with rage, 'What did you say?' he bellowed.

'Sorry, chief. But let's face it... that's a step too far, ain't it? Even for you! She's a woman.'

'Someone *shoot him*, will they?'

The other goons looked at each other, and each attempted to quickly extrapolate the facts and forecast what would happen next by recalling their past experiences with Lassiter. And even though one of the hired helpers managed to draw his revolver from his belt, it was too late. Lassiter pulled what looked like a Philadelphia *muff pistol* from a deep trouser pocket and he fired just one shot. The ball must have hit the fancy guy somewhere between the sternum and ribs because the guy looked down in bafflement at the red splotch that dilated across his dress shirt. As he gazed down, his silly ovoid spectacles dropped from his nose and clattered to the floorboards.

Mayotte looked at all their faces, trying to measure their response to this cold-blooded murder. But the men seemed indifferent to the shooting. In fact they looked *kind of* casual — as if this type of thing happened *every day*.

At that precise moment, the guy who'd gone for rope smashed into the office with a ball of baling twine. 'Will this do, chief?' he asked. Then he gazed into the corner to see that the fancy guy with the red bow collapsed to the ground. 'Lordy! What did *he* do wrong?' he asked.

'He argued with the boss,' suggested one.

'Yeah. He talked *at* the boss as if he was speaking to a coequal...'

'He called him *by his name*...'

'Is he a nutter? He got what he was due, *then*. Oh well, we'll 'ave to get ourselves another academical won't we?' commented the guy with the twine. 'We need a technologist to do all the sums, don't we?'

'Don't worry about *that*,' snarled Lassiter. 'There are plenty more where that shrimp came from. We can get two a dime at Oxford. We'll go shopping next weekend and buy ourselves another brace.'

The guys snickered at this.

'Right get her tied and someone drag her down to the test post. We'll get her lashed onto the post and use her as a target. And someone else get that *mess* cleared away.' Lassiter looked into the corner where his now extinct scientist bled-out, in a heap. 'He's ruining the ambiance with that stain. Someone get a brush and soap and get that cleared-up proper.'

'Hold on!' shouted Mayotte. You haven't heard what I've got to say. I have important information for you. You need to hear me out...' She had to think quickly, despite the fact that she had no information to trade.

But then, by a stroke of luck, the unstoppable force of destiny brought another change of circumstances: two cowboys marched into the room. They were wearing identical basket-weave hats, and identical hair shirts. One held a burned peace pipe in his gloved hands. It was the brothers she'd seen earlier at Toad Blackwing's camp. They had arrived *just in time* to save her skin!

As the twins sauntered into Lassiter's office, Mayotte yelled, from behind the door, from the inconspicuous position, 'These two idiots are gonna tell you they dealt with your problem...'

Ligore Lassiter regarded her, then turned his attention to the two cowboys: 'Well?' he quizzed. 'Are you?'

The brother without the pipe said, 'We dealt with your problem, chief.'

Lassiter chuckled then gestured to the crumpled girl who lay, humiliated, in the recess behind the door. The twins glanced at her, and both smiled and shrugged.

'What are they gonna say next, smartmouth?' Lassiter asked her.

'They'll say the injun has been whacked...' she yelled.

'We was gonna say blotted out...' offered one of the twins, in his defence. 'So she got that wrong, didn't she?'

'And we was gonna say *red man*...' added the other. 'Not *injun*. So that's wrong too.'

Lassiter examined his men's eyes: 'Even so, she predicted the essence of what you were about to say, didn't she?'

'No,' said the first twin. 'We was *actually* gonna say the red man got blotted out. As in charred. We burned the *injun* while he was asleep in his tent.'

Lassiter dismissed the man's attempt to downplay her display of fore-knowledge with a wave of his fingers. He then crouched close to Mayotte and brought his yellow teeth nearer her ears. 'Tell me what they will say next: whisper it! I want to see how good you are...'

'They will say they brought you proof,' she muttered. 'They will show you a pipe they claim is a peace pipe... they will extend the object as proof they did the job.'

'What did she say?' asked one brother, now that Lassiter stood. He contemplated both his henchmen with steady and viperous eyes.

'*You tell me...*' suggested the boss.

'What?' said the other.

'You *tell me* what she whispered into my ear...'

'Um? But how can we, chief? She hush-hushed-it didn't she? We didn't take heed of what she said, did we? Cos the woman spake her words directly into your 'ead, like, didn't she? As if she was giving you a secret divulgement.'

'Try and guess, *anyway*. Give it your best shot.'

'We don't know, boss. Truly, we don't. We ain't into that type of bewitchment. We can't hear something that's not been said open and loud. And neither can we prophesize what someone might say next...'

'No!' Agreed the other. 'She's a witch, that's how she does that magic. How else could she know such things? Why don't you burn her? Isn't she in for burning? Like what they used to do with witches?'

'Yes,' admitted Lassiter, 'She's in for burning. You two will tie her to the test post and we'll use her tethered body for a firing.'

'Good,' said the other. He smiled at the prospect. 'We don't like witches. This one is bothersome...'

'Yeah, this witch is bothersome,' agreed his brother.

'The woodchuck is lying, ain't she? What the brenny-rabbit don't know about what went on with that dead *injun* amounts to nought, don't it?'

'Fool!' shouted Lassiter. 'If that statement were true, and made any sense at all, then she knows *everything* doesn't she? How can I trust you two turkeys?'

'Because you *can*, boss. Because we don't botch nothing.'

'*Fine*,' said Lassiter. 'Anyway, enough about her. What news do you have for me?'

'About the old red man?' one brother asked.

'Yes, *of course* about the old red man...' barked Lassiter, giving an angry stare.

'Well, we burned his tent, didn't we? And we brought you proof we done it.'

The other brother showed Lassiter the blackened pipe. 'This is his peace pipe... as you can see. It's charred by fire. The fire that *kilt* him. They never surrender their peace pipe, do they? This proves we did the job you asked.'

Lassiter gasped, then turned to offer a smile to Mayotte. 'That's what she whispered into my ear,' he muttered.

'No she didn't,' exclaimed the first twin.

'Don't wrangle words with me, you simpleminded buffoon! You bumbled the plan, didn't you? Be honest...'

'No, boss. Truly, we did it exactly as you asked. Here is the proof. His burned pipe.'

'I demand *better* proof. This is not even a peace pipe. Are you two blind? Can't you see the finger holes? This is a sounding pipe, not a smoking pipe. Idiots! Go back to his camp and collect the red man's *skull*. I want his skull in the palm of my hands. I want his cracked skull *here* in my hands, get it? Do you two get it?' Lassiter grabbed the throat of the twin that stood nearest, 'If I don't get the red man's cracked skull in my hands by the end of the day, both of you will be tied to the test post downstairs. We'll make a show of firing the weapon at twin targets. How would you like that?' Lassiter released his grip on the henchman's windpipe. The guy backed away, rubbing his larynx in a frenzied manner, his eyes wide with fear.

'We would *not* like that. Not at all,' squealed the other.

Lassiter turned to him, 'Give me that?' Lassiter pointed at the burned pipe.

The brother handed the artifact over. Lassiter swiped it, then lifted it above his right shoulder, before he slapped it ferociously across the man's face. And although the pipe was scorched, black, crusty, and greatly singed, the swiping blow produced a hammer-like punch that almost knocked the man from his feet. The stooge tried to look along his own nose. It now bubbled with blood.

'Tie her with baling and get her stood up straight. Then bring her down to the test post and tie her *tight* to it. And after you've done those simple jobs, fetch me the red man's cracked skull. So I can take it into my hands. Got that?'

The twins nodded.

~

The twins dragged Mayotte from the floor-boards, secured her wrists behind her, and coiled extra twine around her arms, at elbow height, to stop her thrashing about.

When they had accomplished the roping, Lassiter came over. Meanwhile, she scanned the den and noticed the other meat-heads were busy clearing away the body of the dead scientist, while others produced mops and buckets to wipe away the blood.

'Since you were so informatory just then, I will compensate you with an advantage that I don't often extend to guests, young lady. I don't typically trouble to spell-out what we're accomplishing here to the usual commonplace *illiterate* we have handed to us for trial and error; but I'm prepared to make an exception with you because you don't play according to conventional rules, and *I like that*. We *share* a sense of playfulness, don't we? So I'd like to define Bradiant Induction to you. And, thus, you'll understand something of what will happen to your body, once you have been shackled to the lightning-rod down on the steam shed floor, on those rusted rails. Would you like that?'

Mayotte stuffed her mouth with sputum, then spat into Lassiter's face.

As he rubbed away the jelly with his fingers, he said, 'Be certain to bind her mouth with cloth, so she doesn't holler or yell. And so she doesn't do *that* again. But allow her eyes to remain uncovered. I want to see the terror in those beautiful, *bewitching* eyes when we direct the muzzle of our *scin-rifle* at her face, ha ha!'

One of the twins ripped away his own neck scarf, so the other could mishandle the placement of it. The brother fiddled with the knot because his fingers trembled so much.

Once Mayotte's mouth had been covered, Lassiter came forward, to address her again: 'The physicists claim that everything in the universe is composed of a substance they describe as *radiant matter*. When we scintillate radiant matter, which is the charged particles within all objects, whether the objects are man-made, animate, or inanimate, they will *always* luminesce in unforeseen and extremely explosive ways. I don't pretend to fathom the science of scintillating matter, but in this steam shed we are beginning to appreciate how it works. They tell me that scintillated radiant matter is the fourth *state of matter*. So this is cutting-edge science you will be heling with! You should be proud to be involved! Your sacrifice will help us advance scientific knowledge. *Anyway*, in order to harness its unpredictability and awesome potential, we must learn how to handle the disembodied behaviour of scintillated radiant matter. So that's why we've been working here on lots of experiments. And we think we've refined a technique that has been interpreted by our experts as 'Bradiant Induction.' This technique involves passing an enormously powerful flame through the radiant matter of an object, hoping to make the chosen object, the target, scintillate. The resulting scintillation will facilitate intense deflagration. The scintillation causes an immediate and intense explosion. If we're right about this, then Bradiant Induction will be a game changer! Bradiant Induction will become an impressive and unmatchable weapon because the very substance of any object we target — whether it's a gun, whether it's a fortress, whether it's a frigate, or even whether it's soft human tissue, as you will demonstrate in a few moments — will develop into the powder box, the *gunpowder* if you like, for the resultant explosion. When we use Bradiant Induction on *you*, for example, it will be *your* cells, those tiny little atoms that make your molecules, it will be those that break and burst into a myriad white-hot stars. So *you* will become, all at once, a sparkling powder bomb. *Kaboom!* Of course, we have experienced many failures along the way to this point. For example, it's been hard to get our *scin-rifle* — that's what we call the shooter we use to blast the vigorous flame at our target — it's been hard to get the rifle fiercely hot enough to induce 'Bradiant Induction.' But we're inching ever-closer to getting things exact. Once we arrive at the optimum spark-point, any body, or any *object*, that we fire our *scin-rifle* at will — instantaneously — detonate in a vaporising blaze of silvery light. Once we have developed our weapon, armies won't need to carry volatile incendiaries into battle. And they won't need to re-arm or re-equip their troops. And, with just a handful of men, just a squad actually, if they're equipped with a few *scin-rifles* they will be able to sink battleships, level castles, and flatten defensive walls. Once we've perfected our weapon, we will offer it to the highest bidder.'

~

The twins shuffled and shoved Mayotte out of Lassiter's office and onto the landing.

'Don't neglect to tie her strong to the pole. And when you have completed that, go get me the burned skull of that red man, or you'll be double strapped to the rod yourselves by dusk.'

'Yes, boss,' groaned one brother.

'And the rest of you,' Lassiter growled, turning his mind to the men still cleaning-up the mess in his office. 'Get yourselves down to the side-door and block it off with sandbags, like I advised you before. We don't want no more unexpected visitors, do we? How did she get in? She got in through the open door! I told you that door was a vulnerability.'

'But I thought the main scientist urged us to keep the door unclogged in case we needed a fire escape?' murmured one henchman.

'What?' screeched Lassiter.

'Sorry, boss,' said the man, throwing his arms up. 'It don't matter now, anyway, because the science man is belly up, ain't he?'

'Exactly!' said Lassiter. 'So get to work, all of you.'

Outside on the landing, the twins tugged and pawed Mayotte down the precarious stairtower, and then hauled her onto the yard floor.

'Where we gonna get us a charred skull afore eventide, Malachi?' muttered one thug.

'In a pit I guess, Ezra.'

'Pit? What pit?' asked the brother.

'A grave pit, I spose. We need to raid us a burying ground and dig up a skellington.'

'That's frightfully dire, though, ain't it, Malachi?'

'Taint as dire as being exploderated by that flame cannon though...is it?'

'No, taint,' agreed the other.

They shifted beyond dozens of enormous cylinders, each one silvery glossed and as big as a man.

'Gas jugs,' brother Malachi told her. 'That's where they stash the Pennsylvanian gas. That's our secret ingredient, ha! They pressurise the Pennsylvanian vapours with a compressor and it develops into liquid inside those cylinders. Then we inject it into another compressor, so it's double-compressed, then squeeze it into an accelerator. Later we mix the pressurised gas with methane oils...'

'You don't have to tell her every fink, does you?' challenged the other brother.

'What does it matter? She taint gonna tell nobody now, is she?'

They passed other huge tubs, each one hooked up by a snarl of pipework to others in the row. 'And that's some new liquefied gas, kept in those big tubs there. I don't know 'sactly what that gas is, but I knows the strange stuff has to be kept cool, so me and my twin commonly go collect ice blocks each afternoon and draw 'em back here so scientists can cram those insulating coats with ice to keep them tubs cooler than cool.'

'Yes, that's right tell 'er everything. Tell 'er exactly how we do things...' complained the other.

'Like I already tolt you, what does it matter?'

They headed for the heart of the long space, where the central rails accommodated a gigantic steam engine, though their engine was nothing like any loco, or indeed any mill engine, that Mayotte had ever seen before. It had what she assumed must be a colossal fire-tube boiler, linked to dozens of tubes that headed back to those fuel containers under Lassiter's landing. There was a steam dome almost halfway along the top of the rusted carcass, with a tremendous chimney stack housed upon it, a stack that reached at least the extent of five men. Then there was the typical smoke-box, fire-box, and steam chest you'd see on any steam engine, but these parts were burned black and all the pipes and cylinders from the potential power source seemed to go to a huge blast-pipe that was fitted with a brass nozzle. The brass end bit was not unlike those spigots they fit to firefighting hoses. The snout-shaped thing was bolted to the type of gun carriage they employ at military funerals. So the cannon couldn't be separated from the steam engine because they had locked it to the back. On either side of the cannon were giant red boxes, each two men tall, and these packages steamed and frothed.

'Fire *boilers*,' suggested Malachi. "That's where the fuels are merged before we charge them into the breech. The shooting tube is at the end. That's the stinging bit he'll be pointing at your face.' Malachi smirked at the prospect. 'Not that we will be here to see... shame... but we have to go dig us up a skellington... gratitudes to you...'

Climactically, the brothers tugged Mayotte to a metal post that had been bolted onto the central rail. Behind the pole was space, a long, empty abyss. And, at the far edge of the steam shed space, Mayotte could make out a brick wall.

'Yeah, we built the wall at the far end out of fire bricks like they typically use in a pottery kiln, erm, because, well, sometimes the cannon blasts a flare that, er, well let's say it over-extends itself...'

They arrived at the metal post, turned her around to confront the swell of the muzzle which was pointed her way with its deadly wide-open lips just a few yards from her pitiful body. Then they forced her to straddle the rusted railway line, establishing one foot on each side, before they affixed her to the rod.

'Secure her good and tight,' suggested Malachi. 'This pole you are being fixed to is metalized because we discovered we needed it to be a reliable lightning rod. You see, when the thunderbolt shoots at you, it tends to jerk you in a big shock, a bit like the electricities do in a thunderstorm. Soldiers tell of lightning strikes jerking heavy cannons off their wheels. It's the *same principle* here.'

So the other brother got to work, binding Mayotte to the shooting-post.

' I expect the chief will be down in a moment to press the start-up pumps, study the gauges, and after that he'll show here up to pull *that* trigger. Then it will be *cooking time* for you! I'd like to say it has been a satisfaction meeting you,' offered Malachi, in this farewell speech. 'But it *ain't* been. So I won't. In fact, you gotted me and my twin into a pile of trouble with your yakking and your *predicterizing*... so we consider this sendoff to be befitting.'

'Yeah,' said the other, once he'd completed knotting and hitching, 'Befitting of a witch who has a flappy mouth. So we'll take our leave of you now, and, like they told us on the big ship what brunged us here, *Bon Voyage*, ha ha!'

'Good one,' observed Malachi.

'Fanks!' accepted his twin. 'I thunked that joke up all by myself.'

The twins Malachi and Ezra took a step back to appreciate their tethering job.

Mayotte couldn't see much beyond the cannon-muzzle that was pointed at her body, but guessed that Lassiter had entered the ground floor, ready to fire up the diabolical mechanisms, check the dials and switches, and he was obviously about to come over and trigger the weapon, because both brothers pointed to the fuel tanks, bottles, and canisters and braced themselves for another round of admonitions and reprimands from their boss-man.

Although she couldn't see beyond the muzzle at the top of the cannon, she was free to stare up, toward heaven, or at least an approximation of heaven. So Mayotte peered into the superhigh rafters that kept the steam shed's basilica-like roof from collapsing.

That's when she noticed something *way-beyond* unusual! That's when she saw an *extraordinary* sight. A seraph had emerged from the farthest rafter. And the holy angel treaded her way, though it had to be admitted, the holy figure was exaltedly high in the air. Mayotte guessed that's what the celestial creature *had to be* because the seraph had six wings: two wings that stood tall above a white and crimson mask, two wings that hung low, like huge sleeves from a pure silver vestment, and another two wings that flapped by the figure's hips. The seraph was a magnificent and hypnotic sight, radiant in white, silver, and blood-red.

But Mayotte couldn't believe her eyes and so convinced herself that this spectral heavenly being was *not real* and that her imagination played tricks on her, most likely due to the stress of her terrible circumstances and the fact she hadn't slept properly for at least two days.

Though, even as Mayotte doubted her vision, the twin brothers also became horrified by what they saw in the rafters. They were both so alarmed by the presence of the seraph that they grabbed their pistols from their gun-belts and began shooting, quite randomly, into the air. The two guys began to feverishly shoot bullets into the rafters.

'No, no!' exclaimed Mayotte as the gorgeous seraph wobbled and faltered on the high beam. 'You can't shoot my angel,' she wailed. 'Please!'

However, Malachi and Ezra continued to fire. The sound of their enormous pistol-bangs bounced around the vast cavern-like walls of the steam shed, generating thudding groans of noise that sounded like the first signs of summer thunder.

And *suddenly* the lovely angel appeared to be in great peril. It gazed from its high perch, its six wings fanned out, and its red-smeared visage turned tragically *sepulchral*.

Then something horrible, terrible, happened: the seraph nose-dived from the ceiling beam.

～

Mayotte's eyes blurred with tears. Dewy droplets dampened her clammy skin. She also felt downright sleepy, as if the light of her life had dimmed irreversibly when the redeeming archangel had hurtled headlong from those high timbers. The angel had been her *last* desperate hope, but he had plunged into the hard earth. Now, all she could do was give way to the calamities that surely attended her.

So it was through fuzzy teardrops that she noticed *another* shape move in her direction, to creep along the *same* high joists up in the rafters, though this one moved like a wingless bark-beetle. Stooped in polished black, it skittered and crawled along the length of the beam. When the beetle drew immediately above her approximate position, so she could hardly twist her high enough neck to see it, the creature discharged some kind of satiny entanglement. For a moment, Mayotte speculated it might be threads produced by the beetle's own spinneret, but the complicated mass of fibres slipped close to her position and resembled a rope ladder. She tried to blink away her tears, determined to learn what was about to happen next. She was utterly shocked when she saw that the beetle descended the webbing ladder, manipulating it like a climbing line, and employing it's thick insect arms to lower itself gradually, with its oddly shaped cursorial legs latched onto the threads.

It wasn't until the bark-beetle got down to the floor, and then came up close, that Mayotte identified *it* as possessing human form, not insectoid; and when the beetleish anthropoid grew closer still, she observed the human to be Stormbuckler.

'Sorry I'm late,' he declared. He took a sharp-toothed hacksaw blade from his belt and began to saw at her bindings. 'Your old friend Blackwing insisted he put his war face on... that took some extra time.'

Stormbuckler loosened her from the last of the restraints and, for a moment, she felt too frail to stand. She dropped to her knees. When she went down, Stormbuckler cleared away the scarf that had been knotted around her face.

'We can't rest!' shouted Stormbuckler. 'It's imperative you stand up at once. We *must* fly.'

But Mayotte whimpered and trembled. She buckled heavier into the cold ground. She sniffled.

Stormbuckler presented a tender arm and tried to console her.

'Was that Blackwing up there?' she inquired, giving a sob. 'My protecting angel? Was that the old man? Did they shoot the poor old fellow from the girder?'

'*No*,' responded Stormbuckler, doing his best to yank her upright and balance her on shuddering feet. 'Their bullets missed the old chap!'

'But I saw him fall,' she wailed. '*I saw him fall...*'

'He didn't fall, he *dropped*. That's an entirely different thing. It was intentional. He jumped *onto* his enemy. That was his plan all along. He bore his knife in his grip and he dropped onto the baddie with merciless intent...'

'Are they both—?'

'Yes. They are *both*— come! We must escape. Do you have the strength to climb this rope ladder?'

Mayotte squinted at the length of tangled wibbly wobbly hemp-and-beech. It looked as delicate as a daisy chain. 'You require me to climb that?' she growled. 'It's mighty high.'

'It's the only way out,' declared Stormbuckler.

'But, how? How come you are here? Why did Blackwing jump? I don't understand...'

'I will explain it all *later*.'

'No! Tell me *now*. Or I *shall not* climb your stupid rope.'

Stormbuckler threw an exasperated stare. 'You tax my tolerances sometimes; do you know that? Here I am extricating you from deadly death, and all you do is to *rile me*. Fine! 'The machine had left the American marooned and helpless in the air after his noisy, serpent-like machine became stuck. I thus saved him. I suppose you and the elderly man fled the house while I was saving him.'

'Serpent-like?'

'Don't you think the machine resembles a poisonous spitting cobra?'

'I guess so, now that you point-out the similarity. How did you save him?'

'I flipped the release valve...'

'Um? How did you, um? I mean, how did you learn how his twirling machine operated?'

'Ha ha!' Stormbuckler gave a broad smile. 'That's *exactly* what the millionaire inventor said, *too*.'

'So how?'

'I informed him that his mechano-contraption is identical to any biological machine. It has a heart—in this case, a steam and combustion motor—it has joints, ankles, bones, a skeleton, ligaments, and muscles, as well as fluids that circulate through arteries and a control system that in the case of his machine is controlled by a driver at the top of the framework. In order to figure out what to do next, I visualised the bones and sinews under the skin of his leviscopic engine, that's what he calls it by the way, and his contraption reminded me of a heron, which as you know raises and twists its head to see what threats are nearby...'

'So what did you do?

'I assumed his contraption required fuel. It doesn't eat fish because it isn't a heron. I knew it drank steam and fluids. After figuring out which veins in the circulatory system headed to the machine's heart, I sought to find the valve that managed those energies. I went over to the machine and I disconnected them. The millionaire was saved and his highchair gently descended. That's all there is to it. That concludes my narrative.'

'Not the whole tale, though—what transpired after you saved Lindwürm?'

'He was very appreciative, and as you might imagine, and it surprised him that I understood how his device operated, especially given that he had built the machine in secret in his garage. He told me he had kept it away from others. I then informed him I was familiar with the anatomy of moving things, of muscles, of feathers, of cartilages, of joints, and of operating systems, so he demonstrated how his contraption operated while I observed. I was able to provide ideas that would prevent him from becoming trapped in the air again. He grew thrilled by my suggestions, so after dinner, we returned to his garage with a bigger tool set and we started working on the repairs and improvements that I suggested.'

For a little while, Mayotte was silent: 'I don't know what to say! You are amazing. Remarkable. I under-appreciated you. Didn't you think he must have wanted you to be his senior engineer?'

'He mumbled something about elevating me to chief consultant, but I declined. I turned him down...'

'Turned him down? Whyever would you do such a silly thing?'

Stormbuckler glared back: 'Given what we now know about him and his steam shed 7, do you really think I need to defend my choices?'

'Yes, pardon me; you are correct... You were correct *all along*. I'm the one who didn't see the danger. Oh my goodness, I have been such an absolute dumpling, haven't I?'

Stormbuckler placed his hand on her shoulder and replied, 'No, not at all. But let's get on with this, *please*.'

'One last thing...' she said. 'How did the old man get involved?'

'Well, I had been working all night trying to fix the Leviscopic Engine. Lindwürm explained how the contraption worked in greater detail and I figured-out other problems with it. Just after Lindwürm turned in, he'd been working alongside me all night, but it must have been a little before daybreak — but really early *this morning* — your acquaintance Blackwing appeared at Lindwürm's place and the old man hammered at his garage door. I was worried he man might wake the entire house up, so I opened the side door and asked him what the *heck he was doing*. He seemed in a fearful panic and revealed he thought something abominable was about to happen. *To you!* He told me he suspected *you* had been taken hostage by Lindwürm's men. He demanded I took him, right away, to their secret steam shed. So I got the Leviscopic Engine running, and we pushed the giant garage doors wide, and we sat into the driving seats of his machine, and we trundled all the way *here*. It isn't an especially fast system, but it was swifter than walking.'

Mayotte gazed, open-mouthed.

'When we got here, there was no way into the steam shed, not that we could see, but I had a notion. The key point of this mechano-contraption is to *ascend*, to rise under its own steam, to an extraordinary height. Lindwürm had developed it as a prototype for a whole range of elevating platforms. He hoped his mechanical devices would provide temporary access to unattainable high areas, for workmen and tools. Anyway, I observed that the steam shed had top windows. Actually they're more like vents; it looked as if I might be able to squeeze through the biggest vent situated at the front of the building. So I lined-up the Leviscopic Engine, and we both got into the rising bucket. I engaged the hydraulic pistons, they are powered by twin ignition engines, and the whole thing telescoped up, then the bucket spidered out. It's quite an engine! By then, your acquaintance, Blackwing, had put on what he described as a *war mask*: essentially it was white chalk, elder-gum, and red berry dye that he smeared across his face. He drew out a bone-handled knife too. I said, 'what are you doing with that?' He said, 'Today I complete my hunt.' I begged him to stay inside the bucket and wait for me to get back. I told him *I'd get you* and I suggested he wouldn't be able to squeeze through the narrow opening — but the silly old fool threatened me with his knife and then, well, he went first! He scurried through the air vent as quick as a rat could dash along a waste pipe. I tried to stop him, I tried to draw him back, but he was *too quick* for me. When I got through the gap myself, I saw him standing there... on that shaft. He looked fierce and wild. He held his knife in his fist, and he shouted, 'There he is! That's the devil that abducted my daughter.' And he dropped onto the guy below. I saw the two gun-slingers come to check-over the broken bodies. The thugs ran off in a state of panic. So I balanced on the beam. I came to rescue you. And that's it, you're up-to-date. So haul yourself up this flippin' rope-ladder while we still have a chance, or it'll be the ruin both of us... and I don't think Black-wing would've wanted that...'

'Yes, *you're right,*' commented Mayotte, as she took the first step onto the wobbling ladder. 'He sacrificed himself for me, *for us.* He did it so we could escape this dreadful place. Where did you get this flimsy ladder? Are you sure it will take my weight?'

'It came with the Leviscopic Engine. I believe it is there in case the machinery fails while the operator is up in the air, and needs to get down in an emergency. When you reach the main beam, sprint as fast as you can to the far window. Whatever you do — don't look down!'

Mayotte took a protracted gulp. She put next foot onto the second-lowest rundle, and felt the ladder sway, stretch, and waggle. 'Are you sure this is safe?' she asked.

'I came down it, didn't I?'

She glared at him condescendingly, then she clambered up the bouncy rungs.

When Mayotte arrived at the lofty rafter where she had seen the angel drop, she *did* look down, even though she'd been warned not too! Immediately, she knew it was *a mistake*. Right away she felt shaky and sickened. But Mayotte knew she *had* to *see things for herself*. There, far below, was Toad Blackwing's crumpled body, with his feathered peace-pipe by his side. The old-man's 'wings' were made of feathers and those fathers, and some pelts, were spread across *another* mangled body. This other disfigured body belonged to Lassiter. Mayotte saw crimson blood exuding from Lassiter's heart. But then she received a sharp *prod* from behind. The prod got her moving again. '*Don't* look down I said. Get to the window,' came the voice, from behind.

Mayotte turned and glared at Stormbuckler, then hastened along the remaining portion of the rafter to arrive at the very tight vent. She hoped her gaunt body was skinny enough to slide through the restrictive opening. She wiggled herself in, headfirst, then dragged her arms through the vent, then her legs. She wedged through the opening. And when she became precipitously, and *gloriously*, over-whelmed by a splash of pure dazzling sunlight, her eyes shuttered down. The exuberant intensity of the sun was too much to bear. Then Mayotte almost tumbled sideways, because she became unbalanced.

'Leap into the bucket,' grunted Stormbuckler. 'You're holding things up!'

'Wait a moment, buffoon-head,' Mayotte growled. 'I can't see, can I? My eyes are *only now* adjusting to the glare.'

'Just get on with it,' Stormbuckler sputtered. 'Why do you have to make a pother and flap about *all* that you do?'

'Very well, but I will blame you if I descend to my death,' she responded. Before she added: '*Idiot*.'

She lurched from the window, aiming as carefully she could, for the odd-shaped 'bucket' that sat like a crow's nest above the flimsy rattletrap that wobbled and shuddered below. Soon after she arrived in the bucket, with a bouncing crash that sent the whole thing vibrat-ing, Stormbuckler squinched through the vent too. He sort-of half-catapulted himself into the bucket using his 'bad' leg like a flexible vaulting stick to give his jump more 'spring.' The bucket clattered and balked under his extra weight, and Mayotte became perfectly sure that the whole darned contraption would disintegrate beneath them, and they'd be smashed on the gravels below. But the fangled contrivance somehow survived their misdoings, and the machine remained upright.

Mayotte glanced around the bucket and identified the control mechanisms and levers that, she hoped, Stormbuckler would know how to use to get them back to solid ground. But she also spotted two wick-lamps hanging on the sides.

'Do those lamps work?' she asked.

Stormbuckler shrugged. 'I expect so! Who cares? Why? What does it matter?'

'What are they for?' she asked.

'I assume he fitted them in case an operator needed extra light up high...'

She snatched the first one. 'It smells *funny*,' she advised.

'Would you move over? I need to get to the levers,' Stormbuckler grumbled. 'You're constantly getting in the way...'

'Why does it smell funny?'

'It's filled with distilled petroleum,' he said. 'It's a new invention. Now, remove yourself! I must get to the controls.'

'Do you have a friction match?' she asked.

Stormbuckler scowled at her as if she'd misplaced her senses: 'Why do you want a lamp in broad daylight?'

'Just answer me. Do you have a friction match? *Yes or no*. Why is *everything* so difficult with you?'

'Probably *here*,' Stormbuckler suggested. He opened a modest leather box. 'This is where I found the step-ladder and hacksaw blade.'

Mayotte poked in the box until she encountered what she was needed Then she gathered the *other* paraffin lamp and declared: 'I'm going back...'

'What?' Stormbuckler shrieked. 'Are you insane? We don't have time for nonsense. We only got to this point by the slenderest margin of good fortune. Now you're jeopardizing *everything* we've done to get the heck out of here...'

'Yes, I know. But I've *got to* go back,' Mayotte declared. 'I hoped you'd understand, but you're too nitwittish to follow my reasoning. When I come back, I hope you're still here. But if you're not, then it will be allwhither and nowhere for me! But at least I will have achieved a conclusion to this series of events... for his sake... for the sake of the old man.' And with those words, Mayotte bounced awkwardly onto the window ledge.

~

For several disconcerting seconds she faltered on the threshold, unbalanced, because she carried two oil lamps in her hands, and a match box between her teeth, Then she sunk through the hole again. Back into the mouth of the demon.

Mayotte crawled once more through the vent and pressed into the steam shed. She adjusted herself on the high beam, struggling hard to manage her poise and grace as she managed her equilibrium until she reached the point on the horizontal bar that spanned the fuel flasks and carburetting vessels she'd seen earlier. The table match flared after she knocked it against the vesta case. Mayotte twisted the knob on the side of the lamp, to make the wick bigger, she lit it, and when she felt satisfied that the light developed boldly in the lofted darkness, she surrendered the lantern, and watched it plunge to the steam shed floor. As it crashed to the surface of the steam shed, it burst forth into a proliferating puddle of blue and yellow flares.

Mayotte inched back until she was above the two fallen bodies. She designed to say a prayer over Toad Blackwing, but then elected *not to*... he was a spiritual man, for sure, even pious, he would not appreciate a prayer made to *her* God. So, instead, Mayotte closed her eyes and thought about caring for people and about forgiveness, then struck a second match, lit the extended wick on the second lamp, and dropped it onto his plumes.

After that, she didn't look back. Mayotte scarpered skittishly back to the mouth in the wall. She virtually dived through the vent in a fluid movement, and when she entered into the light, in a single bounce, she lunged into the waiting bucket.

Stormbuckler had already started the engines, and had taken a stance by the machine's control levers.

'Go, go, *go*...' Mayotte shouted.

Stormbuckler yanked on the lever, and the machinery began its squeaky jerky descent.

When they struck ground level, he pushed the lever back, and wrested another hand-crank while also revolving a jackscrew. 'Oh rat-bottoms, I thought this might happen,' he grumbled.

'*Quickly*,' Mayotte cried. 'Won't this chunk of junk drive any faster? We need to leave this place... and I mean emphatically, we need to leave this place right now!'

'No! The power train is jammed. It did this before. I think the jackshaft is on the way out.'

'Can you recommend what we have to do *next* in layperson's terms?'

Stormbuckler nodded. 'Sure. We need to take our chances on foot...'

'Run for it, do you mean?'

'Yup!'

Mayotte was already jerking her legs over the side of the bucket as he mumbled. 'Well, what are you waiting for, dodo-head?' she yelled. 'Come on, idiot, let's run...'

Mayotte shot off, and she run wild across the open ground. She didn't dare glance back to see if Stormbuckler followed because she knew that if she turned, she'd stumble, and if she stumbled, she'd be scorched by the conflagration.

When the hellish eruption blasted-out across the heath, it came not as a firestorm but as a tremendous detonation that battered the wind out of her, and thrust her off her feet. Mayotte sprawled flat in the dirt for protracted moments, struggling to figure out if all her limbs were connected, and whether the skin survived on her bones.

She drew three quick breaths and turned her neck. What she saw defied reasonable description: where previously a long steam shed had stood. Now all that survived of the structure were crumpled stanchions and an enormous crater.

'That was good!' she heard. The words came from nearby.

She inverted her neck to look at where the speech came from, 'For the first time in my life I am delighted to hear your stupid voice,' she said.

'Let's go,' replied Stormbuckler.

'Where to?' she asked.

'I need to get out of this place. I still possess two sovereigns lent to me from Master Eaglehurst. I plan to take the next train out of this place. I propose to travel west. As far west as the train will take me.'

'Why do *you* have to run?' Mayotte asked, picking up from the dirt and smoothing herself down.

'Because Lindwürm knows I stole the Leviscopic Engine. And he'll get reports I travelled here using his machine. And he's not a fool. He'll put two and two together and assume I sabotaged his steam shed, I massacred his men, and I assassinated his best friend. He won't stop pursuing me after this, will he? I'm a marked fellow from now on...'

'I'll come with you,' Mayotte declared. 'Let's get going. We need to run. We must get to the station before the town is sealed-off by the authorities.'

'You don't *need* to come with me,' Stormbuckler suggested.

'Don't you want me?' she asked.

'It's not that,' he replied, picking up speed. He began his awkward jogging motion alongside her. 'It's just that *you* have a life here. Eaglehurst is your sweetheart. Mrs. Oldcorne is your employer. You have a good situation in domestic service. And you have a future.'

Mayotte grinned, but shook her head: 'Yesterday — was it just yesterday? — all the days have rolled into one; but *yesterday* I met a strange man. This strange man offered me a way out of this place and a way out of this life. That man offered me a better future,'

'Who was this mysterious man? What better future?'

'I'll tell you about it on the train as we head west.'

24

Help required?

Tweet the author @neilmach for answers or comments

Ligore Lassiter

ALSO BY THIS AUTHOR

Moondog and the Reed Leopard

A bored teenager named Hopie calls a television show paranormal investigator when a phantom leopard harasses a family member. Moondog, the self-proclaimed praeternatural detective —a standoffish member of the Roma community— has no time for authority, but he reluctantly accepts the case. Meanwhile, Hopie becomes harassed by a co-worker, while the district is plagued by a multitude of monstrously cryptic, supernatural events. Can Hopie and Moondog work together to overcome evil? Will Hopie free herself from the constant hassle of her unwanted admirer?

Moondog and the Dark Arches

Janney is a teenage librarian from a peculiar feudal village. She possesses a remarkable ability: she can fly from her body and hook up to be 'inside' another person. In this state of detachment, she found herself trapped within a young woman who had escaped from a pagan ritual and had jumped from a bridge. Moondog, the preternatural detective, is called-in to investigate these evils. Will he discover the truth? What invisible thing lives beneath the church? And will Moondog hold anyone accountable for this roguery?

Moondog and the Galium Satyr

Moondog teams up with an old adversary to investigate the puzzling disappearance of several maidens from the Roma community.

Meanwhile, a billionaire business tycoon + world-famous oligopolistic neurotechnologist is acquiring vast tracts of territory in the Scottish Highlands, proposing to turn his extensive private property into wilderness. His purpose is to establish the world's greatest pre-hominid habitat and supernatural ecosystem. He hopes the park will become home to rare creatures that humans have helped wipe-out since the last Ice Age. He aims to reintroduce assorted species of untamed creatures, including a number of keystone, non-physical entities. The mogul has already populated his 'rewilding park' with wolves, wild hogs, beavers, and bears. He also proposes to add lynx, a herd of aurochs and a family group of cave lions.

But when Moondog discovers that the mad-science tycoon has ransacked a sacred healing well in the Scottish Borders (the Woolwell Minch) to add to his biodiverse praeternatural portfolio, the investigator becomes uncertain of the billionaire's honorable intentions.

Does the billionaire keep a wild satyr, half-man, and half-beast in his rewilding park? If the reports are true, it will have to be investigated. And is it also true that the billionaire had arranged to introduce a Caspian Calderagon into his artificial ecosystem? Doesn't the miraculous beast need nourishment? Does anyone know what a rare Calderagon eats?

Moondog hopes to bring back the maids that have been lost by his community. And he also wants to see for himself what the billionaire is up to within his 'rewilding park.' He assumes the two mysteries are linked. But Moondog's investigation will mean he will have to pass through a military-style security line at the park, then outwit a small army of guards, before he faces and incapacitates a wild satyr! Will Moondog be able to infiltrate the park and harmlessly release the Calderagon from bondage? Will he track-down the missing maidens? Or has the preternatural researcher finally met his nemesis?

Printed in Great Britain
by Amazon

20154807R10159

Can machinery corrupt a person's soul?

Is it possible to break loose from the trap-cycle of mechanical objectification?

After escaping the Staines parish poorhouse, Stormbuckler rescues one of Asher-John Lindwürm's most essential workers from certain death. After the episode, the American maverick-inventor and self-made steamillionaire, a new guy in town, rewards Stormbuckler by affording him a position in the corporation's drawing department at a recently opened locomobile manufactory. The job comes with a suit of clothes and a generous salary. Meanwhile, parlour-housemaid Mayotte is also looking to improve her lot. She leaves a life of servitude (domestic employment) to join the enterprising (but unorthodox) American inventor's machine-plant, to be his clerical assistant.

Stormbuckler and Mayotte discover that outward appearances are deceptive at the millionaire's manufactory. For a start, people have been disappearing. And Lindwürm engages a gang of armed thugs who protect his ultrasecret ambitions. Lindwürm also employs an evil second-in-command who has schemes of his own and a *very* malevolent disposition.

What mystery links the unfolding events?

ISBN 9798376763926

9 798376 763926

9000